S0-AVO-856

The Death Committee

Books by Noah Gordon

THE RABBI
THE DEATH COMMITTEE

Noah Gordon

The Death Committee

McGraw-Hill Book Company

New York   St. Louis   San Francisco   Toronto   Mexico   Panama

THE DEATH COMMITTEE

Copyright © 1969 by Noah Gordon. All rights reserved.
Printed in the United States of America.
No part of this publication may be reproduced,
stored in a retrieval system, or transmitted,
in any form or by any means, electronic, mechanical,
photocopying, recording, or otherwise, without
the prior written permission of McGraw-Hill, Inc.

Library of Congress Catalog Card Number: 69-18727
First edition   23782

Quotation from "For the Birthday of a Middle-Aged Child" from
Selected Poems by Aline Kilmer. Copyright 1929 by Doubleday
& Company, Inc. Reprinted by permission of Doubleday &
Company, Inc.

Grateful acknowledgment is made to:
The publishers of *Medical World News* for permission to use a quotation from page 72 of the issue of June 16, 1967, which appears
on the frontispiece of this novel;

The publishers of *Massachusetts Physician* and to the publishers of
The New England Journal of Medicine for their cooperation in
allowing use of their titles and simulated material.

Again, for Lorraine:
the girl I married
and the woman she became

In Acknowledgment

Many people showed me kindness while this book was being written. The physicians who suffered my unending questions and gave freely of their encouragement and information must in no way be held responsible for my views or for any errors which may be discovered in my work. They have always had my respect; now they have my gratitude.

I should like to offer thanks to Andrew P. Sackett, M.D., Commissioner, Boston Department of Health and Hospitals, and James V. Sacchetti, M.D., Deputy Commissioner, for making it possible for me to receive instruction and experience at Boston City Hospital as a volunteer surgical technician; to Miss Mary Lawless, R.N., Boston City Hospital Operating Room Supervisor, for teaching me how to behave in the operating room; and to Mr. Samuel Slattery, Operating Room Medical Worker, for causing the research experience to be such a memorable one for me.

In answer to the inevitable question, Suffolk County General Hospital is a product of my imagination and is not modeled after any actual institution, nor is the medical school mentioned in this novel modeled after an existing school.

I am grateful to Lawrence T. Geoghegan, M.D., former Boston City Hospital Chief Surgical Resident, for enabling me to follow his house officers in afternoon rounds, and, for the same privilege, to Mayer Katz, M.D., who became Chief Resident when Dr. Geoghegan went to Vietnam, where Dr. Katz, in his turn, followed.

For allowing me to attend Mortality Conferences in their respective hospitals, I wish to thank Paul Russell, M.D., Director of Transplantation Surgery at the Massachusetts General Hospital; Samuel Proger, M.D., Physician-in-Chief at the New England Medical Center Hospitals; and Ralph A. Deterling, Jr., M.D., Surgeon-in-Chief at New England Medical Center Hospitals and Director of the First (Tufts) Surgical Service, Boston City Hospital.

Because so many people were generous with their help, and because records and memory are imperfect, I wish to apologize to anyone whose name should appear on this page and does not. For their help and cooperation, I wish to thank Paul Dudley White, M.D.; Robert Kastenbaum, Ph.D.; Lester F. Williams, M.D.; Anthony Monaco, M.D.; Don R. Lipsitt, M.D.; Carl Bearse, M.D.; Miriam Schweber, Ph.D.; Blaise Alfano, M.D.; Robert M. Schlesinger, M.D.; Benjamin E. Etsten, M.D.; Richard A. Morelli, M.D.; Rabbi Hilel Rudavsky; Mr. Patrick R. Carroll; and Atty. Charles J. Dunn.

Richard Ford, M.D., Medical Examiner of Suffolk County, who long ago, with tact and sensitivity, introduced a young reporter to his first autopsy, allowed me to stand at his elbow again and proved that the years have made him no less patient and skilled an educator.

A special word of thanks is due to Jack Matloff, M.D., and to John Merrill, M.D., who gave generously of their time and knowledge and who, along with Susan Rako, M.D., performed the added kindness of reading my manuscript.

For her help in preparing the manuscript, I am grateful to Mrs. Ernest Lamb, Jr.; for general assistance, to Miss Lise Ann Gordon; and for their assistance and courtesy, to the staffs of the Framingham Public Libraries, the Framingham State College Library, the Boston Medical Library and the Francis A. Countway Library of Medicine.

For their continued unquestioning support and invaluable judgment, I thank my literary agent, Miss Patricia Schartle, and my editor, Mr. William Goyen. With Lorraine Gordon, they made this book possible.

N. Gordon
1966–1968

Contents

"A person
 gives money
 to the physician.
 Maybe
 he will be healed.
 Maybe
 he will not be healed."
          —*The Talmud*
             Tractate Kethubot: 105

"A resident
 enters one end
 of a tunnel,
 something happens
 on the inside
 and
 gradually,
 after
 six or seven
 more years,
 he emerges
 as a surgeon."
          —*Medical World News*
             June 16, 1967

Prologue

By the time Spurgeon Robinson had been riding the ambulances thirty-six hours on and thirty-six hours off for three weeks, the driver, Meyerson, had long since gotten on his nerves and he was shaken by the gore and troubled by the traumas and didn't like the duty even a little bit. He found that sometimes he could escape by using his imagination, and on this trip he had just about convinced himself that it wasn't an ambulance, it was a goddam space ship. He wasn't an intern, he was the first black man in orbit. The wail of the siren was the jet stream turned into sound.

But Maish Meyerson, the clod, refused to cooperate by acting like a pilot. *"Wehr fahrbrent,"* he snarled at the operator of a stubborn Chrysler convertible, hurling the ambulance around it.

In a city like New York they might have had trouble locating the construction job but in Boston there were still only a few really tall buildings. Because of the red steelmill paint on the naked metal the skeletal structure jabbed into the gray sky like a bloody finger.

It beckoned them right up to the scene of the accident. Spurgeon slammed the door just as the siren whimpered into silence, and the knot of men unraveled around the figure on the ground.

He squatted. The unscathed half of the head told him the patient was a young man. His eyes were closed. A tiny trickle of fluid dripped from the fleshy lobe of one ear.

"Somebody three floors up dropped a spanner," a man with a paunch, the foreman, said in answer to the unasked question.

Spurgeon parted the matted hair with his fingers and beneath the

3

lacerated flesh felt the fragments of bone move loose and sharp like bits of shattered eggshell. It was probably cerebrospinal fluid leaking from the ear, he thought. There was no point in trying to debride the injury while the poor guy lay on the ground, he decided, and took a sterile gauze dressing and dropped it on the wound, where it turned red.

The man's fly was open and his penis was exposed. The fat-bellied foreman saw Spurgeon noticing. "He was taking a leak," he said, and Spurgeon could see it, the workingman easing his urgent bladder and gaining wry satisfaction from christening the building he was helping to raise; the wrench falling, falling, falling with unerring accuracy, as if God were remonstrating against dirty little human acts.

The foreman chewed his unlighted cigar and looked at the injured man. "His name is Paul Connors. Again and again I've told these bastards wear your helmets. Is he going to die?"

"We can't tell much from here," Spurgeon said. He lifted a closed eyelid and saw that the pupils were dilated. The pulse was very thready.

The fat man looked at him with suspicion. "Are you a doctor?"

Black boy?

"Yes."

"You going to give him something for pain?"

"He doesn't feel any pain."

He helped Maish bring out the litter and they loaded Paul Connors into the ambulance.

"Hey!" the foreman yelled as he started to close the door. "I'll ride with you."

"Against the rules," he lied.

"I've done it before," the man said uncertainly. "What hospital are you from?"

"County General." He pulled at the door and let it slam. Up front, Meyerson started the motor. The ambulance lurched forward. The patient was breathing in shallow gasps, and Spurgeon fixed the black rubber otopharyngeal airway tube in his mouth so it wouldn't let his tongue interfere and then turned on the respirator. He placed the mask over the patient's face and the positive pressure oxygen began to be fed in quick short bursts that made noises like a baby burping. The siren gave a small groan of resumption and once more began to unwind a thick ribbon of electronic sound. The ambulance tires whirred against the roadbed. He began to think of how he could orchestrate the incident as a piece of music. Drums, horns, reeds. You could use everything.

Almost everything, he thought as he adjusted the oxygen flow.

You wouldn't want violins.

Dozing with his head on his arms, Adam Silverstone leaned against the hard desk-top in the Chief Resident's office and dreamed it was a bed of dry, tight-curled leaves, the accumulation of many past leaf-falls, on which once he had lain as a boy and peered into a quiet brook-pool in the woods. It was in the late spring of the year he was fourteen, a bad time for him because his father had taken to answering his grandmother's indignant Italian curses with drunken Yiddish insults of his own, and to flee both Myron Silberstein and the old *vecchia* he had simply taken to the highway one Saturday morning and traveled three hours by thumb, without destination, heading only away from the smoke and grit of Pittsburgh and what it represented, until he was dropped off by a motorist on a section of road which ran through woods. Later he had tried half a dozen times to find the place, but he could never remember exactly where it had been, or perhaps by the time he had gotten back to it the forest had been raped by a bulldozer and had spawned houses. Not that it had been anything special; the woods were sparse and scraggly with fallen trees, the trickle of a stream had never housed a trout, the pool was a deep clear puddle. But the water was cold and sun-dappled. He had stretched out on his stomach in the leaves, smelling the odors of cool forest mold, his stomach beginning to feel hunger, conscious of the fact that soon he would have to begin hitch-hiking back, but caring about nothing as he lay and watched little Jesus-bugs walking on the water. What had he experienced in the half hour he had stayed—before the insistent spring dampness crept up through the dry leaves and made him take his shivering leave—that would cause him to dream of the little pool for the rest of his life?

Peace, he decided years later.

That peace was shattered now by the ringing of the telephone, which, still asleep, he answered.

"Adam? Spurgeon."

"Yo," he said, yawning.

"We may have a kidney donor, pal."

He was less sleepy. "Yeah?"

"I just brought a patient in. Compound depressed skull fracture with lots of brain damage. Meomartino's assisting Harold Poole with the neurosurgery right now. He said for me to tell you the EEG showed no electrical activity at all."

Now he was wide awake.

"What's the patient's blood type?" he said.

"AB."

"Susan Garland is AB. That means this kidney goes to Susan Garland."

"Ah—Meomartino says to tell you the patient's mother is in the waiting room. The name is Connors."

"Goddammit." The task of securing legal permission for transplantation was left to the Chief Resident and the Surgical Fellow. Invariably, he had noticed, Meomartino, the Fellow, was busy with other urgent duties when it came time to talk with the next-of-kin. "I'll be right down," he said.

Mrs. Connors was sitting with her pastor, only slightly prepared by the fact that her son had been given Extreme Unction. She was a life-worn woman with a talent for disbelief.

"Ah, don't be telling me something like *that,*" she said, with filled eyes and a tremulous smile, as if she could reason him out of the entire thing. "He *isn't,*" she insisted. "He isn't dying. Not my Paullie."

She was technically correct, Adam thought. By that time, to all intents and purposes, her boy was already dead. The Boston Edison Company was keeping him breathing. Once the electric respirator was switched off, within twenty minutes he would be gone entirely.

He could never tell them he was sorry; it was so inadequate.

She began to weep, achingly.

He waited the long interval until she had regained some control and then as gently as possible he explained about Susan Garland. "Do you understand about the little girl? She'll die, too, unless we give her another kidney."

"Poor lamb," she said.

He didn't know whether she meant her son or the girl.

"Then you would sign the permission slip?"

"He's been torn up enough. But if it will save some other mother's child . . ."

"We hope that it will," Adam said. The permission secured, he thanked her and fled.

"Our Lord gave up his entire body for you and for me," he heard the priest say as he walked away. "For Paul, too, for that matter."

"I never said I was Mary, Father," the woman said.

Depressed, he felt it would help his spirits to see the opposite side of the coin.

In Room 308 Bonita Garland, Susan's mother, sat in a chair and knitted. As usual when the girl saw him from her bed she pulled the sheet up to her neck over nightgowned acorn-breasts, a gesture he carefully refrained from noticing. She was propped against two pillows and reading *Mad,* which somehow relieved him. Weeks earlier during a long sleepless night when she was hooked up to the splashing dialysis machine that periodically washed her blood free of the poisons accumulated because of her ruined kidneys, he had seen her leafing through *Seventeen* and had teased her about reading the magazine when she was scarcely fourteen herself.

"I wanted to be certain I got to it," she had said, turning a page.

Now, ebullient with good news, he stood at the foot of her bed. "Hi, luv," he said. She was going through a fervent emotional involvement with English musical groups, an infatuation to which he prostituted himself shamelessly. "I know a girl says I look like the character who's always on the cover of that magazine. What's his name?"

"Alfred E. Neumann?"

"Yeah."

"You're ever so much better looking." She cocked her head to look at him and he saw that the dark rings had deepened under her eyes and that her face was thinner, with pain-lines around the nose. When first he had seen the face it had been vibrant and impish. Now, even though the freckles showed starkly against the sallowing skin, still it was a face that promised great adult attractiveness.

"Thank you," he said. "You'd better be careful about paying me compliments. Howard might come after me." Howard was her boy friend. They were forbidden by her parents to go steady, she had confided to Adam one night, but they went steady anyway. Sometimes she read him portions of Howard's letters.

He knew she was trying to make him jealous of Howard and was touched and flattered.

"He's coming to see me this weekend."

"Why don't you ask him to make it next weekend, instead?"

She stared at him, alerted by the chronic patient's invisible warning system. "Why?"

"You'll have good news for him. We have a kidney for you."

"Oh, God." Bonita Garland's eyes were exultant. She set down her knitting and looked at her daughter.

"I don't want it," Susan said. Her thin fingers bent the covers of the magazine.

"Why not?" Adam asked.

"You don't know what you're saying, Susan," her mother said. "We've been waiting so long for this."

"I've become used to things the way they are. I know what to expect."

"No, you don't," he said gently. He took her fingers away from the magazine and held them between his hands. "Unless we operate things will become worse. Much worse. After we operate, things will be better. No more headaches. No more nights spent hooked up to the damn machine. In a little while you can go back to school. You can go to dances with Howard."

She closed her eyes. "Will you promise me nothing will go wrong?"

Jesus. He saw her mother, smiling with painful understanding, nod at him.

"Of course," he said.

Bonita Garland went to the girl and took her in her arms. "Darling, it's going to be just fine. You'll see."

"Momma."

Bonita pressed her daughter's head to her breast and began to rock. "Susie-Q," she said. "Oh, thank God, we're lucky people."

"Momma, I am just so scared."

"Don't you be silly. You heard Dr. Silverstone give his word."

He went out of the room and walked downstairs. Neither of them had asked where the kidney was coming from. Next time he saw them, he knew, they would feel ashamed about that.

Outside the hospital there was still traffic but it was thinning. The air blew in from the sea and over the dirtiest part of the city, carrying a rich mixture of smells, most of them bad. He felt like swimming twenty fast laps or making prolonged love, some activity frenziedly physical that might lighten the weight pushing him into the concrete. If he were anything but the son of a drunkard he would have gone to a bar. Instead he walked across the street to Maxie's and had canned chowder and two cups of black coffee. There wasn't a damn thing the kid behind the counter could do to or for the chowder. The coffee was like a first kiss from an ugly girl, nothing to brag about but comforting.

The Surgical Fellow, Meomartino, had established the lines of communication between the Operating Rooms and the donor's next-of-kin. You had to hand it to him, the system worked, Adam Silverstone thought grudgingly as he scrubbed away at his nails.

Spurgeon Robinson was stationed at the door of OR-3.

Upstairs, in the surgical office on the first floor, another intern named Jack Moylan waited with Mrs. Connors. In Moylan's pocket was a slip giving permission for autopsy. He sat with the telephone receiver held to his ear, listening for something to come over the silent open line. At the other end of the line was a first-year resident named Mike Schneider, who sat behind the desk in the corridor outside the OR door.

Ten feet from where Spurgeon stood and watched and waited, Paul Connors lay on the table. It was more than twenty-four hours since he had been brought into the hospital, but the respirator still breathed for him. Meomartino already had prepped him and placed a sterile plastic drape over the abdominal area.

Near him Dr. Kender, the Associate Chief of Surgery, talked softly with Dr. Arthur Williamson of the Department of Medicine.

At the same time in adjoining OR-4, Adam Silverstone, by now scrubbed and gowned, walked to the operating table on which Susan Garland lay. The girl, sedated, stared at him sleepily, not recognizing him behind the surgical mask.

"Hi, luv," he said.

"Oh. You."

"How you doing?"

"Everybody in sheets. You're all so weird." She smiled, and closed her eyes.

At 7:55 in OR-3 Dr. Kender and Dr. Williamson placed the electrodes of an electroencephalograph on Paul Connors' skull.

As it had on the previous evening, the EEG's stylus drew a straight line on the graph paper, confirming their knowledge that his mind was not alive. Twice in twenty-four hours they had recorded the absence of electrical activity in the patient's brain. His pupils were widely dilated and they found no peripheral reflexes.

At 7:59 Dr. Kender turned off the respirator. Almost at once, Paul Connors ceased to breathe.

At 8:16 Dr. Williamson checked for a heart-beat and, finding none, declared him to be dead.

Immediately, Spurgeon Robinson opened the door leading to the corridor. "Right now," he said to Mike Schneider.

"He's gone," Schneider said into the telephone.

They waited in silence. In a very little while Schneider listened intently and then turned from the telephone.

"She signed it," he said.

Spurgeon went back into OR-3 and nodded to Meomartino. While Dr. Kender watched, the Surgical Fellow picked up a scalpel and made the transverse incision which would allow him to remove the kidney from the cadaver.

Meomartino worked with extreme care, aware that his nephrectomy was clean and right because of Dr. Kender's approving silence. He was accustomed to operating before the judging eyes of senior men and was never upset by them.

Still, his self-assurance cracked for a split second when he looked up and saw Dr. Longwood seated in the gallery.

Was it the shadows? Or in his moment of observation were the puffy dark signs of uremic poisoning already discernible beneath the Old Man's eyes?

Dr. Kender cleared his throat and Meomartino bent over the cadaver again.

It took him only sixteen minutes to remove the kidney, which appeared to be a good one, with a single, well-defined artery. While he searched the abdomen with gloved fingers to make sure no occult tumor was present, the communications team, each member by now scrubbed and waiting, took the freed kidney and hooked it to a perfusion system which pumped icy-cold fluids through the organ.

Before their eyes the big red bean of flesh whitened as the blood was washed out of it, and shrank with cold.

They carried the kidney to OR-4 on a tray and Adam Silverstone assisted as Dr. Kender made it part of the girl's body and then removed both of her own kidneys, wasted and wrinkled bits of spoiled tissue that had not functioned for a long time. Even so, as Adam dropped the second one from the forceps to the towel he was newly aware that now Susan Garland's only lifeline was the artery joining her blood supply to Paul Connors' kidney. By that time the transplanted organ was already pinking healthily, warmed by the rush of her young blood.

Less than half an hour after the transplant was begun, Adam closed the abdominal incision. He helped the orderly move Susan Garland to the sterile recovery room and so he was the last man to get to the junior surgeons' room. Robinson and Schneider already had changed from OR greens to whites and had returned to the wards. Meomartino was in his underwear.

"It looked like a score," Meomartino said.

Adam held up crossed fingers.

"Did you see Longwood?"

"No. The Old Man was there?"

Meomartino nodded.

Adam opened the metal locker which contained his own whites and began to pull off the black non-static OR boots.

"I don't know why he would want to watch," Meomartino said in a little while.

"He'll be getting one himself, soon, if we're lucky enough to get a B-negative donor."

"That's not going to be easy. B-negatives are rare."

Adam shrugged. "I suppose Mrs. Bergstrom will get the next transplant," he conceded.

"Don't be so sure."

One of the infuriating things about the relationship between the Fellow and the Chief Resident was that when one of them received information which hadn't reached the other, it was difficult to resist the temptation to act as if he had a direct pipeline to God. Adam rolled the green scrub suit into a ball and tossed it into the half-filled laundry basket in the corner. "What the hell is that supposed to mean? Bergstrom will get a kidney from her twin, right?"

"The sister isn't sure she wants to give one away."

"Jesus." He pulled his whites from the locker and climbed into the trousers which, he noted, were becoming grimy and would have to be replaced with a fresh pair for the next day.

Meomartino left as he was tying his shoes. Adam wanted a cigarette, but the little electronic monster in his lapel pocket sounded its soft snarl and when he phoned in he learned that Susan Garland's father was waiting to see him, so he went straight up.

Arthur Garland was in his early but fattening forties, with uncertain blue eyes and a receding auburn hairline. A leather-goods distributor, Adam remembered.

"I didn't want to leave without talking with you."

"I'm just a house officer. Perhaps you should talk with Dr. Kender."

"I just talked with Dr. Kender. He said everything went as well as could be expected."

Adam nodded.

"Bonnie—my wife—insisted I see you. She said you've been understanding. I wanted to say thanks."

"There's no need. How is Mrs. Garland?"

"I sent her home. This has been very difficult, and Dr. Kender said we won't be able to see Susan for a couple of days."

"The less contact she has, even with people who love her, the less likely she is to pick up infection. The drugs we're using to keep her body from rejecting the new kidney also weaken her resistance."

"I understand," Garland said. "Dr. Silverstone, does everything look all right?"

He was sure that Garland had already asked Dr. Kender. Faced with the man's need for a positive portent, a cabalistic sign to certify that all was under perfect control, he was acutely aware of their real impotence.

"The surgery went smoothly," he said. "It was a good kidney. We have a lot going for us."

"What do you do next?"

"Watch her."

Garland nodded. "A small token." He took a wallet from his pocket. "Alligator. My company handles the line."

Adam was embarrassed.

"I gave one to Dr. Kender, too. Don't presume to thank *me,* you people are giving me back my girl." The trapped blue eyes became shiny, swam, spilled over. Ashamed, the man looked away, at the blank wall.

"Mr. Garland, you're tired as hell. If you don't mind my saying so, why don't you let me give you a prescription for a sedative and then go home?"

"Yes. Please." He blew his nose. "Do you have children of your own?"

Adam shook his head.

"You shouldn't miss the experience. We adopted her, you know?"

"Yes. Yes, I do."

"I fought with Bonnie about that. For five years. I was ashamed. But then we finally got her, six weeks old . . ." Garland took the prescription, started to say something else, shook his head and walked away.

The transplant had been done on Friday. By the following Wednesday Adam felt in his bones that they were home free.

Susan Garland's blood pressure was still high, but the kidney was functioning as though custom-designed.

"I never thought my heart would pound because somebody called for a bedpan," Bonita Garland told him.

It would be a while yet before her daughter could be comfortable. The incision bothered her and she was weakened by the drugs they administered to keep her system from rejecting the kidney. She was depressed. She snapped at well-meant remarks and she wept at night. On Thursday she brightened during a visit from Howard, who turned out to be a skinny boy, painfully shy.

It was Howard's effect on her that gave Adam the idea.

"Who's her favorite radio disc jockey?"

"I think J. J. Johnson," her mother said.

"Why don't you call him and ask him to dedicate some numbers to her on Saturday night? We can invite Howard to visit her. She won't be able to dance or even leave her bed, but under the circumstances it might be an acceptable substitute."

"You should be a psychiatrist," Mrs. Garland said.

"My *private* dance?" Susan said when they told her about it. "My hair's got to be washed. It's grubby." Her mood changed so drastically that, by now carried away, Silverstone telephoned and ordered a corsage, spending for red roses money he had earmarked for other purposes, and dictating a card:

Have a ball, luv.

On Friday her morale was good but it dropped as evening approached. When Adam came by on rounds he found that she had listed several complaints with the nurse.

"What's the matter, Susie?"

"I ache."

"Where?"

"All over. My stomach."

"You've got to expect a little of that. After all, you've had a major operation." He knew that you could fall into the trap of over-coddling. He checked the surgical wound, which was unremarkable. Her pulse rate was up a little, but when he cuffed her arm and took her blood pressure he grinned in satisfaction. "Normal. For the first time. How do you like them apples?"

"Good." She smiled faintly.

"You get some sleep, now, so you can enjoy your dance tomorrow night."

She nodded and he hurried away.

It was six hours later that the floor nurse, coming into her room with medication, discovered that in her sleep the girl had bled to death internally during the quiet hours of the night.

"Dr. Longwood wants the Garland case discussed at the next meeting of the Death Committee," Meomartino said over lunch the next day.

"I don't think that's fair," Adam said.

They were sitting with Spurgeon Robinson at a table next to the wall. He was toying with the horrible stew the hospital served every Saturday. Spurgeon ate his apathetically while Meomartino virtually shoveled it away. How the hell had the cliché evolved which insisted that the rich had sensitive stomachs, Adam asked himself.

"Why not?"

"Kidney transplantation is barely out of the experimental stages. How can we try to affix responsibility for death in an area over which we still don't have a hell of a lot of control?"

"That's the point," Meomartino said calmly, wiping his mouth. "It *is* beyond the experimental stage. Hospitals all over the country are doing this operation with success. If we're going to use it clinically, we have to take responsibility for it."

He could talk that way, Adam thought; the only role he had played in this case had been in removing the kidney from the cadaver.

"She looked perfectly well when you saw her last night?" Spurgeon Robinson asked.

Adam nodded and glanced at the intern sharply. Then he forced himself to relax; Spurgeon, unlike Meomartino, had no ax to grind.

"I don't think Dr. Longwood should be allowed to chair that meeting," Robinson said. "He's not a well man. He runs those Mortality Conferences as if they're the Inquisition and he's Torquemada."

Meomartino grinned. "His health doesn't have a damn thing to do with it. The old bastard has always run the Death Conference that way."

They could tear a man's prospects to shreds in one of those meetings, Adam thought. He put down his fork and pushed his chair back.

"Tell me something," he said to Meomartino, feeling the sudden need to be contentious. "You're the only one on the Service who never refers to Longwood as the Old Man. Is the term too disrespectful for you?"

Meomartino smiled. "On the contrary. It is simply that I believe the term to be one of affection," he said quietly. And went on eating with unabated enjoyment.

Just before he went off duty that night he remembered about the rose corsage.

"Flowers? Yes, they came, Dr. Silverstone," the nurse at the desk said. "I had them sent on to the Garland home. It's what we always do."

Have a ball, luv . . .

I could at least have spared them that, he thought.

"It's all right, isn't it?"

"Sure."

He went up to the little room on the sixth floor and sat and smoked four cigarettes without enjoyment, one after the other, and found himself biting his nails, a habit he'd believed broken long ago.

He thought of his father, from whom he had not heard, wondered about trying to phone him in Pittsburgh and then decided with relief to leave well enough alone.

After a long while he left the room and went downstairs and outside to the deserted street. Maxie's was closed and black. The street lamps made a path through the dark like tracer bullets, interrupted halfway down the block where probably kids had stoned a bulb.

He started to walk.

Then he started to run.

Down to the corner, feeling the concrete sidewalk slam up against his feet.

Around the corner.

On the avenue, moving faster.

A car burred by, the horn hooted, a female shouted something and tittered. In his chest he felt the small choked feeling surge and he ran faster despite the stitch of pain that bubbled to life in his right side.

Around the corner.

Past the ambulance yard. Empty. The green-painted tin shade of the huge yellow light over the ambulance entrance fluttering in the night breeze, telegraphing dancing shadows as he pounded alongside.

Past the loading platform of the warehouse next door where a derelict—seen fleetingly in the dark as a form, a blob, an umbra, his father—drained the last drops from a pint and then sent the empty bottle sailing through the unknown after him as he sped, arms pumping now, chased by a backache and the tinkling crash of broken glass.

Round the corner.

Into the darkest stretch, the back of the moon. Past the blank-eyed houses of the blank-eyed colored slum across the street, mercifully asleep.

Past the parked car where the writhing figures did not break their beat but the girl peered over her lover's shoulder and through the glass at the spectral boneshaker galloping by.

Past the alley where the noise of his feet frightened something small and alive, clawed nails skittering on the hard-packed earth as it fled deeper into the tunnel.

Around the corner.

The street lamps again. His lungs burning, unable to breathe, his head back, a sticking pain in the chest, straining to break the tape as no crowd stood and screamed, he reached Maxie's, staggered and stopped.

Jesus.

He gulped air, swallowed air, knew he was going to be sick, belched loudly and knew he was not.

He was damp under the arms and between the legs, his face was wet. A fool. Panting, he leaned against Maxie's window, which creaked ominously, slid down on it until his buttocks rested on the little red-painted wooden ledge that supported the plate glass.

The ledge gritted beneath him. To hell with it, the whites were already dirty.

He threw back his head and looked up at the starless sky.

They have no right to pray to me, he said. Why don't they ask you for promises?

He dropped the trajectory of his sight a few degrees and he knew the presence of the building only a little lower than heaven, saw the old red brick that had been browned by the dirt and smoke of the city grown around it, felt the stupid patience of the scarred facade.

He remembered the first time he had seen the hospital, only a few months and thousands of years ago.

Book One

The Summer

Chapter 1: Adam Silverstone

The stars had slowly squeezed into hiding in the bleaching sky. As the asthmatic truck left the Massachusetts Turnpike and chugged through the deserted outskirts, the long line of street lamps bordering the river flickered twice and then died in the gloom. The hot day was coming, but the loss of the line of lights ahead gave a brief, deceptive chill and gloom to the daybreak.

He stared through the dusty windshield as Boston approached, thinking that this was the city that had shaped his father, broken him and ground him down.

You're not going to do that to me, he told the passing buildings, the skyline, the river.

"It doesn't look like such a tough town," he said.

The truck driver looked at him in surprise. Their conversation had unraveled its way into tired silence eighty miles back, between Hartford and Worcester, following a tight, terse disagreement over the John Birch Society. Now the man said something indistinct which was lost against the thrum of the truck's motor.

Adam shook his head. "I'm sorry. I didn't understand you."

"What's the matter, you deaf?"

"A little. Just in my left ear."

The man frowned, suspecting mockery. "I said, you got a job waiting?"

Adam nodded.

"Doing what?"

"I'm a surgeon."

The driver looked at him in disgust, confident now that his suspicions were justified. "Sure, you beatnik punk. I'm an astronaut."

He opened his mouth to explain and then thought to hell with him and shut it again and concentrated on the scenery. Poking up through the murk on the other side of the Charles River he could see white spires, undoubtedly Harvard. Somewhere over there was Radcliffe College and Gaby Pender sleeping like a pussycat, he thought, wondering how long he could wait before he called her. Would she remember him? A quotation came to his mind uninvited— something about how often a man needs to see a woman—that once is sufficient, but twice may confirm it.

Within his head the little computer told him who was the author of the lines. As usual, the ability to remember a non-medical reference filled him with bilious discontent instead of pride. A waster of words, he could hear his father say. Adamo Roberto Silverstone, you smug bastard, he told himself, see where the gift of memory is when you're struggling with something from Thorek's *Anatomy in Surgery* or Wangensteen's *Intestinal Obstruction*.

In a little while the man swung the wheel and the truck lumbered off Storrow Drive and down a ramp and suddenly there were lighted warehouse windows, trucks, cars, people, a market district. The driver tooled the van down one street of cobblestones, past a diner whose neon still flashed, and up another long cobblestoned street, stopping before BENJ. MORETTI & SONS PRODUCE. In answer to his horn a man emerged and peered at them from the loading platform. Beefy and balding, in his white smock he looked not unlike one of the pathologists at the Georgia hospital where Adam had taken his internship and first year of residency. *Eh, paisan.*

"What you got?"

The driver belched, a sound like carpet ripping. "Melons. Persians." The man in white nodded and disappeared.

"End of the line, kid." The driver opened the door and climbed heavily down from the cab.

Adam reached behind the seat, took up the worn valpak and joined the other man on the ground. "Can I help you unload?"

The driver scowled at him with suspicion. *"They* do it," he said, jerking his head toward the warehouse. "You want a job, you ask them."

The offer had been made out of gratitude, but Adam saw with relief that it was unnecessary. "Thanks for the lift," he said.

"Yuh."

He carried the suitcase back down the street to the diner, struggling with it, a small bandy-legged man, too big for a jockey, not enough heft for most other sports except diving, which for him had ceased to be a sport five years before. It was at times like this that he regretted not resembling more closely his mother's brawny brothers. He disliked being at the mercy of anyone or anything, including a piece of luggage.

Inside there were wildly enticing food smells and mad diner noise: talk and laughter, the hollow clatter of panware through the small window leading to the kitchen, the solid sound of coffee mugs against the white marble counter, things sizzling on the grill. Expensive things, he decided.

"Coffee, black."

"Bleed one," the straw-haired girl said. She was full-blown and firm fleshed, with pale and milky skin; but she would have an obesity problem before she was thirty. Under her white-draped left breast twin smears of red jam stood out like stigmata. The coffee slopped over the rim of the mug as she pushed it toward him, accepted his dime sullenly and swung away with an insult of hips.

Moo.

The coffee was very hot and he drank it slowly, now and then gulping with great daring and feeling victorious when it became clear that he had not burned his tongue. The wall behind the counter was mirrored. Staring back at him from it was a bum, stubble-faced, wild-haired, wearing a soiled and worn blue work-shirt. When he finished the coffee he got up and carried the suitcase into the men's room. He tested the faucets; both the HOT and the COLD ran cool, a circumstance that failed to surprise him. He went back into the diner and asked the girl for a cup of very hot water.

"For soup or for tea?"

"Just for water."

With an air of patient disgust she ignored him. Finally he surrendered and ordered tea. When it came he paid for it and took the teabag from the saucer and dropped it on the counter. He carried the cup of hot water into the men's room. The floor was covered with layers of grit and, judging from the odor, dried urine. He set the cup on the edge of the dirty sink and, balancing the suitcase on the radiator, opened it to remove his toilet articles. By collecting cold water from the tap in his cupped palm and adding hot water from the cup he managed to soap up his whiskers and rinse his face with water sufficiently warm to soften the bristles. When he finished shaving, the face that looked back at him from the speckled mirror was more civilized. Dr. Silverstone. Brown eyes. Big nose he preferred to think of as Roman, really not tremendously oversized but accentuated by his lack of height. Wide mouth like a cynical slash in the thin face. Face undeniably light-skinned despite the tan and topped by hair of disordered brownness. Such a dull brown. Drab. He took a brush from the suitcase and slapped at his hair. He had always felt slightly guilty about his coloring. *A child should be the color of olives, not of lemons or groats,* he had heard his mother say once. He was groats, a compromise between his blond father and his Italian mother.

His mother had been dark, a woman with unbelievable heavy-lidded black eyes, the bedroom eyes of an earthy saint. He scarcely could remember her face, but to summon her eyes at will he had merely to close his own. On the nights when his father had come home sotted—apostate Myron Silberstein drowning in the strega he had adopted along with pet Italian phrases to demonstrate the democracy of his marriage, sounding his anise-scented shrieks for help (*O puttana nera! O troia scura! O donna! Oi, nafkeh!*)—the little boy would lie awake in the dark trembling at the sick thud of his father's fists against his mother's flesh, the slap of her palm against his face, the sounds often ending in other noises, hot and frantic, slick-liquid and gasping, that made him lie rigid, hating the night.

When he was in junior high school and his mother four years dead, he discovered the story of Gregor Johann Mendel and the garden peas and set to work plotting his own hereditary picture, hoping without admitting it that his brown hair and eyes were a genetic impossibility: that his father's blondness should have been passed on to him, and that perhaps after all he was a bastard, the product of his beautiful dead mother and an unknown male who possessed all the noble virtues so lacking in the man he called Poppa.

But the biology books disclosed that the combination of moonlight and shadow added up to groats.

Ah, well.

At any rate, by this time he was bound to Myron Silberstein with cords of love as well as strings of hate.

To prove it, you damn fool, he told the image in the mirror, you scrape together two hundred dollars and then let him talk you out of it, out of almost all of it. What had shone in his eyes when his hands —those Hebrew-violinist's janitor's hands with coaldust engrained in the knuckles—had closed around the money?

Love? Pride? The promise of life's best surprise, an unplanned drunk? Did the old man still chase after love? Doubtful. Middle-aged impotence common to alcoholics. Sooner or later certain chains bound everyone, even Myron Silberstein.

Only one person, the grandmother, his *vecchia,* had ever been able to cow his father. Rosella Biombetti had been a small woman from southern Italy, white hair in a bun, everything else of course black: shoes, stockings, dress, kerchief, often even mood, as if in mourning for the world. There were pits on her olive face, left there when she was four years old in the Avellino village of Petruro and every one of her parents' eight children had come down with *vaiolo,* the dreaded smallpox. The disease took no one but it scarred six of the children and ruined the seventh, an eight-year-old named Muzi whose mind was burned into soft ash by the high fever, leaving him a Something who eventually became an aging bald man in the East Liberty section of Pittsburgh, Pennsylvania, playing all day with his spoons and bottle caps and wearing a ragged sweater even when layers of July heat shimmered over Larimer Avenue.

Once he asked his grandmother why the old great-uncle was like that.

"L'Arlecchino," she said.

He learned early that the Harlequin was the inner fear pervading his grandmother's life, the universal evil, an inheritance from the Europe of ten centuries ago. A child is dead from a sudden onslaught of unexpected disease? He has been taken by the Harlequin, who covets children. A woman becomes schizophrenic? The lean, devilishly-handsome demon lover has seduced her and eloped with her soul. An arm shrivels with paralysis, a man slowly fades under the ravages of tuberculosis? The Harlequin is plucking vitality from his victim, savoring the living essence like a sweetmeat.

In trying to lock him out she made him a member of her family.

When Adam's female cousins blossomed and bloomed and began to experiment with lipsticks and high pointy bras, the old woman shrieked that they would attract the Harlequin, who stole maidenheads in the night. Little by little, listening to *la vecchia* through the years, Adam picked up details. The Harlequin wore breeches and jacket of multicolored patches and was invisible except under the full moon, which turned his motley into a glittering suit of lights. He was voiceless but his presence could be detected by the tinkling of the bells in his fool's cap. He carried a magic wooden sword, a kind of slapstick which he used as a wand.

The boy sometimes thought it would be a wonderful adventure to be the Harlequin, so all-powerful, so deliciously evil. When he was eleven and having his first damp nightdreams of luscious Lucy Sangano, who was thirteen, on Hallowe'en he decided that he would be the evil spirit. While the other kids ran from door to door for trick or treat he ambled slowly through the suddenly-comfortable dark, envisioning rich scenes in which he tapped the tender young buttocks of Lucy Sangano with his box-lath sword and commanded voicelessly, *Show me everything.*

Rosella warded off the Evil One by using four devices, of which only two, the sprinkling of holy water and the daily attendance at Mass, Adam considered harmless. Her practice of rubbing the doorknobs with garlic he thought a nuisance because of hand-stickiness, and a source of embarrassment in public school because of pungent odor, although he secretly enjoyed the last fugitive scents that remained in his sweaty palm when he held it to his nostrils late at night.

The most powerful protection was gained by tucking the two middle fingers under the thumb, extending the index and little fingers to simulate the devil's horns and dry-spitting between them, following this with the proper words: break the evil-eye, *scutta mal occhio,* poo-poo-poo. Rosella performed this rite many times daily, another form of embarrassment; to some of Adam's peers the finger-sign was a secret signal of another sort, a put-down, a disparaging token of disbelief summed up in one quick unlovely word. To these uninitiates it was hilarious to see 'Damo Silverstone's granny gesticulating with their raffish secret sign. She cost him his first bloody nose and great resentment.

His young soul was rent between the pious superstition of the old lady and the father who carefully remained sober each Yom Kippur so for some important secret reason he could go fishing. Her superstition and her religion had their attractions, but too much of what she said was transparently silly. For the most part he voted silently with his father, perhaps because he was searching so hard for something within the man that he could admire.

And yet, when in her eightieth year and his fifteenth year she sickened and began to fail, he ached for her. When Dr. Calabrese's long black Packard began to be parked in front of the tenement house on Larimer Avenue with increasing regularity, he prayed for her. When she died one morning with a coquettish smile on her lips he cried for her and realized at last the real identity of the Harlequin. He no longer wished to impersonate the jester-inamorato who was death; instead he decided that some day he would drive a long new car like Dr. Calabrese and fight *L'Arlecchino* all the way.

He said goodbye to the old lady at the finest funeral offered by her Sons of Italy insurance, but she never completely left him. Years later, when he had become a doctor and a surgeon and had done and seen things she had never dreamed about in Petruro or even in East Liberty, his initial reaction to misfortune was an instantaneous subconscious search for the Harlequin. If one of his hands was in his pocket the fingers involuntarily assumed the sign of the horns. His father and his grandmother had left him with an unending internal conflict: bullshit, the man of science mocked, while the little boy was whispering, *scutta mal occhio,* poo-poo-poo.

Now in the men's room of the diner he stowed away his toilet articles and then like an ungainly waterfowl, first one leg raised and then the other against the filthy danger of the unpleasant floor, divested himself of the jeans and then of the blue workshirt. The shirt and suit that he dug from the B-4 bag were somewhat wrinkled but presentable. The tie looked not nearly as good as it had eighteen months before, when it was secondhand-new, purchased from a third-year student who was a bad poker player. The dark shoes that replaced the sneakers retained a fair shine.

As he walked back out through the diner the cow behind the counter switched her tail and stared as if trying to decide where she had seen him before.

Outside, it was lighter. A taxi hummed a quiet mechanical song at the curb, the driver lost behind the racing form, dreaming the eternal dream at 8 to 1. Adam asked if Suffolk County General Hospital was within walking distance.

"County Hospital? Sure."

"How do I walk there?"

The cabby allowed one quick grin to break his lips. "The hard way. Way the hell cross town. Too early for a bus, nowhere near a subway." The man put down the racing form, confident of a fare.

How much was in his wallet? Less than ten, he knew. Eight, nine. And a month until pay-day. "Take me for a dollar?"

A look of disgust.

He picked up the B-4 bag and walked down the street, getting to BENJ. MORETTI & SONS PRODUCE when the cab passed him and stopped.

"Get in the back seat," the cabby said. "I cruise all the way, if I pick up somebody else, you get out. For a buck."

He climbed in gratefully. The cab crawled through the streets and he gazed out the open window, perceiving the kind of hospital it would be. The streets were old and sad, lined with tenement houses with broken steps and dribbling ashcans, neighborhoods of poor people crammed together in a glut of poverty. It would be a hospital whose clinic benches were filled each morning with the sick and maimed of one of society's self-built traps.

Tough for you, he said silently to the sleeping victims behind blank windows as the taxi rolled past. But good for me, a teaching hospital where maybe I can learn some surgery.

The hospital complex loomed like a monolith in the early morning light, big parking lamps still burning yellow around the square emptiness of the ambulance yard.

Inside, the entry was gloomy and old-fashioned. An elderly man with sagging wrinkled cheeks and improbable jet-black hair sat behind the reception counter. Adam consulted the letter he had received from the administrator four weeks before and then asked for the Surgical Fellow, Dr. Meomartino. Ah, Italians of the world, we are everywhere.

The man consulted a hospital directory. "Fourth Surgical Service. He might be asleep," he said doubtfully. "Shall I ring him?"

"God, no." He thanked him and wandered outside. Across the street a light flared in a coffee shop and as he walked toward it he could see behind the counter a short dark man adding water to the coffee urn; but the door was locked and the little man didn't look up when he rattled it. He went back into the hospital and asked the man with dyed hair how to get to a Fourth Surgical Service ward.

"Down the hall there straight past Emergency and take the second stairs up one flight. Quincy Ward. Can't miss."

As he approached the Emergency Ward he half-considered volunteering his services. Happily the impulse passed, even before he peered into the big room and saw that it was empty of patients. An intern slumped in a chair reading. A nurse sat across the room and squinted sleepily at her knitting. On a litter in a corner an orderly lay like a sleeping bear, his mouth slightly open.

He climbed the stairs into Quincy Ward, passing in the quiet halls only a skinny blond intern whose open collar drooped beneath his acned chin like a flag on a windless day.

Except for the night lights the ward was dark. The patients lay in rows, some like lumps but others restless and ridden in slumber by devils.

Thou hast been called, O Sleep! the friend of woe, but 'tis the happy that have called thee so. Southey, the computer said.

From one of the beds came the sound of a woman weeping. He stopped. "What is it?" he asked gently. Her face was hidden.

"I am full of fear."

"There is no need to be," he said. Get the hell out of here, he told himself furiously. For all you know, there is every need to be.

"Who are you?"

"I'm a doctor."

The woman nodded. "So was Jesus."

It gave him pause as he walked away.

In the nurse's station he found an elderly R.N. who was accustomed to new doctors. She gave him coffee and fresh hard rolls and butter from the kitchen ward, deliciously free. "All you want, Doctor, it's a rich county. I'm Rhoda Novak." She laughed suddenly. "You're lucky Helen Fultz wasn't on tonight. She wouldn't give anyone spit."

She left before he finished his rolls. He wanted another, but was thankful for little things. A huge man in OR greens came into the station and sighed as he hid a chair beneath his haunches. He had red hair under the operating room cap and despite its size his face was soft and unformed, a boy's face. He nodded to Adam and reached for the coffee pot just as the little signaling device on his uniform buzzed. "Ah," he said. He went to the wall telephone and called in, spoke a few fast words and hurried away.

Adam left his coffee dregs and went after the huge green shape, down a labyrinthian series of corridors to the surgical suite.

The surgery in the Georgia hospital had been clean, brightly lighted, uncluttered and unobstructed. This lighting was dim at best. The corridors seemed to be repositories for extra furniture, spare stretchers, bookcases and random pieces of equipment; during peak hours they probably stacked pre-operative and post-operative patients here as well. The swinging doors to the operating rooms were worn three inches on each side, where the edges of innumerable beds had struck and rubbed, uncovering successive layers of laminated wood like counters of time, the rings within a tree.

There was a stairway and he climbed it to the observation gallery, which was dark and filled with a strange, loud breathing. The sound was the panting of the patient over the intercom, which had been left on and turned up too loud. Unable to find the light switch, he groped his way to a front row seat and dropped into it. Through the glass he could see the man on the table, balding and trapped looking, about forty years old and in obvious pain, watching a nurse set out instruments. His eyes were dull; he would have received a sedative before coming in, and probably scopolamine.

In a few minutes the fat boy who had been drinking coffee in the kitchen came into the OR, scrubbed and gloved.

"Doctor," the nurse said.

Fat boy nodded without interest and started to anesthetize. His sausage fingers toyed with the left arm, finding the antecubital vein without any trouble and slipping in the intravenous catheter. He placed cuffs on the other arm and began to take pressure readings.

"This was one we didn't expect," the nurse said.

"Could sure as hell do without it," fat boy said. He gave the muscle-relaxant with a sleep dose of Pentothol, then he intubated the patient's trachea and took over the job of the man's breathing with a ventilator.

The intern came in, the tall sloppy-looking one Adam had seen in the Ward. Neither the anesthesiologist nor the nurse acknowledged his presence. He began to prep the abdomen, scrubbing it down with antiseptics. Adam watched with interest, wanting to see how things were done here. It looked as though the intern was using a single solution. In the Georgia hospital they had had to wash the field first with ether, then with alcohol, then a third time with Betadine. "I trust you have noted what a smooth-shaven man Mr. Peterson is," the intern said. "A baby's ass by comparison is a veritable forest."

"Richard, as a surgeon you're a fair barber," fat boy said.

The one called Richard finished washing down the belly and began to cover the patient with sterile drapes, leaving exposed only a square foot of flesh framed in a field of cloth.

A surgeon came in. Meomartino, the Surgical Fellow, Adam supposed, but wasn't certain because nobody said hello. A big man with a broken hawk's-nose and an old, almost invisible scar on his cheek, who yawned and stretched, shuddering, "I was dreaming so very nicely," he said. "How's our perforated ulcer? Is he bleeding?"

"I don't think so, Rafe," fat boy said. "Heart rate 96. Respiration 30."

"What's his blood pressure?"

"Hundred-ten over 60."

"Let's go. I'll bet it's like a cigarette hole in there."

Adam saw him take the scalpel from the nurse and make the right paramedian incision, a deliberate parting of flesh that created two lips where before there had been belly flab. Meomartino cut through the skin and the fatty yellow subcutaneous tissue and Adam saw with interest that the intern had been trained to stop the bleeding with sponges instead of clips, at the same time using the pressure of the sponge to spread the margin of the wound so that the glistening gray envelope of the fascia was revealed. That's damned efficient, he thought; it had never occurred to them to do it that way in Georgia. For the first time he felt a flash of happiness; they have things to teach me here.

Meomartino had incised with slow care, but now he cut the fascia swift and clean. To do it that way, in one sure slash that would not cut into the rectus muscle just below, this man had had to do it well a great many times before, Adam knew. For one stupid moment he allowed himself to resent the Fellow for his easy skill. He half-stood to watch but the slob of an intern moved his head and shoulders over the operating field and he couldn't see anything else.

He leaned back in the chair and closed his eyes in the dark and saw in his mind what the surgeon below would be doing: he would lift the fascia and undermine it with the sharp edge of the scalpel and then pry it away with the blunt edge, exposing the midline meeting of the rectus. Then he would elevate the muscle and retract it laterally and go through the peritoneum and into the belly.

Into the belly. For somebody planning to go into general surgery, where so many cases are abdominal, that was the name of the game.

"Here you go, Richard. Here it is," the surgeon said in a little while. His voice was deep. His English was a shade too precise, Adam thought, as if he had learned it as a second language. "Right through the anterior wall of the duodenum. What do we do now?"

"Stitch, stitch, stitch?"

"And then?"

"Vagotomy?"

"Ah, Richard, Richard, I can't believe it. To be so young and so bright and so *half* right, my boy. A vagotomy *and* a drainage procedure. Then it will heal so nicely. A milestone in the annals."

They worked in silence after that, and Adam grinned above them in the dark, feeling the sloppy intern's chagrin as he had felt his own chagrin so many times in similar situations. It was warm in the gallery, colored like the womb. He dozed and dreamed an old nightmare of the two furnaces he had fed during the evenings of his undergraduate junior year, hating the yawning orange mouths that hungered for more coal than he could move.

Sitting in the dark gallery he moaned in his sleep and then jerked himself awake, stiff and wretched, momentarily uncertain of why his mood had changed. And then he remembered and licked his lips and grinned; the damn dream again. He hadn't had it for a long, long time, it must be the new hospital, the unfamiliar situation.

Below him the surgical team still worked. "Help me close the belly, Richard," the Chief Resident said. "I'll suture, you tie. I want it nice and tight."

"You'll get it tight as your childhood sweetheart," Richard said, speaking to Meomartino but looking at the scrub nurse, who gave no sign that she heard.

"I want it much tighter than that, Doctor," Meomartino said.

When he finally nodded, satisfied, and turned from the table, Adam left the gallery and hurried downstairs in time to catch the other man leaving the surgical theater.

"Dr. Meomartino."

The Surgical Fellow stopped. He was shorter than he had appeared when viewed from above. He should have been my mother's child, Adam thought inanely as he hurried to him. But not Italian, he decided, Spanish, perhaps. The color of olives, dark eyes, dark skin despite the usual hospital pallor, hair beneath the OR cap dark with damp but almost completely gray. This man is older than I am, he thought.

"I'm Adam Silverstone," he said, panting slightly. "The new Chief Resident." As appraising eyes took him in he shook a hand like a block of wood.

"You're a day early. I can see you will give me competition," Meomartino said with a slight smile.

"I hitch-hiked. I left myself an extra day and then found I didn't need it."

"Oh? You got a place to stay?"

"Here. The letter said the hospital furnishes a room."

"Usually the Chief Resident uses it only for the nights he's on. I prefer to live away. You and I would be too damn available living here."

"I'll be available. I'm broke."

Meomartino nodded without surprise. "I haven't the authority to assign you a room. But I can help you find a place to flop. For what's left of the night."

The elevator was old and slow. *In Case of Emergency Ring Three Times,* a sign by the bell advised. Adam thought of waiting for this creaking monster in an emergency and felt doubt.

It arrived finally and carried them to the sixth floor. The hallway was especially narrow and dark. The room number was 6-13, which could not be a portent, he told himself. The ceiling slanted; the room was under the old building's eaves. The shades were drawn. In the dim light he could see a terrifying crack in one of the plaster walls, which appeared to be feces-colored. Under the crack and facing the two beds there was a wooden chair flanked by a bureau and a desk, all the color of old mustard. On one of the beds a man in whites was sprawled, the *New England Journal of Medicine* spread open on his chest and abandoned in favor of sleep.

"Harvey Miller. Rotating from that fancy institution across town," Meomartino said, making no attempt to whisper. "Not a bad *hombre* for that place." His tone dismissed all outsiders. Yawning, he waved his hand and went out the door.

The air in the room was stale. Adam went to the window and

raised the bottom four inches. Immediately the blind began to flap; he raised it to conform to the window and the flapping stopped. The man on the bed stirred but did not waken.

He lifted the *New England Journal* from Harvey Miller and lay down. He tried to remember what Gaby Pender looked like, but he found that he could not reconstruct the parts; he recalled only a very deep tan and a marvelous mole on her face, and that the whole was a girl he had liked very much. The mattress was thin and lumpy, a reject from the wards. Wafting up into his open window from the open window below came a sound of pain, more than a groan but less than a scream. Harvey Miller patted his groin in his sleep, unaware that his privacy had been violated. "Alice," he said clearly.

Adam turned to the classified advertising pages of the journal, fantasizing about a future that would offer all the things of life he had never been able to afford as well as sufficient money so that Myron Silberstein's outstretched palm no longer would be a threat to survival. Certain ads he skipped or read scornfully, the invitations to applicants for post-doctoral study, expenses paid with little or no stipend; the notices of research fellowships worth $7,000 a year; the university instructorships that paid a big ten thousand; the deceptively juicy descriptions of inexpensive practices for sale in the large medical centers, Boston, New York, Philadelphia, Chicago, Los Angeles, where there were established practitioners to tie a beginner's hands and send him, tin cup in hand, seeking piece work with the insurance companies at six dollars an hour.

Occasionally an advertisement would cause him to read it several times.

TEN MAN MULTISPECIALTY CLINIC,
corporation, needs general surgeon. Northern Michigan location in the heart of the fishing and hunting
country. New clinic building, and profit-sharing
plan. Beginning salary $20,000. Ownership partici-
pation after two years. Ownership income range
$30,000 to $50,000. Address F-213, *New Eng. J.
Med.* 13-2t

He understood that what he would need one year from now was a region far away from the heady medical atmosphere of the teaching hospitals, away from established competition. The ideal situation would be an ailing or aging surgeon in a remote environment, who was willing to take a gradual profit while phasing out his practice by turning it over little by little to a young associate. That kind of thing would be worth thirty-five thousand from the very beginning, with seventy-five thousand a year not impossible down the road.

On the rare occasions when he had stopped to analyze his feelings about medicine he knew that he wanted to be both a healer and a capitalist, Jesus Christ and the moneychangers all rolled into one. Well, why not? People who could afford to pay their bills got just as sick as the indigent poor. Nobody had asked him to take a vow of poverty. He had had enough of that without vows.

Chapter 2: Spurgeon Robinson

Baby! Spurgeon's Momma whispered, her voice a feather.

Spurgeon, baby, she said again, her voice heavier but rising, a bird that crowded the room with its fluttering.

His eyes were closed but he could see her. She was leaning over his bed like a peach tree heavy with fruit, her body in the fuzzless flannel nightgown all ripe sags and hard planes, her bare toes gnarled like roots beneath the ruined tree trunk legs. He felt ashamed that Momma should come upon him like this, because he knew that under the thin blanket he had a hard on, the result of dreams. Perhaps, he thought, if I pretend to sleep she will go away, but at that instant sleep became impossible due to a thin metallic slap as the timing mechanism in his alarm clock engaged. The clock jangled, a familiar, almost comforting sound that had been rousing him faithfully for years, and he awoke immediately although it took him a moment to remember that he was a grown man, and what he was.

Doctor Robinson, he remembered.

And *where*—a banged-up bitch of a hospital in Boston. His first day as an intern.

In the john at the end of the hall someone was standing on tiptoes before the speckled mirror, scraping at his chin with a razor.

"Morning. I'm Spurgeon Robinson."

The white boy used his towel carefully and then stuck out a good surgeon's hand, not large but strong, with a firm but easy grip.

"Adam Silverstone," he said. "I'm only about three strokes away from a clean shave."

"No hurry," Spurgeon said, although they both knew that there was. The bathroom had wooden floors and the paint on the walls was peeling. On the door of one of the two booths a philanthropist had written *Rita Leary is a nurse who does it like a tender bunny A Spinwall 7-9910*. It was the only reading matter in the room and he finished it quickly, from reflex casting a glance to see if the white boy had noticed him reading it.

"What's the Chief Resident like?" he asked casually.

The razor, about to scrape, paused half an inch in front of the cheek. "Sometimes I like him. Sometimes I don't like him at all," Silverstone said.

Spurgeon nodded and decided to shut up and let the man shave. Waiting like this could make him late on his first day, he thought. He hung up his robe and stepped out of his undershorts and into the shower, not daring to surrender to lengthy luxury but unable to resist after the long night of midsummer heat that had gathered in the room under the roof.

When he came out, Silverstone was gone.

Spurgeon shaved carefully but swiftly, bent like a tense black question-mark over the single old-fashioned sink; on his first day at a new hospital there were precedents to establish. One of them, he thought, was not to be the last man to arrive at the Chief Resident's office for morning rounds.

In his room he pushed his way into whites so stiff with starch that they crackled, clean white socks and the shoes he had polished the night before. He had only a few minutes. Breakfast, he thought regretfully, was out. The elevator was slow; it was going to be a long time before he was accustomed to the molasses pace of the ancient car in the face of a fast schedule. The Chief Resident's office on the second floor was filled with young men in whites, sitting, lounging, standing in proximity, some of them trying to look bored and a few of them succeeding.

The Chief Resident sat behind his desk, reading *Surgery*. It was Silverstone, he saw with embarrassment. A comedian or a philosopher, he thought, and was angry at himself for the gaucherie that had allowed him to ask a complete stranger's opinion about the boss he hadn't met. He let his glance slide over every face in the room.

All ofays. Please God, let me not screw up, he said silently, the prayer he had used for years before every exam.

He stood, shifting his weight from one foot to another. Finally the last man arrived, a transferred first-year resident, six minutes late, the first six minutes of his residency.

"What's your name?" Silverstone asked.

"Potter, Doctor. Stanley Potter."

Silverstone stared, eyes unblinking. The new men waited for a sign, a revelation, a preview.

"Dr. Potter, you've kept us waiting. Now we're keeping patients and nurses waiting."

The resident nodded, smiling in embarrassment.

"Do you understand me?"

"Yes."

"This is a clinical and educational duty, not a show put on for your adolescent amusement, to be attended tardily or at random. If you intend to serve on this service, you'll move and think and act like a surgeon."

Potter smiled miserably.

"Do you understand me?"

"Yes."

"Good." Silverstone looked slowly around the room. "Do you all understand me?"

Several of the new men nodded almost happily and exchanged with one another covert glances of great significance, their question answered.

A bastard, they told each other with their eyes.

Silverstone led the way, followed by a long line of residents and interns. He stopped only at certain beds, chatting for a moment with the patient, speaking briefly of the case history, asking a question or two in a sleepy, almost disinterested voice and then pushing on. The group made its way around the perimeter of the large room.

In one of the beds a colored woman whose red hair came from a cheap bottle stared through him as he stopped in front of her and she was surrounded by a silent wall of white-clothed young men.

"Hello," Silverstone said.

She looked very much like half a dozen hookers in the old neighborhood, Spurgeon thought.

"This is . . ." Silverstone checked the chart. ". . . Miss Gertrude Soames." He read for a few moments. "Gertrude has been in the hospital before for a number of symptoms which can be attributed to the fact that she's had some liver cirrhosis—which probably can be attributed to the usual fact. There appears to be something palpable there."

He threw back the sheet and lifted the rough cotton gown, exposing thin shanks rising to a melancholy muff and a belly with two old incision scars. He probed her abdomen first with the fingertips of one hand and then with both, while she turned her gaze upon him now. Spurgeon thought of a dog wishing but not daring to bite.

"Right here," Silverstone said, taking Spurgeon's hand and placing it.

Gertrude Soames looked at Spurgeon Robinson.

You're the same as me, her eyes said. Help me.

He glanced away, before his eyes could say, I can't help you.

"Feel it?" Silverstone asked.

He nodded.

"Gertrude, we have to take something called a liver biopsy," the Chief Resident said cheerfully.

She shook her head.

"Oh, yes."

"No," she said.

"We can't take it if you don't want us to. You have to sign a paper. But there's something wrong with your liver, and we won't know how to help you unless we make this test."

She was silent again.

"It's just a needle. We put in a needle and when we take it out there's a speck of liver on the end, not very much but for our purposes plenty, enough for us to test."

"That's a painful thing?"

"It hurts just a little bit, but there's no choice. It has to be done."

"I'm not your damn guinea pig."

"We don't want a guinea pig. We want to help you. Do you understand what may happen if we don't?" he asked gently.

"You say it that way, I understand." Her face remained as stone, but the dull eyes shone suddenly, and there were tears that ran down toward her mouth. Silverstone took a tissue from the bedstand and reached to wipe her face, but she jerked her head away.

He replaced the gown and adjusted the sheet. "You think it over for a while," he said, patting her knee, and they moved away.

On the male side of the ward a large man, so wide he seemed to fill the bed to overflowing, lay propped up by three pillows and watched them guardedly as they approached him.

"Mr. Stratton here is a truck driver for a soft drink bottling concern," Silverstone said, eyes on the chart. "A couple of weeks ago a wooden case fell off his truck and struck him below the right knee." He pulled down the sheet and revealed the man's leg, stocky but white and unhealthy-looking, with an ugly ulcerated sore about four inches in diameter.

"Does your leg feel cold, Mr. Stratton?"

"All the time."

"Soaks and antibiotics have been tried, but this isn't healing properly, and the leg has lost color," Silverstone said. He turned to the resident he had lacerated for tardiness. "Dr. Potter, what do you think?"

Potter smiled again, looking wretched, but said nothing.

"Dr. Robinson?"

"An arteriogram."

"Head of the class. Where would you inject the dye?"

"Femoral artery," Spurgeon said.

"What, I need an operation?"

"We're not talking about an operation, at least not yet," Silverstone said. "Your leg feels cold because the blood isn't circulating in it as well as it should. We've got to find out why. We're going to inject some dye into an artery in your groin and then take some pictures."

Mr. Stratton's face reddened. "I can't take that kind of business," he said.

"What do you mean?"

"Why don't you just keep on soaking it like Dr. Perlman's been doing?"

"Because Dr. Perlman tried that and it didn't do you any good."

"Try it some more."

There was a long moment's silence.

"Where's Dr. Perlman?" the man said. "I want to speak to Dr. Perlman."

"Dr. Perlman is no longer Chief Resident here," Silverstone said.

"I'm told he's now Captain Perlman and on his way to Vietnam. I'm Dr. Silverstone, the new Chief Resident."

"I couldn't even take the shots when I was in the Merchant Marine," the man said. Someone snickered on the fringe of the group circling his bed, and Silverstone turned and stared coldly.

"It's supposed to be funny, a guy my size afraid of you bastards," Stratton said. "But it isn't funny, believe you me. First guy puts his hand on me, I'll beat the crap out of him."

Silverstone placed a hand lightly, almost absentmindedly, on the patient's chest. They looked at one another. Incredibly, moisture glittered in Mr. Stratton's eyes.

Nobody snickered. His face, Spurgeon thought wonderingly, was shaped by the same sharp fear that had etched the face of the aging prostitute across the hall, expressions so similar she might have been his sister.

This time Silverstone did not reach for tissues. "Now, you listen," he said, a man talking to an errant child. "You pay attention. You can't afford to waste time. If you give us trouble—*any* trouble —about examining you, we won't ever have to worry about your beating the crap out of us. You won't be able to beat the crap out of Little Orphan Annie, pal. You'll either have one leg or you'll be dead.

"Do you understand me?"

"Butchers," Mr. Stratton whispered.

Silverstone turned on his heel and walked away, followed obediently by fourteen shadows dressed in white.

They gathered in the surgical amphitheater for the Mortality Conference.

"What the devil is the Mortality Conference?" Jack Moylan, the intern next to Spurgeon, whispered after glancing at the mimeographed first-day schedule.

Spurgeon knew. They had held Mortality Conferences in New York, although as a student he had been ineligible to attend.

"A place where your mistakes fly home to roost," he said.

Moylan looked puzzled.

"You'll end up calling it the Death Committee like everyone else. The entire surgical staff meets to review deaths on the Service and decide if they were preventable—and if they *were,* why they weren't prevented. It's a method of continuing education and surgical quality control. A responsibility-fixer, a kind of professional pin-the-tail-on-the-donkey."

"Jesus," the other intern said.

They sat in the rising tiers of seats, drinking coffee or Pepsi in cardboard cups. One of the nurses passed plates of Oreos and Uneeda Biscuits. In the front of the room Silverstone and Meomartino sat at opposite ends of a small table piled with case records. For administrative and teaching purposes, the house officers were divided into two groups, the Blue Team and the Red Team. Cases concerning the Red Team were handled by Meomartino, while the Blue Team was overseen by Silverstone.

Next to an empty seat at the beginning of the first row, the Associate Chief of Surgical Services, Dr. Bester Caesar Kender ("when in trouble it's Bester C. Kender"), a cigar-chewing former Air Force colonel who had made a national name for himself as the Service's kidney surgeon and transplant innovator, was telling an earthy story to Dr. Joel Sack, head of Pathology. They were a study in physical contrasts, Kender a big, hirsute man with a florid complexion and the slow sound of his Maine potato-country origins still in his speech, Sack bald and fussy-looking, a wry chipmunk of a man.

Sitting together were the two Chinese on the staff, Dr. Lewis Chin, a native Bostonian and a Visiting Surgeon, and moon-faced Dr. Harry Lee, a third-year resident from Formosa; and, as if for comfort, the two females, Dr. Miriam Parkhurst, another Visiting, and Dr. Helena Manning, a cool, assured girl who was a first-year resident.

Everyone rose when the Chief of Surgery entered the room, Spurgeon sloshing cola over the edge of his cup onto the leg of his beautiful fresh whites.

Dr. Longwood nodded and they sat obediently.

"Gentlemen," he said.

"I welcome those of you who are new to Suffolk County General Hospital.

"This is a busy municipal institution which offers you a brutally heavy work load and demands a great deal from you in return.

"Our standards are high. It is expected that each of you will do no less than fulfill your promise.

"The meeting about to commence is the Mortality Conference. It is that portion of the week which is most important to your continuing professional development. Once you leave the operating room the surgery you perform there becomes a thing of the past. At this meeting your failures and mine will be hauled out and examined under the searching scrutiny of our peers. What happens here, perhaps even more than what happens in the operating room, is what will turn you into surgeons."

He took a handful of crackers, settled himself in the front row and nodded to Meomartino. "You may begin, Doctor."

As the Surgical Fellow read the details it was apparent that the first case was routine, a 59-year-old male with advanced liver carcinoma who had not sought help until too late.

"Preventable or unavoidable?" Dr. Longwood asked, brushing crumbs. Each senior man voted unavoidable, and the Chief concurred. "Long past the time of no return," he said. "Points up the need for early diagnosis."

The second case was that of a woman who had died of heart failure while being treated medically in the ward for gastric lesions. There had been no previous heart disease history, and the autopsy had revealed that the lesions had in fact been non-malignant. Again each of the surgeons declared the death unavoidable.

"I agree," Dr. Longwood said, "but I must remark that if she had not died of coronary disease we would have been treating her wrongly. She should have been opened and explored. An interesting article in *Lancet* two months ago emphasized that the five-year survival rate for medically treated gastric tumors—undetermined whether benign or malignant—is ten per cent. When the patient is explored to find out just what's happening in there, the five-year survival rate rises until it becomes fifty-to-seventy percent."

This is a class room, Spurgeon thought, relaxing and beginning to enjoy himself; only a class room.

Dr. Longwood introduced Dr. Elizabeth Hawkins and Dr. Louis Solomon. Spurgeon felt the small change in the atmosphere, noticed Dr. Kender, the kidney transplant man, lean forward, nervously jiggling something is his ham-like hand.

"We are happy that Dr. Hawkins and Dr. Solomon have accepted our invitation to meet with us today," Dr. Longwood said. "They are residents in the Pediatric Service, where they were nearing the end of the internship at the time of occurrence of the next death to be discussed."

Adam Silverstone read of five-year-old Beth-Ann Meyer, who had suffered thirty percent body burns when scalded by boiling water. Two skin grafts later in the hospital's pediatric ward she had vomited one night at three o'clock, and cast-up foodstuffs had occluded her windpipe. It had taken a resident in anesthesiology sixteen minutes to respond. When he got there the small patient was dead.

"There was no excuse for the amount of time taken by the anesthesiologist in responding, of course," Dr. Longwood said. "But tell me . . ." the cool eyes traveled from Dr. Hawkins to Dr. Solomon, ". . . why didn't you do a tracheotomy?"

"It happened so fast," the girl said.

"There was no tracheotomy kit," Dr. Solomon said.

Dr. Kender held up, between his thumb and forefinger, the object he had been shaking in his fist. "Do you know what this is?"

Dr. Solomon cleared his throat. "A pen knife."

"I'm never without it," the kidney surgeon said quietly. "I could open a windpipe with it on a trolley car."

Neither of the pediatric residents answered. Spurgeon could not take his eyes from the pale face of the girl. They are handing it to these people cold turkey, he thought. They are saying to them: You —*you*—killed this child.

Dr. Longwood glanced at Dr. Kender.

"Preventable," the Associate Chief said through the cigar.

At Dr. Sack.

"Preventable."

At Dr. Paul Sullivan, a Visiting Surgeon.

"Preventable."

At Dr. Parkhurst.

"Preventable," she said.

Spurgeon sat there as the word rolled like a cold stone around the perimeter of the room, no longer able to look at either of the pediatric residents.

God, he thought, don't ever let this happen to me.

He was assigned to Quincy Ward with Silverstone, and they walked there together. It was a busy hour for the nurses, the time of scut work, of changing simple dressings and of taking temperatures, of serving juice and carrying bedpans, of delivering pills and completing records. They stood in the corridor while the resident looked at the notes he had made during morning rounds and Spurgeon watched two giggling student nurses making beds until finally Dr. Silverstone looked up.

And the Lord spake, Spurgeon thought, saying . . .

"Harold Krebs, post-op prostatectomy, Room 304, needs two units of whole blood. Start an I.V. on Abraham Batson in 310. And then pick up a cut-down kit and we'll place a central venous catheter in Roger Cort, 308."

There was a spare, wispy-haired old woman, with the head nurse's stripe on her cap, sitting in the records station. Spurgeon reached past her with a muttered apology and took the telephone.

"Do you have the number of the blood bank?" he asked her.

Without looking at him she handed him a telephone directory.

When he dialed it, the number was busy.

A very pretty brunette nurse with a good body displayed in a nylon uniform came into the station and began to write a message on the blackboard: *Dr. Levine please call WAyland 872-8694.*

He dialed the blood bank again. "Damn."

"Can I help you, Doctor?" the young nurse said.

"I'm just trying to get the blood bank."

"That's the hardest number in the hospital to get. Most of the interns just go down and pick up the bloods themselves. The person to see down there is Betty Callaway."

He thanked her and she hurried out of the station. He leaned past the head nurse again and replaced the telephone. Old white witch, he thought, why didn't *you* tell me? Hell, I don't even know how to find the damn blood bank, he realized in dismay.

He leaned over and looked at the head nurse's name tag. "Miss Fultz," he said. She continued to write in her records.

"Can you direct me to the blood bank?"

"Basement," she said, without looking up.

He found it after three inquiries and ordered the bloods from Betty Callaway, waiting impatiently while she looked up Harold Krebs's blood type. Riding back upstairs in the slow elevator he cursed himself out for a jackass, fighting landlords like a little tin version of Stokely when he should have been wandering around the hospital, learning where everything was.

The way things had started he would not have been surprised to discover that the patient in 304 had invisible veins, but Harold Krebs turned out to be a man with a good, well-defined venous system made for accepting catheters, and he got the transfusion going without trouble.

Now, the intravenous for 310. But where were the I.V.'s kept? He couldn't ask Miss Fultz, he thought, and then swiftly changed his mind; why allow the old witch to frighten him off?

"Hallway closet," she said, head still bent.

Old lady, you look at me, he said silently. It's just black skin, it doesn't hurt your eyes. He got the I.V. and of course Abraham Batson in 310 turned out to be what he had expected in 304, a dried-up little man with hair-line veins and the puncture marks to show that others had tried and failed. It took eight additional stabbings amid groans and looks and mutterings from the pincushion, and then he was able to flee.

Jesus, the cut-down kit.

"Miss Fultz," he said.

This time she looked at him. He was enraged by the contempt in her eyes, which were faded blue.

"Where will I find a cut-down kit?"

"Three doors down on the left."

He got it and found Silverstone in the women's side of the ward.

"God. I was about to send out an alarm," the resident said.

"I spent most of the time being lost."

"Me, too." Together they went to Room 308.

Roger Cort was carcinoma of the bowel. If a man stared hard enough, Spurgeon thought, he could see the angel perched on Roger Cort's right shoulder.

"You ever do a cut-down?"

"No."

"Watch closely. You'll do it yourself next time."

He watched while Silverstone sterilized the ankle and injected Novocaine and then snapped on sterile gloves and made a tiny incision anterior to the medial malleolus. He made two stitches, one above and one below, slipped in the cannula and tied it in with the second stitch, and in a few seconds glucose was dripping into Roger Cort's bloodstream. Silverstone made it look easy. I'll be able to do that, Spurgeon thought. "What's your next pleasure?" he asked.

"Coffee," Silverstone said, and they went for some. The pretty brunette nurse poured it for them.

"What do you think of our ward?" she said.

"What's the secret sorrow of your head nurse?" the Chief Resident asked. "She hasn't done more than grunt at me all morning."

The girl laughed. "Oh, she's a hospital legend. She doesn't talk to doctors unless she likes them, and she likes very few doctors. Some of the visiting men have known her for thirty years and they still get grunts."

"What an inheritance," Silverstone said gloomily.

At least, Spurgeon thought, it isn't my color she hates. She hates everybody. Somehow the thought made him happy. He finished his coffee and left Silverstone and changed several dressings without having to ask Miss Fultz where anything was. I'd better start exploring this place, he thought, wondering suddenly what he would do if somebody were to go into heart failure. He didn't know where the defibrillator was, or the resuscitator. A nurse was hurrying down the corridor. "Can you tell me where the Code 99 equipment is kept?" he asked.

She stopped as if she had run into a glass wall. "You have a Code 99?"

"No," he said.

"Are you expecting an emergency, Doctor?"

"No."

"Well, I've got a woman vomiting her guts out," she said indignantly and hurried away.

"Yes, ma'am," he said, but she was gone. Sighing, he set out to search, an explorer in a strange and foreign land.

At eight p.m., thirty-six hours after he had begun his career as an intern, Spurgeon opened the door of his room on the sixth floor and winced as the heat flooded out to meet him.

"Hoo-whee," he said softly.

He had slept here only a few hours on the preceding night, interns being on first call, with the resident being bothered only for matters of some seriousness. Eight or nine times he had been awakened to prescribe drugs that would bring to patients the sleep denied to their intern.

He put down the paper sack he was carrying and threw the window open wide. He pushed out of his shoes without untying the laces, stripped out of his whites and peeled off a sodden undershirt. From the bag he took a six-pack of beer and, tearing the aluminum tab from a can, drank one-third of its contents in one long, cold swallow. Then, sighing, he went to the closet and got the guitar.

Sitting on the bed he finished the can of beer and began to pluck the strings and sing softly, the tenor part of a madrigal.

> *There's a rose in my gar-den*
> *And it has one sharp thorn,*
> *And I prick myself on it*
> *At least twice a morn.*
> *And I hasten to plead*
> *As I hasten to bleed:*
> *Wipe the blood*
> *Off the rose*
> *In my gar-den . . .*

Hell, no, he thought sorrowfully, the mood was all wrong in this place.

What his own material had always needed was an admiring audience, a willowy chick telling him, "clever Spurgeon" with her eyes, the slight promising pressure of a knee as she sat next to him on the piano bench, and guys hustling drinks for him as if he were Ellington and urging him to play this song or that.

He missed that gig, he realized.

"Your fault, Uncle Calvin," he said aloud.

Uncle Calvin had thought for sure he'd end up playing piano in some Harlem joint, knocking himself out for cakes or worse. He grinned and opened another can and drank to the stepfather whose money had made him a doctor despite the fact that Spurgeon refused to train himself to take over the business the old man had sweated most of his life to develop. And then drank to himself, swimming in his own sweat in the tiny hotbox of a room.

"Uncle Calvin," he admitted aloud, "this ain't exactly my idea of success."

He walked to the window and looked out at the lights that were beginning to pop into life as the city darkened. Got to get away from this clothes-closet, he told himself. Somewhere down there was a comfortable pad where maybe he could have a second-hand piano.

"You bastards," he told the city.

He had stayed at the Statler for three days while answering apartment ads in the *Herald* and the *Globe*. Real estate people had reacted warmly to calls from Dr. Robinson, but always when he showed up to look at the apartment it had just been rented.

"You ever hear of Crispus Attucks?" he asked the last Realtor.

"Who?" the man had said nervously.

"He was a colored man, like me. He was the first American killed in your goddamned Revolution."

The man had nodded brightly and smiled with relief as he walked away.

There must be nice buildings that have been broken, he thought.

Well, he told himself, maybe he had been looking at apartments that were *too* nice. The thing was, he could afford a nice place. A check was going to come once a month from Uncle Calvin, even though he had explained that now he would get paid by the hospital. They had argued at length until he had understood that the third Thursday of each month, when he signed that check, Calvin would be giving away two things, money, which he valued because there had been a time when he hadn't had it, and love, the most miraculous thing in his life.

Old Uncle, he thought tenderly. Why haven't I been able to call him my father?

There was a time, remembered clearly but as a bad dream, when they had been poor niggers, before his mother had married Calvin and they had become wealthy Negroes. He had slept in a cot next to his mother's bed in a small dreary room on West 172nd Street. There was faded brown wallpaper with watermarks around the top edge of one of the walls, left there long ago when something had overflowed on the floor above or a steampipe had leaked. He always thought of the marks as tearstains because when he cried his mother would point to them and tell him that if he didn't stop bawling his cheeks would have marks on them like the ones on the wallpaper. He remembered a creaky rockingchair with a worn plaid pad, the two-burner gas range that worked badly so that water took a long time to boil, the small card table on which no food could be left overnight because of the hungry things that came out of the walls.

He remembered these things only when he could not elude their memory. He preferred to think of Momma, of how she had been when she was young.

When he was small his mother had left him each day with Mrs.

Simpson, who lived in three rooms on the floor below and had three children of her own and a relief check instead of a husband or a job. Momma got no relief check. She worked as a waitress in a whole series of restaurants while he was a boy, the labor leaving her with bad feet and thickened legs. Even so, she was exceedingly pretty. She had given birth to him when she was a young girl, and above the spoiled legs her body had ripened but remained slim and hard.

Momma sometimes cried in her sleep and she was always wiping disinfectant onto the seat of the toilet they shared with the Hendersons and the Catletts. Sometimes at night after he said his prayers he would whisper her name over and over in the dark. Roe-Ellen Robinson . . . Roe-Ellen Robinson . . .

When he was little and she heard him whispering her name she would let him come into bed with her. She would put her arms around him and hug and squeeze till he shouted, and she would scratch his back and sing him songs—

> *Oh, the river is deep and wide, hallelujah!*
> *Milk and honey on the other side . . .*

—and tell him what a good life they would have when they got to the land of milk and honey, and he would lay his head on her big soft breasts and go to sleep happy, happy, happy.

He went to the neighborhood school, an old red-brick building with windows that were broken faster than the city could replace the glass, a concrete play-yard outside and a peculiar miasma inside, composed mostly of the smell of coal-gas and the scent of bodies unaccustomed to private baths and hot water. When he had started the first grade his mother had told him to be sure and learn to read because his father had been a reading man, always with his nose in a book. So Spurgeon learned and grew to like it. When he got into the higher grades, fourth and fifth and sixth, it was harder to read in school because there was generally some kind of disturbance, but by this time he had found his way to the public library and he took books home all the time.

He ran with two kids in particular, Tommy White, who was very black, and Fats McKenna, who was light yellow and very skinny, which was why he was called Fats. At first the thing he liked about them was their names, but after a while they became his friends. They all liked a girl named Fay Hartnett who could sing !ike

Satchmo and lipfart like a funky trumpet. Mostly they just hacked around the neighborhood of West 171st Street, played stickball, praised the Gi'nts and criticized the Yankees and their lousy white teachers. Once in a while they pinched something, two of them keeping a shopkeeper's attention while the third swiped, usually something to eat. On three Saturday nights they had rolled drunks, Tommy and Spurgeon each holding an arm behind the man's back while Fats, who thought he looked like Sugar Ray, did the physical part.

They had watched closely the changes occurring in Fay Hartnett's body, and one night on the roof of Fats' building she showed them how to do something some older boys had showed her how to do. They bragged about it to the four winds and a couple of nights later she performed the same service for them and a large group of their friends and acquaintances. Two months later she dropped out of school and from time to time they would see her on the street and snigger because her stomach was blowing up as if she had swallowed a basketball and somebody was pumping it full of air. Spurgeon felt neither guilt nor responsibility; the first time he had been second and the second time he had been seventh or eighth—way back in line. And who knew how many other parties there had been, to which he hadn't been invited. But sometimes he missed hearing her sing like Louie.

He couldn't imagine Momma doing that woman-thing that Fay had done, spreading her legs and squirming all wet and excited like that, and yet he knew somewhere deep inside that she probably did do that, sometimes. Roe-Ellen always knew a lot of men and every once in a while she would pay Mrs. Simpson to let Spurgeon sleep overnight in her place with her two boys, Petey and Ted. One man in particular, Elroy Grant, a big handsome man who ran a dry-cleaning store on Amsterdam Avenue, kept hanging around Momma. He smelled of strong whiskey and paid no attention to Spurgeon, who hated him. He chased around with a lot of women and one day Spurgeon found Roe-Ellen on the bed crying and when he asked Mrs. Simpson what was the matter she told him Elroy had married a widow who owned a saloon in Borough Hall and had closed the dry cleaning store and moved to Brooklyn. Momma moped around for weeks after that, then finally she snapped out of it and announced that Spur would have to be especially grown-up because she had enrolled in a secretarial course after work and would be spending four nights a week at the Patrick Henry High School on upper Broadway. The nights she didn't go to school he always made certain to be home; they became his holidays.

Roe-Ellen attended the classes for two years and when she had completed the course she could type 72 words a minute and take a hundred words a minute in the Gregg system of shorthand. She expected to have a hard time finding a job but two weeks after she went out looking for work she was hired for the secretarial pool at the American Eagle Life Insurance Company. Every night she came home starry-eyed and with tales of new wonders, the fast elevator, the wonderful girls in the secretarial pool, the number of letters she had done that day, the short hours, the joys of resting her legs while putting in a full working day.

One day she came home looking almost frightened. "Honey, I saw the President today."

"Eisenhower?"

"No. Mr. Calvin J. Priest, President of the American Eagle Life Insurance Company. Spur, honey, he's *colored!*"

It didn't make sense. "You must have made a mistake, Momma. He's probably a real dark ofay."

"I'm telling you he's as black as you are. And if Calvin J. Priest can do something wonderful like becoming president of the American Eagle Life Insurance Company, why shouldn't Spurgeon Robinson? Baby, baby, we're going to see the land of milk and honey yet. I promise you!"

"I believe you, Momma."

Their vehicle to the land of milk and honey, of course, was Uncle Calvin.

By the time he was a man grown, Spurgeon *knew* Calvin Priest, as he was after Spurgeon had met him and as he had been before their meeting. He was able to obtain this knowledge because Calvin was a communicative man who used his voice to make contact, reaching out toward Roe-Ellen and her son with words like hands. The bits and pieces of his life were gleaned by Spurgeon over a long period of time, during many conversations, after listening to unending reminiscences and rambling stories, until he had the true picture of the man, his step-father.

He was born during a tropical storm on September 3, 1907, in the peaches-country town of Justin, Georgia. The initial in his name stood for Justin, the name of the community's founding family in whose home Calvin's maternal grandmother, Sarah, had once worked as a house girl and a slave.

The last surviving member of the Justin family, Mr. Osborne Justin—attorney, town clerk, elderly practical joker as well as the inheritor of certain traditional roles—had offered old Sarah ten dollars if her daughter would name the baby Judas, but the old lady was both too proud and too shrewd. She named the baby after the white man's family, despite—or perhaps because of—the fact that according to local legend their relationship in their younger days was far more than that of slave girl and master's son, and fully aware that custom demanded that the old white man make the gift to the child anyway, to acknowledge the tribute paid to his family name.

Calvin grew up as a rural Negro. As long as he was in Georgia he never heard himself identified without an emphasis on the middle name—Calvin *Justin* Priest—and it was perhaps this link with a privileged background and portent of proud things to come which led him to be allowed extended schooling. He was a religious boy who enjoyed the drama of prayer meeting and for a long time he thought he would be a preacher. It was a happy boyhood, despite the fact that both his parents were carried off by the epidemic of influenza that leaked into the countryside from the cities, tardy but just as deadly, in 1919. Three years later Sarah knew that although God had granted her a rich and long life, it was nearing its end. She dictated a letter to young Calvin, who transcribed it painstakingly and sent it off to Chicago, the place of opportunity and freedom. It offered Sarah's burial money, one hundred and seventy dollars, to former neighbors named Haskins if they would take her grandson to their home and to their bosom. She was certain that Osborne Justin would see to her burial; it was a chance for one last joke at his expense.

The reply came in the form of a penny postal card on which someone had scrawled in pencil:

SIND THE BOY.

Before he returned to Georgia he was a man.

Moses Haskins turned out to be a mean brute who beat Calvin and his own brood with regular impartiality, and he ran away before he had lived with the Haskins family a year. He sold the *Chicago American,* shined shoes, then lied about his age and labored in a stockyard packing house. The work was bitterly hard—who would have thought dead animals could weigh so much?—and in the beginning he did not think he would last, but his body toughened and the money was good. Still, two years later, when the opportunity arose to become a roustabout with a traveling carnival, at less money, he seized it eagerly. He traveled the wide country with the show, drinking it all in, the glories of it, the high places and the remote valleys, the different kinds of people. He did a little of everything that required a strong back, packed and repacked the canvas, raised and lowered the tents, fed and watered the miserable animals: a few mangy cats, some monkeys, a pack of trained dogs, an old bear, a clipped-winged eagle that sat chained to its perch, white tailfeathers drooping. The eagle died in Chillicothe, Ohio.

When Calvin had been with the carnival for ten months the show took to the southland, and the day they pulled into Atlanta he helped raise the tents and then told the foreman he had to go away for a few days and he took a bus and sat in the back until it arrived in Justin.

Sarah had died several years before and he had already cried for her, but he wanted to see where she was buried. But he couldn't find his grandmother's grave. When he sought out the preacher that night the man grumbled because he was tired from a long day of picking peaches, but he got a flashlight and came with Calvin and searched until he found the grave, small and unmarked and—what Sarah had never been in life—in the charity corner.

The next day Calvin hired a man to help him. There was no open plot next to his mother but there was one not too far away, and he and the other man dug a grave. They moved his grandmother. The box in which she was buried crumbled some when they lifted it, but it was in surprisingly good shape after two years in the wet red clay. He stood there that evening as the preacher rolled the fine-sounding biblical phrases into the darkening sky. Somewhere high, high up, a bird hovered proudly. An eagle, he decided; but totally different from the captive carnival bird that had died. This one moved so free through air it owned that as he watched it he began to cry. He realized that by relegating the old nigger lady to a pauper's grave, Osborne Justin, attorney, town clerk, elderly practical joker and inheritor of certain traditional roles, had had the last laugh after all.

Calvin left money with the preacher to pay for a stone and then he took the bus back to the carnival. He never used his middle name again. From that day on he was simply Calvin J. Priest.

When the American economy fell apart he was twenty-two years old. He had seen the country, its width and its depth, the giant cities and the sleepy little towns, and he had found that he loved it desperately. He knew it was a country that didn't really belong to him, but seventeen hundred dollars of it did, wrapped securely in the brown sock.

The market crashed while the carnival was beginning its autumn southern tour, and as businesses failed and corporations fell the deepening of the depression could be read in the dwindling attendance at each performance, until in Memphis, Tennessee, the show performed to eleven people and failed.

He got himself a room there and spent the fall season trying to figure out what he was going to do next. At first he just loafed. It had been a dry summer and he spent lots of his days fishing with a pitchfork and gunny sack, an art once taught to him by a roustabout from Missouri. He would go to the exposed bottom of the receded river and violate the dry cracked upper mud until he came to the rich wet underneath, where the catfish had buried themselves like fat black jewels until the winter rains. He harvested them like potatoes and lugged the bag full of horned pout home to help his landlady skin and clean them, and she fried the sweet white meat and the whole boardinghouse ate and sang hosannas to his skill with rod and reel. At night he lay in his bed and read in the newspaper about white men who used to be millionaires jumping out of the windows of skyscrapers, while he put his hand into his pocket and stroked the money like a man absentmindedly touching his sex, trying to decide whether to go North.

The landlady had a tramp of a daughter named Lena with eyes like white pools in her brown face and straightened hair and a hot mouth that played on his body and one night he lay in the room with the girl, trying to make love on the mattress under which the money was hidden, and their lovemaking being spoiled by the sound of somebody's broken heart.

When he asked the girl who was crying she told him it was her mother.

When he asked her why, she told him the white bank in which her mother had kept her burial money had just failed, and she wept for the funeral she would never have.

After the girl had left him he thought about Old Sarah and the burial money she had once pinned to his underwear. He remembered the mean pauper's grave in Justin, Georgia.

The following morning he walked around Memphis. Then after lunch he hiked out of the city, past the outskirts and into open country. After five days of looking, the land he decided on was two acres of tired meadow nestled between a stand of pines and a snaggle-banked river. It cost him six one-hundred-dollar bills and his hands trembled as he paid the money over and collected the deed, but nothing could have stopped him because he had thought it all out and he knew this was something he was going to do.

It cost him another twenty-one dollars and fifty cents for a fine big black and white sign saying *Shadowflower Cemetery*. He took the name from the verse of the Book of Job that had been Sarah's favorite, *He cometh forth like a flower and is cut down; he fleeth also as a shadow and continueth not.*

He found his landlady in the kitchen of the boardinghouse, boiling up a big pot of clothes, her red eyes streaming in the lye steam. There was a pitcher of buttermilk and he sat and drank three glasses without saying anything, then he put a nickel and a dime on the table to pay for the refreshment and began to talk. He told her his plans for Shadowflower, about the beautiful plots, bigger than any white man's; about the singing birds in the pines, and even about the big catfish in the river which, although he had not seen them, he somehow knew had to be there.

"It's no good, boy," she said. "My burial money's gone."

"You must have *some* money. You got boarders."

"No real money I can spare. Not even for burial."

"Well, now." He touched the coins he had left on the table. "You got this."

"A nickel an' a dime? You gonna give me a buryin' place for a nickel an' a dime?"

"Tell you what," he said. "You come up with a nickel an' a dime each and every week and the burial place is yours right now."

"Man," she said, "what if I die three weeks from this very moment?"

"It would be a real loss."

"What if I *never* die?"

He smiled. "Then we both gonna be happy, sister. But you know all people gotta die some day. Ain't that right?"

"That's surely right," she said.

He sold her two other plots, one for each of her daughters. "You got friends lost their burying money when the banks failed, same as you?"

"I surely do. A buryin' place for a nickel and a dime! I can't hardly believe it."

"Give me their names and I'll drop around and see them," Calvin said. It was the beginning of the American Eagle Life Insurance Company.

Spurgeon remembered the day Momma brought Calvin home. He was sitting in the room doing homework when the key grated in the locked door and he knew it had to be Momma. He got up to greet her and when the door opened there was a man with her, not tall, half-bald, silver-rimmed spectacles, quizzical brown eyes that looked directly at him, weighing him, judging him and evidently liking what they observed because the man smiled and his hand took Spurgeon's, pumping it in a sure, dry grasp.

"I'm Calvin Priest."

"The President?"

"What? Oh." He laughed. "Yes." He looked slowly around the room, seeing the waterstained ceiling, the murky wallpaper, the broken borax furniture.

"You can't live here any more," he said to her.

Her voice broke in her throat. "Mr. Priest," she whispered. "You have the wrong idea about me. I'm just a plain, ordinary colored girl. I'm not even really a secretary. What I've been most of my life is a waitress."

"You're a lady," he said. When Roe-Ellen told the story again and again for the rest of her life she always said that his exact words were, "You're *my* lady," Don Quixote to Dulcinea.

Neither Spurgeon nor Calvin ever contradicted her.

By the following week he had installed them in the apartment in Riverdale. She must have told him a lot about them. When they got there, a quart of Borden's Grade-A was on the dining room table in an ice-filled champagne bucket, next to a bowl of Gristede's honey.

"You mean we made it, Momma? This is it?" Spurgeon asked.

Roe-Ellen couldn't answer him but Calvin rubbed the woolly head. "You crossed the river, son," he said.

They were married a week later and left for a month in the Virgin Islands. A fat, happy woman named Bessie McCoy stayed with Spurgeon. She did crossword puzzles all day long and cooked fine meals and left him alone except for an occasional query about esoteric words he could never supply.

When the newlyweds returned, Calvin devoted several weeks to the task of selecting a good private school for him, deciding ultimately on Horace Mann, a fine liberal prep school whose campus was not far from the apartment house in Riverdale, and after entrance examinations and interviews to Spurgeon's enormous relief he was accepted.

His relationship with Calvin was a good one, but once he asked his step-father why he didn't do more for others of their own race.

"Spurgeon, what can I do? If you took all my money and split it up among all the brothers in just one tenement block of Harlem, there wouldn't be a single man there who wouldn't run out of cash sooner or later. You've got to realize that men are all the same. Remember that, boy: *all the same*. Whatever their color, the only way they're divided is into those who are bone lazy and the ones who are willing to work."

"You can't believe that," Spur said in disgust.

"Of course I believe it. Nobody's going to be able to help them unless they get off their rusty-dusties and help themselves."

"Without education or enough opportunities, how can they help themselves?"

"I did, didn't I?"

"You. You were a million-to-one long shot. To the rest of us you're a freak, don't you realize that?"

If anything in his young clumsiness he had meant it as a compliment, but the bitter despair in his voice sounded like scorn to the man. For months after that despite their mutual efforts there was a thin wall of glass between them. That summer—Spur was then sixteen—he ran away and shipped out to sea, telling himself he was trying to find out what his dead sailor father had been but in reality testing himself against the legend of his stepfather's independence at an early age. When he came back that fall he and Calvin were able to pick it right up again. The old warmth was there, and neither ever again dared ruin it by resuming the argument about their race. Eventually, the reason for argument died in the boy's mind, and he came to think of the inhabitants of places like Amsterdam Avenue in the way he thought of white folks.

They were "those people."

Ultimately, life with Calvin confused him badly. In Riverdale, black of skin and white of world, he neither knew what he was nor what kind of man he was expected to become. He was aware nowadays of the racial pride he gave Calvin (even the Justins of Justin, Georgia, never had a doctor in the family). But years after he had left Riverdale Spur thought immediately of the apartment house with the white doorman when he heard the Godfrey Cambridge comedic routine about the wealthy Negroes who, when informed a nigger lurked nearby, shrieked and looked around wildly, screaming in great anguish, "Where! Where? *Where?*"

The little room under the hospital roof was unbearably hot and far removed from both Amsterdam Avenue and the comfortable air-conditioning of Riverdale. He got up and peered from the window; the sixth floor of the hospital, he saw, was recessed. Directly below, the roof of the fifth story jutted out about ten feet, and after a moment he took a pillow and a blanket and dropped them out the window. Then, carrying the guitar and the carton of beer, he clambered over the sill.

There was a slight salt breeze, and he lay gratefully on the roof with the pillow against the wall. Below him were the fantastic lights of the city and over on the right began the slice of broad darkness that was the Atlantic Ocean and far out a steady yellow flicker like a feisty wink, a lighthouse.

Through the open window in the room next to his he heard Adam Silverstone unlock the door, come in and then go out. There was the sound of a dime in the coin drop of the wall telephone in the hall, and then Silverstone asked somebody if he could speak to Gabrielle.

It isn't like eavesdropping, he thought; what the hell else can I do—jump off the roof?

"Hello, Gaby? Adam. Adam Silverstone. Remember, from Atlanta? . . ."

He laughed. "I *told* you I'd be up. I've got a residency at County Hospital . . .

"Oh? I have this thing about writing. Really. I don't write to anybody . . .

"I did, too. It was wonderful. I've thought about you a lot."

He sounded very young, Spurgeon thought, and without the confidence he displayed as a doctor. He sucked at the can of beer, thinking about the kind of life this white boy must have had. Jew, he thought, that's a Jewish name. Probably doting parents, new bicycle, dancing school, temple, Colonial house, Adam stay in your room that's a nasty word, bring her home dear let us meet her.

"Look, I'd like to see you. How about tomorrow night? .... .

"Oh," he said flatly, and Spurgeon, listening, grinned sympathetically in the dark.

"No, I'm on the ward again by then, thirty-six hours on, thirty-six off. And the next couple of times I'm off I'm going to have to do a little moonlighting, to make some loot . . ."

"Well, I'll get to see you eventually," he said. "I'm a patient man. I'll call you next week. Be a good girl."

There was the sound of the receiver returned to the cradle and slow footsteps back into the room.

The white boy's ass was dragging. Chief Resident or not, his first shift in this place was probably as rough as mine, Spurgeon thought. "Hey," he said loudly. He had to say it twice before Silverstone looked out the window.

Adam saw Robinson sitting on the roof in his BVD's with his knees crossed like a black Buddha and he grinned.

"Come on out. Beer."

He came and Spurgeon handed him a beaded can. He sat on his haunches and drank and sighed, closing his eyes.

"That was quite an initiation we had," Spurgeon said.

"Amen. Jesus. It will be days before we know where the hell everything is around here. They might at least have given us a tour."

"I heard somewhere that more people die in hospitals the first week in July, when new residents and interns come in, than any other time."

"Wouldn't surprise the hell out of me," Adam said. He drank again and shook his head. "That Miss Fultz."

"That Silverstone."

"What's the Chief Resident like?" Silverstone said blandly.

"Sometimes I like him, sometimes I don't."

They found suddenly that they were laughing.

"I like the way you handle patients," Spurgeon said. "You take pretty good care of yourself."

"I've been taking care of myself for a long time," Silverstone said.

"Stratton let us give him his arteriogram. No more trouble."

"That colored girl, Gertrude Soames, signed her way out of the hospital this afternoon," Adam said. "She's committing suicide."

Maybe not enough to live for, boy, Spur said silently. There were two cans of beer left. He handed one to Adam and kept the last one for himself. "Little warm," he apologized.

"Good beer. Last beer I had was Bax."

"Never heard of it."

"Soapsuds and hoss piss. Big down South."

"You don't talk like a Southerner."

"Pennsylvania boy. Pitt, Jefferson Medical. You?"

"New Yorker. N.Y.U. all the way. Where'd you intern?"

"Philadelphia General. Took the first part of my residency at Atlanta Surgical."

"Hostvogel's clinic?" Spurgeon said, impressed despite his desire not to be. "Get to see much of the big man?"

"I was Hostvogel's resident."

Spurgeon whistled soundlessly. "What brought you here? The kidney transplant program?"

"No, I'm going into general surgery. The transplant stuff is just the frosting on the cake." He smiled. "Being Hostvogel's resident wasn't as good as it sounds. The great man loves to operate. House officers down there hardly get to hold a knife."

"Lord."

"Oh, he doesn't do it out of meanness. It's just that if any cutting is to be done, he can't give it up. Maybe that's what keeps him a great surgeon."

"Is he really great? As good as they say?"

"He's great, all right," Silverstone said. "He's so great he feels pulses nobody else in the world can feel because they aren't there. And statistics were invented just for him. I remember a medical society meeting when he announced that because of a surgical technique of his invention only three prostatectomies in a thousand developed trouble, and this old redneck surgeon who had used the method stood up and drawled, 'Yeah, suh, an' all three of 'em are my patients.' " He grinned. "A great reputation, a lousy teacher. After spending my time mostly watching I said hell with it and came here to learn surgery instead of flourishes. Longwood can't match Hostvogel's glitter, but he's a fantastic teacher."

"He scared the hell out of me at the Mortality Conference."

"Well, according to scuttlebutt, that's no act. That Chinese resident—Lee?—told me the tradition at this hospital dates back to years ago, when Longwood's predecessor, Paul Harrelmann, was fighting for the Chief-of-Service job against Kurt Dorland. The way they competed was in committee. They challenged each other, debated, needled, questioned, demanded justification of technique. Harrelmann finally was given the job and Dorland went away to become famous in Chicago, of course. But they had shown that the Death Committee could be used to keep the staff practicing the best possible surgery." Silverstone shook his head. "It isn't a gentle group. I never expected anything like that."

Spurgeon shrugged. "It isn't unique. Even without someone like Longwood pushing, at a lot of places it isn't only the new boys who have to sit up straight during the meeting. Those old pros know how to cut each other up pretty good." He looked at Silverstone curiously. "You sound as if it's new to you. Didn't you have a Mortality Conference down there in the land of peach cobbler and Lester Maddox?"

"Oh, yeah. Maybe they do one token autopsy for teaching purposes. Fella named Sam Mayes, Hostvogel's second-in-command, will sit around with two or three of the docs, talk about how Jerry Winters' boy has been accepted to med school over in Florida, maybe cuss out the forces of socialized medicine down in Washington and comment on the shapeliness of a new nurse's ass. Then they'll yawn and somebody'll say 'Too bad about this pour soul, unavoidable death, of course,' and they'll all nod and go home and diddle their wives."

They were silent for a moment. "I like it better the way it is here," Spurgeon said finally. "It's less comfortable—in fact, it scares the bejesus out of me—but it's sure to keep us sharp, maybe guarantee that we won't become what the public is beginning to think doctors are like."

"And what's that?"

"You know—Cadillac drivers. Fat cats. Rich philistines."

"Screw the public."

"Easier said than done."

"What do they know about what it takes to force yourself into medicine? I'm twenty-six. I've been stone-poor twenty-six years. I am personally looking forward to the longest, most expensive, luxury-assed Cadillac money can buy. And lots of other things, *material* things, I'm going to get with the money I earn as a surgeon."

Spurgeon looked at him. "Hell, you want those things, you don't have to suffer through a long residency. You've interned. You could go out tomorrow and earn good money."

Adam shook his head, smiling. "Ah, there's the fallacy. *Good,* but not *big.* What pays real money in this world is board-certification. That takes time to acquire. So I'm putting in the time. For me, the next year will be the best kind of self-torture, the last moments of humping before the orgasm."

Spurgeon had to grin at the simile. "You come up before that Death Committee a few times, you can join a monastery," he said.

They drank again, then Adam pointed the beer can at the guitar. "You play that thing?"

Spur picked it up and tinkled a few bars, *Oh, I wish I was in the land of cotton* . . .

Adam grinned. "Goddam liar." Several blocks away an ambulance siren called, the lonely banshee sound growing as it bore upon them.

When it had dwindled, Spurgeon chuckled. "I was talking to an ambulance driver today, a nice beer-bellied con man named Meyerson. Morris Meyerson. Call me Maish, he says.

"Anyway. Last month he was sent out in the wee hours to pick up this fella in Dorchester. Seems the patient has insomnia, and one night he couldn't sleep. The sound of a dripping faucet in the kitchen was driving him crazy, so he climbed out of the sack and went downstairs to fix it."

He belched. "Pardon. Now, get this.

"He's one of these people who sleeps in pajama tops only? No bottoms, understand? So he goes down into the cellar to get his monkey wrench or something, and in the cellar is where they keep their big, mean old Tom cat? On the way back up into the kitchen he forgets to shut the cellar door, and he's on his hands and knees under the sink, turning off the water—no bottoms, remember—when tommycat comes pussyfooting up and in, sees this strange object and—" the black hand rose, fingers transformed into claws, and then fell.

"Well, of course the man goes straight up in the air and hits his head a terrible clout on the bottom of the sink. His wife is awakened by the commotion, runs down from the bedroom to find him laid out and calls the hospital. It is just a slight concussion and by the time Meyerson and his intern respond, the man has regained consciousness. They're taking him out of the house when Meyerson asks him how it happened, and when the man tells him, Maish laughs so hard the stretcher slips out of his hand and the man falls and breaks a hip. Now he's suing the County."

It was their mutual fatigue more than the story that broke them up. They laughed together, shook, chortled, wept, would have rolled in their silliness had they not been close to the edge of the roof. The sudden, unexpected joy came from down deep in their bellies, uncoiling springs of tension wound tight by the thirty-six hours just past. Cheeks wet, Adam kicked happily, his foot striking one of the dead soldiers. The empty can skittered on the tar paper and then disappeared over the side.

It fell.

And fell.

And finally clattered on the cement courtyard below.

They waited in silence, resuming breathing at the same time. "I'd better look," Adam whispered.

"Let me. Natural camouflage." He crept forward and inched his head beyond the lip of the roof.

"What do you see?"

"Nothing going on down there but a tin can," he said. He lay with his cheek on the lip of the roof, the shingles still warm from the long day's sun, his head spinning from weariness and mirth and too much beer. This place may work out just fine, he told himself.

Later that night he was less optimistic. It was hotter, the dark marked by heat lightning but no rain. Spur lay naked on his bed, missing Manhattan. When all sound of movement had ceased next door and he felt sure that Silverstone was asleep he picked up the guitar and played softly in the dark, at first noodling but then seriously improvising, the running unnamed melody one he had never heard before but which said for him what he was feeling, a combination of loneliness and hope. It was ten minutes before he stopped playing.

"Hey," Silverstone said. "What's the name of that thing?"

He didn't answer.

"Hey, Robinson," Silverstone called. "Man, that was great. Play that again, will you?"

He lay quiet. He couldn't have played it again if he had wanted to. This place, he thought; no privacy but fine acoustics. The lightning flashed, occasionally calling forth a muttering of thunder. Twice more there were ambulance wailings. Fantastic sound to get into a piece of music, he thought. You'd have to use horns.

Eventually, without realizing it was possible, he made it into sleep.

Chapter 3: Harland Longwood

Early in August, after his attorneys had set up the irrevocable trust, Harland Longwood telephoned Gilbert Greene, chairman of the hospital board, and asked him to come to his office to review the terms of his will, in which he had named Greene as executor.

He felt that the trust was well-conceived. The income from a block of blue-chip securities would endow a new chair for Kender in the medical school. Longwood's salary as Chief of Surgery was more than adequate for his immediate needs, but he had a New Englander's innate aversion for dipping into capital.

The bulk of his estate would not be added to the trust until after his death, when a faculty board of advisors would be named to spend the income for the benefit of the medical school.

"I hope that advisory group won't have to be formed for a long time," Greene said after he had read the papers.

The remark was as close as he had ever heard the banker come to making an emotional statement.

"Thank you, Gilbert," he said. "Can I offer you a drink?"

"A little brandy."

Dr. Longwood opened the portable liquor stand behind his desk and poured from one of the old blue bottles. Only one glass, none for himself.

He was particularly fond of the little liquor cabinet, all lovely deep mahogany and old silver. He had bought it one afternoon at an antique auction on Newbury Street, only two hours after voting in favor of Bester Kender's appointment to the hospital staff. Kender already had made a name for himself as a transplantation innovator in Cleveland, and that afternoon Harland Longwood had been newly conscious of the emergence of younger and brighter men in his world. He paid more than the little antique bar was worth, partly because he knew that Frances would have liked it and partly because he told himself with black humor that if ever the young turks moved him into a quiet corner he could fill the bottles with his favorite booze and anesthetize the long afternoons away.

Now, ten years later, he was still the Chief of Surgery, he reminded himself with some satisfaction. Kender had attracted other young geniuses to the staff but each shed his bright light over a narrow field. It still took a grizzled old general surgeon to put all the pieces together and run the place like a surgical service.

Greene sniffed, sipped, rolled the brandy on his palate, swallowed slowly. "It's a generous gift, Harland."

Longwood shrugged. They shared the same commitment to the hospital and the medical school. Although Greene wasn't a medical man his father had been Physician-in-Chief and he had been named to the board almost automatically as soon as his position in the banking community had made him an asset to the hospital. Longwood knew that Gilbert's will carried stipulations that would benefit the hospital even more than his own.

"Are you certain you haven't allowed your loyalty to this place to cause you to neglect the other beneficiaries?" Greene asked. "I notice that the only other bequests are for ten thousand dollars apiece to Mrs. Marjorie Snyder of Newton Centre and Mrs. Rafael Meomartino of the Back Bay."

"Mrs. Snyder is an old friend," Dr. Longwood said.

Greene, who had known Harland Longwood all his life and had thought he knew all his old friends, nodded with the lack of surprise of a man who had read a good many surprising wills.

"She has a comfortable annuity and neither needs nor desires financial help from me. Mrs. Meomartino is my niece Elizabeth. Florence's girl," he added, remembering that at one time Gilbert had been half in love with Florence.

"Whom is she married to?"

"One of our Surgical Fellows. He's pretty well fixed. Family money."

"I must have met him," Greene said with reluctance. Longwood had noticed that Gilbert hated to admit not being able to identify the hospital's younger people, as if it were still a small, intimate organization.

"There's nobody else," Dr. Longwood said. "That's why I wanted to endow the chair for Kender without delay. It's long overdue."

"The Harland Mason Longwood Chair of Surgery," Greene said, tasting the title as he had tasted the brandy.

"The Frances Sears Longwood Chair," Dr. Longwood said.

Greene nodded. "That's very nice. Frances would have liked that."

"I'm not sure. I think it might have embarrassed her," he said. "I want you and the others to understand that this isn't going to lower the department's budget, Gilbert. That isn't the purpose of the gift at all. I want to utilize some of the funds this is going to free."

"In what way?" Greene said guardedly.

"To pay for a new surgical instructorship, for one thing. We haven't been developing our own faculty people. I think we'd best start, and damned soon."

Greene nodded thoughtfully. "That sounds all right to me. Do you have a candidate in mind?"

"Not really. There's Meomartino, but I don't know yet if he's interested. And a young fellow named Silverstone who's just joined us and who looks awfully good. There's no need to make up our minds now. That's the Department's job. We can keep our eyes open and let the nominating committee get us the best man available in time for next July."

Greene rose to leave. "How are you really, Harland?" he said as they shook hands.

"I'm fine. I'll let you know when I'm not," he said, aware that Greene was receiving reports about his condition.

The board chairman nodded. He hesitated. "I was thinking just the other day about those Saturday afternoons we used to have out at the farm," he said. "They were good times, Harland. Really splendid."

"Yes," Dr. Longwood said, astonished. I must look much worse than I had thought, he told himself, to wring this much sentiment out of Gilbert.

He dropped back into his chair after Greene had left and thought of the summer afternoons when, a young Visiting Surgeon, he would make afternoon rounds and then lead three cars full of people—house officers, staff men, an occasional trustee—to the farm in Weston where they would play hilarious softball on a rough, slanting meadow until it was time to eat the Saturday suppers of frankfurters, baked beans and brown bread that Frances had prepared.

It was following one of those good Saturday afternoons that she had taken ill. He had known immediately it was her appendix, and that there was plenty of time to take her to his own hospital.

"Are you going to remove it yourself?" she had asked, smiling despite her pain and nausea because it was so damn funny being one of his patients.

He shook his head. "Harrelmann. I'll be there, Darling." He didn't ever want to operate on her. Not even an appendectomy.

In the hospital he had turned her over for the work-up to the young Puerto Rican intern named Samirez.

"My wife is allergic to penicillin," he had said in case she forgot to mention it.

He had repeated it two more times before he had kissed her and hurried off to find Harrelmann. Later they had discovered that the boy knew almost no English at all. He hadn't taken a case history from Frances because he could neither ask the questions nor understand the answers. Evidently the only word that had come through clearly was "penicillin," and dutifully he had given her 400,000 units intramuscularly. Before Harland had even located Dr. Harrelmann, Frances had gone into anaphylactic shock and was dead.

Although his friends had tried to keep him away from the Mortality Conference, he had attended and had quietly insisted on the presence of an interpreter so that Dr. Samirez could understand every word. Under Harrelmann's watchful, analytic eyes he had treated the boy with consideration and great control. But he had been mercilessly thorough. A month after the committee had declared the death preventable and Dr. Samirez had resigned his internship and returned to his island home, Dr. Harrelmann had invited Harland to lunch and had persuaded him to head the department upon his own retirement.

He had had to give up his private practice, but he never had regretted that. He broke as much as possible with the pattern of their former life. He had sold the farm the following autumn, passing up a profit of five thousand dollars from a Worcester accountant named Rosenfeld in order to sell to a lawyer from Framingham named Bancroft. Rosenfeld and his wife seemed like nice people and he never told any of his friends about their offer. He knew it was the kind of thing that would have made Frances furious at him and yet he couldn't bear the thought of the farm she had loved being used for the pleasure of people who were so different from what she had been.

He shook his head and replaced the brandy bottle after a slight battle with himself.

He never had been much of a drinker, but lately he had developed a small enjoyable habit, fed by the rationalization that the alcoholic content of brandy was almost completely metabolized and therefore could be considered a form of self-prescription.

When the first symptoms had appeared he had suspected that his prostate was enlarged. He was 61, just the age when that became likely.

The prospect of undergoing prostatectomy was annoying; it meant he would have to take time off and he was just beginning a project he had been working toward for years, the writing of a new general surgical text.

But it soon became apparent that it wasn't his prostate.

"Have you had a sore throat recently?" Arthur Williamson had asked him when finally he had invited the internist to examine him. It was precisely the question he had been expecting and therefore it annoyed him.

"Yes. It lasted only a day. About two weeks ago."

"Did you have a culture?"

"No."

"Did you take an antibiotic?"

"It wasn't streptococcus."

Williamson had stared at him. "How do you know?"

But they both suspected that it had been, and somehow he knew with a curious resigned certainty, even before the tests were done, that the infection had damaged his kidneys. Williamson turned him over to Kender immediately.

They had placed an arteriovenous shunt into a vein and an artery in his leg.

From the start he was a very bad patient, fighting the kidney machine emotionally the instant they mated its tube to the shunt. The
apparatus was noisy and impersonal and during the blood-
cleansing procedure, which took fourteen hours, he lay restlessly on
the bed and suffered violent headaches, inefficiently attempting to
work with the three-by-five file cards on which he had accumulated
the material for the first chapter of the book.

"Often the kidneys pick right up and begin to function again after
a few sessions with the machine," Kender told him encouragingly.

But he performed the obscene rite with the damned machine
twice a week for a month and it was apparent that his kidneys were
not responding, and that only the apparatus was going to keep him
alive.

They gave him standing appointments, every Monday and
Thursday evening at 8:30.

He took himself off all surgery schedules. He considered resign-
ing and then decided, dispassionately, he hoped, that he was too
valuable as an administrator and a teacher. He continued to make
daily rounds.

On the Thursday of his seventh week on the machine, however,
without any planning at all he simply did not go to the Kidney Laboratory. He left word that they should put another patient on the
machine in his place.

He thought that perhaps Kender would attempt to persuade him
to return to the machine, but the next day the kidney man made no
attempt to see him.

Two nights later he noticed that his ankles were swollen with
edema. He lay awake most of the night and then in the morning for
the first time in years he called his secretary and told her he
wouldn't be in that day.

A couple of capsules allowed him to sleep until two o'clock. He
awoke feeling nervous and irritable, made himself some canned
soup he didn't really want, then took an additional grain-and-one-
half and went back to sleep until five-thirty.

For want of anything better to do he showered and shaved and
put on some clothes. Then he sat in the darkening living room without switching on a lamp. In a little while he went to the hall closet
and took down from the back of the shelf a bottle of Chateau
Mouton-Rothschild, 1955, that had been given to him three years
before by a grateful patient who had advised him to save it for an

occasion. He opened it with only a little difficulty and poured a glass, then he went back into the parlor and sat in the dusk and sipped the warm, dusky wine.

He was thinking very clearly. Going on this way simply wasn't worth it. It was not so much the pain as the indignity.

The sleeping capsules were really very mild and one would have to take a great many, but there were more than enough in the little bottle.

He attempted to think of life-situations in which he might be needed.

Liz had Meomartino and their little boy, and God knew he had never been able to help her with any of her problems.

Marge Snyder would miss him, but they had given one another very little for years. She had lost her husband just before Frances had died and they had been lovers in the period of great mutual need, but it had been over for a very long time. She would miss him only as an old friend, and she had an orderly life in which he would leave no vacancy.

At the hospital perhaps there would be a gap, but although Kender would prefer to remain a transplantation specialist he would as an obligation assume the responsibilities of Surgeon-in-Chief, and Longwood knew he would be very good, undoubtedly even brilliant, in the role.

That left only the book.

He went into the study and looked at the two battered four-drawer file cabinets full of case histories, and at the stacks of reference cards on the desk.

Might it actually turn out to be the great contribution he imagined?

Or was he, after all, indulging in the last gasp of a once-vital vanity, anxious only that there be an opportunity for medical students to consult Longwood instead of Mosely or Dragstedt?

He took the bottle of sleeping capsules and placed it in his pocket.

Defiantly, he had another glass of wine and then left the apartment. He got the car and drove through the cloudy early darkness to Harvard Square, thinking that perhaps he would go to a movie, but they were showing an old Bogart and he continued right on through the square, observing that Frances wouldn't recognize it, all bare feet and beards and exposed thighs.

He circled the Yard and parked not far from the Appleton Chapel. Without knowing why he got out of the car and entered Appleton, which was quiet and deserted; what religion had always been to him.

Soon there were footsteps: "Can I be of help to you?"

Longwood didn't know whether the polite young man was a chaplain but he saw that he was hardly older than an intern.

"I don't believe so," he said.

He went outside again and into the car. This time he knew where he was going. He drove to Weston and when he had reached the farm pulled the car off the road so that he was parked overlooking the meadow where they had held their ball games.

He couldn't tell very much in the dark but it seemed to be unchanged. A few feet from the car a great old silver-gray beech still stood; he was glad it had survived.

Almost unbelievingly he felt a once-familiar pressure growing in his bladder.

Perhaps it was the wine, he thought with a rising excitement.

He left the car and walked to a point midway between the car and the big tree. Facing the old stone wall he unzipped and took himself out and concentrated.

After a long while two drops emerged and fell, as if from a turned-off faucet.

Headlights appeared and approached and he jerked himself back into his trousers like a little boy surprised by an opening door. The car flared past and he stood trembling, an idiot, an *idiot,* he thought in outrage, trying to pee in the dark on a bed of lily-of-the-valley he had planted there a quarter of a century before.

A raindrop kissed him coldly on the forehead.

He wondered whether, when the time came, the Death Committee would decide that the failure of Harland Longwood had been Preventable or Unavoidable.

If through some trick of reincarnation he were to preside at that meeting, he would place the responsibility squarely on Dr. Longwood, he thought.

For so many wrong decisions.

Awed, he saw it with perfect clarity.

All of life was a Mortality Conference.

The case history began with the first moment of responsible existence.

And sooner or later—at first creeping up and then with stunning swiftness—the moment when the history was about to be completed came to every man. And he was confronted with the sum of his own imperfect performance.

And so vulnerable, so terribly vulnerable.

Gentlemen, let us consider the Longwood case.

Preventable or Unavoidable?

By the time he got back into the car the rain was falling steadily, as if drawn from the sky by his pelvic muscles.

When he turned the car around, the light of his headlamps illuminated the sign at the end of the driveway and he saw that the Bancrofts had sold the place to people named Feldstein.

He hoped the Feldsteins were as nice as the Rosenfelds.

In a little while he began to laugh, and soon he was laughing so hard he had to pull the car to a stop again by the side of the road.

Oh, Frances, he said to her, how without knowing it could I have turned into this stupid malfunctioning old man?

Remembering, he still felt inside like the young man who had knelt naked before her the first time they had made love.

And after worshiping all his life at a shrine like that, he thought, he couldn't suddenly begin to believe in a saving God simply because now he needed to be saved.

Nor, he knew with sudden frightened clarity, after fighting death all his life could he now help himself to die.

When he reached the hospital he found Kender still in the Kidney Lab, going over x-rays with young Silverstone.

"I'd like to go back on the machine," he said.

Kender peered up at a film. "They're busy for the rest of the night," he said. "I can't get you on until morning."

"What time?"

"Oh, say ten o'clock. When you're through with the machine I want you to have a blood transfusion."

It was a statement, not a request; Kender was speaking to a patient, he realized.

"We don't think the machine is the permanent answer for you," Kender was saying. "We're going to try to get you another kidney."

"I know how difficult it is to choose kidney recipients," Dr. Longwood said stiffly. "I don't want any special favors."

Dr. Kender smiled. "You're not getting any. Your case was selected on its teaching merits by the Transplant Committee, but you have a rare blood type, and of course it may take a long while for us to find a cadaver donor. In the meantime, you'll have to be dependable and show up here twice a week for the machine."

Dr. Longwood nodded. "Good night," he said.

Outside the laboratory, the closed doors shut off the sound of the machines and it was quiet. He had almost reached the elevator when he heard the door open and close and the sound of the hurrying footsteps.

He saw when he turned that it was Silverstone.

"You left this on Dr. Kender's desk," Adam said, holding out the bottle of sleeping pills.

Longwood searched the younger man's eyes for pity but found only watchful interest. Good, he thought, this one might make a surgeon.

"Thank you," he said as he took the bottle. "That was quite careless of me."

Chapter 4: Adam Silverstone

The thirty-six hour shifts made the days and the nights run into one another curiously, so that during periods of overwork sometimes if Silverstone didn't look out a window he was uncertain whether it was dark or light outside.

He found that Suffolk County General was something he had been seeking for a long time without knowing it.

The hospital was old and shabby, not as clean as he would have liked; the unwashed poverty of the patients was nerve-wracking; the administration pinched pennies in nasty little ways like not issuing clean whites to the house officers often enough. But the Service practiced a tremendously exciting brand of university surgery. From the beginning he operated often, cases of more interesting variety during the first month than he had done in half a year in Georgia.

He had experienced a sinking feeling when he had first heard that Rafe Meomartino was married to the Old Man's niece, but he had to admit that the good cases were divided impartially between the two of them. He recognized that there was an inexplicable coldness between Meomartino and Longwood, and he had come to realize that Rafe might actually be at a disadvantage because of the relationship.

The only uncomfortable portion of his existence occurred when he found himself on the sixth floor, which in a moment of absent-minded stupidity he had turned into a cold and lonely place.

The worst part of the whole soap episode was that he really liked Spurgeon Robinson.

He had come into the bathroom one morning while the intern was shaving and they had talked baseball while he got out of his clothes and stepped into the shower.

"Hell," he muttered.

"What's the matter?"

"I don't have any damn soap."

"Take mine."

Adam had looked at the white soap in Robinson's hand, and he had shaken his head. "No, thanks."

He had relaxed under the warm spray and a few minutes later —without thinking?—he had picked up the thin sliver of used soap in the tray and had lathered his body with it.

As Robinson was leaving he had glanced into the shower. "Ah, I see you found some after all," he said.

"Yes," Adam said, suddenly uncomfortable.

"That's the piece I used yesterday to wash my black ass," Spur had said pleasantly.

Money no longer was an immediate threat. He became a moonlighter through the kind offices of the chubby anesthesiology resident the OR nurses called the Jolly Green Giant, whom he always thought of as fat boy but whose name had turned out to be just plain Norman Pomerantz. One day Pomerantz wandered into the staff room and while pouring himself coffee asked whether anybody was interested in covering the Emergency Room several nights a week at a community hospital west of Boston.

"I don't give a damn where it is," Adam said before anyone else could answer. "If it pays anything I'll take it."

Pomerantz laughed. "It's in Woodborough. You get paid out of hospitalization insurance."

So he auctioned off his sleep and was not at all unsatisfied with the bargain. The first night he was off-duty at Suffolk County General he took the elevated train to Park Square and a bus to Woodborough, which turned out to be a baroque New England manufacturing village lately transformed into a sprawling and populous bedroom suburb. The hospital was good but small, the work hardly stimulating—lumps and bumps, gashes and slashes; the most complicated procedure he ran into was a Colles' fracture of the wrist—but the money was lovely, the following evening he sat on the Boston-bound bus and realized almost with awe that he was solvent. Of course, it had come right out of his hide; he hadn't been to bed for sixty hours—thirty-six hours on duty at Suffolk County General and then another twenty-four at Woodborough—but the sudden feeling of affluence was worth it. When he got back to his room in the hospital he slept for eight hours and then woke feeling light-headed, fuzzy-mouthed and curiously rich.

He made the bus ride to Woodborough every time he was off-duty. As his body became more exhausted he took to grabbing small greedy catnaps—on litters, sitting in the staff room, once even while leaning against a corridor wall, cherishing the sleeping moments like a child savoring a ball of hard candy.

He felt even more alone than usual. One night he lay on his bed and listened to Spurgeon Robinson play the kind of guitar he hadn't known existed. He thought the music told him a lot about the intern. In a little while he got up and went downstairs to a package store and bought a sixpack of beer. Robinson opened the door when he knocked and stood there for a moment without saying anything, looking at him.

"You busy?" Adam asked.

"No. Come on in."

"I thought we might go out on the roof again and have a brew."

"Crazy."

The perfect host, he opened the window and snatched the bag, letting Adam go over the sill first.

They drank and made small talk and then suddenly they ran out of conversation and were ill at ease until Adam belched and glared.

"Goddammit," he said, "I'm sorry. You and I can't go around angry at one another, like a couple of little boys. We're professionals. There are sick people depending on our ability to communicate."

"I get mad and I shoot my mouth off," Spurgeon said.

"Well, hell, you were right. I don't like to use *anybody's* soap—"

Spurgeon grinned. "I wouldn't use yours on a bet."

"—But the more I think about it the more I know that isn't why I refused *your* soap," he said softly.

Spurgeon just looked at him.

"I've never known a colored guy really well. When I was a kid in an Italian neighborhood in Pittsburgh, gangs of black kids used to come in and fight us. Up to now, that was the most genuine part of my inter-racial contact."

Spurgeon still didn't comment, and Silverstone reached for a fresh beer. "You've known a lot of whites?"

"In the past twelve years, man, I've been surrounded and outnumbered."

They both looked out over the neighboring rooftops.

Robinson held something out and he reached for it, thinking it was a beer but discovering that it was a hand.

Which he shook.

Out of his first Blue Shield check he repaid the advance in salary he had gotten from the hospital the day he arrived, and when the second check came he went to a bank and opened a savings account. In Pittsburgh there was the old man, silent for the present but certain to speak up momentarily to plead a touch. He vowed to resist: my entire fortune for disaster, but not one cent for booze. Although he didn't withdraw the money and begin to haunt the used-car lots, for the first time in his life he experienced a desire to be a reckless spender. He wanted to own a vehicle in which to park and wrestle with someone, perhaps Gaby Pender.

After six weeks he still hadn't seen her. He had talked with her several times on the telephone, but he had refrained from asking her out, feeling impelled to go to Woodborough and increase his little hoard of cash.

When they *did* go out, he told himself, he would be able to afford to spend some money.

But on the other end of the line she became perceptively puzzled and increasingly cool with each call, and finally he decided he would have to tell her what he was doing with his off-duty time.

"But you'll drop dead of exhaustion," she said, horrified.

"I'm about ready to slow down."

"Promise me you'll take next weekend off."

"I will if you'll go out with me. Sunday night."

"You *sleep.*"

"After I see you."

"Okay," she said in a little while. She sounded happy to surrender, he thought optimistically.

"Big night on the town."

"Listen," she said. "I have an idea for a wonderful evening. The Boston Symphony is broadcasting tonight from Tanglewood. I'll bring my portable radio and we can spread a blanket on the grass of the Esplanade and listen to the music."

"You're trying to save me money. I can afford a better evening than that."

"More expensive but not better. Please. It will give us a chance to talk." She agreed to be ready at six so they would have more time.

"You're crazy," he said, loving the blanket part.

By Sunday afternoon his anticipation was at its crest. It was a quiet day. Thinking ahead, he took care of all the routine detail work early, so nothing would develop into a tardying nuisance. There was a big old clock over the nurses' station with hands at twenty-five minutes to five, like the hands of a Charleston dancer paralyzed immediately after fanning his knees. Eighty-five long minutes, he thought. He would shower and change and leave the hospital protected on all fronts, Banned, Crested and Lavorised, beard shaved, face lotioned and powdered, shoes shined, hair beaten down and hopes high, to pick up Gaby Pender.

He leaned back in his chair and closed his eyes. The great building was like a sleeping dog, he thought; it could nap contentedly, but sooner or later . . .

The telephone purred.

The old bitch was already awake, he thought wryly and answered it: Emergency, with three burns cases. "Coming," he said, and went. In the elevator he continued to worry, concerned now lest this would turn out to be something that would make him late for his date.

The smell of fire met him in the hallway.

There was a man and two women. He saw that the women were not too badly off, and they had already been sedated; score two points for the Emergency Room resident, the kid named Potter, who needed the credits. He had performed a trach on the man, probably his first—(add one point for guts and then deduct five points: in this case he should have waited another couple of minutes and done it in the operating room) and was busily and shakily fussing with an aspiration catheter, trying to suction secretions.

"Has Meomartino been called?"

Potter shook his head, and Adam telephoned the Surgical Fellow. "We could use some help down here, Doctor."

Meomartino hesitated. "Can't you handle it alone?" he said crisply.

"No," he said, and dropped the telephone receiver back into its cradle.

"God, look at all this stuff I'm pulling out of the lungs," Potter said.

Adam looked and shouldered him aside. "Those are gastric contents from the stomach. Don't you realize he's aspirated?" he said in disgust. He began cutting whatever clothing it was possible to pull away from the seared flesh. "How did it happen?"

"Fire marshal's investigating, Doc," Maish Meyerson said from the doorway. "It was in a delicatessen. Near as we could figure, they had an explosion from a deep-fryer. Their joint was closed for painting and repairs. From the smell, though, they had the fryer full of a mixture of kerosene and cooking oil. It probably ignited just before it covered them."

"Lucky for him it wasn't a pizzeria. Nothing worse than third-degree mozzarella burns," Potter said, striving to recover some of his cool.

The man groaned and Adam made sure he hadn't yet been sedated and then gave him five mg. of morphine and told Potter to clean all of them up as much as possible, which under the circumstances was not much; fire was such filthy stuff.

Meomartino appeared, stony-faced but relaxing slightly when he saw that more hands really were needed, and drew bloods from the women for lab determinations and cross-match while Adam did the man, then they gave the patients their first electrolytes and colloids through the needles with which they had taken the blood. By the time they had moved the whole show into OR-3 a nurse had gone through the male patient's wallet and he had a name and age, Joseph P. for Paul Grigio, 48. Meomartino supervised Potter taking care of the women while Adam placed the urinary catheter in Mr. Grigio and then did a cut-down on the long saphenous vein of the ankle, inserting a polyethylene cannula and anchoring it with silk ligatures to establish the intravenous life line.

He had partial-thickness burns over thirty-five percent of his body surface—face (lungs?), chest, arms, groin, a small section of his legs and back. Once he had been muscular, but now there was flab. How much reserve strength was there in that middle-aged body?

Adam was aware suddenly that Meomartino was watching him as he assessed the patient.

"No chance. He won't be with us tomorrow," the Surgical Fellow said as they stripped off their gloves.

"I think he will," Adam said unwillingly.

"Why?"

He shrugged. "Just a feeling. I've seen a good many burns." Immediately he was angry at himself: he hardly qualified as a burns specialist.

"In Atlanta?"

"No, in Philadelphia. I worked as a diener in the morgue while I was in medical school."

Meomartino looked pained. "It's not exactly the same thing as working with them while they're alive."

"I know. But I feel this guy will make it," he said stubbornly.

"I hope so, but I don't *think* so. He's all yours." Meomartino turned to leave and then stopped. "I'll tell you what. If he does make it, I'll buy the coffee at Maxie's for a week."

Goddam sport, Adam thought, watching him leave with the women.

He administered tetanus prophylaxis and then followed the man as he was taken up to the ward. Using the Evans rule to estimate the amount of fluid replacement needed for a 170-pound male, he came up with 2100 cc. of colloid, 2100 cc. of saline and 2000 cc. of water for urinary excretion. Half of this would have to be dripped into the vein in the first eight hours, he knew, along with massive doses of antibiotics to fight the bacteria that would set up housekeeping all over the charred and dirty surface of the burned area.

As they pushed the bed off the elevator on the second floor he saw the time with a sudden sense of dismay.

6:15.

He should have been getting ready for Gaby. Instead he faced at least another twenty minutes before he could leave his patient.

Room 218 was empty, and he placed Mr. Grigio in it in isolation and then concentrated on how he would treat the burn locally, wondering what Meomartino was using on the other patient in the women's ward.

Miss Fultz was seated in the nurses' station working on the inevitable records with her massive black fountain pen. As usual, he might have been the shadow of a gnat. Tiring of waiting for her to look up, he cleared his throat. "Where can I find a large sterile basin? And I need a few other things."

A freshman nurse was scuttling past. "Miss Anderson, give him what he needs," the head nurse said quietly, without missing a penstroke.

"Joseph P. Grigio is in 218. He'll need special nurses for at least three shifts."

"No specials are available," she told her desk.

"Why the hell not?" he said, more annoyed at her refusal to talk to him than he was at the problem.

"For some reason, girls no longer are becoming nurses."

"We'll have to transfer him to Intensive Care."

"The care in Intensive Care is not so intensive. It's been overloaded since a week ago last Tuesday," she said, her great lance of a pen making tight little circles in the air before slashing down to pin a period to the page.

"Put in an order for specials. Let me know as soon as you hear something, please."

He accepted a white sterile bowl from Miss Anderson and mixed his witch's brew. Ice cubes, to cool and anesthetize the burn and keep the swelling down as much as possible. Saline, because plain water would have acted as a leaching agent on the body electrolytes. Phisohex for cleansing; it curdled in swirls as he stirred the mixture. All he lacked was dragon's blood and tongue of newt.

He started to take gauze pads from a cupboard and then, noticing sanitary napkins on a higher shelf, took three boxes of Kotex, ideal for the job.

"Ah—you aren't by chance available to give this patient a little help?"

"No, Doctor. Miss Fultz has me doing three other things, including running bedpans for the whole ward."

He nodded, sighing. "Would you do just one thing for me? Make a quick phone call?" He wrote Gabrielle Pender's name and number on a prescription pad and tore off the blank. "Tell her I'm afraid I'm going to be a little late."

"Sure. She'll wait. I would." The girl grinned and then was gone, leaving him to ponder small-buttocked Scandinavian attractiveness, but not for long. He took the basin gingerly to Room 218, sloshing only a little onto the polished corridor floor, and dropped the pads into the brew. A gentle squeeze to get rid of excess moisture, and then he laid each wet pack on burned flesh, starting at the head and working downward until Mr. Grigio wore a crazy suit of sodden Kotex. When he had covered the shins he started all over again, replacing the oldest air-warmed pads with cold, wet ones.

Mr. Grigio slept, riding the opium wave. Ten years before, his face no doubt had been handsome, the face of an Italian swordsman, but the Mediterranean good looks had been diffused by the rising hairline and the deepening jowl. Tomorrow morning, Adam knew, the face would be a grotesque balloon.

The burned man stirred. *"Dove troviamo i soldi?"* he moaned.

He was wondering where he could get money. Not from the insurance company, Adam knew silently. Poor Mr. Grigio. The fat and kerosene had been placed on the oven and now, with the fire marshal's office interested, for Mr. Grigio the fat was in the fire.

The man stirred fitfully and murmured a name, perhaps that of the woman, haunted by his conscience or a prescience of the pain to come if he lived. Adam dipped the pads in the icy bowl, wrung them, applied them, the wrist watch he had shoved up his arm ticking mockingly.

Shortly after using up and replenishing the contents of the fourth iced bowl, he paused and noticed that Miss Fultz was standing next to him, holding out a thick mug.

Astonished, he accepted the tea.

"I believe I've lined up a special nurse for tonight," Miss Fultz said. "She's due on at eleven, and I'm perfectly free between now and then. It's only an hour. You run along."

"I *did* have an appointment," he said, finding his vocal powers. 10:05!

In the nearest telephone booth he dialed Gaby's number and

reached an amused feminine voice. "This must be Doctor Silver-stone?"

"Yes."

"This is Susan Haskell, Gaby's roommate? She waited and waited. About an hour ago she told me when you called I should say she'd meet you on the Esplanade."

"She went *alone* to wait in the dark by the river?" he asked, thinking of mugging, thinking of rape.

There was a pause. "You don't know Gaby very well, do you?" the voice said.

"*Where* on the Esplanade?"

"Near that bandstand shaped like a shell, you know?"

He didn't, but the taxi driver did. "There ain't a concert tonight," the cabby said.

"I know, I know."

When he got out of the cab he walked away from Storrow Drive into the darkness, over soft grass. For a little while he thought she was not there but then he saw her sitting a good distance away on her blanket spread under a lamp post as if it were a sheltering pine.

When he dropped next to her on the blanket he got the full warmth of her smile and forgot he was tired.

"Was it something earth-shaking, the thing you almost stood me up for?"

"I just got through. I was sure you wouldn't wait." He indicated his whites. "I didn't even take the time to change."

"I'm glad you finally could come. Are you hungry?"

"Starving."

"I gave your sandwiches away."

He looked at her.

"You didn't show up. These three high school boys came along, and they didn't ravish me or anything. One of them was a little dar-ling who let it slip they didn't have money for supper. There's a plum."

He accepted it and ate it because he could think of nothing charming to say. It was embarrassingly juicy. He felt grimy and at a disadvantage and he wanted to impress this girl but he realized sud-denly that while he had been aching to see her again, her roommate had been absolutely right, he didn't know her at all; in fact he had been with her only three hours, one of which was spent in the middle of a very crowded party in Herb Shafer's sister's living room in Atlanta.

"I'm sorry you missed Symphony," she said. "Is this the kind of thing that happens a lot?"

"Not a whole lot," he said, unwilling to frighten her off.

He lay back on the blanket and later he remembered discussing music with her and her graduate program in psychology and then he closed his eyes and when he opened them again he realized he had been sleeping but he didn't know for how long. She was sitting, looking out at the river, just patiently waiting. He wondered how he could have forgotten that face. If the nose had been a plastic job she would have received a hairline more than her money's worth. The eyes were brown, quiet now, but very alive. Her mouth was maybe a bit wide, upper lip thin, hinting at bitchiness, lower lip generously full. The dark blonde hair, glossy in the overhead lamp light, had sunstreaks in it. The mole was beneath the left eye, accentuating the cheekbones. Her features were not regular enough to make her a really pretty girl. She was small enough but too sexually attractive to be called cute. A little too thin, he decided.

"That's the deepest tan I've seen in a long time. You must live on the beach," he said.

"I have a sun lamp. Three minutes a day, all year round."

"Even in the summer?"

"Sure. More privacy in my bedroom."

There would be no white patches or strap marks. He felt a weakness in the knees.

"One of the boys at school says I have such a passion for physical warmth because I come from a broken home. I love hot days."

"You analyze each other in psychology class?"

She smiled. "After class. All the time." She lay back beside him on the blanket. "You smell of strong male juices," she said, "and as if you've been to a fire."

"God, is it that bad? I planned to come to you smelling like a flower."

"Who wants a man to smell like a flower?"

Their heads were very close on the blanket and it took little effort for him to kiss her.

He kissed the mole.

Her portable radio softly gave them the theme music from *Never on Sunday*.

"Can you hasapiko?"

"I'd like to learn," he said lecherously.

"The Greek dance."

"Oh, that. No."

He got up with regret when she insisted and she showed him. He had a good diver's natural rhythm and he picked up the basic step. Holding hands, they danced to the languid beat and then more wildly as the music from the radio rose to crescendo, Zorba and his woman on the soft grass of the Esplanade, but of course he made a mistake and they collapsed, laughing and out of breath, and he kissed her again and felt the warmth of her under his mouth, in his arms.

It was pleasant. They lay there without talking and with a nice sense of privacy, the traffic barreling along Storrow Drive behind them and the river in front of them satisfactorily dark as far as the lights of Memorial Drive on the Cambridge side; in the middle, one blurry white sail.

They were, of course, spotlighted under the lamp post.

The sail was moving. "I'd like to take a boat ride," he said.

"There are a couple of rowboats at the boat club, right behind the concert shell."

He held out his hand and she took it and they ran to the dock. There were no oars but he helped her into one of the boats anyway. "We can pretend. I'll be Ulysses," he said, still feeling Hellenic. "You're a siren."

"No. I'm just Gabrielle Pender."

They sat in the stern facing the far shore and the lights that should have spoiled it but didn't, Cambridge Electric and the Electronic Corporation of America and all the others. He kissed her again and when he stopped she said, "He was married."

"Who?"

"Ulysses. Remember poor Penelope, waiting back in Ithaca?"

"He hadn't *seen* her in twenty years. But, okay, I'll be somebody else." He buried his face in her hair. God, she smelled fine. Her barely-perceptible breath quickened as he kissed her neck and her fine pulse made little hammer blows on his lips. The boat rose and fell on tiny waves that came to them from the river mouth a few miles away and lapped under the dock.

"Ah, Adam," she said between kisses. "Adam Silverstone, who are you now? Who are you really?"

"Find out and let me know," he told her.

The mosquitoes drove them inland. He helped her to fold the blanket and they stowed it in her car, a battered blue 1963 Plymouth convertible parked off Storrow Drive. They walked to a cafeteria on Charles Street and sat at a table against the wall and drank coffee.

"Was it a case that kept you at the hospital?"

He told her about Grigio. She was a good listener; she asked intelligent questions.

"I'm not afraid of fire or drowning," she said.

"That means you *are* afraid of something."

"We've had a lot of cancer. On both sides of the family. My grandmother just died of it."

"I'm sorry. How old was she?"

"Eighty-one."

"I'd settle for that."

"Well, so would I. But my Aunt Louisa, for instance. A young, beautiful woman. I'd hate to die before I was *old,*" she said. "Do a lot of hospital patients die? High numbers, I mean?"

"On a ward like ours, a few a month. In our service, if a month goes by without a death, the Chief Resident or the Surgical Fellow throws a party."

"Do you give lots of parties?"

"No."

"I couldn't do what you do," she said. "I couldn't watch the pain and the dying."

"There's more than one way to die. Plenty of pain to watch in psychology, isn't there?"

"Sure, in clinical. That's why I'm going to end up testing sweet little boys to see why they won't come out from under the bed."

He nodded, smiling.

"What's it like to watch somebody die?"

"I remember, the first time . . . I was a student. There was this man . . . Well, I saw him on my rounds. He was simply fine, laughing and joking. While I was fixing his I.V. his heart stopped. We tried everything in the book to bring him back. I remember looking at him and asking myself, 'Where did it go? What was it that went away? What turned him from a *person* into . . . this?"

"God," she said. Then, "I've got this lump."

"What?" he said.

She shook her head.

But he had heard. "Where?"

"I'd rather not say."

"For Christ's sake," he said. "I'm a doctor, remember?" Probably the breast, he thought.

She looked away. "Please. I'm sorry I mentioned it, I'm sure it's nothing. I'm the kind who worries."

"Then why don't you make an appointment with a doctor for an examination?"

"I will."

"Promise me?"

She nodded, smiled at him, changed the subject: told him about herself. Parents divorced; father remarried and running a resort in the Berkshires, mother remarried to a cattleman in Idaho. He told her his mother had been Italian and was dead and that his father was Jewish, but he carefully avoided saying anything else about him, aware that she noticed and did not press.

When they finished three cups of coffee apiece she insisted on driving him back to the hospital. He didn't kiss her goodnight, partially because the hospital entrance was not at all private and partially because he was too damned tired to think about being Zorba or Ulysses or anybody but a sleeping form in the bed in the room on the top floor.

Nevertheless, he stopped the elevator on the second floor and walked as if magnet-drawn to Room 218. One quick check, he promised himself, and he would go to bed.

Helen Fultz was leaning stiffly over Joseph Grigio.

"What are you doing?"

"The eleven to seven nurse never showed up."

"Well, I'm here." His guilt manifested itself in annoyance. "Go to bed, please." How old was she, he wondered. She looked done in, her gray hair wisping down over the lined, tight-lipped face.

"I'm not going anywhere. It's too long since I did a little old-fashioned nursing. Paperwork turns you into a clerk." Her tone brooked no argument, but he argued. In the end they compromised. It was past midnight. He said she could stay until one o'clock.

The presence of a second person, he found, made a great deal of difference. She maintained her neurotic silence but she brewed coffee hotter than Gaby's flesh, blacker than Robinson's. They spelled each other in applying the dressings when their hands protested the repeated immersions in iced saline.

Joseph Grigio kept on breathing. This old terror, this silent gray bitch, this tired aging woman had kept him alive. Now with the help of a surgeon he might yet recover and prove an ass. Shakespeare.

At two a.m. he drove her from the room, braving her eyes. Alone, it was harder. His eyelids drooped. A small ache appeared in the cramped muscles of his back. The left leg of his once-white trousers was coldly damp where saline from the wet-packs had dripped.

The hospital was quiet.

Quiet.

Except for occasional little sounds. Pain cries, muted hollow drumming of urine into bedpan, rubber-heel tattoo across linoleum floors; blending to the background like cricket-shrill and birdcalls in the country, felt but not actually heard.

Twice he dozed briefly, jerking himself awake to hastily change the ice-water packs.

I'm sorry, Mr. Grigio, he silently told the recumbent form on the bed.

If I had not been hungry for money I would be more rested now, better able to take care of you. But I am hungry for money with good reason and I needed the money from that moonlighting. Really needed it.

Only please don't die because I fall asleep.

God, don't let that happen to me. Don't let that happen to him.

His hands dipped into the icy water.

Throttled the cold cloth.

Applied the chill pack.

Took the fabric meant for warm female loins, warmed now instead by fire absorbed from braised male flesh, and dropped it into the bowl for rechilling.

He repeated the procedure again and again while Joseph Grigio breathed soft unconscious sighs, occasionally whimpering unintelligible Italian phrases. His burned face and body were perceptibly swollen now.

Listen, Adam told him.

This is a hell of a lot of trouble if you die. You will not die on me, you pitiful incendiary son of a bitch.

You had better not, he threatened.

Once he thought he heard the harlequin walking through the corridors of the ward.

"Stay away from here," he said aloud.

Scutta mal occhio, poo-poo-poo.

Repeating the litany as he drove his hands into the cold wet.

He lost track of the hours, but it no longer became a battle to stay awake. He had spurs of pain which kept him headed into consciousness. Sometimes he almost wept with the pain as he reached into the bowl whose ice he had replenished three more times in the course of the night. His hands became gnarled and blue, the fingers difficult to bend, their tips puckered and empty.

Once, in his own agony he forgot about the patient, abandoned him. He rose, rubbed his hands, stretched, arched his back, flexed his fingers, batted his eyes, walked to the men's room and relieved himself, washed his hands with wonderful warm water.

When he got back to Room 218 the packs on Mr. Grigio were warm, far too warm. Furiously he squeezed new ones, applied them, dropped the used ones in the bowl.

Mr. Grigio groaned, and he answered with a groan of his own.

"You haven't been here all night?" Meomartino said.

He didn't answer.

"Cristos. Obviously you'll do anything to win coffee."

He heard the voice as through a telephone, although the Surgical Fellow stood next to him.

It was morning, he realized.

Mr. Grigio still breathed.

"Get the hell upstairs and go to sleep."

"A nurse?" he said.

"I'll get somebody, Dr. Silverstone," Miss Fultz said. He hadn't seen her standing in the doorway.

He got to his feet.

"Shall I send up some breakfast for you? Or coffee?" Miss Fultz asked.

He shook his head.

"Come on, I'll go up with you," Meomartino said.

As they entered the elevator Helen Fultz spoke to him again. "Do you have any special instructions, Dr. Silverstone?"

He shook his head. "Wake me if he gets into trouble." He found it necessary to speak very carefully.

"She'll call *me*," Rafe Meomartino said in disgust.

"Certainly, Dr. Silverstone. Sleep well, sir," she said as though Meomartino were not present.

Meomartino studied him strangely as the car ascended. "How long have you been here, six, seven weeks? Not even two months. And she's talking to you. It took me two *years*. Some guys never make it. Six weeks is the shortest time I ever heard."

Adam opened his mouth to say something, but it turned into a yawn.

He sank into sleep at seven-fifteen and was awakened sometime after eleven-thirty by a barrage on the door of his room. Meyerson, the ambulance driver, stood outside looking at him with friendly contempt.

"Message from the office, Doc. You didn't answer the page."

His head pounded. "Come in," he whispered, rubbing his temples. "Goddam dream."

Meyerson looked at him sharply and with new interest. "What was it about?"

He and Gaby Pender had died. They had simply ceased to be alive but had not gone anywhere; he had been unaware of change, of after-life or lack of it.

Meyerson listened with interest.

"You didn't dream of numbers?"

Adam shook his head. "What do you want with numbers?"

"I'm a mystic."

A mystic? "What happens to the soul after death, Maish?"

"How good do you know your Talmud?"

"The Old Testament?"

Meyerson looked at him strangely. "No. Jesus Christ, where did *you* go to Hebrew school?"

"I didn't."

The ambulance driver sighed. "I don't know much, but that much I know. The Talmud is the book of old laws. It says the good souls get to be put under Jehovah's throne." He grinned. "I figure it must be one goddam big throne or damn few of us are any good. One or the other."

"And the ones with evil souls?" he asked against his will.

"Two angels stand at opposite corners of the world and play catch with the bad guys."

"You're putting me on."

"No. Fling the poor *momsers* back and forth." Meyerson remembered his errand. "Listen, they said a collect call from Pittsburgh. You want to accept it, get Operator . . ." he consulted a slip, ". . . 284."

"Oh God.

"Thanks. Hey!" He called him back. "Got change for singles?"

"Just my seein' an' raisin' money."

"What?"

"My gambling stake, poker money."

"Oh. Let me have a little?" He passed over two bills and accepted silver.

"Just you and the broad in the dream? No numbers?"

He shook his head.

"That's two people. I'll play 222. Nigger pool. Want I should put half a buck down on it for you?"

Some mystic. "No."

"Maybe 284, the operator's number?"

"No."

Maish shrugged and went away. Adam's head hurt and his mouth was dry as he went to the wall telephone in the hall.

It had to come eventually, he thought.

He's finally fallen off a bridge. Or jumped.

Or perhaps he's in a hospital, maybe burned like Mr. Grigio. It happens all the time, kids set fire to drunks.

But the call was *from* his father, the operator said. Five quarters, a nickel, a dime.

"Adam? That you, son?"

"Pop, what's the matter?"

"Well, I need a couple hundred. I want you to get it for me."

Relief and anger, a kind of emotional see-saw.

"I gave you money last time I saw you. Because of that I came here like a tramp. I had to borrow money myself, an advance from the hospital."

"I know you haven't *got* it. I said *get* it for me. Listen to me. Take another loan."

"Why do you need it?"

". . . Sick as a dog."

Suddenly it was easy. He had to be drunk right now or he would not be playing the game so stupidly. Sober he was shrewd and dangerous. "Go to the medical school and tell Maury Bernhardt, Dr. Bernhardt, that I sent you. He'll call me and I'll tell him to give you whatever care you need."

"I need money, the *money.*"

There was a time, he thought, when I would have hocked something to see that you got it.

"No more from me."

"Adam."

"If you've drunk up the two hundred, and it sounds as if you have, sober up and get a job. I'll send you ten dollars eating money."

"Adam, don't do this to me. Be merciful. Son . . ." The sobbing came on cue. He was intelligent; he could cry simply by facing reality. It was pretending hard enough to *laugh* that was difficult.

Adam waited until the spasm had passed, weakening only slightly. "I'll add five to that. Fifteen dollars, but that's all."

At toll rates, his father blew his nose leisurely in Pittsburgh. When he spoke again the old gentleman-among-churls arrogance was back in his voice. "I've got a quotation for your collection, word-waster."

"Pop . . ." But then he waited warily.

> " 'I'm sorry you are wiser,
> I'm sorry you are taller . . .'

"Got it?"

Adam repeated it.

"Yes," Myron Silberstein said, and hung up, oh the old bastard, a man who cherished exits.

He stood there with the telephone to his ear, not knowing whether to laugh or to cry, his eyes closed against the insistent drumming in his head, growing louder. For his thoughts, he felt himself seized by the angel, lifted, hurled through the icy darkness, caught by the terrible waiting hands and hurled again. When he replaced the receiver the telephone rang immediately and he obeyed the operator's demand for thirty cents more.

He went back to bed but all hope of sleep was gone. He didn't know the quotation. Surrendering finally, he dressed and went to the hospital library to consult *Bartlett's*. It was by Aline Kilmer, whose husband Joyce had been killed while a young man and presumably still lovable. There were two more lines:

> *I'm sorry you are wiser,*
> *I'm sorry you are taller;*
> *I liked you better foolish,*
> *And I liked you better smaller.*

Despite himself he felt the stab, as his father had known he would. I should simply forget about him, he thought, write him out of my life.

Instead he sat down and wrote a short note and enclosed the fifteen dollars, sending it with an air mail stamp he stole from the nurses' station while Helen Fultz pretended not to notice.

Gaby Pender.

She had him mesmerized, with her over-all tan and her juicy plum. He thought of her constantly, telephoned her too often. She had gone to the student health service, she told him when he asked; the lump had turned out to be nothing, not even a lump, just muscle and imagination. Gratefully, they talked of other things. He wanted to see her again, as soon as possible.

Susan Garland came between them by dying. Saving Joseph Grigio's life didn't make up for losing Susan Garland's: he found that in medicine there was no such thing as evening the score.

His spirit became infected with a world-weariness that frightened him, but he couldn't cast it off. Perhaps Gaby's fear of mortality had made him more sensitive than was desirable, he thought. For whatever the reason, he discovered within himself a deep well of fury at their impotence to deal with the waste of beautiful lives.

For the first time since leaving medical school he felt great doubt as he made his rounds in the ward. He found himself seeking confirmation of professional opinions, shying away from making independent decisions that a few weeks before would not have caused him to hesitate.

He turned his anger inward, finding fault with everything about Adam Silverstone.

His body, for example.

The old diving days were gone but he was still young, he told himself peevishly, looking in the mirror and thinking of the soft white grubs his Uncle Frank used to spade up in the spring when he turned the soil for his tomato garden.

When he stood in his underwear and looked down he could see a soft roundness of belly, the kind of an abdomen that should belong only to a woman not long pregnant.

He picked up sneakers and a sweat suit at the Harvard Coop and began to run regularly, half a dozen times around the block whenever he finished a stretch of duty. At night the darkness gave him privacy but when he ran in the morning he sometimes galloped through a gauntlet of nurses' titters.

One morning a small colored boy, about six or seven, looked up from sifting the dust in the gutter. "Man, who chasin' you?" he called softly.

The first time, conserving wind, Adam didn't answer. But when the question was placed again each time he circled the block, he began to fling replies like mini-confessions.

"Susan Garland."

"Myron Silberstein."

"Spurgeon Robinson."

"Gaby Pender."

He suffered a compulsion to answer the question honestly. Therefore as he came around the block on his final trip, legs pumping and arms flailing, "I'm chasing myself!" he flung over his shoulder at the child.

The morning they discussed the case of Susan Garland he discovered something new about the Mortality Conference.

He learned that when you were personally involved in a case being scrutinized, the Death Committee suddenly became a different animal.

It was the difference between playing with a house cat and with a leopard.

He sipped coffee that gave him an immediately acid stomach while Meomartino presented the case history and then Dr. Sack gave the post-mortem report.

The autopsy had revealed that there had been nothing wrong with the transplanted kidney, which let Meomartino off the hook immediately.

There had been no problem with the anastomoses or any other factor in Dr. Kender's transplantation technique.

That left only one man, Adam realized.

"Dr. Silverstone, at what time did you last examine her?" Dr. Longwood asked.

He was aware suddenly of the eyes of everybody at the meeting. "Just before nine p.m.," he said.

The Old Man's eyes looked larger than usual because the weight loss had made his long ugly facial features almost gaunt. Dr. Longwood ran his fingers through his thin white hair thoughtfully. "There was no sign of infection?"

"None at all, sir."

The nurse had found her dead at 2:42 a.m.

Dr. Sack cleared his throat. "The time isn't relevant. She would have bled to death in a relatively short period. Perhaps an hour-and-a-half."

Dr. Kender knocked the ash from the end of his cigar. "Did she complain of anything?"

She wanted her hair washed, Adam thought idiotically. "General malaise," he said. "Some abdominal pain."

"What were the signs?"

"Her pulse was up slightly. Her blood pressure had been elevated but was normal when I checked it."

"What did that fact say to you?" Dr. Kender asked.

"At the time, I thought it was a favorable sign."

"What does it indicate to you now, knowing what you do?" Dr. Kender said, not unkindly.

They were being easy on him, Adam realized; perhaps it was a sign they thought well of him. Still, he felt nauseated. "I imagine she was already losing blood internally when I examined her, which accounted for the lowered blood pressure."

Dr. Kender nodded. "You simply hadn't seen a sufficient number of transplant patients. You can't be blamed for that." He shook his head. "I wish to make it clear, though, that in the future when you're faced with something inexplicable in one of my patients, you are to summon one of the staff men. Any Visiting Surgeon on this Service would have known immediately what was taking place. We could have given her blood, gone in like Flynn and attempted to repair the artery, placed a deep drain behind the kidney and shot her full of antibiotics. Even if the kidney had been irreparable, we could have removed it."

And Susan Garland would be alive now, Adam thought. He was numbly aware he had been walking around with the subconscious knowledge that he should have called in a Visiting Surgeon that night. It was why he had been consulting Visitings lately even for the routine things.

He nodded at Kender.

The transplant specialist sighed. "The damned rejection phenomenon is still the thing that's plaguing us. We're good enough surgical mechanics to transplant anything, physically—hearts, limbs or puppy-dogs' tails. But then the recipient's antibodies go to work to reject the transplant, and to prevent this we poison the system with chemicals and leave the patient wide open to infection."

"When you do the next transplant—the kidney for Mrs. Bergstrom—do you plan to use lighter dosages of the drugs?" Dr. Sack asked.

Dr. Kender shrugged. "We'll have to go back to the lab. We'll do more animal studies and then decide."

"Let's return to the Garland case," Dr. Longwood said calmly. "How would you classify the death?"

"Oh, my, preventable," Dr. Parkhurst said.

"Preventable," Dr. Kender said, sucking at his cigar.

"By all means," Dr. Sack said.

When it was Meomartino's turn he had the grace merely to nod silently.

The Old Man fixed Adam with those huge eyes. "On this Surgical Service, Dr. Silverstone, whenever a patient bleeds to death it will be assumed that the mortality could have been avoided."

Adam nodded again. There seemed to be no point in saying anything.

Dr. Longwood rose and the meeting was over.

Adam scraped his chair back from the table and got the hell out of the amphitheater.

When he came off duty that evening he traced Dr. Kender to the animal lab and found him setting up a new series of drug experiments with canines.

Kender greeted him genially. "Pull up a chair, son. You seem to have survived your ordeal by fire."

"Not without getting singed," Adam said.

The older man shrugged. "You deserved to get your ass singed, but it was a mistake most of us would have made with your inexperience in transplantation. You're doing fine. I happen to know Dr. Longwood has his eye on you."

He found himself tingling with pleasure and relief.

"Of course, I wouldn't rely on that if you come up before the Mortality Conference on a regular basis," Kender said thoughtfully, pulling at his ear.

"I won't."

"I don't think you will. Well, what can I do for you?"

"I think I'd better learn something about this end of it," Adam said. "Is there anything I can do around here?"

Kender cast him an interested glance. "When you've been here as long as I have, you'll learn never to refuse when somebody volunteers to work." He went to a cabinet and took out a tray full of small bottles. "Fourteen new drugs. We get them by the dozens from the cancer people. All over the world investigators are developing chemicals to fight cancer. We've found that most agents that are effective against tumors also will kick the hell out of the body's ability to reject or fight foreign tissue." He selected two books from his shelf and handed them to Adam. "If you're really interested, read these. Then drop around again."

Three evenings later Adam was back in the animal lab, this time to watch Kender transplant a canine kidney and to exchange the two books for a third. His next visit was delayed by greed and the opportunity to sell his free time in Woodborough. But a week later, coming off duty one night, he found himself walking to the lab and pushing open the old, paint-chipped door. Kender gave him an unsurprised greeting and coffee and talked with him about a new series of animal experiments he wanted begun.

". . . Do you think you understand all that?" he asked finally.

"Yes."

He grinned and reached for his hat. "Fine and dandy. Then I'll go home and shock my wife."

Adam looked at him. "You want me to start it alone?"

"Why not? A medical student named Kazandjian will be here in half an hour. He works as a technician and knows where to find everything." He picked a notebook from the shelf and slapped it down on the desk. "Keep careful notes. If you get confused, the whole *shmeer* is outlined here."

"Fine and dandy," Adam said faintly.

He sank into a chair, remembering that he was scheduled to cover the Emergency Room in Woodborough the next day.

But by the time the medical student arrived he had studied the notebook and was happy about being there. When he helped Kazandjian to prep a bitch named Harriet, mostly collie with lustrous brown eyes and terrible breath, she licked his hand with a warm, rough tongue. He wanted to buy a bone and sneak her into the room on the sixth floor but he remembered Susan Garland and instead steeled himself and put her under with a stiff jolt of Pentothal. He scrubbed and got ready just the way he would have for a human patient and while Kazandjian prepped a German Shepherd named Wilhelm he removed a kidney from Harriet and then while Kazandjian perfused Harriet's kidney he removed a kidney from Wilhelm and from that moment he forgot they were dogs. The veins were veins and the arteries were arteries, and he knew only that he was performing his first kidney transplants. He worked very carefully and cleanly and when finally Harriet owned one of Wilhelm's kidneys and Wilhelm owned one of Harriet's it was almost one a.m., but he could feel Kazandjian's silent respect, which pleased him more than if the student had put it into words.

They gave Harriet a minimum dose of Imuran and Wilhelm a maximum dose; it was not one of the new agents—in fact it was the one they had used on Susan Garland—but Kender wanted to do studies with the established drugs first, in order to be ready for the upcoming transplant on Mrs. Bergstrom. Kazandjian asked some intelligent questions about immunosuppression, and after they had returned the dogs to their pens the student brewed coffee over a Bunsen burner while Adam explained how the antibodies in the recipient's system were like defensive soldiers reacting as though the transplanted tissue were an invading army, and how the function of the immunosuppressive drug was to strike a hard enough blow against the defensive forces so they wouldn't be able to fight off the foreign organ.

By the time he was back in his room it was nearly two o'clock. He should have been able to fall into bed like a log but instead when he reached for sleep it eluded him. He was keyed up by the experience of the transplantations and haunted by a terrifying compulsion to telephone Arthur Garland and apologize.

It was after four o'clock when finally he fell asleep. Spurgeon Robinson's alarm woke him at seven. He had dreamed of Susan Garland.

Have a ball, luv.

Around eight o'clock, he decided to get up and take a short run and then a very long shower, a combination which he had found sometimes could be substituted for rest.

He got into his sweat suit and sneakers and went downstairs and began to trot. When he turned the corner and came to the Negro slum he saw that the little boy had already fled from whatever den his family occupied.

The boy squatted in the gutter, sifting dust. His dark face lighted as Adam padded wearily toward him.

"Man, who chasin' you?" he whispered.

"The Death Committee," Adam said.

Book Two

Fall and Winter

Chapter 5: Rafael Meomartino

The only sounds in Rafe Meomartino's office were the woman's voice and the singing of compressed air as it bled through the pipes that ringed the ceiling of the small room. The humming noise filled him with a sense of nostalgic euphoria, inexplicable until one morning he realized it was the same feeling he had experienced in another world, in another life, while sitting on the verandah of a club —*El Ganso Oro,* the Golden Goose, one of his brother Guillermo's haunts on the Prado—stunned then by too much alcohol but with the hot Cuban wind making a rasping moan in the palm trees similar to the sound he heard now from the hospital's air pipes.

She looked tired, he thought, but it was more than fatigue that marked the difference in the faces of the two sisters. The woman in Room 211 had a soft, almost slack mouth, slightly weak, perhaps, but also very feminine. This twin's mouth was . . . *female* rather than feminine, he decided. There was no weakness. If the chiseled features projected anything through the make-up it was a suggestion of brittle protective gloss.

As he observed her, his fingers touched the tiny angels embossed in bas relief on the heavy silver case of the pocket watch on the desk. Playing with the watch was a weakness, a nervous fetish he fell into only when under tension; realizing, he abandoned it.

"Where did we finally catch up with you?" he asked.

"Harold's, in Reno. I was just finishing two weeks."

"Three nights ago you were in New York. I caught you on the Sullivan show."

She smiled for the first time. "No, the show segment was taped weeks ago. I was working, so I didn't even get to see it."

"It was very good," he said truthfully.

"Thank you." The smile automatically flashed brighter and then went away. "How's Melanie?"

"She needs a kidney." As Dr. Kender informed you on the telephone, he thought, before you hinted to him that probably it was not going to be one of yours. "Are you planning to remain in Boston for a while?"

She recognized the real question. "I'm not certain. If you need to reach me, I'm at the Sheraton Plaza.

"Registered as Margaret Weldon," she added as an afterthought. "I would just as soon not let it be known that Peggy Weld is here."

"I understand."

"Why does it have to be mine?" she asked.

"It doesn't," he said.

She looked at him, suspending her relief.

"We could transplant a kidney into Mrs. Bergstrom from a cadaver but we wouldn't get an immunological match as close as yours and your sister's."

"Is that because we're twins?"

"If you were identical twins your tissues would be a perfect match. But from what Melanie has told us, you're fraternal twins. If that's so, the match won't be perfect but your tissues would be accepted by your sister's body more readily than any other we could find." He shrugged. "It would give her that much more chance."

"A girl has only two kidneys," she said.

"Not every girl."

She was silent. She opened her eyes and looked at him.

"You only need one kidney to live. Lots of people have been born with one kidney and have lived to ripe old age."

"And some people have donated one kidney and then something has gone wrong with the other one. And they've died," she said quietly. "I've done my homework."

"That's right," he admitted.

She took a cigarette from her bag and absently lit it herself before he could move.

"We can't minimize the risks. We can't even, with any morality, urge you to do it. It's completely a personal decision."

"There are lots of things involved," she said wearily. "I'm supposed to go to the West Coast to make a movie about the days of the big bands. It's what I've been waiting for."

This time he remained silent.

"You don't understand how it is between some sisters," she said. "I did a lot of thinking about it on the plane last night." She smiled mirthlessly. "I'm the older sister, did you know that?"

He smiled and shook his head.

"Ten minutes. You'd think it was ten years, the way my mother always carried on. Melanie was the baby doll with the pretty name and Margaret was the dependable older sister. All our lives I've been the one who's had to take care of *her*. From the time we were sixteen we were singing in joints where we were afraid to use the toilet and I had to make sure she wasn't off behind the bandstand with some lousy trumpet player. Six years of that. And after one good season with Leonard Rathbone's television show we began to make it and we got booked into Blinstrub's and our agent introduced her to his Boston cousin. And that was the end of the sister act."

She got up and walked to the window and stared out at the parking lot. "Look, I was happy for her. Her husband is a nice, square kid. College graduate, makes a decent living. He treats her like a queen. I didn't give a damn about the act. I started out all over again as a single."

"You've done very well," Meomartino said.

"I've earned every last bit of it. It meant starting all over, going back to the same dreary dives, always on the road. It meant every summer touring with the USO in Greenland and Vietnam and Korea and Germany and who knows where all, hoping somebody would see me. It meant a lot of other things, too." She looked at him coolly. "You're a doctor, it's no news to you that a woman needs a sex life."

"No great big news."

"Well, it's also meant a lot of terrible one-night stands because I've never stayed in one place long enough to develop a relationship."

He nodded, vulnerable as always to an honest woman.

"I finally got lucky and made a couple of novelty sides the little goons all bought. But who knows what kind of records they'll be buying next year, or for that matter, next month? My agent tells everybody I'm twenty-six, but I'm thirty-three."

"That's hardly old."

"It's old to be making your first movie. And it's too old to make it big for the first time on TV and in the clubs. This success should have happened to me ten years ago. My figure's harder to keep all the time and in a few years I'll have neck wrinkles. If I don't push hard right now it'll all be over. So you're not asking me to give her just a kidney. You're asking me to give her more than I ever want to give her again."

"I'm not asking you to give her anything," Meomartino said.

She ground out her cigarette. "Well, don't," she said. "I have my own life to lead."

"Would you like to see her?"

She nodded.

Her sister was asleep when they entered her room.

"We'd better not wake her," Meomartino said.

"I'll just sit here and wait."

But she opened her eyes. "Peg," she said.

"Hello, Mellie." She leaned over and kissed her. "How's Ted?"

"Fine. What a marvelous thing, to wake up and find you here!"

"And the two little Swedes?"

"They're wonderful. They watched the Sullivan date. Hey, it was so good, I was so proud." She looked up at her sister and sat up in bed. "Ah, no, Peg. Don't."

She took her twin in her arms and stroked her head. "Please, Peggy. Peggy, darling, don't do that . . ."

Rafe walked back to his office. He sat at his desk and tried to rid himself of paper work.

You don't know how it is between some sisters.

But I know how it is between some brothers, he thought.

The compressed air continued to moan in the pipes. Despite himself his hand went out to the pocket watch, his fingers nervously touching the embossed angels on the tarnished silver lid until he opened the watch and stared through the old-fashioned Roman numeraled face into events he desperately did not want to recall.

The pattern had been established when Rafael was five and Guillermo was seven.

Leo, the family handy man—a large, shambling human animal who loved him—tried to tell him one day after he caught Rafael prepared to leave a second-story window equipped with paper wings Guillermo had tied to his shoulders.

"He will be your ruin, that little bastard, may your mother forgive me," Leo said, spitting through the open window. "Never listen to him, remember what I tell you."

But Guillermo was always so interesting to listen to.

Weeks later, "I have something," he said.

"Let me see."

"It is a place."

"Take me."

"It is a place for big boys. You still siss your pants."

"No," Rafael said hotly, afraid he was going to cry, feeling the little tug in his groin right this minute, remembering that only three days before he had not made it to the bathroom in time.

"It's a wonderful place. But I don't think you're a big enough boy for me to take you. If you siss your pants there the old lady witch will get you. She turns herself into any animal she wants. And then it's goodbye."

"You're fooling me."

"I'm not. But it's a great place."

Rafael was silent. "Have you seen her?" he asked finally.

Guillermo glared at him. "I never siss my pants."

They played, after a while wandering into their parents' room. Guillermo stood on the bed to reach the top drawer of the bureau and took out the red-velvet box in which the watch was placed by their father each night and from which it was removed each morning.

He opened it and banged it shut, open and shut, a satisfying noise.

"You will be punished," Rafael said.

Guillermo made a rude noise. "I can touch it because it will be mine." The watch was passed on to the elder son, as had been explained to the boys. Nevertheless, he replaced it in the drawer and strolled back to his room, Rafael trailing.

"Take me, Guillermo. Please."

"What will you give me?"

Rafael shrugged. His brother chose the three toys he knew were closest to the smaller boy's heart: a red soldier, a picture book about a sad clown, a teddy bear named Fabio, hunchbacked because he clutched it so tightly when he slept with it every night.

"Not the bear."

Guillermo gave him a look as hard as a marble and then agreed.

That afternoon when they were supposed to be napping Guillermo led him down a path through the forest of stunted pines behind the house. It took them ten minutes, following the old, twisting path, to reach the small clearing. The smokehouse was a large, windowless box. Unpainted, its timbers were bleached by the sun and silvered by the rains.

Inside, it was night.

"Go ahead," Guillermo urged. "I'm right behind."

But as he entered, leaving the world of light and green, the door behind him swung shut, and with a click the bolt was thrown.

He bawled.

In a moment he stopped.

"Guillermo," he said, laughing. "Don't fool me."

Whether he opened or closed his eyes, light remained bunched up behind his lids. Purple shadows swung by him, at him, through him, shapes he did not want to recognize, the color of the blood of the great swine which had hung here. Several times his father had taken him to the slaughtering. He remembered the smells and the blood and the grunting, the wild rolling of the eyes.

"Guillermo," he shouted, "you can have Fabio."

The silence was black.

Crying, he threw himself forward to smash unexpectedly into the unseen wall he had envisioned several feet beyond. A great pain at once replaced his nose. As his knees gave, a projecting nail tore the softness of his cheek, narrowly missing his right eye. Something wet was on his face, which hurt, hurt; and in the corner of his mouth, salt. As he sank to the coolness of the hard dirt floor he felt a soft warm spreading, a terrified trickling down the inside of his thighs.

In the dark corner, leaves rustled and a small thing scurried.

"I'll be a big boy. I'll be a big boy," Rafael screamed.

Five hours later, after the searchers shouting his name had passed him again and again, someone—the handyman, Leo—had thought to open the smokehouse door and look inside.

That night, sedated, tenderly bathed, the slash in his face sutured and his nose grotesque but cared for, he slept in the arms of his mother.

Leo had reported that the smokehouse had been bolted from the outside. Fabio was discovered in the kidnapper's bed, and Guillermo confessed and was duly beaten. On the following morning he presented himself to his brother and delivered an eloquent and contrite apology. Ten minutes later to the amazement of their parents the two boys were playing together and Rafael laughed for the first time in twenty-four hours.

But he had an I.Q. of 147 and even at the age of five he was intelligent enough to know that he had learned something.

His life was shaped by avoidance of his brother.

Meomartino men studied abroad; when Guillermo had elected to go to the Sorbonne, a year later Rafael became a freshman at Harvard. He roomed for four good years with a Portland, Maine, boy named George Hamilton Currier, a raw-boned baked beans heir whose family's canned product was a staple in three out of ten American kitchen cupboards. Beany Currier gave him his first and only nickname—Rafe—and constant exposure to his views of the glories of medicine as a career. Guillermo had decided to study law at the University of California—it was traditional for Meomartino males to train for one of the professions even though their working lives were spent husbanding the family sugar interests— and when Rafe left Cambridge with second honors, almost as an afterthought he decided to study medicine in Cuba. His father had died of a stroke several years earlier. His mother's world, which always had revolved about the warm glow of her husband, now maintained its stability through a similar orbit about her youngest child. She was a beautiful woman with a sweet but harried smile, an old-fashioned Cuban lady whose long slender hands tatted lace with easy skill, but a woman modern enough to collect abstract art and to go immediately to the family physician when finally she discovered the lump on her right breast. The terrible word was never spoken in her presence. The breast was removed with dispatch and kind words.

Rafe's years in *La Facultad de Medicina de la Universidad de la Habana* were good ones, the kind which do not enter a lifetime more than once, combined of youth and immortality and certainty in everything he believed. From the beginning the hospital smell was more heady to him than the sickening-sweet odor of sugar-cane bagasse. There was a girl, a classmate named Paula, small and dark and warm, with slightly buck teeth, with legs less than perfect but a behind like a pear and an apartment near the university and absolute clinical dependability in the matter of birth control. She glowered and lost interest at the mention of Batista, so he learned not to mention Batista, hardly a problem. There were times when he arrived at her apartment to find a small group, never more than half a dozen fast-talking men and women who fell strangely silent when he entered the room, in which case he would immediately and cheerfully depart.

He cared nothing of the webs she spun without him in secret sessions, intrigue adding only another ingredient to the spice called Paula. As for the meetings, there had always been secret meetings in Cuba, who got excited about meetings? Dreaming and plotting futures that never arrived was part of the atmosphere, like the sun, like the lovers on the grass, like jai alai, like cockfighting, like the mysterious stains left on the marble sidewalks of the Prado when you stepped on the dark blue berries that dropped from the low-cropped trees. He minded his own business and nobody bothered to invite him to meetings since he was of the Meomartinos, a family which enriched those in power despite inevitable periodic changes in government.

Guillermo came home when Rafael was in his last year of medical school, the year of internship at *El Hospital Universitario General Calixto García.* Carlos hung his law degree on the wall of an office at the sugar mill and spent his time pretending to draw charts showing the relationship between sugar cane, brown sugar and blackstrap molasses. Often the pen wobbled in his hand due to a passionate predilection for double-and-triple-distilled beverages, domestic and imported. Rafael saw little of him, the internship filling all his hours, the days evaporating under the heat of overwork, too many sick people, too few doctors.

Two days after he received the degree of *Doctor en Medicina* his uncle Erneido Pesca came to call. His mother's brother was a tall, thin man with military bearing, a once-gray mustache in a wrinkled and pouchy face, and a penchant for Partagás cigars and well-pressed white linen suits. He removed his Panama to reveal his blue-gray mane of hair, sighed, asked for a drink—by which he meant rum—and looked on with disapproval as his nephew poured himself a scotch.

"When will you enter the firm?" he asked finally.

"I thought," Rafael said, "that perhaps I would busy myself with medicine."

Erneido sighed. "Your brother," he said, "is a fool and a dissolute weakling. Perhaps worse."

"I know."

"Then you must enter the firm. I will not last forever."

They argued, quietly but heatedly.

In the end, a compromise. He would have the office next to Guillermo's at the sugar mill. He would also have a laboratory at the medical school, Erneido would see to it. Three days a week at the mill, two days a week at the medical school; this was as far as Erneido would bend as head of the family and successor to his father.

Rafe agreed with resignation. It was more than he had hoped for.

The Dean, an academic veteran wise in the procurement of endowments, personally showed him to the large but shabby laboratory, filled with enough equipment to support three researchers instead of one and presented to Rafe along with the title of research associate.

He was proud when he showed the lab to Paula, like a little boy with a new toy. She looked at him in puzzled amusement. "You never mentioned research," she said. "Why now all the interest in research?" She had taken a position with the government health service and was leaving to become health officer in a small mountain village in Oriente Province, in the Sierra Maestra.

Because I am up to my ass in bagasse, because I do not wish to drown in sugar, he thought. "It's needed," he said, convincing neither of them.

In the laboratory next to his was a Ph.D. biochemist named Rivkind, who had come to Cuba from Ohio State under a small grant from the Cancer Foundation. His reason for being there, he admitted to Rafael, was that it was cheaper to live in Havana than in Columbus. The only time Rivkind began a conversation was to complain bitterly because the University would not buy him a lousy two-hundred-and-seventy-dollar centrifuge. Rafe owned one in his new lab, a fact he was too embarrassed to mention. They did not become friends. Every time Rafe stepped into Rivkind's cramped, crowded cubicle, the American seemed to be working.

In desperation, he decided to work himself.

He became a writer. He wrote a list.

> *Leptospirosis, a mean little bugger.*
> *Leprosy, a ragged begger.*
> *Jaundice, a yellow bastard.*
> *Malaria, something to sweat about.*
> *Other febrile diseases, many hot problems.*
> *Elephantiasis, one big problem.*
> *Dysentery-like diseases, a lot of shit.*
> *Tuberculosis, can we hack it?*
> *Parasites, living off the lean of the land.*

He carried the list folded in his pocket for days, pulling it out to read until it was tattered and doomed.

Which problem should he concentrate on first?

He became a reader. He drew great piles of books from the library and on Monday and Tuesday of each week he sat in his private laboratory surrounded by stacks of volumes and he read, taking copious notes, some of which he managed to save. On Wednesday, Thursday and Friday he went to his office at the sugar mill and collected other literature, *Pythium Root Rot and Smut in Sugar Cane, The Genesis and Prevention of Chlorotic Streak,* market reports, U.S. Department of Agriculture tracts, sales treatises, confidential memos, an entire sugar library lovingly gathered for him by Uncle Erneido. These he read with less interest. By the third week he was ignoring the sugar literature entirely, bringing a medical volume to the sugar plant office in his briefcase and reading like a thief, the door locked.

Often in the late afternoon there would be a tentative scratching at the door. "Sssst. Let's go out tonight and change our luck," Guillermo would say in a voice already whiskey-hoarse. It was an invitation he tendered often, one which Rafe refused with what he hoped was brotherly affection. Could Pasteur have founded microbiology, could Semmelweis have put the skids to puerperal fever, could Hippocrates have written the goddam oath, if they were all the time screwing off to get laid? He spent his evenings in the laboratory, puttering, practicing, breaking glass retorts, growing molds, looking at his eyelashes in the microscope mirror.

Paula came to Havana one afternoon from the small village in the Sierra Maestra where she was stationed as a health officer.

"What are you working on?" she asked.

"Leprosy," he said, making up his mind.

She smiled at him skeptically. "I will not be back in Havana for a long time," she said.

He understood that she was saying goodbye. "Are there so many sick people depending on you?" The idea filled him with envy.

"It isn't that, it's a personal thing."

Personal? What was personal? They discussed her monthly periods like baseball scores. The only personal thing in her life was politics. Fidel Castro was somewhere in those mountains raising periodic hell. "Don't get into trouble," he said, reaching out a hand to touch her hair.

"You'd care?" Her eyes surprised him with their tears.

"Of course," he said. Two days later she was out of his life. He was not to think seriously of her again until the single remaining time he would hear her voice.

Having told her that he was working on leprosy, he spent a lot of time poring through *Index Medicus,* drew up long lists of source material, gathered fresh stacks of journals from the library and settled down for more reading.

It led him to nothing.

He simply sat in his expensive laboratory, watching dust-motes float in the beam of sun which slanted in through the somewhat-dirty windows, trying to think of a program of research.

If he had been able to think of something bad, he would not have been so frightened.

He came up with nothing at all.

Finally he exorcised all fright. He gazed at his reflection in the mirror, critically but honestly, admitting for the first time that what he saw was not a researcher.

Up and down the corridor and over three floors, sometimes almost running, he gave things away, the Cuban Santa Claus of modern medicine—all the small portable equipment, all the retorts, all the lovely unused supplies. He picked up the centrifuge and carried it into Rivkind's small lab. The microscope, a useful object in public health work, he packed tenderly and sent off to Paula in the fierce mountains where she was a real doctor. Then he left his key and a short but grateful letter of resignation in the Dean's mailbox and walked from the building, his heart trailing great painful drops, almost visible.

So.

He was not a medical researcher.

He would listen to his father's genes and be a sugar man.

He went to the office at the *central* every day.

At Uncle Erneido's left elbow (Guillermo at his right) he sat in on sales meetings, production meetings, key hirings, key firings, scheduling sessions, shipping conferences.

No longer a big, overgrown little boy playing at man of science.

Now, he knew, a big, overgrown little boy playing at man of business.

Every evening when he left the office he would go to one of several drinking clubs by prearrangement and in a little while Guillermo would show up with the women, mostly semi-professionals but sometimes, like an appetizer, not; as they crossed the room to where he was sitting and waiting Rafe made a game of trying to guess correctly and he was often wrong. One pair he had classified as call girls turned out to be two schoolteachers from Flint, Michigan, facing their need to feel guilty but used.

Guillermo, he soon realized, was second-rate in this as in other matters. They went to tritely-wicked places, drug pads, sex circuses, the clichés which knowing and wiser *Habaneros* hooted at as traps for self-conscious Yanqui tourists, the Hemingway seekers. He found himself drifting toward a bloated future. He could see himself in ten years, dull-eyed and uncaring, sucking the sugar teat and swapping filthy tales with Guillermo in the bars along the Prado. And yet he felt curiously powerless to pull out, as if he were a Hindu figure frozen against his will in a lewd stone frieze, cursing the sculptor.

Later, there was never any doubt in his mind that he was saved by Fidel Castro.

For a couple of days everyone stayed in his own home. There was some self-righteous wrecking and looting, places like the Deauville Casino where Batista had split the take with American gamblers.

Castro men were everywhere, wearing a variety of dirty dress. Their uniforms were the red and black *26 de Julio* armbands, the loaded rifles and the beards that made some of them Christ-like and some merely goatlike. The firing squad executions commenced in the Havana Sports Palace and were continued daily, sometimes with matinees.

One afternoon, sitting in the almost-deserted Jockey Club, Rafe was called to the telephone. He had told nobody where he was going. Someone must have followed me, he thought. "Hello?"

The woman on the other end of the line called herself "a friend." He recognized Paula's voice at once.

"This week is a good one for traveling."

Little children playing at melodrama, he thought, but against his will felt the soft kiss of fear. What had she heard?

"My family?"

"Also. It should be a long trip."

"Who is this?" he asked charitably.

"Don't ask questions. Another thing, your telephones at home and at the office are tapped."

"Did you get the microscope?" he asked, an end to charity.

Now she was weeping, hard and wrenchingly, trying to talk.

"I love you," he said, hating himself.

"Liar."

"No," he lied.

The phone went dead. He stood there holding the receiver, feeling numb and grateful, wondering what he had let get away when he had so carefully kept her out of his needs. Then he replaced the receiver and hurried to see his uncle.

They did not sleep that night. They could not take the land with them, the buildings, the machinery, the long good years. But there were negotiable securities, jewelry, the most valuable of his mother's paintings, like money in the bank. Considered as Meomartinos they would be poor; considered by most standards they would have financial comfort.

The boat Erneido procured was no fishing boat. It was a power launch, a 57-foot Chris-Craft with twin 320 General Motors diesels, a stateroom, a carpeted salon and a galley: a fast and comfort-able boat built to pleasure rich men. He gave his mother one and one-half grains of Nembutal as they left the beach at Matanzas the following midnight. She slept soundly.

He and his mother stayed in Miami only ten days. Guillermo and Uncle Erneido, mapping a legal campaign they hoped might some-how retain the Meomartino properties for the family *in absentia,* set up a residence-headquarters in two rooms of the Holiday Inn. They looked upon Rafe's decision to go North as a temporary aberration.

His mother enjoyed the train trip to Boston on the East Coast Champion. They went directly to the Ritz through the lemon-freeze air of New England spring. For several weeks after that they were tourists, chasing the worlds of Paul Revere and George Apley, his mother's strength trickling like sawdust from a doll with a torn heel. When she began to run a low-grade fever, he found her a famed cancer man at the Massachusetts General Hospital and stayed near her until the fever disappeared. Then he resumed his prowling search —for what? —without her.

It was March, cool and cruel. The lilacs and the magnolias along Commonwealth Avenue were tight hard buds, brown and black, but in the Public Gardens across the street from the Ritz, beds of hot-house tulips made splashes of color against the unawakened sod.

He made the short excursion to Cambridge and paced the Yard, looking at the pinkcheeked schoolboys, some with Castro beards, studying the robust, no-nonsense 'Cliffies with their green felt book-bags, feeling no sense of home-coming.

He had a reunion with Beanie Currier, now a second-year resi-dent in pediatrics at the Boston Floating Hospital for Infants and Children. Through Beanie he met other young house officers, drank beer with them in Jake Wirth's and listened to their talk. He real-ized gladly one morning that he was hardly through with medicine. He started to look the field over from new perspectives, slowly and carefully. He began to study hospitals and surgical departments. He spent whole evenings walking through the corridors of wards at the Massachusetts General, Peter Bent Brigham, Carney, Beth Israel, Boston City, the New England Medical Center. The moment he saw Suffolk County General Hospital he felt a curious abdominal flut-tering, as if he had just seen a girl he wanted very much. It was a big old monster of a hospital, crammed with the indigent. He wouldn't send his mother there but he knew it was the kind of place where surgery would be learned with a knife in his hand. It drew him, warmed his blood with its noises and smells.

Dr. Longwood, the Chief of Surgery, was less than cordial. "I don't know that I can encourage your application," he said.

"Why not, sir?"

"Let me be frank, Doctor," he said with a cold smile. "I have both personal and professional reasons to be wary of foreign-trained physicians."

"Your personal reasons are none of my business," Rafe said carefully. "Do you mind disclosing your professional ones?"

"Like hospitals all over the country, we have had our troubles with foreign house officers."

"What kind of troubles?"

"We've grabbed them as an answer to our physicians-shortage. And we've found they can't always take a proper case history. And they often can't speak sufficient English to comprehend what is necessary during emergencies."

"I believe you'll find I take an adequate history. I've spoken English fluently all my life, even before I attended Harvard," he said, noting the Harvard degree on Dr. Longwood's own office wall.

"Foreign medical schools haven't covered the same broad areas with the thoroughness of American medical schools."

"I don't know what will happen in the future, but my medical school always has been approved in this country. It has a distinguished past."

"You would have to repeat internship here."

"That would be satisfactory," Rafe said quietly.

"And you would have to pass the test of the Educational Council for Foreign Medical School Graduates. I might add that I was one of those responsible for getting the test established."

"All right."

He took the examination at the State House in the company of a Nigerian, two men from Ireland and a covey of miserable, perspiring assorted Puerto Ricans and Latin Americans. It was the simplest of tests in the most basic medical principles and the English language, almost an insult to a man who had been graduated from the College magna cum.

According to American Medical Association regulations, he submitted his diploma from *La Facultad de Medicina de la Universidad de la Habana,* accompanied by a certified Berlitz translation. On July 1, in whites and an intern again, he reported for duty at the hospital. He found that Longwood treated him the way he had treated the lepers along the Havana waterfront, politely but with a forced tolerance. He had no large laboratory; no one would have dreamed of buying him a centrifuge or anything else; he found that when he held a scalpel he still felt comfortable and unafraid, and he was confident that he would become better as time passed; he walked the polished brown linoleum of the corridors with long, happy strides, restraining his impulse to shout.

It was at the Massachusetts General Hospital. His mother was waiting in an office on the eighth floor of the Warren Building for her weekly examination and a fresh supply of time-buying steroids. He wandered into the coffee shop on the ground floor of Baker and ordered a cup of black from a girl in one of those blue smocks with the word *Volunteer* embroidered in red over the left breast. She was dark-blonde, attractive in a quietly sophisticated, heavy-lidded way that didn't generally appeal to him, perhaps because it included exactly what turned Guillermo on about a woman, just a hint of past ruttishness.

He was half through with the coffee when the girl left the counter and came over to his table carrying a tray on which were a magazine, a cup of tea and a dessert plate with a danish pastry.

"May I?"

"Of course," he said.

She made herself at home. It was a small table and her magazine was large. It jogged his saucer when she placed it on the table, causing sloshing but no spilling.

"I am sorry!"

"Nonsense, no harm done."

He drank, staring out the glass walls into the corridor. She read, sipped, nibbled at her pastry. He was aware of a subtle, undoubtedly expensive perfume, musk and roses, he decided. Involuntarily he closed his eyes and simply breathed in. Next to him she turned a page.

He risked a quick sidelong glance and was caught at it—direct gray eyes, very powerful depths, a hint of crow's-feet in the corners, grin lines or sin lines? Instead of looking away, to his embarrassment he didn't move his head but slammed his eyelids down again like guilty trapdoors.

She laughed like a child.

When he opened his eyes again he saw that she had taken a cigarette from her purse and was feeling around for a match. He struck one, secure in the knowledge that his surgeon's hands would not tremble, and then, as her fingertips brushed his hand to guide the flame to the end of the cigarette, trembling. The moment gave him a chance to look at her. Her blonde hair was not her own shade, an expensive rinse but nonetheless discernible. Her skin was good: the nose slightly prominent, curved, passionate; the mouth a trifle wide but full.

They both realized at the same time that he was staring. She smiled and he felt like an adventurer.

"Are you here with a patient?"

"Yes," he said.

"It's a very good hospital."

"I know," he said. "I'm a doctor, an intern at Suffolk County General."

She cocked her head. "What department?"

"Surgery." He held out his hand. "My name's Rafe Meomartino."

"Elizabeth Bookstein." For some reason she was laughing, a fact he found annoying. He hadn't thought of her as a silly woman. "Dr. Longwood is my uncle," she said as she shook his hand.

Cristos.

"Oh?"

"Yes," she said. She had stopped laughing but she was watching his face and smiling. "Oh, dear. You don't like my uncle. Not at all."

"No," he said, smiling back. He was still holding her hand.

To her credit, she didn't ask for reasons. "They tell me he's a good teacher," she said.

"He is that," Rafe said. The answer appeared to satisfy her. "Your name. Where did you get the Bookstein?"

"I'm a divorced lady."

"Are you anybody's divorced lady in particular?"

She took her hand back but the smile stayed. "Not in particular."

He saw his mother coming through the door, looking much smaller than he remembered her looking only yesterday, moving much slower than she once had moved.

"Mama," he said, standing. When she came over he introduced them. Then, politely, he said goodbye to the girl and walked slowly out of the coffee shop, matching his pace to his mother's.

When they made subsequent visits to the hospital he looked for her but she was not in the coffee shop; the volunteers worked erratic schedules, coming in more or less as they pleased. He could have found her telephone number —he did not bother even to consult the book —but he was working very hard at the hospital, and his mother's illness, increasing in intensity, weighed heavier on his shoulders with each passing day. Her flesh seemed to become thinner and transparent, to stretch tighter across the delicate framework of her bones. Her skin developed a kind of luminosity that he was to recognize instantly in cancer patients whenever he saw it for the rest of his life.

She talked more of Cuba. Sometimes when he came home he would find her sitting in the dark of her room by the window, looking down at the traffic sliding silently over Arlington Street.

What was she seeing, he asked himself: Cuban waters? Cuban forests and Cuban fields? The faces of ghosts, people he had never known?

"*Mamacita,*" he said one night, unable to be completely silent. He kissed the top of her head. He wanted to reach out, stroke her face, pull her gently to him, place his arms around her in such a way that nothing could reach her, so anything that might harm her would have to go through him first. But he was afraid that he would frighten her, so he did nothing.

Within seven weeks the aspirin and codein had proven ineffectual. The cancer man replaced them with Demerol.

Eleven weeks after that, he returned her to the very nice, sunny room in Phillips House at the Massachusetts General Hospital. Charming nurses filled her veins regularly with the gift of poppies.

Two days after his mother went into coma the cancer specialist told him gently but matter-of-factly that he could continue to do a number of things to prolong the agonized functioning of her vital organs or he could discontinue to do them, in which case she would die rather quickly.

"We are not talking about euthanasia," the elderly physician said. "We are talking about deciding not to give support to a life in which there is no longer hope for real living; only, perhaps, for intermittent periods of terrible pain. I never make this decision alone when there is a relative. Think about it. It is a decision you will be faced with again and again as a doctor."

Rafe did not take much time to think about it. "Let her go," he said.

On the following morning he entered his mother's hospital room to see a dark shade bending over her, a tall, skinny priest whose freckled baby face and carrot hair above his black cassock was a joke.

Oil already glistened on his mother's eyelids, reflecting winks of light.

". . . May the Lord forgive you whatever sin you have committed," the priest was saying, his dipped thumb making the sign of the cross on her twisted mouth, his voice an abomination, the worst kind of South Boston accent.

You unwholesomely sober young man, what serious sins could *she* possibly have committed, Rafe wondered. The juvenile thumb dipped again. "Through this holy anointing . . ."

Ah, God, as they say, you are dead. If you existed, why would you screw us around like this? I love you. Do not die. I love you. *Please.*

But he said nothing aloud.

He hovered at the foot of his mother's bed, feeling suddenly the aloneness, the awful isolation, the knowledge that he was a speck of pigeon waste in the terrible, terrible emptiness.

In a little while he observed clinically that there was no respiration. He went to her, unknowingly shrugging off the priest's hand, and took her into his arms.

"I love you. I love you. Please." His voice was loud in the silent room.

His mother went out in expensive but lonely splendor. Rafe made certain there were flowers in profusion. The casket was like a copper Cadillac with blue velvet upholstery. The last thing he did

for her was pre-pay for the Solemn High Mass of Requiem in St. Cecilia's. Guillermo and Uncle Erneido flew up from Miami. The
housekeeper and the floor maid from the Ritz came and sat in the
last row. A trembly drunk who muttered to himself and knelt at the
wrong times sat alone in the corner, four seats away from the
church custodian. Other than that, St. Cecilia's was completely
empty, a polished echo smelling of floor wax and incense.

At the graveside in Brookline they were alone, shivering with
sorrow and fear and the bone-piercing cold. When they returned to
the Ritz-Carlton, Erneido excused himself and went to bed with a
headache and pills. Rafe and Guillermo went to the lounge and sat
and drank scotch. It was like bad old times, drinking and not listening to Guillermo. Finally, through an alcoholic haze, as from a distance he understood that Guillermo was telling him something of
great importance.

". . . Giving us arms, planes, tanks. Training us. They will fight
right by our side, those Marines are wonderful fighters! We'll have
air cover. We'll need every officer, you will have to contact everybody you know. I am a captain. You no doubt will be a captain,
too."

He concentrated hard and realized what his brother was talking
about, then he laughed without mirth. "No," he said. "Thank you."

Guillermo stopped talking and looked at him. "What do you
mean?"

"I need no invasions. I plan to stay here. I'm going to apply for
citizenship papers."

Sixty percent horror, thirty percent hatred, ten percent contempt,
he decided, watching his brother's veiled Meomartino eyes.

"You don't believe in Cuba?"

"Believe?" Rafe laughed. "I'll tell you the truth, big brother. I
don't believe in *anything,* not the way you mean. I think all move-
ments, all large organizations in this world are lies and profit for
somebody. I believe, I suppose, in people doing as little harm as
possible to other human beings."

"Noble. What you really mean is you have no balls."

Rafe stared at him.

"You never had balls." Guillermo downed his drink and snapped
his fingers for service. "I have balls enough for all the Meomartinos.
I love Cuba."

"You're not talking about Cuba, *alcahuete.*" They had been talking in Spanish; suddenly, for unknown reasons, Rafe found that he had lapsed into English. "You're talking about sugar, how can you pretend differently? How will it help the poor slobs who really *are* Cuba if we boot Fidel in the *nalgas* and take back all our marbles?" He took a furious swallow of scotch. "Would whoever we set up to take his place treat them differently?

"Never," he answered his own question. To his chagrin he found himself trembling.

Guillermo waited him out coldly.

"Few men in our movement are sugar men. We have some of the best," he said, as if talking to a child.

"Perhaps all of them are patriots. Even if they are, their reasons undoubtedly are just as bad as yours."

"It's wonderful to be omniscient, you spineless son-of-a-bitch."

Rafael shrugged. Guillermo had been a loving son in his fashion. Rafe knew the thoughtless insult had been directed at him and not at their mother. At last, he thought with a strange sense of relief, we are calling each other, aloud, the names we have always kept in hidden places.

Nevertheless, Guillermo obviously regretted his choice of words. "Mama," he said.

"What about her?"

"Do you think she can rest peacefully in a grave with snow on it? She should be returned to sleep in Cuba."

"Why don't you go to hell," Rafe said furiously. He got up without finishing his drink and walked away, leaving his brother sitting and staring into his glass.

Guillermo and Uncle Erneido left that evening after shaking his hand like strangers.

Four days later the last nor'easter of the spring struck New England a white blow, dumping four inches of snow along the coast from Portland to Block Island. Late that afternoon Rafe took a taxi to Holyhood Cemetery. The storm had passed but the wind blew snow devils that whirled their way up the sleeves of his topcoat and down beneath his collar. He walked to the grave, getting snow in his shoes. The mound was still raised; despite the wind, veins of trapped snow stood out between the frozen earth-clumps. He stood there as long as he could, until his nose ran and there was no sensation in his frozen feet. When he returned to his room he sat in the dark by the window as she had been accustomed to sit, watching the traffic continue to move over Arlington Street. No doubt some of the same machines; automobiles died slower than people.

He moved out of the Ritz to a converted brownstone rooming house one block from the hospital. Across the hall lived two lissome male students, perhaps in sin. Upstairs was a cross-eyed girl he thought was a hooker, although there was no sign that she entertained even a boy friend in her room.

He spent most of his spare time at the hospital, reinforcing his reputation for competent earnestness and insuring that he would be selected for a residency in the following year, but refusing to live there formally because he didn't wish to acknowledge to himself that he had need of a refuge.

Spring caught him vulnerable and unaware. He forgot to get his hair cut; brooded about the possibility of an after-life and decided in his wisdom that nothing lay beyond; considered psychoanalysis until he read in an article by Anna Freud that the individual was beyond the analyst's reach when in mourning and when falling in love.

The invasion of the Bay of Pigs shook him out of his lethargy, unpleasantly. He first heard the news over a portable radio in the women's side of the ward. The report was optimistic about the success of the invasion but was sketchy and gave very few facts, save that the landing had occurred in the Bay of Pigs.

Rafe remembered it well, a seaside resort area where sometimes his parents had taken him when he was a little boy. Along the shore each morning while their parents slept, he and Guillermo had collected great piles of sea-treasure that stank by evening, and small, smooth white stones like petrified bird's eggs.

With each new report the news got worse.

He tried calling Guillermo person-to-person in Miami without success but finally reached Uncle Erneido.

"There is no way to tell where he is. He is somewhere there, with the others. It appears to be very bad. This goddam country, which was supposed to be our friend . . ."

The old man could not continue.

"Let me know as soon as you hear something," Rafe said.

In a very few days it was possible to reconstruct part of the terrible picture and guess the rest: the enormity of the defeat, the magnitude of the attacking Brigade's unpreparedness, the obsolescence of the equipment, the absence of air support, the arrogant bungling of the CIA, the obvious anguish of the young American President, the invisibility of the United States Marines when they were so desperately required.

Rafe spent a lot of time imagining what it must have been like, the sea at their backs, the swamp and Fidel Castro's Soviet-armed militia everywhere else. The dead, the paucity of facilities to treat the wounded.

Walking slowly through the hospital, he *saw* certain things for the first time.

A resuscitator, a pacemaker.

A suction machine.

Beds offering warmth and rest for patients in shock.

The *fantastic* operating room suites, the teams of people.

God, the blood bank. All the Meomartinos were rare blood types.

He had never made a secret of the fact that he was a Cuban; a number of staff members and a few of the patients muttered words of sympathy, but most avoided the subject. On several occasions conversation ground to a sudden guilty halt when he entered a group.

Suddenly he found that he could sleep at night; as soon as he entered his bed he sank into the deep, anesthetic slumber of a man seizing escape.

One day in May the heavy silver watch with angels on the lid arrived like a white feather from Uncle Erneido by registered mail. The note which accompanied it was brief but contained a number of messages.

> *My Nephew,*
>
> *As you are aware, this family watch is part of the Meomartino inheritance. It has been guarded with honor by those who kept it in trust for you. Guard it as well as you are able. May you pass it along to many generations of Meomartinos.*
>
> *We do not know how your brother died, but we have it on the best authority that he perished, and that he acquitted*

> *himself well before his destruction. I will attempt to learn
> more as time goes on.*
>
> *I do not expect that we will meet in the near future. I am
> an old man, and whatever energies I have left I will use the
> best way I know how. I hope and trust that your medical
> career goes well. I despair of seeing my Cuba liberated.
> There is not a sufficient number of patriots with men's
> blood in their veins to wrest from Fidel Castro that which is
> rightfully theirs.*
>
> *Your uncle,*
Erneido Pesca

He placed the watch in his bureau and left for the hospital. When
he returned forty hours later and opened the drawer it was there
waiting for him. He stared at it and then closed the drawer and put
on his coat and left the rooming house. Outside the afternoon was
trying to decide whether it was the shank of spring or the edge of
summer, with rain clouds gathering. He walked over the pavements
of Boston, block after block for a long time through the afternoon
heat.

On Washington Street, feeling hunger like sudden surprise, he
turned into a saloon in the shadow of the elevated. The Boston
Herald-Traveler was a block away. It was a good tavern, a workingman's bar full of newspapermen eating or drinking their suppers, some of the pressmen still wearing square hats of folded news
sheets to keep the ink and grease from their hair.

On the end stool he ordered veal cutlet parmigiana. A television
set above the mirror spewed forth a news broadcast, the latest as-
sessment of the catastrophe at the Bay of Pigs.

Few of the invaders had been evacuated.

A large percentage of them had been killed.

Virtually all survivors had been taken prisoner.

When the veal arrived he didn't bother to cut it. "Double scotch."

He had that one and then another, which made him feel better,
and then a third, which made him feel very bad. Needing air, he
dropped a bill on the mahogany and walked away on tired legs.

Outside, the new night sky was low and black, the wind like a
series of wet towels blown from the sea. He sought refuge when a
taxi stopped.

"Take me to any good bar. And wait, please."

Park Square. The name of the place was The Sands. The lighting was dim but the scotch was definitely unwatered. When he came out the taxi was there, a ghostly charger that galloped him, meter ticking, to the neon-bright pleasure palaces of the living. They worked their way north, pausing frequently. Alighting before a tavern on Charles Street, grateful for fidelity, Rafe pressed a bill into the driver's hand, realizing his mistake when the taxi went away.

When he left the place on Charles Street all objects were blurs, some brighter than others. The wind off the Charles River was rude and wet. Rain drummed and hissed along the pavement at his feet. His clothing and his hair accepted it until they could hold no more and then they streamed like the rest of the world. The rain, hard and cold, bit into his face, making him unaccountably nauseous.

He passed the Massachusetts Eye Infirmary and the wet outlines of the Massachusetts General. He was uncertain at which point the moisture within him rose to meet the wetness outside but he suddenly found that from deep, deep down he was crying.

For himself, certainly.

For the brother he had loathed so and would never see again.

For his dead mother.

For the father he scarcely remembered.

For his lost uncle.

For the days and places of his childhood.

For the lousy world.

He had reached a lighted canopy outside a spotlighted haven where man-made fountains splashed in the rain.

"Screw off," the Charles River Park doorman said in sotto voce menace. He edged aside to let two women pass, smelling bruised roses. One of the girls had entered the cab. The other came back and held out her hand as if to touch him. "Doctor?" she said unbelievingly.

Remembering her from somewhere, he tried to speak.

"Doctor," she said, "I don't recall your name. We met in the coffee shop at the General. Are you all right?"

I am a coward, he said, but no sound came.

"Elizabeth," the other girl called from the cab.

"Is there something I can do?" she asked.

Now the other girl had left the cab. "We're *already* late," she said.

"Don't cry," Elizabeth said. "Please."

"Elizabeth," the other girl said, "what do you think you're *doing?* How long do you think those guys are going to *wait?*"

Liz Bookstein put her arm around his waist and began to steer him down the red-carpeted canopy, the color of blood, toward the entrance to the hotel. "Tell them I said I was sorry," she said without turning around.

The first time he awoke he saw in the dim light of the nightlamp that she sat sleeping on the chair next to the bed, still wearing her dress but with her girdle and stockings and shoes on the floor and her bare feet tucked under her as if against the chill. The second time there was the gray light of first dawn in the room and she was awake and looking at him with those eyes he remembered now with no trouble at all, not smiling or saying anything but just looking and in a little while without wanting to, he slept again. When he awoke fully the bright sun of mid-morning streamed through the windows and she was in the same chair, still wearing her dress, her head fallen to one side, oddly defenseless and very beautiful in sleep.

He did not remember having been undressed, but when he got out of bed he was naked. To his embarrassment he had a giant erection, and he padded hastily into the bathroom. He was a very bad drunk, he reflected with gloom as he purged his body of poisons.

In a little while she tapped on the door.

"There's a new toothbrush in the medicine chest."

He cleared his throat. "Thank you."

He discovered it next to a razor, a shock until he told himself fiercely that it was hers, for use on her legs. In the shower he discovered the soap was impregnated with the crushed roses but shrugged and became a Sybarite. He allowed himself to shave and then opened the door a crack while he finished off with the towel.

"May I have my clothes?"

"They were filthy. I sent them out, everything but your shoes. They'll be back in a while."

He tied his lower half into the damp towel and walked out.

"Well. You look better."

"I'm sorry I took your bed," he said. "Last night when you found me —"

"Don't," she said.

He sat in the chair and now she came toward him in her bare feet.

"Don't apologize for being the kind of man who can cry," she said.

He remembered everything in a quick rush of memory and he closed his eyes. Her fingers touched his head and he stood and put his arms tightly around her, feeling her full warm palms and outstretched fingers on his bare back. He knew she felt him through the towel but she didn't move away.

"All I meant to do was take you in out of the rain."

"I don't think so."

"You know me so well already. I think you might be the one. I've been looking so hard."

"Have you?" he said sadly.

"Are you some kind of South American?" she asked in a few moments.

"No, Cuban."

"Why do I have to get so involved with minority groups?" she said into his chest.

"I think maybe because your uncle is such a bastard about things like that."

"Yes, but be nice. Please don't turn out to be nasty. I couldn't stand it." She lifted her face and he discovered that he had to bend his head to kiss her mouth, which was already slack and moving. He fumbled behind her neck to undo the buttons of the wrinkled dress. When finally he gave up and she stepped back to do it herself the towel slipped away from him, the articles of clothing falling one by one to join it on the blue rug. Her released breasts were small but years beyond the bud stage, being in fact slightly overripe, with nipples like fingertips. She wore stockings of suntan on her neat, plump feet and good but muscular legs—a tennis player?—with full thighs like a welcoming committee.

Yet he found to his horror a few moments later that it was just as it had been on the previous evening when, famished, he had ordered a meal and found it impossible to eat.

"Don't worry," she said finally, pushing him gently until he lay back on the mattress with his eyes closed, the springs sighing as she got up.

She was very adept.

In a very little while when he opened his eyes her face was covering his universe, a very serious face like that of a small girl intent upon a problem; there was the beginning of perspiration sheen where the nostrils flared at the corners of the cruel curving nose; the gray eyes were very wide, irises wild jet, pupils warm and liquid, all-encompassing; the eyes widened, wider, locking with his and drawing in his gaze until he allowed it to slide inside hers, deep, deep, with a tenderness that was strange and new.

Perhaps, God, he thought fleetingly, a peculiar moment to get religion.

Months later, when for the first time they felt able to discuss that morning with words—this was long before she had become restless again and he had begun to feel her love slipping like sand between his fingers—she told him that she had been ashamed of her skill, sad that she was not able to offer him the gift of innocence.

"Who can?" he had asked her.

Now the moaning noise of the trapped air in the pipes became a hollow whistling. Disgusted, Meomartino abandoned all attempts to concentrate on the paperwork and shoved his chair back from the desk.

Peggy Weld appeared in the doorway, her eyes reddened and her face washed free of makeup. Her mascara must have run, he told himself.

"When do you want to take my kidney?"

"I don't know, exactly. There are a lot of preliminaries. Tests and things."

"Do you want me to move into the hospital?"

"Eventually, but not just now. We'll let you know when."

She nodded. "You'd better forget what I told you about reaching me at the hotel. I'm going to stay in Lexington with my brother-in-law and the children."

She was infinitely more attractive with her face scrubbed, Meomartino thought.

"We'll get things started," he said.

Chapter 6: Spurgeon Robinson

Spur existed in the exact center of a familiar desert island and it moved with him wherever he went. Some of the patients seemed grateful for his help but he knew others couldn't take their eyes from the purple of his hands against their pale skin. One very old Polish lady pushed his fingers from her wrinkled belly three times before she allowed him to press her abdomen.

"You doctor?"

"Yes, ma'am."

"Real doctor? Been school, ever'ting?"

"Yes."

"Well . . . I don' know . . ."

With the Negro patients most of the time it was easier but not always, a few of them automatically sizing him up as a shufflefoot. If I'm down here in bed nigger-poor and full of pain and being poked and hurt by the man all the time, what are *you* doing up there in that white suit and living the fine life?

He was never completely at ease in his role as a Negro professional surrounded by ofays, the way, for example, the orientals on the staff were able to take for granted their complete acceptance. One day in the OR he saw Dr. Chin and Dr. Lee waiting to assist Dr. Kender as the Associate Chief of Surgery pushed into his gown. Alice Takayawa, one of the nurse-anesthetists who was nisei, had just pulled a stool close to the patient's head and sat down. Dr. Chin's face grew bland as he held open Dr. Tyler's gloves.

"Sir, you're familiar with both the Blue Team and the Red Team?"

Dr. Kender waited.

"Meet the Yellow Team."

It drew a great laugh, was repeated all over the hospital, and served to make the Chinese doctors even more popular than they had been before. It was the kind of thing Spur could never have said while sober to a white superior about his color. Except for his friendship with Adam Silverstone, those first few weeks he never really knew from hour to hour how he stood with the rest of the staff.

Just strolling by himself one morning about three a.m. on his way to a coffee break, he had seen Lew Holtz and Ron Preminger stop a third intern named Jack Moylan in the hallway. They whispered, with much shaking of the shoulders and many covert glances in the direction of Emergency. Moylan made a face at first as if at a bad smell, but then he grinned and walked toward Emergency.

Holtz and Preminger continued down the hall, smiling widely, and both said hello. Holtz looked as though he were going to stop and say something else, but Preminger tugged his sleeve and they kept on walking.

Spurgeon had another ten minutes. He sauntered over to Emergency himself.

A black boy—probably sixteen years old—sat on the wooden bench alone in the dimly lit corridor. He looked at Spurgeon. "You a specialist?"

"No. Just an intern."

"How many doctors they need? I hope she's going to be all right."

"I'm sure they'll take good care of her," he said carefully. "I just came down for coffee. Want some?"

The boy shook his head.

He dropped the dime and the nickel into the machine and then withdrew the filled cup and sat on the bench near the boy. "Accident?"

"No . . . uh, it's personal. I explained it to the doctor inside."

"Oh." Spurgeon nodded. He sipped the coffee slowly. Someone had abandoned a *Daily Record* on the bench. The tabloid was only slightly wrinkled from buttock-pressure, and he picked it up and read the baseball stories.

Jack Moylan came out of Emergency two doors down from

where they were sitting. Spurgeon thought he heard him laughing as he walked away down the hall. He was certain he saw Moylan shake his head.

":Remember, now, I'm a doctor," Spurgeon said. "If you tell me what happened, maybe I can help."

"They got a lot of colored doctors here?"

"No."

"We, uh, were parked, you know?" the boy said, deciding to trust him.

"Yuh."

"We were doin' it. You know what I mean?"

Spurgeon nodded.

"It was the first time for her. Not for me.

"The, uh, thing came off me and stayed in her."

Spurgeon nodded again and sipped coffee, keeping his eyes on the cup.

He started to explain about douching, but the boy stopped him.

"You don't understand. I read all about that. But we couldn't even reach it to get it out of her. She became, wow, hysterical. We couldn't go to my brother or her mother either. They'd kill us. So I drove her straight here. The doctor inside there has been calling in specialists for almost an hour."

Spurgeon took a last swallow, draining the coffee, and set the cup carefully on the newspaper. He got up and walked into Emergency.

They were in an examining room with the curtains drawn. The girl had her eyes closed. Her face, turned to the wall, was like a clenched brown fist. She was on the table in lithotomy position, with her feet in the stirrups. Potter, peering through an otolaryngologist's head-mirror covering one eye, was using a thin flashlight as a pointer, delivering a learned lecture to an intern standing behind the girl's head. The intern was from anesthesiology. Spurgeon didn't know his name. He was convulsed with silent laughter.

Potter looked frightened when the curtain parted, but when he recognized Spurgeon he grinned. "Ah, Dr. Robinson, I'm glad you were free for consultation. Dr. Moylan sent you?"

Spurgeon picked up a pair of forceps and without looking at either of the other men he found and removed the offending object and let it drop into the waste basket. "Your friend is waiting to take you home," he said.

She left very quickly.

The intern from anesthesiology had stopped laughing. Potter just stood there looking at him through the stupid round mirror on his forehead. "It was harmless, Robinson. Just a gag."

"You goddam scum."

He waited a moment for trouble but of course none came and he left Emergency and went back up to the ward, trembling only slightly.

If he had to make an enemy on the staff, Potter was the one he would have chosen, a prize screw-up. Detailed to show an intern how to strip out a varicose vein in the leg, he had been talked through a dry run of the procedure by Lew Chin. When the Visiting Surgeon was summoned into the adjoining OR to help with a cardiac arrest, Potter had gone right ahead, mistakenly stripping out the femoral artery instead of the vein. Dr. Chin, so angry he could scarcely talk, had tried to repair the damage, attempting to replace the vital artery with a nylon graft. But it was a shambles; the graft was impossible and a woman who had entered the operating room for a simple procedure was returned to the ward following an amputation. Dr. Longwood had spoken pointedly of the case in a discussion of the week's complications. But less than a week later Potter, performing the most basic of hernia repairs, had tied off the spermatic cord along with the hernial sac. The blood supply in the area was completely compromised, and within days the man had irreparably lost the function of one testicle. This time the Old Man had reviewed the case more acidly, reminding the staff that medicine did not yet have access to a spare parts bin.

Spurgeon had felt sorry for Potter, but the resident's arrogant stupidity made continued sympathy impossible, and now he was content to be disdainfully ignored whenever he met Potter in the corridor. The Emergency Room incident had the opposite effect on Jack Moylan, who tried to be extra-friendly, a bribe he despised.

Only a few people had been involved, and most of his fellow-workers treated him as before. He and Silverstone had integrated the sixth floor. Otherwise he lived alone on his island, on rare occasions even preferring his solitude.

In mid-September there were a few crisp days and then a spell of heavy heat, but he could feel in the air that blew in through his open window every morning, a curious mixture of sea ozone and city stink, that even Indian summer soon would be dying. On his next day off, a Sunday, he stripped the blanket from the bed and took his bathing suit and drove the old Volks bus to Revere Beach, a nicer beach than Coney, of course, but not nearly as nice as Jones. It was almost deserted when he got there at ten-thirty, but after lunch, which for him was a hot dog and a bottle of Miller's, people came.

He picked up his blanket and decided to explore, trudging along the water's edge until he had left the municipal beach. The facilities here were still public, but they were not maintained. The sand was ash-gray and sparse instead of trucked-in white and deep, and there were large stretches of bruising rocks. But there were fewer people. In the immediate vicinity four jocks with Charles Atlas bodies were striking poses full of ego and muscle; a fat man with a pale belly lay in the sand like a mushroom, his face covered with a towel; two children ran leaping like dancers along the creaming lip of the breakers, yelping little animals; and a Negro girl lay spread out for the sun.

He walked on past the girl in order to have more time to look at her, then he turned around and came back to a spot within twelve feet of where she lay on her back, eyes closed. There were fine patches of sand elsewhere and there were rocks where he spread his blanket; they dug into his flesh when he sat down.

She was lighter than he, a kind of chocolate to his purple-black. She wore a one-piece knit bathing suit, very white, designed for modesty but doomed to failure by the girl's structure. Her hair was black-frizzly and cut so close it adorned her fine head like a rich skullcap. She was something no white girl could ever hope to be.

After a while three of the jocks got tired of making specific muscles jump and flung themselves into the Atlantic. The fourth, who appeared to have been sired by Johnny Weismuller out of Isadora Duncan, trotted disdainfully over the discouraging terrain and squatted by the lady's blanket. Ah, he was all muscle, clear through to the top of his head: he spoke of the weather, the tides, offered largely to buy her a Coca-Cola. Finally, conceding defeat, he retired in gloom to make a bicep like a post-natal breast.

Spurgeon hung back, content simply to watch, forewarned that this was not a woman for a casual approach.

An undetermined time later she donned her bathing cap, rose and entered the sea. Clinically trained, he was interested to note that it made him physically ache to watch her.

He left the blanket and made the long trek back to the blue Volks bus, walking quickly but forcing himself not to run. The guitar was where he had left it, on the floor under the second seat. He carried it back to the blanket, burning the soles of his feet piteously on the hot rocks. He felt sure that when he got back she would be gone forever, but she was sitting on her blanket, having evidently taken a long swim and, despite the cap, dampened her hair. She had removed the cap and was sitting back with her weight propped against her arms. From time to time she would shake her head as her hair dried in the sun.

He sat down and began to stroke the strings. At parties and at hired gigs he had stunted on innumerable occasions, trying to make it with a girl by using only notes, no words. Sometimes it had worked and sometimes it had bombed. He suspected that more often than not when it had worked anything would have worked, eyes, smoke signals, a singing telegram or a crooked and wiggling finger.

Nevertheless, one used whatever weapons.

The guitar spoke to her shyly, with forthright, bravely sexless insincerity.

I want to be your friend, nameless miss.

I want to be as a brother to you.

Believe me.

The girl stared out to sea.

I want to talk with you of the fallacies of Schopenhauer.

I want to argue with you about the best art movies.

I want to watch television with you on a rainy afternoon and give you half of my oatmeal cookies.

She threw one quick glance, clearly puzzled.

I want to chuckle at your puns, no matter how pathetic.

I want to laugh with joy at all your jokes, even when they make no sense to me. His fingers flew, making runs and peals of joyous little laughing sounds, and she turned her head . . . and . . . ah, she smiled!

I want to kiss that amused African mouth. Steady, perfidious guitar.

You are a black blossom I alone have discovered on this wonderful dirty-gray beach.

The music now was hardly sexless. It whispered to her, stroked her.

The smile faded. Now she turned her face away from his eyes.

I must bury my face in the round brown of your belly.
I dream now of dancing naked with you, your behind in the palm
of my hand.

The girl rose. Picking up her blanket without folding it, she left
the beach, hurrying but unable to disguise or ruin her marvelous
walk.

Goddam hot-pants guitar.

He stopped playing and saw for the first time a forest of ugly
knees. The four jocks, the fat man, the two children and several
strangers were standing next to his blanket, transfixed.

"Hooo-whee," he whispered, gazing after her.

The thirty-six hours that followed were not good. That night he
prepped four people for surgery, a job he loathed; shaving a patient's belly or scrotum, with unexpected moles to nick and unsus-
pected blemishes to slice off and mocking little hair follicles that
eluded the keenest Weck blade, was quite different from shaving
one's own familiar if homely face. He assisted Silverstone faithfully
at an appendectomy Monday morning and as a reward was allowed
to snare and snip an evil set of infected tonsils.

He came off-duty Tuesday at eight and was on the beach at 10:
30. The morning was overcast and blowy and there were very few
people when he got there. He watched the gulls and learned a lot
about delicate aerodynamics. About 11:30 the sun broke through
and he wasn't so cold anymore and by the time he came back from
lunch some people had begun to arrive, but it remained breezy and
there was no trace of the girl.

He spent the early afternoon stepping over legs, searching for
sensual brown ones. But he didn't find the right pair, so he practiced
his crawl and sidestroke and took naps, periodically starting awake
to sit up and stare around the beach. Finally he picked up a six-year-
old named Sonia Cohen and they built Jerusalem out of the sand, an
interfaith project that was destroyed by a Roman wave at 4:07. The
little girl sat down by the waters and wept.

He left the beach at the last possible moment, returning to the
hospital with enough time only for the quickest of showers and re-
porting for duty at the ward with sand from Sonia's shovel still
gritty on his scalp.

The ward shift was dull but easier to tolerate. By then he had accepted the fact that he would never see the girl again, and he had convinced himself that she couldn't have been as spectacular as he remembered her. On Thursday night that cretin Potter self-diagnosed a virus, which probably meant he had something else, and ordered himself to bed. Adam shuffled the duty roster with the result that Spurgeon drew four hours of Emergency Room duty.

When he got there he found Meyerson sitting dully on a bench, reading a newspaper.

"What do I have to know, Maish?"

"Very little, Doc," the ambulance driver said. "Just remember that if somebody comes in who looks as though he's about to sign off, admit him to one of the wards, *fast*. Old unwritten rule."

"Why?"

"During peak hours this joint is packed. Sometimes patients have long waits. *Very* long waits. Word gets around that somebody kissed off in Emergency, the first thing lots of people are going to think is *anybody* could die in that goddam place before they take care of you."

It made him steel himself for a workout, but they were four quiet hours, not at all like the frenzied activity he had expected. He read three times the single notice on the bulletin board.

TO: All professional personnel

FROM: Emmanuel Brodsky, R.N., Ph.B., Chief Pharmacist

SUBJECT: Missing prescription pads

It has come to the attention of the Pharmacy Department that a number of books of prescription pads has been reported missing from several clinics over the past two weeks. This summer an amount of barbiturates and amphetamines also was discovered to be missing. Because of the growing drug problem, the Pharmacy Department suggests that *neither prescription blanks nor drugs should be left where they might fall into irresponsible hands.*

Early in the evening Maish brought in a woman alcoholic who told him unconvincingly that her ill-used body had become a mass of contusions when she had fallen down the stairs. He knew that someone—her husband, a lover?—had beaten her. X-rays proved negative, but he waited to release her until he could get a chief resident to come downstairs, following hospital policy that only senior residents could make final dispositions of patients on the accident floor. Adam had the night off and was working in Woodborough. Meomartino finally arrived and sent the woman home to hot baths. It was exactly what he would have done himself twenty minutes earlier, Spurgeon thought, scorning hospital rules.

A colored couple named Sampson came in shortly after 10 p.m. with their four-year-old child screaming and dripping blood from a lacerated palm. He placed half a dozen sutures after removing glass shards; somehow the little boy had fallen from the bathroom sink while holding a medicine bottle.

"What was in the bottle?"

The woman blinked. "Just some old stuff. I forget. It was reddish. I had it a long, long time."

"You're lucky. He might have swallowed the contents. By now perhaps he'd be dead."

They shook their heads as if cut off from him by a language problem.

These people, he thought.

All he could do was give them a small bottle of ipecac and hope if the boy ever swallowed anything poisonous but non-corrosive they would remember to dose him immediately so he would vomit while they waited for the doctor.

If they called the doctor, he thought.

Just after midnight a police prowl car brought in Mrs. Therese Donnelly, shaken but furious.

"I've a riddle for you. What does an Irishman become when you make him a cop?"

"I give up," he said.

"An Englishman." The officer at her side kept a carefully expressionless face.

Mrs. Donnelly was seventy-one. Her car had run into a tree, forcibly. She had struck her head on impact but insisted she was all right. It was only the third accident she had had in more than thirty-eight years of careful driving, she emphasized.

"The other two very *teeny* ones, you understand, with neither of them my fault. Men show their true nature, silly jackasses, when you put them behind a wheel." Exuding, with her indignation, the faint fumes of bottled spirits.

"I've got one for *you,*" he said, pulling from somewhere the line he undoubtedly had read years ago in a long-incinerated comic book: "If Ireland should sink, what would float?"

Both the policeman and the old lady concentrated but said nothing.

"Cork," he said.

She screamed her delight. "What's the biggest part of a horse?"

Over her head he and the police officer exchanged grins like a secret fraternity handshake.

"No, ye dirty things! The answer is the mane part."

Senility, he wondered? She was alert enough to be acerbic, protesting throughout the physical examination, which was unremarkable.

He ordered pictures of the skull and was reading the wet x-rays when her son arrived. Arthur Donnelly was beefy-faced and visibly anxious.

"Is she all right?"

The films showed no skull fractures. "She appears to be. But at her age, I think it unwise to allow her to drive."

"I know, I know. It's one of her greatest pleasures. Since my father passed away the only thing she enjoys is driving herself over to visit some girl-friends. They play cut-throat bridge, maybe take a little nip."

Or two, Spurgeon thought. "She seems fine," he said. "But considering the fact that she's seventy-one, perhaps we'll keep her overnight under observation."

Mrs. Donnelly became stony-faced at the suggestion. "What's a fool?" she asked.

"I give up," he said helplessly.

"Somebody who can't understand that after what I've been through I want to sleep in the bed that's my own."

"Look, we know this place," her son said. "My brother Vinnie —you know him, Vincent X. Donnelly, the state rep?"

"No," Spurgeon said.

Donnelly looked annoyed. "Well, he's a hospital trustee and I know he'd want her to go home."

"We can give your mother every care here, Mr. Donnelly," Spurgeon said.

"Screw that. We *know* this place. It's no bed of roses. You people have enough humanity on your hands without worrying about our old lady. Be a good fella and let me take her home to her own mattress. We'll call in Dr. Francis Delahanty, who's known her for thirty years. We'll even hire nurses to come to the house. For as long as you want."

He telephoned Meomartino, who listened impatiently while he outlined the findings.

"I'm watching a cardiac arrest, among other things," Meomartino said. "I've yet to get any sleep tonight. Do you really need me down there?"

It was a tacit vote of confidence at best, but he grasped at it. "I can handle it," he said. He released the old woman from the hospital, beginning to feel like a physician.

The rest of the night was quiet. He went on his own special late rounds, gave some medications, changed a few dressings, said goodnight to the weird old building and even managed three hours of uninterrupted rest before morning, returning to bed at the end of his shift to sleep until noon.

While walking toward the house officer's dining room for lunch he changed his mind almost in mid-stride and without bothering to go upstairs for his bathing things he left the hospital and drove to Revere Beach.

Sonia Cohen was nowhere to be seen, but the girl was lying there at the place he had first seen her, watching him as he walked toward her with sand in his brown suede shoes.

He thought he saw something—a brief flash of unguarded gladness?—before she looked at him as though she had never seen him before.

"May I sit with you?"

"No," she said.

He clumped in his sand-filled shoes to the rockiness not far away, the place for silent admirers, where he had spread his blanket the first day. The rocks burned his flesh through the cloth of the chinos when he sat.

He just stayed there dumbly, watching her. The sun was very hot.

The girl attempted to behave as if she were alone on the beach, from time to time moving with aimless grace to enter the water, swimming with pleasure that appeared unaffected and genuine, and then leaving the water to sit again on the old U.S. Navy blanket in the golden heat.

It was the kind of early fall day that sometimes comes to New England directly from the tropics. He sat beneath the beating sun and felt the juices flow from his pores until they dampened his kinky close-cropped hair, rolled down his cheeks in drops like rain and caused his clothing to stick to his body.

He had missed lunch. By three o'clock his head felt hollow and light, a cinder burnt weightless by the great searing sun. His eyes smarted from his own salt. When he kept them open now he saw three girls who moved in graceful unison, like a smart modern ballet team. Periodic strabismus, he told himself, thinking how wonderfully efficient the eye muscles ordinarily are.

Shortly after three-thirty she gave up and fled as she had on the day before. This time, however, he followed her.

He was waiting outside the bath-house when she came out, wearing a yellow cotton dress now and carrying the blanket and her bathing things. He went to meet her.

"Look," she said.

He saw that she was afraid.

"Please," he said. "I'm not a pervert or a pimp or anything like that. My name's Spurgeon Robinson. I'm respectable, extremely —even dully, but I don't dare take a chance that I won't meet you again. There's nobody here to introduce us."

She started to walk away. "Will you be here tomorrow?" he asked, following.

She didn't answer.

"At least tell me your *name.*"

"I'm not what you're looking for," she said. She stopped and faced him and he liked the hard scorn in her eyes. "You want a little thrill-girl to liven up a dull day at the beach. I don't have any thrills to give you, mister. Why don't you just try somewhere else."

Next time she looked around was when she reached the bottom of the stairs at the Elevated.

"Just tell me your name.

"Please," he said quietly.

"Dorothy Williams."

Standing there and staring up as she climbed the steep stairs was hardly the respectable thing to do, but he could not tear his eyes away until she had dropped the token into the turnstile at the top and disappeared through the revolving doors.

Pretty soon a train like a ground-trembling dragon blotted out the light overhead and when it went away, so did he.

The sun shone but the heat was gone, no doubt for good. He wore his bathing trunks anyway and somehow was unsurprised to find her there when he arrived. They greeted each other shyly and she offered no objection when he spread his blanket next to hers, where the sand was softest.

They talked.

"I looked my eyes out all week."

"I was in school. Yesterday was my first free day."

"You're a student?"

"A teacher. Junior high school art, seventh and eighth grades. You're a musician?"

He nodded, realizing it was not a lie and not wanting to get into the rest of it yet, wanting to learn all about *her.* "Do you paint, sculpture in stone, make things out of clay?"

She nodded.

"Which?" he said. "I mean, what's your special thing?"

"I'm fair at all of it, good at nothing. That's why I teach. If I had real talent—if I could work the way you play—I'd want to go at it all the time."

He smiled and shook his head. "That's an amateur's line. 'Do or die for creativity, all you terribly talented people, while the rest of us unfortunates watch you in comfort.' "

"You have no right to call me a hypocrite," she said.

Even her displeasure pleased him. "I'm not doing that. But my initial impression is that you're not a girl to take risks."

"A maiden-aunt of a girl."

"Hell, no. I didn't say that."

"I *am* kind of an old maid," she conceded.

"How old?"

"Twenty-four last November."

It surprised him; she was only a year younger than he. "You figure that's it, you're too withered for the marriage thing?"

"Oh, it has nothing to do with getting married. I'm talking about a frame of mind. I'm becoming very conservative."

"A colored child has no right being conservative."

"Do you feel strongly about things, politically?"

"Dorothy, I'm black," he said. It was the first time he had called her by name; she appeared pleased, either by that or by his answer.

He began to build sand castles and the girl knelt and dug a hole in the beach so they could get wet sand from its bottom, then she began to use some of the moist sand herself, modeling a face, her eyes on his features and her long, delicate fingers stroking the sand in a way that made his bones turn to jelly. She was right about her talent, he thought, looking at the face in the sand, which did not bear a very good likeness to his own.

Finally when they were messy with sand she sprang up without warning and ran into the water and he followed through a frigid breeze, discovering to his relief that the water covered his skin like warm silk compared to the cooler air. She headed straight out and he splashed valiantly to stay with her. Just before he would have had to quit, she turned and they began to tread water, bodies close but not touching. "You're a crazy swimmer," he panted, a pain in his chest.

"We live near a lake. I'm in the water a lot."

"I didn't learn to swim until I was sixteen years old, on the Riviera." He saw that she thought he was joking. "No, honestly."

"What were you doing there?"

"I never knew my father. He was a merchant seaman, on oil tankers. My mother remarried when I was twelve, to a marvelous guy. My uncle Calvin. When I asked about my real father, all they ever told me was he was dead. So the summer I was sixteen I decided to try to see the world the way *he* had seen it. Now it seems kind of stupid, but I guess I thought somehow I might be able to find him. At least, *understand* him."

She treaded water with very little motion, the white suit submerged, her smooth brown shoulders above the surface looking naked and lovely. "It doesn't seem stupid," she said. On her upper lip, above the ample pink mouth, the faintest white dusting had appeared as the sea water dried in the sun. He would have preferred to erase it with his tongue, but he reached up a wet thumb and passed it gently over her lip.

"Salt," he explained as she drew back. "Well, I couldn't get a job on a tanker, which was lucky for me. But I told them I was eighteen and I got taken on the *Ile de France* as a piano player. The first night in Le Havre there was a heavy mist and I just hung around on the streets and looked at things and said no to the whores and tried to imagine I was older and tougher and had a wife and a baby son waiting for me back in the States, but of course it was no good. I couldn't begin to imagine how it really had been for my father."

"God. That's the saddest thing I ever heard."

He decided to take advantage of her sadness, moved in like a clumsy courting sea lion to reach for her mouth with his own. She started to pull away and then, changing her mind, placed her hands on his shoulders and her lips softly over his for a brief moment, a sea-tasting kiss with no passion but a great deal of tenderness.

"I can remember things lots sadder than that," he said, reaching for her again, and she showed her fine teeth and placed both feet against his chest and pushed away from him, not really a kick but sufficient to cause him to go under and inhale ocean, and when he stopped coughing they both agreed it was time to leave the water.

They swam in and all was shivering and goosebumps and he offered to rub her warm with the towel and she refused. She ran along the beach to warm up and he quickly realized it was even better than following her when she walked. Too soon it was over and they returned to the blanket and she opened what he had thought was a knitting bag and shared a very good lunch with him. "But you still didn't explain about learning to swim," she said.

"Oh." He swallowed tuna salad on rye. "I made the round trip all summer, Manhattan to Southampton to Le Havre, with a two-day layover and then back the way we came. It's a classy boat and I was saving money, but all I was seeing was water. I was too scared even to take the night-boat into Paris. Then, right about this time of year, the ship tied up in Le Havre for a week-long overhaul.

"There was an assistant purser, a guy named Dusseault. His wife ran a suckers' boutique in Cannes, and he offered me a lift if I'd help him drive his Peugeot. The trip took thirty hours. While he made it with his wife I sat on the beach every day and stared at bikinis. A gang of French teeny-boppers kind of adopted me. This one little girl taught me to swim in three days."

"Did you make love to her?" she asked in a little while.

"She was a white girl. I had vivid memories of Amsterdam Avenue. In those days I'd sooner have slit my throat."

"And now?"

"Now?" For years the little French girl had been a principal figure in his sexual and social fantasies. Repeatedly he had asked himself what might have happened if he had stayed, come really to know her, courted her, done the marriage thing with her, become a European. At times the lost dream had made him numb with longing and regret; most of the time, however, he decided that the result would have been disaster. The lovely young girl probably would have grown into a shrewish woman, the people would in time have lost their color blindness, the snake would have wriggled his way into Eden. "Now . . . I think you ask too damned many questions," he said.

He asked her to have dinner with him and she refused. "My parents are expecting me."

"I'll drive you home."

"It's too far," she said, but he insisted. She laughed when she saw the wagon-bus. "You're not a musician. You're some kind of delivery boy."

"A band leader *is* a delivery boy. You transport a bass player, a couple of horns, a wailer and a cat lugging a whole set of drums."

She was silent.

"What's the matter?"

"Nothing," she said.

"You act afraid."

"How do I know who you are?" she burst out. "A man I allowed to pick me up at a public beach. You could be a pusher. You could be lots worse."

His laughter spilled out. "I'm a beachcomber," he said. "I'm going to take you to a desert island and plait frangipani into your hair." He almost told her about the medical thing then and there but he was enjoying himself and his amusement was spontaneous enough to reassure her; her mood changed and she became voluble and almost gay. He was deriving kicks just being with her and before he knew it the Volks was lumbering off the Massachusetts Turnpike at a place called Natick. The house was only a couple of minutes from the toll road, a painfully-neat bungalow of weathered shingles in an otherwise-white neighborhood. The mother was thin and spare, with sharp features that hinted at long-forgotten white rape. The father was a brown and quiet man who looked as though he spent his spare hours manicuring lawn, snipping hedge, casting anxious glances of comparison at nearby Anglo-Saxon and Semitic lawns and shrubs.

The parents shook his hand uncertainly but were plainly pleased that the girl had brought someone home. There was a child, a three-year-old named Marion with kinky black hair and café-au-lait skin. He found himself involuntarily looking from one face to the other, noting the duplicated features.

Her child, he told himself.

Mrs. Williams had a finely-tuned native perception. "We call her Midge," she said. "Because she's so small, you know. The daughter of my youngest, Janet."

They took him out to sit in the arbor behind the house, a deep-shade place fragrant with grapes but laden with mosquitoes. While Spurgeon slapped, Mr. Williams poured beer he had helped to make himself.

"Quality control. Sample the product as it goes through operations. Run chemical and bacteriological checks on every batch during fermentation." He had started in the brewery as a sweeper and then had worked six years as a shipper, he confided while his wife and daughter remained silent with the patience of what clearly was long practice. He had had to take a whole battery of tests to win the job. And then the kicker:

"Over three white men!"

"Wonderful," Spurgeon said.

"Education is what's wonderful," Mr. Williams said. "That's why it pleases me to see Dorothy a teacher, doing what she can for the young people." He cocked his head. "What might you do, son?"

He and the girl spoke at the same time.

"He's a musician."

"I'm a doctor."

Her parents were clearly puzzled. "I'm a doctor," he said. "A surgical intern at Suffolk County General Hospital."

They looked at him, the parents with wonder, the girl with loathing.

"How do you like chicken pie?" Mrs. Williams said, smoothing her apron. He liked it the way it was served, steaming, crumble-crusted and containing more lean chunks of chicken than vegetables, with new summer squash and little potatoes he figured they grew themselves in the large vegetable garden behind the house. Dessert was chilled rhubarb-applesauce followed by lemony iced tea. While the ladies cleared the dishes Mr. Williams played old Caruso records, scratched but interesting.

"He could shiver a glass with just his voice," Mr. Williams said. "Some years back, before I became a quality control man, I used to pick up a dollar now and again on a weekend, you know? On a Saturday morning I was cleaning out a garage over in Framingham Centre and this uppity lady came out and just laid a big pile of Caruso records on the trash.

" 'Ma'am,' I said, 'you're throwing away a piece of your culture.' She just gave me a mean look, so I moved the records into the back seat of my car."

They listened to the great dead voice soar, the little girl light as a snowflake on Spurgeon's knee, while from the kitchen came the sound of dishes being washed by hand. After Caruso, Spurgeon shuffled through the pile of records looking for dixie or progressive, and finding nothing good. There was an old upright piano, battered and repainted, but of true tone when he sounded the scales. "Who plays?"

"Dorothy took some lessons."

The ladies had just returned. "I took exactly eight lessons. I play three children's songs all the way through, plus a handful of fragments. Spurgeon plays like a professional," she told her parents wickedly.

"Oh, play us some hymns," her mother pleaded.

What the hell, he thought. He sat on the revolving piano stool and played "Steal Away," "Go Down Moses," "Rock of Ages," "That Old Rugged Cross" and "My Lord, What a Morning." There wasn't a decent voice among the four of them, and any white trash who insisted that all Negroes are born with rhythm should have heard her old man. But he was listening to the girl, not the way he would listen to a professional singer, but as one person listening to another person, and hearing her voice, thin and reed-like and full of emotion, singing with her mother and father like this, he felt like a fish who has been toying with a lure and suddenly realizes the barb is in his throat.

They said a number of warm things about his playing and he mumbled hypocrisies about their singing and then her parents went to put the child to bed and make coffee. As soon as they were alone she treated him as though he weren't worth stepping on.

"Why did you have to lie?"

"I didn't."

"You told them you're a doctor."

"I am."

"You told *me* you were a musician."

"I am. I was a musician before I became a doctor, but I'm a doctor now."

"I don't believe you."

"Your loss."

Her father came back, and then her mother carrying a tray, and they had coffee and banana bread. He saw that it was dark outside and said he would have to be leaving.

"Are you a church-going man?" her mother said.

"No, ma'am. I guess I haven't been to church six times in the past five years."

She was silent for a moment. "I admire you for telling the truth," she said at last. "What church do you attend when you go?"

"My mother's a Methodist," he said.

"We're Unitarians. If you'd care to come with us tomorrow morning, you're welcome."

"I heard somewhere that a Unitarian is somebody who believes in the fatherhood of God, the brotherhood of man and the neighborhood of Boston."

Henry Williams threw back his head and shouted his mirth, but Spurgeon saw Mrs. Williams' compressed lips and realized that he was being a damned fool. "I'll be on duty at the hospital the next two Sundays. I'd like very much to sit next to Dorothy in church in three weeks, if the invitation still holds."

He saw that both parents were looking at her.

"I haven't been going to church," she said clearly. "I've been going to Boston Temple Eleven."

"You're a Muslim?"

"She's not," her mother said quickly. "She's just very interested in their movement."

"Some things in that religion make sense," Henry Williams said uncomfortably. "No question about that."

He thanked them and said goodbye and the girl walked him to the front porch.

"I like your mother and father," he said.

She leaned back against the front door and closed her eyes. "My father and mother are Uncle Tom and his old lady. And you," she said, opening her eyes now and looking at him, "you had them eating out of your hands like a charlatan. You tell me you're one kind of man and tell them you're something else again."

"Come to the beach with me next weekend."

"No," she said.

"I think you're a very beautiful girl. But I don't beg. Thank you for bringing me home."

He got as far as the gate before her voice stopped him. "Spurgeon."

The whites of her eyes gleamed in the dark on the vine-grown porch. "I don't beg either. But come before lunch and bring a warm sweater. We'll go for a walk." She smiled. "I froze my fanny waiting for you on that miserable beach."

The hospital was just as he had left it. The same smell of sick poverty hung heavy and sullen in the air. The elevator creaked and groaned as it rose slowly. On impulse he got off at the fourth floor and checked into the ward. It was understaffed, some of the nurses having come down with the same Coxsackie virus which had felled Potter and several other staff members.

"Please," a voice said. Behind a drawn curtain the very old Polish woman, with limbs like sticks covered with suppurating sores, lay dying slowly in the terrible odors of her body wastes. He cleaned her, washed her tenderly, gave her a grain and a half of numbness, adjusted her urinary catheter, quickened the flow of her intravenous fluid and left her dying more sweetly than she had been dying before.

As he passed Silverstone's office on the way back to the elevator the door opened.

"Spurgeon."

"Hello, there, boss-man."

"Come in, will you?"

He felt good again, having already forgotten the old woman whose life was ebbing and remembered the young woman whose life was ripening. "What's the word, baby?"

"You had a patient in Emergency the other night named Mrs. Therese Donnelly?"

The riddle lady. A tiny knot of apprehension formed in his chest. "Yeah, sure. I remember the case."

"She came back into the hospital six hours ago."

The knot grew, tightened. "You want me to stop in and take a look at her?"

Adam's eyes were direct and unblinking. "It might be a good idea for both of us to look over the pathologist's shoulder in the morning," he said.

Chapter 7: Adam Silverstone

In the inner world of Adam Silverstone pathologists were accorded great respect but little envy. He had done their vital job often enough to realize it required a scientist's knowledge and a detective's skill, but on an emotional level he had never understood why anyone would choose it as a life's work over the practice of medicine with the living.

After all this time he still disliked post-mortems.

A surgeon came to know the human body as a wonderful meat machine wrapped in a remarkable epidermal package. The entire thing throbbed with multiple processes. Its juices and fibers, the awesome complexities of its wonderful substance, pulsed with life and constant change. Chemicals reacted to enzymes; cells replaced themselves, sometimes criminally; muscles pulled levers and limbs moved on ball joints; pumps, valves, filters, combustion chambers, neural networks more complex than the electronic circuitry of a giant computer—everything *worked* while the physician tried to anticipate the needs of the whole integrated organism.

In contrast, the pathologist labored over decaying objects in which nothing worked.

Dr. Sack came in, dour with desire for his morning coffee. "What brings you here?" he greeted Adam. "Thirst for knowledge? Wasn't your patient, was she?" He prepared coffee for himself in a huge chipped green mug marked MOTHER.

"No, but she was treated on my Service."

Dr. Sack grunted.

When he had drained the last of his coffee they accompanied him to the white-tiled autopsy room. Mrs. Donnelly's body was on the table. The instruments were prepared and waiting.

Adam looked around approvingly. "You must have a good diener," he said.

"Damn right," Dr. Sack said. "He's been with me eleven years. What do you know about dieners?"

"I worked as a diener when I was a student. For the medical examiner in Pittsburgh."

"For Jerry Lobsenz? God rest him, he was a good friend of mine."

"Of mine, too," Silverstone said.

Dr. Sack was in no great hurry to begin. He sat in the room's single chair, reading slowly and carefully through the case history while they waited.

Finally he left his chair and went to the body. Holding the head in his hands, he moved it from side to side. "Dr. Robinson," he said after a moment, "will you come here, please?"

Spurgeon went and Adam followed. Dr. Sack moved the head again. In death, the old woman seemed to be denying something stubbornly. "Do you hear?"

"Yes," Spurgeon said.

Standing next to him, Adam was able to detect the small grating sound. "What is it?"

"We'll soon know for sure," Dr. Sack said. "Help me to turn her. I think we're going to find a fracture of the odontoid process," he said to Spurgeon. "In short, the poor old thing broke her neck when she struck her head in the automobile accident."

"But she wasn't in pain when I saw her," Spurgeon said. "There was no pain at all."

Dr. Sack shrugged. "There would not necessarily have been pain. She had old, brittle bones that would have broken easily. The odontoid process is just a little thing, a bony prominence of the second cervical vertebra. Her son reported that last night she was feeling very well, had eaten with good appetite, in fact, just an hour before her death. She was confined in bed, with three pillows behind her for support. Having slipped down, she threw herself back on the pillows rather petulantly. I would guess that the jarring, plus a partial turning of her head on the neck bones, drove the loose fragment into the spinal cord, making death almost instantaneous."

He performed the laminectomy, cutting into the back of the neck to expose the knobs of the cervical spine, slicing expertly through the red muscle and the whitish ligaments. "Notice the spinal dura, Dr. Robinson?"

Spurgeon nodded.

"Exactly like the membrane that wraps the brain." With his gloved fingertip and the scalpel he held the incision wide so they could see the area of hemorrhage and the cord crushed by the fragment of bone, the death-dealer.

"There it is," he said cheerfully. "You didn't order neck x-rays, Dr. Robinson?"

"No."

Dr. Sack pursed his lips and grinned. "I predict that you will next time."

"Yes, sir," Spurgeon said.

"Turn her again," Dr. Sack said. He looked at Silverstone. "Let's see how well old Jerry taught you," he said. "Finish it up for me."

Without hesitation Adam accepted the scalpel from him and made the broad, deep Y-incision over the sternum.

When he looked up a few minutes later he saw satisfaction in Dr. Sack's eyes. But he glanced over at Spurgeon and his feeling of pleasure died. The intern's eyes were on Adam's knife but his features were rigid and wracked with misery.

Whatever he was seeing was a long way from the little group around the table.

Adam sympathized with Spurgeon. But the numbing knowledge that he had been solely responsible for not preventing death was an occupational Gorgon that sooner or later confronted every physician, and he knew instinctively that the intern had to be allowed to face it in his own way.

He had problems of his own in the animal lab.

The German shepherd named Wilhelm, the first dog he had given a large dose of Imuran, had developed a clinical pattern almost exactly like the one that had killed Susan Garland. Within three days Wilhelm was dead of an infection.

The mongrel bitch named Harriet, to whom he had given a minimum dose of the immunosuppressive drug, rejected the transplanted kidney the day before Wilhelm died.

He operated on a long series of canines, some of them old and ugly and some of them scarcely more than puppies and so beautiful he had to steel his heart from remembering the quaint insane newspaper ads of the anti-vivisection groups who preferred to sacrifice children to save animals. As he worked he zeroed-in on the most effective dosages, lowering the maximum quantities and raising the minimum ones, carefully recording the results in Kender's coffee-stained notebook.

Three of the dogs that received large amounts of the drug developed infections and died.

Four of the animals receiving smaller dosages sloughed-off the transplanted kidney.

When he had narrowed down the field of choices it was evident that the range of effective but safe dosage was razor-thin, with rejection of the transplanted kidney on one side of the line and an open invitation to infection on the other.

He went on to test other drugs and had completed animal studies on nine of the agents when Dr. Kender admitted Peggy Weld to the hospital for a pre-operative physical.

Kender studied the lab notebook carefully. Together they translated the animal weights into terms of human weight and calculated proportionate drug dosages.

"What immunosuppressive are you going to use on Mrs. Bergstrom?" Adam asked.

Kender cracked his knuckles without answering, then tugged at his ear. "Which would you use?"

Adam shrugged. "In the agents I've tested so far, there don't seem to be any panaceas. I'd guess four or five are unsatisfactory. A couple, I would say, are about as effective as Imuran."

"But no better?"

"I don't believe they are."

"I agree with you. Yours is about the twentieth study we've done here. I've done ten or twelve of them myself. At least our transplant team is familiar with the drug. We'll stick to Imuran."

Adam nodded.

They placed the transplantation on the operative schedule for

Thursday morning, with Mrs. Bergstrom in OR-3 and Miss Weld in
OR-4.

He was solvent and doing much less moonlighting but he was still
not getting enough sleep, now because of Gaby Pender. They
toured the museums, went to Symphony and a couple of parties.
One evening they stayed in her apartment and necked with wonderful progress but her roommate came home. On days when they
couldn't see each other, they talked on the telephone.

Then early in November she told him casually that she had to
drive to Vermont for four days and asked him if he could come with
her. He considered the implications, and then her choice of words.
"What do you mean, you *have* to?"

"I have to go see my father."

"Oh."

Why not, he thought. He was assigned to the Bergstrom transplant, but they could leave Thursday night.

He was supposed to be off for only thirty-six hours but he traded
with Meomartino against a future double shift so they would have
more time.

Miriam Parkhurst and Lewis Chin, the two Visiting Surgeons,
had done an emergency in OR-3 during the early hours of Thursday
morning, a dirty case, which meant the entire operating room had to
be scrubbed before Mrs. Bergstrom could be moved into it. Adam
waited in the corridor outside the OR with Meomartino, next to the
rolling litters on which the twins lay, sedated but conscious.

"Peg?" Melanie Bergstrom said drowsily.

Peggy Weld raised herself on one elbow and looked at her sister.

"I wish they had given us a rehearsal."

"This one we can ad-lib."

"Peg?"

"Mmmm?"

"I never in all this time said thank you."

"Don't start now, I couldn't stand it," Peggy Weld said drily. She
grinned. "Remember how I used to take you to the ladies' room
when we were kids? In a way, I'm still taking you to the ladies'
room."

High on Pentothal, they fell into a giggling fit which dwindled into silence.

"If anything happens to me, take care of Ted and the girls," Melanie Bergstrom said.

Her sister didn't answer.

"Promise, Peg?" Melanie said.

"Oh, shut up, you stupid girl."

The doors of OR-3 swung open and two orderlies came out, pushing the wheeled kick-buckets before them with their feet. "It's all yours, Doc," one of them said.

Adam nodded and they moved Mrs. Bergstrom into the OR.

"Peg?" she said again.

"I love you, Mellie," Peggy Weld said.

She was weeping as Adam pushed her litter into OR-4. Without having to be told, fat boy gave her another jolt in the arm before they transferred her to the table.

Adam went in to scrub. When he came back the anesthesiologist was already seated on his stool near her head, playing with his dials. Rafe Meomartino, whose assignment was in the other OR, was standing over Peggy Weld, gently caressing the wetness from her face with a piece of sterile gauze.

It went flawlessly. Peggy Weld had very healthy kidneys, and Adam assisted while Lew Chin removed one of them, then he perfused the kidney and hung around the other OR to watch while Meomartino helped Kender with the transplant.

After that, the rest of the day was anticlimactic and slow-moving and he was very happy to see Gaby when she drove up to get him that evening.

On the road they did very little talking. The scenery was very nice in a stark and autumnal way but in a little while it grew dark and there was nothing to see outside the car but moving shadows; inside, by the slight light of the dashboard, she was a silhouette, lovely and changing in slight detail now and then when she pulled around a more sensibly driven automobile or braked to avoid running through a truck. She drove too fast; they hurtled along as if racing the devil or Lyndon Johnson.

She saw him looking at her and she smiled.

"Watch the road," he said.

As they penetrated the foothills the temperature dropped. He rolled down the window and smelled the bite of fall in the air that poured down on them from the plum-colored hills, until Gaby asked him to close the window because she was afraid of catching cold.

Her father's resort was named Pender's North Wind. It was a large and rambling country estate which in a gentler era had seen grander days. She turned the car off the driveway between two stone gargoyles and they followed a long and rattling gravel drive to a Victorian mansion that loomed unbelievably, lights burning only in the central portion of the ground floor.

As they got out of the car something nearby, an animal or a bird, shrilled a high, mournful cry, repeated over and over again in a restless, sorrowing litany.

"God," he said, "what's that?"

"I don't know."

Her father came out to meet them as Adam pulled their bags from the car. He was a tall man, lean and fit-looking, wearing workpants and a blue sweatshirt. His hair was gray but heavy and waving. He had the kind of clean-profiled good looks which must have been especially impressive when he was much younger, and even now he was a handsome man.

But he was afraid to kiss his daughter, Adam saw. "Well," he said. "So you made it, with a friend. Glad you brought somebody along this time."

She introduced them and they shook hands. Mr. Pender's eyes were bright and hard. "Call me Bruce," he commanded. "Leave the bags. We'll see that they get taken care of." He led them down a side walk, past a putting green with the last of the moths flitting around the overhead light, to pause before a silent gleaming expanse of water. "You never saw this, did you?"

"No," she said.

"Olympic size. Could swim a goddam army, hold professional races in it. Still, you should have seen them pack it full of flesh this summer on a good hot weekend. Cost me a bundle, but it was worth it."

"It's very nice," she said in a curiously formal voice.

He led them through a side door, down a flight of inside stairs, through a tunnel and soon they were in a basement bar. The room was built for perhaps two hundred people. In front of the large fireplace, in which flames sprang and crackled over the corpses of three logs, a woman and two little girls sat and waited, their identically-slender bare feet extended toward the fire, which gleamed in reflection on thirty nail-polished toes like small blood-red shells.

"She brought a friend," her father said. Pauline, Gaby's step-mother, was a carefully-tended redhead, her generous body still young, but not as young as her hair would have proclaimed. The girls, Susan and Buntie, were her daughters by a previous marriage, eleven and nine and in the silly stage. Their wary mother said little; when she spoke, every word seemed planned in advance.

Bruce Pender threw another log on the fire, already too warm for Adam's taste. "You've eaten?" They had, so long ago that Adam was hungry now, but they both nodded. Mr. Pender poured drinks with a heavy hand.

"What do you hear from your mother?" he asked Gaby.

"She's fine."

"Still married?"

"So far as I know."

"Good. Fine woman. Too bad she's the way she is."

"I think it's time you children went to bed," Pauline said. The girls protested but acquiesced, pushing into their shoes and bidding sleepy goodnights. Adam noticed that Gaby kissed them with warmth she was unable to display to their mother or her father.

"Pauline will be right back," Bruce said when they were alone. "The house is right down the road."

"Oh, you don't live in the hotel?"

Pender smiled and shook his head. "All summer long and every weekend during ski season, this place is a madhouse. Musical beds. More than a thousand guests, mostly singles who come up here to raise hell and have orgasms."

"You can see that my father has a great delicacy," Gaby said.

Pender shrugged. "Spade a spade. I make money running a legalized bagnio. All the economic advantages, none of the legal risks. A New York crowd but good spenders, beautiful amounts of cash."

There was a silence. "Silverstone," he said. He cocked an eye at Adam. "You a Jewish boy?"

"My father is. My mother was Italian."

"Oh." He poured more liquor for himself, for Gaby and for the absent Pauline. Adam placed his hand over his glass.

"Last summer one morning about two a.m.," Pender said, "we came damn near having a drowning in the lawn fountain. Not in the pool, mind you. In the *fountain*. The ingenuity. Two college kids, drunk as skunks."

Gaby said nothing and sipped her drink.

"Some of the girls are cupcakes, too. Pauline keeps me on short leash." He sipped thoughtfully. "This is her place, of course. I mean, it's in her name. Gaby's mother cleaned me out. Made me pay through the pocketbook."

"She had grounds, dear Father."

"Grounds, hell." He drank.

"I can remember the scenes of my childhood, Daddy. Do you and dear Pauline treat Suzy and Buntie to the same kind of advantages?"

Pender looked at his daughter expressionlessly. "I figured with a guest here, maybe you'd be fit to be with," he said.

Outside the mournful trilling noise began again. "What *is* that?" Adam asked.

Pender seemed willing to change the subject. "Come on," he said. "I'll show you."

On the way out he switched on an outside light that illuminated a section of back lawn behind the swimming pool. In a chicken-wire cage a large raccoon paced like a lion, its small eyes baleful red behind the black face mask.

"Where did you get it?" Adam asked.

"One of the college kids knocked her out of a tree with a pole and covered her with a bread carton."

"Are you going to keep her here as a . . . tourist attraction?"

"Hell, no, they're dangerous. A bitch coon like this will kill a dog." He picked up a broom and poked the stick through the wire, digging into the animal's ribs. The raccoon turned; its paws like dainty ladies' hands gripped the shaft, the mouth ripped at it, splintering. "Right now she's in heat. I've got her here to attract the boar coons." He pointed to two smaller boxes at the fringes of the pool of light. "Traps."

"What will you do with them if you catch them?"

"Delicious roasted, with sweet potatoes. Delicacy."

Gaby turned away and walked back inside and they followed her. They were settling down before the fire with fresh drinks when Pauline came in.

"Brrr," she said, complaining of the night chill. Snuggling next to her husband, she asked Gaby about school. Bruce put his arm around her and pinched a round melon breast once, asserting ownership. Adam looked away. The two women continued to talk, appearing not to have noticed.

The conversation lagged and picked up, sometimes desperately. They discussed the theater, baseball, politics. Mr. Pender envied California because it had Ronald Reagan, muttered into his glass that the G.O.P. had been tainted by Rockefeller and Javits, insisted that the United States should muster its strength and obliterate Red China in a Fourth of July shower of atomic explosives. Adam, by this time fascinated with the enormity of his aversion for the man, could not bring himself to be sufficiently serious about mass insanity to argue.

Besides, he was incredibly sleepy. Eventually, after he had yawned three times, Pender picked up the almost empty bottle of bourbon and signaled that the evening was over. "We usually put Gabrielle in the house with us. But seeing she brought a playmate, we've given you adjoining rooms on the third floor."

They said goodnight to Pauline, who sat pensively scratching the sole of one narrow white foot with sharp fingernails that matched the color of her bloody toes. Pender led them upstairs.

"Goodnight," Gaby said coldly, evidently to both men. She went into the room without looking at them and closed the door.

"Anything you want, you'll have to get. Gabrielle knows where everything is. You've got the whole goddam building to yourself."

How could a man leer like that when the girl he thinks is about to have intercourse is his own daughter, Adam wondered.

He was aware that Gaby was listening on the other side of the closed door.

"Goodnight," he said.

Pender waved and went away.

Jesus.

He lay down on the bed fully clothed. He could hear Pender make his way down the stairs to laugh briefly with his wife, and then the sound of the two of them leaving the hotel. The old building was very quiet. In the room next door he could hear Gaby Pender moving around, evidently getting ready for bed.

The rooms were separated by a bathroom. He walked through it and tapped on the closed door.

"What is it?"

"Feel like talking?"

"No."

"Well, then. Goodnight."

"Goodnight."

He closed the two bathroom doors, got into pajamas, shut off the light and lay in the dark. Outside the open window crickets shrilled a fierce serenade, perhaps with foreknowledge that the frost which would kill them was somewhere right over the horizon. The raccoon trilled, a desperate weeping sound. Gaby Pender went into the bathroom and through the closed door he could hear the tinkling and then the flushing of the john, sounds which despite his long clinical experience caused him to lie rigid, hating her father.

He got up and clicked on the light. There was stationery in the desk bearing the resort's letterhead. He used his pen and wrote quickly, as if scribbling a prescription:

> *Commissioner*
> *Division of Fish and Game*
> *Montpelier, Vermont*
>
> *Dear Sir:*
> *A large female raccoon, captured illegally, is being held in a cage at this resort as a lure for the illegal capture of male raccoons. I have witnessed that the creature is being mistreated and would be pleased to testify to this. I may be reached at the Department of Surgery at Suffolk County General Hospital in Boston. Your prompt investigation is requested, since the raccoons are destined to be eaten.*
> *Yours truly,*
> *Adam R. Silverstone, M.D.*

He put it in an envelope, wet the flap with his tongue and sealed it carefully, found the book of stamps in his wallet and affixed one, then he placed the letter in his valpac and returned to bed. For about a quarter of an hour he lay and tossed, certain despite his overwhelming weariness that now he would not be able to sleep.

The old hotel creaked as if lecherous ghosts bed-hopped from room to room, shaking liberated chastity belts instead of chains. The crickets shrilled their swan song. The raccoon wept; and raged. Once he thought he heard Gaby crying but decided that perhaps he had been mistaken.

And fell asleep.

He was awakened—almost immediately, he felt—by her hand.

"What is it?" he said, thinking at first that he was in the hospital.

"Adam, take me away from here."

"Of course," he said stupidly, neither asleep or awake. And then shut his eyes against the light as she snapped it on. He saw that she wore slacks and a sweater. "You mean *now?*"

"Right now." Her eyes were reddened from crying. He felt a wave of tenderness for her, and pity. At the same time his weariness pushed his head back against the pillow.

"What will they think?" he said. "I don't believe we should simply disappear in the night."

"I'll leave a note. I'll tell them you were called back by the hospital."

He closed his eyes.

"If you won't come with me I'll go alone."

"Go write the note. I'll get dressed."

They had to feel their way down the broad staircase in the dark. The moon was low now but threw a light through which they made their way to the car easily. The crickets had fallen asleep, or whatever they did when they stopped singing. Behind the pool the poor raccoon still trilled.

"Wait," she said.

She switched on the headlamps and knelt in their light to select a large rock. When he started to follow her she stopped him. "I want to do it alone."

He sat on the cadaver-skin leather seat, which was wet with dew, and shivered while she smashed at the lock of the cage, wondering whether he would have mailed the letter informing on her father. In a moment the trilling stopped. He heard her running back toward him and then a bumping noise, and her curse.

When she reached the car she was laughing and sobbing, sucking a skinned palm. "I was afraid it would bite me, and when I ran away I tripped over one of the traps," she said. "I almost fell into the goddam swimming pool."

He started to laugh with her; they laughed all the way down the long driveway, past the stone gargoyles and onto the highway. When he stopped laughing he saw that she was crying. He considered taking over the wheel from her so she could cry in safety, and then decided he was so tired it didn't really matter.

She was a soundless weeper; they were far more devastating to watch, he thought, than the more dramatic kind.

"Listen," he said finally and with difficulty, his voice thick with fatigue, as if he were high. "You don't have the corner on horrible parents. With your father it's sex, with mine it's the bottle."

He told her the essential details about Myron Silberstein, matter-of-factly and without emotion, leaving out very little: the story of an itinerant musician from Dorchester who drifted into a job in the pit of the Davis Theater in Pittsburgh and one night met a much younger and inexperienced little Italian girl.

"I'm sure he married her because of me," he said. "He started drinking before I had any memories of him and he hasn't stopped yet."

When they were once more on Route 128 and the car was boring into the night in the direction from which it had come, she touched his arm.

"We can be the start of new generations," she said.

He nodded and smiled. Then he went to sleep.

When he awoke they were just crossing the Sagamore Bridge.

"Where in hell are we?"

"We had the free time all arranged," she said. "It seemed a pity simply to go home and waste the holiday."

"But where are we going?"

"A place I know."

So he remained quiet and let her drive. Forty-five minutes later they were in Truro, according to the roadsign illuminated briefly as she turned the car off Route 6 and onto a Cape Cod road, two ruts of white sand divided by a track of sawgrass. They topped a small rise and high above them and to the right a revolving finger of light searched the black sky at the edge of the sea. The sound of the surf was there suddenly, as though someone had switched it on.

She had slowed the car almost to a stop. He didn't know what she was looking for, but whatever it was, she found it and turned the car off the road. He saw nothing, only the inky blackness, but when they got out of the car he was able to see the more solid darkness that was a small building.

A very small building, a cottage or a shack.

"Do you have a key?"

"There is no key," she said. "It's bolted from the inside. We go through the secret entrance."

She led him around to the back, small pine trees tearing at them with invisible fingers. The windows were boarded up, he saw on closer inspection. "Give the boards a yank," she said.

He did and the nails came out easily, as though they had made the trip many times. She slid the window up and wriggled over the low sill. "Watch your head," she said.

He bumped it anyhow, on the upper bunk. The room was closet sized, making even his room at the hospital appear to be spacious by comparison. The crude wooden bunks took up most of the space, allowing only walking access to the door. The illumination came from bare light bulbs, turned on by pull strings. There were two other chambers identical to the one through which they gained entrance; a minuscule bathroom with shower, no tub; and an all-purpose room with kitchen facilities, a rickety rocker and a moth-eaten sofa full of bumps and sags. The decor was classical Cape Cod: clam shells for ash trays, a lobster pot for a coffee table, sand dollars and starfish on the mantel, a rigged surf rod propped in one corner, in another corner a gas stove which she primed expertly and lit with ease.

He stood there, swaying. "What can I do?" he asked.

She looked at him and for the first time was able to take the full measure of his fatigue. "Oh, God," she said. "Adam, I'm sorry. Really." She led him to a lower bunk, took off his shoes, covered him tenderly with a brown woolen blanket that tickled his chin, comforted him with eye-kisses that closed both his lids, and left him alone to sink into the sound of the surf.

He awoke finally to foghorns like giant stomach-rumblings, the scent and sizzle of frying food, and the feeling that he was traveling steerage on a very small ship. A smoky mist made the window as blank as Little Orphan Annie's eyes.

"I was hoping you'd sleep late," she said, turning bacon. "But I got so damn hungry I had to drive to the camping ground store for food."

"Who owns this shack?" he asked, still entertaining visions of arrest.

"I do. It was left me in a small trust set up by my grandmother before she died. Don't worry, we're legal."

"Jesus, an heiress."

"There's plenty of hot water. It's a good heater," she said proudly. "Tooth paste in the cabinet."

The shower restored his enthusiasm, but the contents of the medicine cabinet dampened them again somewhat. There was what at first he feared was a douche bag but turned out to be an enema, accompanied by physics and nose drops and eye drops and aspirin and pain-killers of several varieties, as well as a welter of vitamins and unlabeled pills and medicines, a neurotic's accumulated do-it-yourself kit of medical indulgences.

"God," he said testily when he emerged, "will you do me a favor?"

"What?"

"Get rid of that . . . *junk* in your cabinet."

"Yes, Doctor," she said, too meekly.

They breakfasted on canned peaches, bacon and eggs and frozen corn sticks that stuck to the toaster and had to be eaten as crumbs.

"You make better coffee than anyone," he said in mellower humor.

"Intimate knowledge of the coffee pot. I lived here alone for a year."

"A whole year? You mean right through the winter?"

"Especially right through the winter. Under those circumstances a good cup of coffee can be absolutely life-saving."

"Why did you want to hole up?"

"Well, I'll tell you. I was jilted."

"Really?"

"Really."

"The damned fool."

She smiled. "Thank you, Adam. That's very sweet."

"I mean it."

"Well, anyway. On top of my less than perfect parental situation —with which you have become somewhat familiar—it left me in a real emotional hang-up. I figured what was good for Thoreau was good for the country. I simply took some books and came here. To think things out. Try to find out who I really am."

"Did you? Find out, I mean."

She hesitated. "I think so."

"You're lucky."

He helped her with the dishes. "It looks like we're fogged in," he said, as they stacked their cups and saucers.

"Oh, no, we're not. Get a jacket. I want to show you something."

Outside the hut she led him over a path almost obliterated by the low, thick vegetation. He recognized bayberries and here and there a leafless beach plum. The fog was so thick he could see only where he was walking and the fine waggle of her tight blue jeans directly ahead of him.

"You know where you're going?"

"I could go with my eyes closed. Careful, now. From here on in we go slowly. We're almost there."

It appeared to be a sheer drop. They stood on the lip of a sea cliff, the mist like a wall in front of them, but below them a drop—into solid fog—which his imagination told him was horrifying, a replica of the hundred-foot plunge he had used to take for money in Benson's Aquacade.

"Is it steep? And far down?"

"Very steep. And pretty far down. It frightens people when they see it for the first time. But it's quite safe. I get to the bottom by sitting down and riding a little sandslide on my rear."

"Well, look at the vehicle."

She grinned, accepting it as a compliment. While he squatted nervously a few feet behind her, she dangled her feet over the edge of the cliff, her eyes closed as she sniffed the cold salt fog.

"You love it," he accused.

"The coastline's always changing, yet it's still the way it was when my grandfather had the shack built for my grandmother. There's a Realtor in Provincetown who keeps offering me a small fortune for it but I want my kids to see it like this, and their children. It's part of the John F. Kennedy National Seashore, so nothing else can be built here, but the ocean keeps nibbling away at the land, a few feet every year. In fifty years or so the cliff will be worn back almost to the house. I'll have to have it moved back or the ocean will get it."

It seemed to him that they hung suspended in the fog. Far below, the surf boomed and hissed. He listened and shook his head.

"What's the matter?" she asked.

"The fog. It's an alien atmosphere."

"Not so much on land. In the water, it's completely alien, it's almost a mystical experience," she said. "When I lived here, sometimes I wouldn't bother with a bathing suit and I'd go skinny-dipping in the fog. It was indescribable, like becoming part of the sea."

"Isn't it also dangerous?"

"You can hear the surf, even from far out. It tells you where the land is. A couple of times . . ." She trailed off uncertainly, and then, as if making up her mind, went on. "A couple of times I swam straight out but I didn't have the courage to keep going."

"Gaby. Why would you want to keep going?" Behind them in the fog a bob-white began to call. "Did the man who jilted you mean that much to you?"

"No, he was a boy, not a man. But I was . . . I thought I was dying."

"Why?"

"I had pains that tormented me. Patches of numbness, overwhelming weariness. The same symptoms my grandmother had had while she was dying."

Ah. The collection of nostrums in the medicine cabinet suddenly were a pathetic part of the narrative. "It sounds like a textbook case of hysteria," he said gently.

"Of course." She allowed a handful of sand to drift through her fingers. "I know I'm a hypochondriac. But at the time I was convinced that a horrible sickness was going to take my life. Being convinced that you have that kind of disease can be just as bad as actually having it. Believe me, Doctor."

"I know."

"I guess the swimming was a way of seeking out what I feared, an attempt to get it over with."

"Jesus, but why did you come here? Why didn't you go to a doctor?"

She smiled. "I had *been* to doctors. And doctors. I simply didn't believe them."

"Do you believe them now when they say you're all right?"

She smiled. "Most of the time."

"I'm glad," he said. Somehow he knew she was lying.

Around them the fog seemed to lighten. Overhead a glow began to spread through the mist.

"What did your parents think of your living out here alone?"

"My mother had just remarried. She was . . . preoccupied. She sent me an occasional letter. My father never even sent me a postal card." She shook her head. "He really is a bastard, Adam."

"Gaby . . ." He sought the right words. "I don't like him, but we're all weak, each of us in some kind of a bag. I'd be a hypocrite to condemn him. I'm sure I've done most of the things for which you loathe him."

"No."

"I've been on my own most of my life. I've known a lot of women."

"You don't understand. He's never given me anything. Never anything of himself. He paid my college tuition, then sat back and waited for me to be properly grateful."

Adam didn't say anything.

"I have a feeling that you worked your way through college," she said.

"I got through Pitt because of my Uncle Vito."

"Your uncle?"

"I had three uncles. Joe, Frank and Vito. Frank and Joe were built like bulls, they worked in the steel mills. Vito was tall, but he was fragile. He died when I was fifteen."

"He left you some money?"

He laughed. "No. He didn't have any money. He was a towel man in the locker room of the East Liberty branch of the Pittsburgh Y.M.C.A."

"What's a towel man?"

"Haven't you ever been in the locker room of a Y.M.C.A.?"

She smiled and shook her head.

"Well, he hands out the towels, of course. And among other things he pushes the little buzzer that lets people into the pool. Every day after I got out of school and delivered my *Pittsburgh*

Press route I'd walk over to Whitfield Street and Vito would let me into the swimming pool. When finally they caught on that I wasn't paying dues, everybody had gotten to know me and they gave me a Newsboy Club scholarship. A great 'Y' coach named Jack Adams took me in hand and I was a fancy diver by the time I was twelve. I dove so much I picked up an ear infection and that's why sometimes now I have trouble hearing."

"I never noticed. You're deaf?"

"Only very slightly, on the left side. Just enough to keep me out of the army."

She touched his ear. "Poor Adam. Did it bother you a lot when you were growing up?"

"Not really. As a diver I represented the 'Y' and my high school, and I got through four years of Pitt on a full athletic scholarship as a member of the swimming team. Living high off the hog. Then my first year in medical school I found myself suddenly poor again. To get enough money for food and a bed I picked up and delivered clothing at all the dorms for a dry cleaner every morning. Every evening I covered the same route with a carton of sandwiches."

"I wish I had known you then," she said.

"I wouldn't have had time to talk to you. After a while I had to drop both the cleaning service and the sandwich route, school was too demanding. For two terms I worked in a hash house for my meals and borrowed from the university for my room. That first summer I worked as a waiter at a hotel in the Poconos. I had an affair with one of the guests, a wealthy Greek woman who was married to a man who wouldn't divorce her, the president of a chain of specialty stores. She lived in Drexel Hill, not far from where I went to school in Philadelphia. I saw her all the time, for almost a year."

She sat and listened.

"It wasn't only that we had an affair. Sometimes she gave me money. I didn't have to work. She'd call me on the telephone and I would come to her house and afterwards she often tucked a bill into my pocket. A large bill."

Her head was turned away from him. "Stop it," she said.

"Finally I stopped seeing her. I couldn't stand myself any longer. I got a job shoveling coal, where I really had to sweat for my money, as if to expiate."

From far away another bob-white began to answer the first bird.

Now she was looking at him. "Why tell me?"

Because I am a fool, he thought wonderingly. "I don't know. I never told anyone before."

She reached out and touched his face again. "I'm glad." In a moment she said, "May I ask you a question?"

"Of course."

"Making love with that woman . . . you know, a casual affair. Was it any different from the same thing with someone you love?"

"I don't know," he said. "I never loved any of them."

"That's like . . . animals."

"We are animals. There's nothing wrong with being animals."

"But we should be more."

"It's not always possible."

The fog was breaking. Shining through it he became conscious of an enormous sun-reflector, more ocean than he had ever looked at. The beach was broad, white, marked only by jetsam and driftwood on the upper reaches and on the lower strands shining and hard and pounded so smooth by the breakers that it glittered in the sun.

"I wanted you to see it," she said. "I used to sit here and tell myself that if you piled all the ugly hurts down there they would be washed out with the tide."

He was thinking of that when to his horror she sounded a whoop and disappeared from view over the edge of the precipice, which fell to a dizzying conclusion far below at what was at least a hundred-degree angle. Her buttocks left a straight furrow in the soft red sand. In a moment she was laughing up at him from the bottom. It left only one thing he could do. He sat down on the edge and closed his eyes and then he slid. Him the Almighty Power hurled headlong flaming from the eternal sky with hideous ruin and combustion down to bottomless perdition. John Milton. There was sand in his shoes and no doubt his landslide had not been large enough: His rump was raw. The girl was howling with laughter. When he opened his eyes he realized that when she was happy she was extremely pretty; no, more than that, she was the most beautiful girl he had ever seen.

They combed the beach, finding a number of smelly sponges but no treasure; watched a dogfish undulate its way through a clear little cove; picked up eight unbroken sand-dollars; gouged red clay out of the cliff and fashioned a pot which cracked as it dried in the cold breeze.

When they became chilled they tried unsuccessfully to stamp the sand from their shoes and climbed straight up the cliff on the rickety wooden stairs and went back into the warm cabin. The sun streamed through the window bathing the lumpy sofa. While he started a fire she lay down and when the fireplace was roaring she made room for him and he lay next to her and they closed their eyes and allowed the sun god to turn their world into a large red pumpkin.

After a long time he opened his eyes and rolled over and kissed her very gently and, more gently still, touched her with his fingertips. Her lips were warm and dry and salty. There was quiet except for the outside sounds of the sea and the screams of a gull and the inside sounds of the fire and their breathing. He was touching her breast through the blue sweat shirt, aware that they were both remembering her father turning the same gesture into a contemptuous brand with which he had marked his wife.

This is different, he said to her silently. Understand that. Please understand that. He could feel within her a faint trembling like a suppressed shudder, more fear than desire, he knew, and somehow, despite all the girls and the women, the fear was transmitted to him so that he, too, trembled; yet he continued to allow his hand to bridge the space between them until he felt the trembling subside, his and hers. She kissed him this time, tentatively at first and then with a rush of feeling that made it seem as though she wanted to devour him, leaving him shaken; finally by unspoken agreement they drew apart and helped each other with things like buttons and zippers and snaps, hastily. It was as he had expected: there were no white patches, no strap marks, he saw in glimpses that turned his legs to water.

"You have a little pot belly," she observed.

"I've been running," he said defensively.

"You're very firm," he said.

"Not all the time."

Then they were lying close and perfect together again. God, how sweet in the warm sun. She was kissing his defective ear and crying and he realized with a sudden new feeling that he wanted to take nothing, he yearned only to be giving, to give to her tenderly all that he owned in the world, everything that was Adam Silverstone.

Eventually they felt hunger.

"Tomorrow," she said, "we'll get up in time for the early tide at Head-of-the-Meadow. I'll catch you some small but plump flounders and you can clean them for me like a good surgeon and I'll broil them for you over charcoal, basted with fresh lime juice and lots of butter."

"Mmmm . . ." Then: "What about *today?*"

"Today . . . we have some eggs left."

"I don't think so."

"Portuguese soup?"

"What is it?"

"*Specialité de la région.* Noodles and vegetables, mostly cabbage and tomatoes, cooked with pork. There's a good place in Provincetown. Served with hot crusty white bread. Followed, if you like, by good cold tap beer."

"That's it, Charlie."

"I'm not a Charlie." They shot sparks at each other again and he grinned.

"I am aware."

They wandered about the room picking flung clothing from the floor and dressing with only a little self-consciousness and then they went out to the car and drove slowly through the perfect day five miles down Route 6 past the dunes to Provincetown. They had the soup, hot and smoky-tasting, full of delicious chunks, and then they got to the fish pier just as a boat was coming in and Gaby bargained shamelessly until for thirty-five cents she bought a beautiful large fluke, still flipping, insurance against the possibility that the following morning would be rainy or that they would oversleep and not go fishing.

When they got back to the cabin she put the fish in the refrigerator and came to him and took his face in her palms and held it hard. "Your hands smell of fluke," he complained and then kissed her for a long time and looked at her and they both knew he was going to make love to her again without giving her a chance to wash the fish off her hands.

"Adam," she said shakily, "I want to give you six children. At least six. And to stay married to you for seventy-five years."

Married, he thought.

Children?

This crazy broad.

"Gaby, listen . . ." he said anxiously.

She drew back and he reached for her again so he could be holding her as he talked but she wasn't having any, she was looking straight at him.

"Oh, lord," she said.

"Look—"

"No," she said. "I don't want to look. I'm not very smart. That's no surprise to me, I've always known it. But you. God," she said. "Poor Adam. You're *nothing.*"

She ran into the bathroom and locked the door. He heard no weeping but in a little while there was the sound of something terrible, the broken noise of retching, the flushing of the john.

He knocked at the door, feeling terribly guilty. "Gaby, are you all right?"

"Go to hell," she gasped, crying now.

After a long while he heard the sound of running water as she washed and finally the door opened and she emerged.

"I want to leave," she said.

He carried the bags to the car and she turned off the gas and locked the door from the inside and climbed through the window, on which he replaced the boards. When he attempted to get behind the wheel she snarled at him. Her driving on the return trip was suicidal, resulting finally in a citation for speeding on Route 128 in Hingham, the state trooper bitingly sarcastic as he protected the public good and welfare.

After she got the ticket she drove more cautiously but the coughing began, a series of rasping asthmatic spasms that shook her whole frame as she hunched over the wheel.

He endured the sound as long as he was able. "Get off the highway and find a drug store," he said. "I'll write out a prescription for ephedrine."

But she continued to drive.

Dusk was falling when finally she pulled the car to a stop in front of the hospital. They hadn't interrupted their travel to eat and Adam was weary once more, hungry and emotionally frazzled.

He placed his bag on the sidewalk.

He could hear her coughing as she jammed her foot down on the accelerator. The Plymouth jolted into the center of the street, in and out of the path of an oncoming taxi whose driver cursed and leaned on his horn.

Adam stood on the sidewalk, realizing suddenly that they hadn't remembered to take the fish out of the refrigerator. Next time Gaby used her cabin there would be another disgusting reason for remembering their interrupted holiday. He felt borne down by conflicting emotions, worry, guilt and regret. He had filled her up to her ears with seamy confessions of the most degrading sort, and then he had allowed himself to . . .

Damn it, he thought, did I make any promises?

Did I sign a contract?

But in sudden self-disgust he knew that while he had treated her body with tender gentleness he had torn her soul like an animal.

He threw back his head and looked up at the old monster of a building.

Well, I'm back, he told the hospital.

The lights were going on as darkness fell and the hospital looked back at him with many eyes. He thought of what was going on inside, all the ants within the hill, wondering how many patients now in the wards would be operated on by him in the week to come.

As a human being I'm a sorry mess and a fool, he thought, but I can function well as a surgeon, and that has to count for something. God give them wisdom that have it; and those that are fools, let them use their talents. Will Shakespeare.

He picked up his bag. The front door opened like a mouth and the grinning building swallowed him.

After he had unpacked he went down to the ward to steal a cup of coffee and almost at once he was doubly sorry to be back.

Mrs. Bergstrom had been doing fine, Helen Fultz told him, but since early that afternoon there had been signs that she was rejecting the kidney. Her temperature was 101.6° and she complained of malaise and pain in the wound.

"Is the kidney putting out urine?" he asked.

Miss Fultz shook her head. "It's been doing beautifully, but to-day its output went way down."

He looked at the chart and saw that Dr. Kender was attempting to abort the rejection by administering Prednisone and Imuran.

The crowning touch to garnish the day, he told himself.

He thought briefly of going to the animal lab and working but could not force himself to do it. He had had enough of dogs and women and surgery for the moment. Instead he went upstairs anxious to take sleep as though it were a healing draught, relishing the prospect of unconsciousness.

Chapter 8: Spurgeon Robinson

Spurgeon Robinson spent a good deal of his time worrying.

If one of your cases had to be presented to the Mortality Conference, he reasoned, it should be when things were going well. At a time like this, with a kidney transplant showing an increasing number of rejection signs and with the Old Man beginning to look like hell, there would be staff people at the meeting in a mood to tear somebody apart.

He began to wonder what he would do if he were thrown out.

When he should have been sleeping he found himself thinking of Mrs. Donnelly's riddles. One night he dreamed the incident in the Emergency Room occurred again, only this time instead of releasing the woman from the hospital and sending her home to die, his great skill as a physician allowed him to realize instantly that there was a fracture of the odontoid process. He awoke that morning with happiness in every cell, and for a while he lay there and wondered why, and then he remembered it was because he had saved Mrs. Donnelly. Finally, of course, he knew it had been a dream and nothing would alter the reality that he had killed her. He lay in his misery, unable to get out of bed.

He was a Doctor of Medicine. They couldn't take that away.

If he were dropped from internship, the only thing open would be a salaried position somewhere. Uncle Calvin would dearly love to give him a medical appointment with American Eagle Life, advancement guaranteed. And some of the large drug manufacturers hired Negro M.D.s. But he knew if they fired him from the house staff, if he couldn't have medicine the way he wanted it, he would go back to where he'd been a few years ago and try to have music the way he wanted it.

He began to make excuses to go to Peggy Weld's room, to draw the singer into conversations about music.

At first he could see that she considered him another young guy who played a little and thought he was a musician, but then they discovered a name they knew in common.

"You mean *you* played Dino's on 52nd Street. In Manhattan?"

"My little group. Three other guys, me on piano."

"Who's the manager?" she challenged.

"Vin Scarlotti."

"He sure is. I've sung there myself, a couple of times. You must be good. Vin's tough to please."

But he ran out of excuses to talk music with her, and she had her sister on her mind. He stopped bothering her.

Coming off-duty after thirty-six hours, aching for sleep, he sat on his bed and played the guitar, forcing himself to practice music in a way he had not done for a number of years.

He *needed* a piano.

That afternoon after a nap he took the elevated into Roxbury and got off at the Dudley Street station where a lot of colored people got off and walked down Washington Street until he came to the kind of place he was looking for, a sleazy ghetto joint with the windows painted red and black, the dead neon sign showing a poker hand and the name of the club in white tube glass, the Ace High. Night club was too grand a word, it was a cheap colored saloon, but in a corner was an upright.

He ordered a scotch-and-milk he didn't want and carried it to the piano. The scratched Baldwin was out of tune but when he began to play, it was balm music. He forgot all about what Uncle Calvin would say when his boy came dragging home and told him he couldn't make it like white folks. He even forgot about the dead Irish lady and her riddles.

In a little while the bartender came over. "Can I get you something else, friend?" he asked, glancing at the drink on the piano, which Spurgeon had barely touched.

"Yuh, I'll have another."

"You play real good, but we already got a piano player. Fella named Speed Nightingale."

"I'm not auditioning."

He brought the second drink and Spur paid a dollar-eighty. After that the bartender left him alone. At the end of the afternoon he walked away from the piano and sat on one of the stools at the bar and ordered another.

The bartender's eyes flicked to the two glasses still on the piano, only one of them empty.

"You don't have to order just to talk to me. Want to ask me something?"

"I'm a doctor over at the county hospital. I can't keep a piano in my room. I'd like to come here and play a couple of afternoons a week, like I did today."

The bartender shrugged. "No skin off me, I don't give a damn."

But it turned out that he did. He was especially fond of Debussy, which he appreciated with scotch-and-milk in lieu of applause. Spurgeon tried to pay for the drink but gave up gracefully; a professional never insults a music-lover.

A few days later when he again went to the club there was a lean brown man, zulu-haired and with a thin line of mustache, standing at the bar talking with the bartender. Spurgeon nodded and went straight to the piano. All the way down he had been hearing music in his head and now he sat and played it. Bach. *The Well-Tempered Clavier.* And then bits and pieces from *French Suites* and *Chromatic Fantasy and Fugue.*

In a little while the lean brown man came over with two scotches-and-milk.

"You play big long-hair piano." He held out a glass.

Spurgeon took it and smiled. "Thanks."

"You know how do something little more relaxed?"

He took a sip and then set the glass down and did a little Shearing.

The man pulled a chair over to the lower part of the keyboard and his left hand took over the bass and his right hand sneaked in on the harmony and Spur moved over and began to work on the treble keys in improvisations that became wilder as the bass demanded it by setting a faster pace. The bartender stopped polishing glasses and just listened. First one of them dominated, then the other. They fought it out until sweat glistened on their faces, and when they stopped by mutual agreement Spur felt as though he had been running a long way through a rainstorm.

He held out his hand and it was slapped.

"Spurgeon Robinson."

"Speed Nightingale."

"Oh. This music box is yours."

"Hell it is. Belongs to the place. I'm just a hired hand. Thanks for tuning it, sucker. I haven't sounded this good for a long time."

They moved to a table and Spurgeon bought a round.

"Bunch of us get together and jam all the time, early mornings, little place on Columbus Avenue, down there in the housing project. Apartment 4-D, Building 11. Real music. Come on over."

"Hey." He took out his notebook and wrote down the address. "I'm going to do that."

"Yeah. We play a little, burn a few, have a ball. You want to turn on, somebody usually brings some good stuff."

"I don't use it."

"Not *none* of it?"

He shook his head.

Nightingale shrugged. "Come anyhow. We're democratic."

"Okay."

"Good stuff harder to get in this town than a good gig, lately."

"That right?"

"Yeah. Understand you're a doctor."

"Who told you that?" Behind the bar the man studiously polished glassware. Spur waited. In a moment it came, as by now he knew it would.

"Bring some stuff to one of our little sessions, we sure would appreciate it."

"Now, where would I get it, Speed?"

"Hell, everybody knows all kinds of stuff just layin' around in hospitals. Nobody goin' to miss just a little bit. Are they, Doc?"

Spurgeon stood and dropped a bill on the table.

"Tell you what," Nightingale said. "Forget all about that. Just sign me a few prescription blanks. I'll get us some real bread."

"So long, Speed," he said.

"Damn good bread."

As he passed the man behind the bar on his way out, the music-lover didn't even look up from the glass-polishing.

He found catharsis in the music that made him looser in the OR, able to be sharper and more intense as a surgeon. Through comparison he discovered he was not bad. That Friday, he found himself scheduled for the operating room to assist Dr. Parkhurst and Stanley Potter. Inevitably he and the resident had to work together, but each occasion was an unpleasant experience with no banter and the time passing slowly.

That morning they grafted on Joseph Grigio, the burns case, transplanting fresh skin from the thigh to the chest. Then they had an appendectomy in a very obese patient named Macmillan, a sergeant in the Metropolitan District Commission police department. The man's grossness forced them to cut through what seemed to be interminable fat, and then Dr. Parkhurst sliced off the worm and left them to tie the appendix stump and close.

Spurgeon was snipping while Potter held and tied. It seemed to him that the resident was pulling the Chromic O catgut too hard around the stump. He was certain of it when the suture began to disappear into the tissue.

"You've got it too tight."

Potter looked at him coldly. "This is just the way I've always done it, very successfully."

"The suture looks as though it may cut through the serosa."

"It will be all right."

"But . . ."

Potter was holding the suture, staring at him sardonically and waiting for him to snip.

Spurgeon shrugged and shook his head. This guy is a resident and I'm an intern, he thought. He snipped like a good little boy.

He didn't go back to the Ace High. Instead, that Sunday he asked Mrs. Williams if he could practice once in a while on their piano. It was a bad instrument and driving to Natick wasn't as convenient as taking the subway to Washington Street, but the music pleasured Mrs. Williams and it gave him a chance to see Dorothy.

On Tuesday evening, while outside the first winter snow fell, they sat whispering together in the living room, with her mother and father and the little girl all sleeping nearby behind partially closed doors, and she told him she knew something was eating away at him.

He found himself whispering hoarsely about the old lady who had died because of him and about the Death Committee and of the fact that he could always make a good living out of music.

"Oh, Spurgeon."

She pulled his head down and he rested softly, the way he had with Roe-Ellen when he was a little boy. Dorothy bent to kiss his closed eyes and he felt it flowing from her as she held him, sympathy, desire, the willingness to make things right in his world.

But when he acted on this belief he managed only to earn a bitten lip while she clawed the back of his hand and he learned that she still retained a belief in one of the Muslims' basic tenets.

He was unable to believe it. In the neighborhoods, both black and white, that had fashioned him, there were few twenty-four-year-old virgins. It filled him with awe but he smiled at her despite the lip-pain.

"A piece of flesh. Thin, often very fragile. Having nothing to do with intimacy. What does it mean? We're already intimate."

"You know this house, this yard? What is it but lumber, glass, a few trees, half a dozen shrubs. Do you know what it is to my father?"

"Middle-class respectability?"

"Exactly."

He hooted. "Lord, what an analogy. You want so badly to conform you end up being non-conformists. There isn't another property on this street as well-tended as your father's. And I'd give odds that pelvic examinations wouldn't disclose an army of twenty-four-year-old virgins, either. You think you have to be stricter with yourselves than all those white folks to buy your way into their kind of world?"

"We're not trying to conform. We think a lot of white people are losing something they once had, something very valuable. We're trying to gain it," she said, reaching into his pocket for a cigarette. He lit a match. In the flare of the soft, quick light the African face made his hand tremble and the match went out, but the cigarette tip glowed as she drew smoke. "Listen," she said, "you thought Midge was my child, didn't you? Well, you were on the right track. She's my sister's. My unmarried sister Janet's."

"Your mother told me. I didn't know there wasn't a husband."

"No husband. You know how Lena Horne looked when she was young? Add a kind of . . . happy wildness. That's my baby sister."

"Why haven't I met her?"

"She comes home once in a while. She plays with Midge then as if she were a little girl herself, but not like a mother. She says she doesn't *feel* like a mother. She's living in Boston with a bunch of white hippies."

"I'm sorry."

She shrugged. "Janet says with them her color doesn't matter. She never seems to learn. Midge's father was a baseball player up from Minneapolis to try out with the Red Sox for a few weeks. He played third base. And my sister."

"She's not the first girl to make that kind of mistake," he said gently.

"She should have known white baseball players don't date young colored girls to further the cause of American democracy. By the time he was back in the minor leagues she was missing her first period." She snubbed out the cigarette. "She would have been happy to give the child up, but my father is the strangest man. He took the baby and wouldn't sue the baseball player for support and he gave Midge his own last name. He looked all his white neighbors in the eye and he dared them to tell him his family was the kind of trash he had been working away from all these years. To my knowledge nobody ever said a word to him. But my father, a good part of him . . ."

He took her into his arms.

"She's always been his favorite," she said into his shoulder. "He'd deny that but I know it to be true."

"Honey, you can't make it all up to your father by living like a nun," he said softly.

"Spur, this no doubt is going to chase you away from here lickety-split, but I'm going to say it. He goes around all day holding his breath because he thinks there's a chance that something serious is developing between us, that you might ask me to marry you. A black son-in-law who's a doctor, my God."

He moved his palm against her back. "I don't think it will chase me away." This time when he kissed her she kissed him back.

"Maybe it should," she said breathlessly. "I want you to promise me something."

"What?"

"If I should ever . . . lose control . . . I want you to swear . . ."

He was exasperated for only a moment, and then he had to fight hard to keep the grin from his face. "When you get married your husband will get the whole package, including the seal," he told her soberly. Then he threw back his head and roared, making her terribly angry and waking her parents. Mr. Williams came out in his robe and slippers and Spurgeon saw that he slept in his long underwear. Her mother emerged blinking and muttering and without her upper plate. Mrs. Williams was beginning to accept him on her own terms, he noted. She made him hot cocoa before returning to bed but his laughter had awakened Midge and when the little girl started to cry she tongue-lashed him unabashedly for being too loud and extremely inconsiderate.

When he got back to the hospital it was after two a.m. On the way up to his room he checked a few patients, among them Macmillan. He found the big police officer groaning and febrile. The chart showed that his temperature and pulse rate were each one hundred.

"Did Dr. Potter see this man tonight?" he asked the nurse.

"Yes. He's been complaining of discomfort and tenderness. Dr. Potter said he has a very low pain threshold. He ordered 100 mgs. of Demerol," she said, pointing out the order on the chart.

Something else to worry about, he thought as he waited for the elevator.

When he got to bed he lay and peered into the darkness at the alternative paths his life could take.

If they kicked him out, perhaps some of his former professors could help him get into one of the New York hospitals.

But he would have to leave Dorothy. He couldn't afford to marry her yet; he wouldn't want Uncle Calvin to support his wife.

The Mortality Conference that would consider the Donnelly case was only a week away . . .

It was the last thought he had until he awoke in the false light of early dawn, the sheets damp with perspiration despite the fact that the room was cold.

He could remember clearly that he had dreamed both of the girl and of the Death Committee.

When he came into the ward on Saturday he saw that Macmillan had become much worse. The man's face was flushed, his lips dry and cracked. He was groaning with pain he said came from deep within his rigid abdomen. His pulse hammered 120 times a minute and his temperature was 102°.

Potter had departed on a much-publicized excursion to the fleshpots of New York City. Oh you miserable slob, I hope you enjoy it, Spurgeon thought, I hope you catch everything. He went to the telephone and got Dr. Chin, the Visiting Surgeon who was on call. "We've got a guy here who's pursuing a classical septic course," he said. "I'm almost certain it's peritonitis." He described the case.

"Call the OR and schedule him right away," Dr. Chin said.

When they took him downstairs and opened, they found that the stump of the appendix had blown. Swollen with edema, the tissue had forced itself against the tight ring of catgut like cheese against a sharp knife, and with the same results.

"Who tied this goddam thing?"

"Dr. Potter," Spurgeon said.

"That guy again." The Visiting shook his head. "The tissue is waterlogged. It's too friable to play with. If we touch it with a forceps it will fall apart. We're going to have to pull the cecum up to the abdominal wall and do a cecostomy."

Under the older surgeon's patient direction, Spurgeon cleaned up Potter's mess.

Monday morning there was a duty rotation and he found himself facing five weeks in the Emergency Room, up tight inside because it was a place where he had already failed once; a place where things happened very fast; where, when decisions had to be made, they had to be made quickly. A repeat of the Donnelly incident, he knew, and . . .

He tried not to think about it.

He drew ambulance duty with Maish Meyerson, an intensive debating course, an introduction to The News of the World in Review, an oral scratch sheet, a seminar in philosophy. The ambulance driver's views were always definite and often irritating and by noon Spurgeon was weary of him.

"Take the race situation," Meyerson said.

"Okay, I got it."

Maish looked at him suspiciously. "Wait, you won't smile, two armies, one white, one black, the country will be a bonfire."

"Why?"

"You think all whites are liberals in Brooks Brothers suits?"

"No."

"Bet your ass, no. To a lot of us the colored man is a threat."

"I'm a threat to you?"

"You?" Meyerson said with scorn. "No, you're an educated punk, a doctor. A black white man. I'm more nigger than you are, I'm a white nigger. It's the black niggers who are a threat to me, and there are a hell of a lot of black niggers. I'm going to help myself first. Charity begins at home."

Spurgeon said nothing. Meyerson gave him a sidelong glance. "That makes me a bad guy, right?"

"Damn right."

"You're better?"

"Yes," Spurgeon said, but less emphatically.

"In a pig's eye. Ever hear yourself talk to a colored patient? You sound like you're doing the poor slob an enormous favor out of the goodness of your heart."

"Do *me* a favor. Just don't talk," he said, glaring.

Triumphantly Meyerson sneaked up behind a slow woman-driven convertible and goosed her with quick, impatient growls of the siren, even though the ambulance was empty and they were cruising back to the hospital.

He pushed the hours by somehow.

That evening he found himself feeling very sorry for Stanley Potter.

"Are you certain?" he asked Adam.

"I saw it myself," Adam said. "He was in the junior surgeon's room reading the paper and having a cup of coffee when he was called down to the Old Man's office. In a little while he came back looking as though he'd been trompled on, and he cleaned out his locker and carried his things away in a paper bag. Goodbye, Dr. Stanley Potter."

"Amen. But I'll be next."

He hadn't realized he had spoken aloud until he saw Adam looking at him.

"Don't be an ass," Adam said sharply.

"Two more days, man. That Death Committee's going to tear me into tiny pieces."

"No doubt. But if they were going to throw you out of here, pal, they wouldn't wait for any committee meeting. They didn't waste much time with Potter, did they? Because he was a general fuck-up. You're an intern who made a mistake. A woman died and that's a lousy shame, but if they threw out every doctor who made a mistake there wouldn't be a doctor left in the hospital."

Spurgeon didn't answer. Let them withhold the residency if they want to, he said silently. Just let me remain an intern.

He had to stay in medicine.

He needed his music as a way of escaping into beauty from the ugliness of the disease he saw everywhere he looked in the hospital. But with the world going to hell forty different ways he couldn't even pretend to himself that he wanted to spend the rest of his life playing the piano.

Wednesday morning he was less certain. The day started ominously. Adam Silverstone was in bed with a spiking temp, the latest victim of the virus that was making patients of the hospital staff. Spurgeon hadn't realized how much he had depended on Adam's silent support.

"Anything I can do for you?" he asked miserably.

Adam looked at him and groaned. "Oh, Jesus, just go down and get it over with."

He skipped breakfast. Outside it was snowing heavily. Some of the Visitings had telephoned to say they would not be in for the meeting, which he considered good news until it was announced that the Death Committee meeting was transferred from the amphitheater to the library, where the intimacy would make it more of an ordeal.

At 9:50 when he was paged and told to report to Dr. Kender's office he responded numbly, positive he would be notified of his dismissal prior to the Mortality Conference: this week they were cleaning out the misfits.

When he arrived there were two men with Kender, who introduced Lt. James Hartigan of the Narcotics Bureau and Mr. Marshall Colfax, a Dorchester pharmacist.

"Did you write these, Dr. Robinson?" Kender asked quietly.

Spurgeon took the prescriptions and leafed through them. Each was written for twenty-four tablets of morphine sulphate, quarter grain, prescribed for names that were not familiar. George Moseby, Samuel Parkes, Richard Meadows.

Each was signed with his name.

"No, sir."

"How can you be sure?" the lieutenant asked.

"In the first place, until I finish my internship I have only a limited license to practice medicine, which means I write orders that are filled in the hospital pharmacy, but I don't issue outside prescriptions. Second, that's my name but not my signature. And every doctor has a Federal Narcotics Registration Number, but the number on these prescriptions isn't mine."

"There's no need for concern on your part, Dr. Robinson," Kender said quickly. "You're not the only doctor here whose name has been used. Merely the latest. I'll ask you, of course, not to mention this to anyone."

Spurgeon nodded.

"What caused you to suspect that these prescriptions weren't right?" Kender asked Mr. Colfax.

The druggist smiled. "I began noticing how very neat they were. And so complete. Take abbreviations, for example. Almost every doctor I've met just scrawls prn, you know, for *pro re nata?*"

"What does it mean?" Hartigan asked.

"Latin for 'according as circumstances require,' " Spurgeon said.

"Yes. Well, take a look at these scripts," Colfax said. "It's written out. When I checked back I saw that every single prescription was exactly alike, as if the man who wrote them had copied them all at one sitting."

"He made a mistake, though," Hartigan said. "When Mr. Colfax read the prescription to me over the phone I knew it was a phoney right away. He used a six-numeral Federal number. We don't have that many physicians in Massachusetts."

"Did you pick up the person who passed these?" Kender asked.
Hartigan shook his head.

"I asked him some questions the last time he came in, just before
I called the police," Colfax said. "I must have frightened him
away." He smiled. "I'm a lousy detective."

"On the contrary," Hartigan said. "There aren't many druggists
sharp enough to pick up something like this. Can you describe the
man to Dr. Robinson?"

Colfax hesitated. "Well, he was a Negro . . ." He looked away
uncomfortably.

Look at our faces, Spurgeon told him silently.

"He had a mustache. I'm afraid I don't remember much else."

Speed Nightingale?

Hartigan smiled. "I realize that isn't very much to go on, Dr.
Robinson."

It would be unfair to name Nightingale, Spurgeon realized; there
were a great many mustached black men, a number of whom used
drugs. "It could be anybody."

Hartigan nodded. "A lot of people can get their hands on blank
prescriptions. Workers at the printing plant, people all over the
hospital, patients and their families when you people turn your
backs." He sighed.

Dr. Kender looked at his watch and pushed his chair back from
the desk. "Is there anything else, gentlemen?"

Both of the visitors smiled and stood.

"In that case, I'm afraid that Dr. Robinson and I have a conference to attend," Dr. Kender said.

At 10:30 Spurgeon sat in one of the side chairs at the long, highly
polished table and nibbled cookies and sipped cola, gazing straight
ahead at a wall decorated with a drug company print of Marcello
Malpighi, discoverer of capillary circulation, who looked a little
like Dr. Sack wearing a beard and a rug.

They straggled in, one by one, and he finally joined them in rising
for the entrance of Dr. Longwood.

Meomartino presented a case, a long one.

Meomartino presented another goddam case. Not *the* case. Maybe, he thought prayerfully, they wouldn't take it up. Just *perhaps*
there would be no time left, but when he lifted his eyes to the clock

he saw there would be more than enough time, and his stomach gave a lurch and he thought he would be the first intern in the history of the hospital to be ill all over the shiny table and the bottles of Pepsi and the cookies and the Chief of Surgery.

And then Meomartino was presenting again and he heard all the details he knew so well. Her name, and her age, and the facts of the automobile accident, the date he had seen her in Emergency, her past history, the films that had been made in X-ray and oh God the films that had not been made, how he had released her on his own, how she had gone home—

Hold on now, he thought with sudden urgency. What is going on here?

O you sneaky bastard.

What about the call I made to the Surgical Fellow? The call I made to *you,* he thought numbly.

But Meomartino was finishing up, telling how the riddle lady had come back to the hospital for the last time, dead on arrival.

Dr. Sack described what they had learned at the post-mortem, briskly presenting the findings in a few minutes.

Dr. Longwood sat back in his chair. "This is the worst kind of case to lose," he said. "Yet, inevitably, we lose patients like this. Why do you suppose that happens, Dr. Robinson?"

"I don't know, sir."

The hollow eyes held him. He saw with a terrible kind of fascination that a fine tremor had begun to jerk Dr. Longwood's head almost imperceptibly.

"It's because this type of case demands that we recognize an injury we don't see every day. An injury which is correctable and yet which, if uncorrected, can cause death."

"Yes, sir," Spurgeon said.

"Nobody has to tell me the kind of pressures and the heavy work load carried by our house officers. A good number of years ago I was an intern and a resident here, and then a Visiting Surgeon before I assumed a full-time position with this hospital. I know we get patients who are neglected, complicated and thrown at us in such number that some private institutions wouldn't believe what we accomplish.

"But it's precisely the poor shape of many of our patients and the demands on our time which make it necessary for us to be doubly alert. Which make it necessary for *every* intern to ask himself if he's fully aware that *every* diagnostic procedure, *every* necessary x-ray has been taken.

"Did you ask yourself these things, Dr. Robinson?"

The tremor had become more pronounced. "Yes, I did, Dr. Longwood," he said steadily.

"Then why did this woman die?"

"I suppose I didn't know enough to help her."

Dr. Longwood nodded. "You lacked the experience. Which is why an intern should never take it upon himself to release a patient from this hospital, even though the patient may complain bitterly about being kept waiting until an experienced doctor can find time to release him. No patient ever died of complaining. Our responsibility is to protect him from himself. Do you know what would have happened if you hadn't released her?"

He sought for Meomartino with his eyes but the Surgical Fellow was absorbed in the case history. "She would be alive," he said.

There was a silence and he looked back toward Dr. Longwood. The cavernous blue eyes that had bothered him throughout the meeting were still directed at him but he saw that their glint was gone and that they were focused far beyond him.

"Dr. Longwood?" Dr. Kender said.

"Harland," Dr. Kender said gently. "Shall we poll the staff?"

"What?"

"Shall we poll the staff, Harland?"

"Yes," he said.

"A preventable death," Dr. Kender said.

Dr. Longwood ran his tongue over dry lips and looked at Dr. Sack.

"Preventable."

At Dr. Parkhurst.

"Preventable."

Preventable.

Preventable.

Preventable.

Spurgeon tried again to catch Meomartino's eye but could not. It had to have been an unintentional omission, he told himself, sitting there and studying Marcello Malpighi's portrait.

When he arrived at Silverstone's room on the sixth floor he thought Adam was going to climb the wall in his rage.

A rage directed at Spurgeon, he discovered to his astonishment.

"How could you let Meomartino get away with a thing like that?"

"He didn't tell me to release her. It's true I called him on the telephone, but he didn't tell me a damn thing, man. He just asked me if I really needed him and I said I could handle it myself."

"But you called him," Adam said. "It was his responsibility to tell you to hold the patient until he could get down there. The committee would have known that."

Spurgeon shrugged.

"I'll go to the Old Man."

"I'd rather you didn't. He looks so bad I'm not sure he's capable of handling this kind of situation."

"Then go to Kender."

He shook his head.

"Why not?"

"Because," he said, "there *is* a rule that interns shouldn't release patients, and I *did* break that rule. Because Meomartino did *not* tell me to send her home. Because if I was going to do any complaining I should have done it at the conference."

"Robinson, you are the most stupid person I ever met in my entire life," he heard Adam call after him as he left.

Meomartino had revealed himself to be less than a man, he told himself as he clumped in misery to the elevator.

But during the torturous ride from the sixth floor to the basement, with an old sick dread he forced himself to recognize the reason he had not called attention to the telephone call during the committee meeting.

He had been terrified of all those white, white faces.

The day continued as it had begun.

Disastrously.

He and Meyerson were idle and bored with one another until mid-afternoon. From 3:30 until almost 8:30 they had six pick-ups, four of them long and difficult hauls, then at 8:35 they were sent out to pick up Mrs. Thomas Catlett, a case of expected childbirth, 31 Simmons Court, Charlestown. But Meyerson turned off the Expressway and wended through streets that hadn't been widened since they were declared broad enough for Paul Revere's horse. Ultimately he pulled into a No Parking zone in front of Shapiro's Book Store on Essex Street.

"Where are you going?" Spurgeon asked warily.

"I'm hungry. I'll pick up a sandwich and a drink at the delicatessen, you'll drive while I eat. Okay?"

"Better make it fast."

"It's all right, relax. Want me to bring you something? A corn beef?"

"No, thanks."

"Pastrami? They steam the meat."

"Maish, I don't want to waste time."

"We got to eat."

Spurgeon surrendered, handing over a dollar from his wallet. "Swiss on white. Coffee, regular."

He sat in the front seat of the ambulance and studied the books in the windows of Shapiro's as the seconds turned into minutes and Maish had not reappeared. In a little while he got out of the ambulance and walked to the corner and peered through the plate glass window of the Essex Delicatessen. Framed by a giant ring of salami in the window, his torso hidden behind a pyramid of knockwurst, Meyerson stood in line, talking earnestly to two taxi drivers.

Spurgeon knocked at the window, ignored the hundred-and-twenty-odd eyes that at once were turned upon him, and pointed to his watch.

Maish shrugged and pointed at the counter.

Lord, he hadn't been waited on yet.

He turned and walked the other way, past the book store, to the end of the block. Beyond lay Chinatown, a flashing neon jungle of palm trees and dragons.

He walked back. For a while he leaned against the side of the ambulance.

Finally he could stand it no longer. He went to the Essex and entered.

"Take a check," the man at the entrance said.

"I'm not staying."

"So on the way out, you give it back."

Maish was seated at a corner table with the cab drivers, the plate before him empty except for a few meat crumbs. His bottle still contained an inch of beer.

"Get the hell out into that ambulance," Spurgeon said.

Maish looked at the taxi drivers and lifted his eyes. "New man," he said.

In the ambulance he handed Spurgeon a brown paper bag and twenty cents change. "I figured I better gobble it inside," he said. "This way I can drive. I know Charlestown. I figured you might get us lost."

"We'd better make tracks to pick up that maternity case. That's what *I* figure."

"After we get her there she'll take a day and a half to deliver. I guarantee."

They went through Chinatown to the Expressway. "Eat," Maish commanded, the Jewish mother of the ambulance corps. The sandwich was like cardboard on his nervous tongue, the coffee nauseatingly cold, gulped as they rumbled over the Tobin Memorial Bridge. "You got twenty-five cents?" It was the driver's job to pay tolls, but Spurgeon shelled out, making a mental note to collect later.

The streets all looked the same. The houses all looked the same. It took Maish ten minutes to admit he couldn't find Simmons Court, another five minutes before he abandoned the City Directory map.

After lengthy consultations with two policemen and a Navy shore patrol they found it, an unlighted cul-de-sac at the end of a snow-rutted private street. The Catletts lived on the third floor, of course. The apartment was dark and dirty, smelling of relief checks. There were children frightened out of sleep and a silent, sullen man. The woman was porcine from a life of starches, trouble and too-frequent breeding. They got her on a litter and lifted, grunting in unison. The oldest girl laid a brown paper bag on the stretcher with her mother.

"My nightie and things," the woman told Spurgeon proudly.

They moved toward the door and then Spurgeon stopped, the stretcher digging into the backs of his knees. "Don't you want to tell her goodbye?" he asked the man.

" 'Bye."

" 'Bye," she said.

She was very heavy. They maneuvered her down the narrow, creaking double flight of stairs and out of the dark smell of the hallway.

"Watch the ice," Maish the Leader warned.

Their arms and legs were taut and trembling when finally they pushed her into the ambulance.

She screamed.

"What's the matter?" Spurgeon asked.

It was almost a minute before she could answer. In his first fright he did not think to look at his watch.

"I got a pain."

"What kind of a pain?"

"You know."

"Was that the first one?"

"No. I already had lots."

"Meyerson, you'd better get going," he said. "Use your little toy whistle."

Maish hit the siren immediately, the show-off, the cretin, and they moved across the empty courtyard and down the empty street, as in every apartment lights blossomed and a black or a brown face peered from a window.

He sat down near her and put his feet on the opposite wall to steady his knees while he used them to write against.

"I MIGHT AS WELL TRY TO WORK UP THE FIRST PART OF THE CASE HISTORY," he roared against the onslaught of the siren. "WHAT WAS YOUR FULL NAME, MOTHER?"

"WHAT?"

"YOUR FULL NAME?"

"MARTHA HENDRICKS CATLETT. HENDRICKS MY MAIDEN NAME." She spelled hoarsely.

He nodded. "WHERE BORN?"

"ROCHESTER."

"NEW YORK?" She nodded. "THOMAS YOUR HUSBAND'S NAME. MIDDLE INITIAL?"

"C. CHARLIE." Her face twisted and she shrieked, rolling on the litter.

This time he glanced at his watch. 9:42. The contraction lasted almost a minute.

"WHERE WAS YOUR HUSBAND BORN?"

"CHOCTAW, ALABAMA. DAMN LIAR."

"WHY?"

"TELLS KIDS HE'S PART INDIAN."

He nodded, grinning. He was beginning to like her. "WHERE DOES HE WORK?"

"UNEMPLOYEDEEE," the shout turning into a scream of anguish. He glanced at his watch again. 9:44. Two minutes.

Two minutes?

I can't deliver a baby, he thought dazedly.

His experience was limited to five days of obstetrical training during his third year in medical school, two years before.

Had he paid attention?

"YOU GOT A BEDPAN, DOC?"

"CAN'T YOU WAIT?"

"I DON'T THINK SO."

That did it; he knew the child was almost there. He lurched toward the front of the ambulance and touched Meyerson's shoulder. "PULL OVER AND STOP."

"WHY?"

"I WANT TO BUY YOU ANOTHER GODDAMMED CORNED BEEF SANDWICH," he screamed.

The ambulance slowed, halted, swallowed its siren-wail with a sound like a hiccough. It was suddenly very quiet except for the swoosh-swoosh-swoosh of cars passing very fast and very close.

He looked out and felt faint. They were on the bridge.

"You got those smoke signals, you know, traffic flares?" he asked Meyerson.

Maish nodded.

"Well, put them out so we won't get killed."

"You want me to do anything else?"

"Rub two sticks together and start a fire. Boil lots of water. Pray. Stay the hell away from me."

"Aaaagh," the woman said.

There was a small tank of nitrous oxide under the litter platform, and a face mask. And an obstetrical pack. He dragged them out. He began to think very hard. She certainly was not primipara, a first-time mother. But had there been five children, which would make her a multip? "How many kids do you have, mother?"

"Eight," she said, grunting.

"How many boys?" he asked, although he didn't give a damn. She was a grand-multip, which meant that there was a good chance she would drop the baby like a bomb.

"First two boys, all the rest girls," she said as he took off her shoes. There were no stirrups, of course; he lifted her feet and propped them against the benches on either side of the litter so the blood would flow back into her trunk instead of pooling in the legs.

Meyerson opened the door, letting in traffic noises. "Doc, got some change? I'll walk to a phone, call the hospital."

He gave him a dime.

"I have to make some other calls."

He gave him a handful of change, thrust him out of the ambulance, locked the door from the inside. The woman groaned. "I'm going to give you a little something for the pain, mother."

"Go to sleep?"

"No. Just like a good drunk."

She nodded and he gave her a whiff or two of nitrous oxide, guessing at the amount, being very conservative in case of error. It took effect quickly.

"Glad," she murmured.

"Of what?"

"Colored doctor. Never had colored doctor."

My God, poor lady, he thought. I would gladly allow the baby to be delivered by George Wallace or Louise Day Hicks if the one were an obstetrician or the other a midwife, and either were here.

He opened the obstetrical pack, which contained not much: a bulb for suctioning, a couple of hemostats, scissors and forceps. Pulling her dress up to her bosom, he exposed thighs like oaks and a pair of brown silk underpants, which he proceeded to cut from her.

She began to cry. "Present from my second-oldest girl."

"I'll buy you new ones."

Exposed, the stomach was awesome, an expanse of dusky flesh, fat-dappled and childbirth-mottled, on which her husband had lain and struggled in the only pleasure a poor black man could afford, the only joy that costs no money, cheaper than the movies, cheaper than booze, to deposit the tiny seed that had grown into this thing big and tight as a watermelon against her skin.

So low, so low.

I have a question from the peanut gallery, Doctor Robinson. How do I get an object as large as this fat woman's undoubtedly fat baby through an opening which—although I have seen smaller —is still relatively small?

So small.

It was an opportunity, he realized grimly, to lose *two* patients, to score strike two and strike three simultaneously, as it were.

There was a bottle of Zephiran. He took off the cap and poured it liberally over the vulva and the perineum, then he poured some on each of his hands and waved them until dry; not a satisfactory substitute for the dermasurgical scrub, but the best one available.

The woman was huffing, puffing, pushing, trying to blow her house down.

"How you doing, mother?" She merely grunted.

Please, Lord.

There was a great gush of water all over his white pants, Niagara Falls the color of straw. Her eyes were closed, the great leg-muscles knotted. A small bald head appeared in the opening, wearing the hair of the mother's unprepped genitalia like a tonsure.

Two more contractions and the head was clear. Spurgeon used the bulb to suction liquid out of the tiny mouth and then realized that she was having a tighter time with the shoulders. He made a small epesiotomy which bled very little. Next time she contracted he helped with his hands, and the entire baby was out in the cold world. He put two clips on the cord and cut between them, and then made a point of looking immediately at his watch; it was important for legal reasons that the time of birth be recorded.

One of his hands was holding the tiny neck and head, the other held the small rump, warm velvet, soft as . . . a baby's ass. Music-writer, music-maker, try and put this happening into sound, he told himself, and he knew it could not be done. The baby opened his mouth and made a prune of his face and gave a small cry, at the same time sending a stream of urine from the tiny penis—a well-hung boy.

"You have a fine son," he told the woman. "What's his name going to be?"

"What's your name, Doctor?"

"Spurgeon Robinson. You're going to name him after *me?*"

"Hell, no. Name him after his daddy. Just wanted to know your name."

He was still laughing a moment later when Meyerson and the police officer knocked on the door of the ambulance.

"Anything to help, Doc?" the policeman asked.

"I have everything under control, thank you." Behind them traffic was backed up for half a mile. The horns, he realized for the first time, were deafening.

"Wait a minute. Come in and hold Thomas Catlett for a moment, will you please?"

Delivery was just like any surgical procedure as far as the possibilities of shock were concerned. He started an intravenous dripping into her, dextrose and water.

He covered her with a blanket, deciding that he would wait for more aseptic conditions to deliver the placenta. Then he took the baby from the policeman.

"Mr. Meyerson," Dr. Robinson said with great dignity, "will you please drive us off this damn bridge?"

When they reached the hospital yard the first flash bulb made him blink as soon as he opened the ambulance door.

"Hold up the baby, Doc. Get in close to the mother," a cameraman ordered.

There were two photographers, three reporters. Two television crews.

What the hell, he asked himself, and then he remembered all the change Meyerson had needed to make telephone calls. He looked around wildly.

Maish was in the process of disappearing through the ambulance entrance. Like a leaf before the wind—no; like the March Hare —Meyerson scuttled.

Much later, he reached his room. He peeled off his whites, which smelled strongly of blood and amniotic fluid. The shower down the hall beckoned but for a long time he simply sat on the bed in his underwear, doing little thinking but feeling very fine.

Champagne, he thought finally. He would shower and change and get two splits of very fine champagne. One he would share with Adam Silverstone. The other he would share with Dorothy.

Dorothy.

He went out and dropped two dimes into the hall telephone and dialed Dorothy's number.

Mrs. Williams answered.

"Do you know what time it is?" she said sharply when he asked for Dorothy.

"Yuh. That's one of the things about a doctor's life. You better get used to that, Momma."

"Spurgeon?" Dorothy said in a moment. "What happened at the Conference?"

"I'm still going to be an intern."

"Was it awful?"

"They rubbed my nose in it the way you do to a puppy."

"Are you all right?"

"I'm fine. The world's greatest living authority on the odontoid process." Suddenly husky, he found himself babbling to her about the big fat soul sister and the sweetest little soft-assed well-hung baby boy delivered to life because Dr. Robinson was a fearless front-line physician.

"I love you, Spurgeon," she said, very quietly but distinctly, and he could picture her standing there in the kitchen in her nightgown with her beautiful hand cupping the receiver and her mother hovering like a great dark butterfly.

"Listen," he said. But loudly, not caring if Adam Silverstone or anybody else in the universe heard him. "I love you, too, even more than I want your nubile Nubian body. Which is a good deal more than considerably."

"You're crazy," she said in her old maid school teacher's voice.

"Uh-huh. But when your ticket into the great white middle classes is finally punched, I'll be the canceling instrument."

He thought she was laughing, but he couldn't be sure because she had hung up on him. He blew a loud, wet kiss into the buzzing telephone.

Chapter 9: Harland Longwood

As his illness wore on Harland Longwood became accustomed to it, as if it were an ugly and hated garment he couldn't cast off for economic reasons. He found himself able to sleep less and less at night, a mixed misfortune since he accomplished his most effective writing when the apartment building in Cambridge was muffled in black velvet and the world intruded through his closed windows with a minimum of sound.

He wrote swiftly, using material accumulated with painstaking slowness over the course of many years, and completing a careful second draft of each chapter before proceeding to the next. When he had finished three chapters, he knew it was time for the test, and after a great deal of deliberation he chose three eminent surgeons, each living far enough from Boston so that word of Longwood's illness would not yet have reached him. The chapter on thoracic surgery went to a professor at McGill, the chapter on hernia went to a surgeon at Loma Linda Hospital in Los Angeles, the chapter on surgical technique to a man at the Mayo Clinic in Minnesota.

When their critiques arrived he knew he wasn't simply chasing a foolish, ego-born dream.

The McGill professor spoke glowingly about the thoracic section and requested permission to publish it in a journal he edited. The Mayo surgeon offered high praise but pointed out an additional area for discussion that would be of value, which added three weeks of labor to Longwood's task. The Californian, a jealous pedant with whom he had contended for years, grudgingly conceded the value of the material and added three hair-splitting editorial corrections with which Longwood disagreed and which he ignored.

He wrote with a pen, filling lined paper with a cramped, spidery script. Occasionally now the need for sleep overcame him in the daylight hours when he had finished a stretch of writing on the book, and for the first time in his life he began to stay home from the hospital with frequency, grateful for Bester Kender's ability to take over.

He felt safe enough now to mention the book to Elizabeth one day at lunch and was touched when she volunteered to type the manuscript, believing that she wished to watch over him. For two days she played at the typewriter like a child with a toy, and on the third morning after twenty minutes she got up and spent a long time before the mirror putting on her hat.

"I promised Edna Brewster I'd go shopping with her, Uncle Harland," she said, and when he nodded she kissed his cheek.

In a few days it was Bernice Lovett who was ill and needed visiting.

Two mornings later she said Helen Parkinson had insisted that she help the committee planning the new Vincent Club show.

After that her presence was needed by Susan Silberger, Ruth Moore, Nancy Roberts, while the pile of untyped manuscript grew at the side of the typewriter.

He wondered who the man was this time.

The Latin American wasn't strong enough to keep her steady, he thought, finally justified in his disapproval of Meomartino.

Always she stayed at the apartment a little while and then left, having carefully named the woman with whom she would spend the day. It took him only until the Helen Parkinson morning to figure things out.

"In case your husband calls, you mean," he said when she told him.

Liz looked at him and then smiled. "Now, don't you be silly and say things we'd both regret, Uncle Harland," she said.

"Elizabeth, you came here to help me. Would you like to talk with me about . . . anything? Is there no way I can help you?"

"No," she said.

Instead of thinking about it he called a secretarial agency and arranged for the services of a part-time typist.

The worst times were the nights he spent with the dialysis machine, held fast by needle fingers while the tubes turned bright red as it sucked the blood from him like a vampire and he lay unable to move from the bed through the long hours, the prisoner of the thing which now gave him life.

It was not noisy, but it splashed quietly. He knew it was an inanimate product of man's mechanical ability, yet at times the splashing seemed like soft mocking laughter.

Whenever he was freed he fled it in relief and later that day went out on the town like a sailor on leave, a drink at the Ritz-Carlton, dinner at Locke-Ober at which he often broke the rules of his diet, feeling that the low-sodium restriction literally deprived him of some of the salt of living. Invariably he ordered lots of after-dinner brandy. He never had been close with money but now he astonished Louie, the waiter who had served him for thirty years, by the lavishness of his tips.

Wracked with desire to finish the book, he worked every night; he wrote as quickly as he dared, observing himself with the detachment of a stranger watching a horserace and wondering with ironic amusement who was going to win.

Once or twice Elizabeth left the little boy at the apartment with him and Longwood played on the floor with his great-nephew while the sun streamed in through the windows, and in his weakness he felt the same age as the boy, content to wheel the toy cars Miguel had brought with him, the blue one pushed by the small chubby hand and the red one by the long bony fingers that lately had held surgical instruments, around the rug and through the chairs and under the dining-room table. Sometimes in the afternoon he took the boy for real rides in a real car, short trips usually, but one afternoon he found himself on Rte. 128 with the accelerator held down and the speedometer needle going up, up, up and the car being hurled down the straight ribbon of road.

"You're going too fast, dear," Frances said mildly.

"I know," he said, grinning.

Then he heard what he thought was an ambulance and by the time he realized his mistake the state trooper had pulled his motorcycle alongside and he stopped the car by the side of the road.

The trooper looked at his gray hair and the physician's registration plates on the car. "Is it an emergency, Doctor?"

"Yes," he said.

"Want me to escort you?"

"No, thank you," he said, and the trooper nodded and saluted and went away.

When he looked again Frances had disappeared before he had had a chance to ask her what to do about Elizabeth, and the little boy was sleeping on the front seat, curled up like a kitten. He began to tremble, but he forced himself to resume driving and returned to Cambridge at twenty miles an hour, hugging the right side of the road.

He never took the boy for a ride in the real car again.

The cannulas festered in his flesh. They moved the shunt several times until the small incision scars decorated his leg. The toxins had been accumulating in his system and one afternoon his entire body began to itch. He scratched until blood came and then he lay in bed and writhed, the tears streaming down his face.

That night he went to the hospital for dialysis, and when they saw the marks of his scratching they prescribed Benadryl and Stelazine, and Dr. Kender told him he would have to go on the dialysis machine three times a week instead of two. They gave him Monday, Wednesday and Friday at 9 a.m. instead of Tuesday and Thursday nights. That meant that even if he felt well on those days he couldn't come into the hospital to work. He still telephoned Silverstone or Meomartino every night for a report on the Service, but he stopped making any attempt to go on rounds.

Occasionally when he was alone he wept. Once he looked up to see Frances sitting near his bed.

"Can't you help me?" he asked her.

She smiled at him. "You have to help yourself, Harland," she said.

"What could we have done for this man, gentlemen?" he asked the Death Committee.

But no voices answered.

He made no attempt to go back to Appleton Chapel or any other church, but one night as he sat and worked on the book he felt a sudden new certainty that he would finish it. The knowledge was very strong. He felt it not in a burst of colored lights or rising music the way such moments were always displayed on the bad movies televised every Easter morning. It was simply a quiet, forceful promise.

"Thank you, sir," he said.

The following morning before he reported to the machine he went into Mrs. Bergstrom's room and stood by her bed. She appeared to be asleep but in a few moments she opened her eyes.

"How do you feel?" he asked.

She smiled. "Not very well. How about you?"

"Do you know about me?" he said with interest.

She nodded. "We're in the same boat. You're the doctor who's sick, aren't you?"

So even the patients knew. It was the kind of information that swept through a hospital.

"Is there anything I can do for you?" he said.

She licked her lips. "Dr. Kender and his people are taking care of everything. You shouldn't worry. They'll take care of you, too."

"I'm sure they will," he said.

"They're wonderful. It's good to have somebody you can put your trust in."

"Yes, it is," he said.

Kender came in and told him they were waiting to place him on the machine. They left the room together and in the corridor Longwood turned to the younger man. "She has a terrible faith in you. She believes that you are infallible."

"That happens. It's not a bad thing. It helps us," Kender said.

"It's unfortunate, of course, that I am aware of your limitations," he said.

Kender nodded. "Yes, it is, Doctor," he said.

Longwood lay down and let the nurse connect him to the machine. In a moment it began to splash mockingly. He lay back and closed his eyes. Gently scratching the itch, he began at the beginning and told God everything.

Chapter 10: Rafael Meomartino

Meomartino got home that night as Huntley was saying goodnight to Brinkley. Liz was lying on the living room couch in a house dress, her shoes on the floor and her hair just slightly disarranged and her fatigue accentuating the faint lines around her eyes. She turned her head and offered her cheek to be kissed. "How was your day?"

"Terrible," he said. "Where's the boy?"

"In bed."

"This early?"

"Don't wake him. He's worn himself out, and me, too."

"Daddy?" Miguel called from his room.

He went in and sat on the bed. "How are you?"

"Good," the boy said. He was afraid of the dark and they kept a lamp on the bureau with a small bulb burning.

"You can't get to sleep?"

"No," he said. When he took his hand out from under the covers Rafe saw it was dirty.

"Didn't you have a bath?"

Miguel shook his head, and Rafe went into the bathroom and ran a warm tub and then carried the boy from his bed and undressed him and bathed him very gently. Ordinarily Miguel thrashed and splashed but now he was sleepy and he lay still. He was beginning to grow faster than his flesh could keep up. His hip-bones protruded and his legs and arms were thin.

"You are getting to be big," Rafe said.

"Like you."

Rafe nodded. He rubbed him down with a towel and dressed him in clean pajamas and carried him back to the bedroom.

"Make a tent," Miguel asked.

He hesitated, weary and hungry.

"Please," the boy said.

So he went into his study and came back with an armload of books. He took a blanket from the bed and spread it across the space between the bed and the bureau, anchoring each corner of the blanket with four or five books. Then he snapped off the light and he and his son crawled into the tent. The acrylic carpet was softer than sod. The little boy snuggled up to him and gripped him with his arms.

"Tell me about the rain. You know."

"It is raining very hard outside. Everything is cold and wet," Rafe said obediently.

"What else?" He yawned.

"In the forest the small animals are trembling with cold as they dig under leaves and the earth to get warm. The birds have placed their heads under their wings."

"Aw."

"But are we cold and wet?"

"No," the boy murmured.

"Why?"

"A tent."

"That is absolutely right." He kissed the still baby-soft cheek and began to touch his son gently between the thin shoulder-blades, half pat, half stroke.

In a little while the quiet, even breathing told him the child was asleep. Carefully, he disengaged, then crawled out and disassembled the tent and returned Miguel to his bed.

In the living room Liz was still lying on the couch.

"You didn't have to do that," she said.

"What?"

"Bathe him. I would have given him his bath in the morning."

"I don't mind bathing him."

"He's never neglected. I am some things and I'm not some other things, but I am a good mother."

"What's for dinner?" he said.

"I have a casserole. I just have to turn on the oven to heat it."

"You stay there," he said. "I'll do it."

Waiting for the food to warm, he thought that a drink would revive both of them. He was searching for the bitters in a kitchen cabinet when he saw the Beefeater's bottle behind a round oatmeal box. It was still cold when he touched it, having obviously been in the refrigerator until just before he came home.

There comes a time, he thought, when you face things.

He placed the bottle on a tray with two glasses and carried it into the living room.

"Martini?"

She looked at the bottle but said nothing. He poured the drink and handed it to her.

She sipped. "It should be colder," she said. "But otherwise I couldn't have made a better one myself."

"Liz," he said, "why the scene from *The Lost Weekend?* You want to drink during the day? Drink during the day. You don't have to hide the bottles from me."

"Hold me," she said in a moment. "Please."

He lay down beside her and held her in his arms, balancing on the edge of the narrow sofa.

"Why have you been drinking?"

She leaned back and looked at him. "It helps," she said.

"With what?"

"I become frightened."

"Why?"

"You don't need me anymore."

"Liz—"

"But it's true. When I first met you, you needed me terribly. Now you've grown very strong. Sufficient unto yourself."

"Must I be weak to need you?"

"Yes," she said. "I'm going to spoil things, Rafe. I know it. I always do."

"That's nonsense, Liz. Don't you see how silly that is?"

"Before this it never really mattered. After I messed things up with Bookstein and we were divorced I was actually happier. But I can't stand the thought of messing things up again."

"We're not going to mess anything up," he said helplessly.

"When you're home everything is all right. But the damned hospital takes you back every thirty-six hours. Next year when you go into practice it will be worse."

He traced her lips with his finger, but she moved her head. "If you could go to bed with the hospital I'd never see you," she said.

"Next year it will be better," he said. "Not worse."

"No," she said. "When I remember my Aunt Frances I always remember her waiting for my uncle to come home. She almost never saw him. He sold his practice and went to work at the hospital only after she was gone. When it was too late."

"You won't spend your life waiting for me," he said. "I promise you."

Her arms tightened around him. To keep from falling from the couch he held her where the back of the thigh spread, a solid grasping place. In a little while her breathing became slow and even against his neck; she fell asleep like the little boy, he thought. He felt desire but did nothing about it, unwilling to spoil the comfortable intimacy. Presently he dozed himself, dreaming unaccountably that he was a small boy again asleep in his bedroom in the big house in Havana. It was an incredibly clear and realistic dream, down to the certain knowledge that his mother and father were in the big carved-wood bed in the master bedroom down the hall and Guillermo was asleep next door.

The buzzer on the stove in the Boston apartment awakened them together, the sleeping dream-family and the man whose flesh-and-blood wife leaped up to turn off the oven timer before it disturbed their son.

Meomartino lay there on the sofa.

The television was still broadcasting news and he watched a thirteen-year-old South Vietnamese who had been adopted by an American infantry regiment against his parents' wishes. The soldiers had given the boy cigarettes and beer and a rifle and already he had killed two Vietcong.

"How did it feel to kill two men?" the TV reporter asked.

"It felt good. They were bad," the boy said, although he had never seen his two slain countrymen until just before his small finger had pressed the G.I. trigger and the automatic rifle, constructed to work so simply that the mentality of the user was not a factor, had fired.

Rafe got up and turned off the set.

She doesn't know a damned thing about me, he thought.

Sometimes now he dreamed again of war.

The nightmares always began as the Bay of Pigs and included

Guillermo, but usually they became Vietnam. As a naturalized citizen who was a physician he faced a military call as soon as he finished the final year of residency, and many of the young doctors who had been in the hospital the previous year were now in Vietnam. Already one had been killed and one wounded. This was a war that did not respect doctors, he reflected gloomily. Surgeons had been sent out on the line instead of enlisted medics, and hospitals in Saigon were as exposed as aid stations.

His wife was half right, he decided. He *had* become stronger.

By now he faced with courage the fact that he was a coward.

It was very unusual. The note merely said *Are you free for lunch?* It was signed Harland Longwood. No title. If it had been business, Surgeon-in-Chief would have been typed neatly below the signature. That meant the meeting probably would have something to do with Liz. The only personal subject Rafe discussed with his wife's uncle was his wife.

He stopped at the old man's office and told his secretary he was available for lunch. He had eaten alone with Dr. Longwood only once, five days before he and Liz had been married. They had gone to the Men's Bar at Locke-Ober, where amid all the pewter and polished mahogany Dr. Longwood had tried to suggest, delicately and glumly, that while she was far too good for a foreigner she was still a handful of problems, alcoholic and sexual and others that he merely hinted at, and Dr. Meomartino would be doing a great favor for all concerned and especially for himself if he were to stop seeing her at once.

And so they were married.

This time Longwood took him to Pier Four. The soft-shelled crabs were very fine. The wine was mellow and precisely chilled. It helped Rafe through the arduous small talk.

Over the black coffee, which he drank alone, he ran out of patience. "What's on your mind, sir?"

Dr. Longwood took a small sip of brandy. "I am curious about where you will be going next year."

"I suppose into private practice. If by some miracle I escape the army."

"Your wife is a woman with problems. She requires stability," Longwood said.

"I understand that."

"You haven't made arrangements yet, for next year?"

It told Rafe at once the reason for the invitation to lunch. The old man was afraid he was going to take Liz and the boy half a world away.

Longwood really had begun to look very ill, he thought pityingly. He looked away, out over the crowded restaurant. "I've made no arrangements yet, although I suppose it's time for me to start. Boston is top-heavy with surgeons, and if I were to open an office here I'd have to compete with some of the best men in the world. I might try to join one of them as an associate. Do you know of anyone with a busy practice who is looking for help?"

"There are one or two men." He took a cigar case from an inside pocket, opened it, offered one to Rafe, who refused. Dr. Longwood clipped the cigar and leaned over as Rafe snapped the lighter, then nodded his thanks as he puffed to start the ash. "You have some independent income. You don't need a large initial salary. Correct?"

Rafe nodded.

"Have you thought of a career with a medical school?"

"No."

"We'll be adding an instructor of surgery in September."

"Are you offering me the appointment?"

"No, I'm not," Dr. Longwood said carefully. "We'll be talking with several other people. I think your only competition might be from Adam Silverstone."

"He's a good man," Meomartino said reluctantly.

"He's well thought of, but so are you. If you were to go after the job I'd be careful not to influence the selection, of course. Still, I believe you'd stand an excellent chance on your merits."

Rafe saw with wry inner amusement that the old man offered praise to him with the same lack of enthusiasm he displayed himself when talking of Adam's merits.

"A university job means research," he said. "Silverstone has been working with Kender's dogs. I have learned to my great edification that I'm not a researcher."

"It doesn't have to mean research. In the scramble for grant money and laboratory buildings, medical schools have lost sight of their reason for existence—the students—and we've started to realize this. Good teachers are going to be increasingly important, because teaching is going to be increasingly difficult."

"At any rate, there's my military service," Rafe said.

"We request deferments for medical faculty people," Dr. Longwood said. "The deferments are renewable annually."

His eyes said nothing but Rafe had the uncomfortable feeling that now Longwood was smiling inside.

"I'll have to think about it," he said.

For the next two days he tried to tell himself there was a chance he wouldn't go after the job.

Then the morning of the Mortality Conference came and he sat in dumb shame while Longwood nailed Spurgeon Robinson to the library wall, though he knew he could take the brunt of the attack —share the crucifixion—with a statement that the intern had called him before releasing the woman from the hospital.

All it would have taken was a simple declarative sentence.

Afterwards he attempted feebly to convince himself that he didn't make it because Dr. Longwood looked so ill he had wanted the meeting to finish as quickly as possible.

But he was aware his silence had been the first step in his candidacy.

That evening, on his way to the dining room, he met Adam Silverstone emerging from the elevator.

"I see you've left the sick-bed," he said. "Feeling better?"

"I'll live."

"Perhaps you should rest a bit longer. Those viruses can be nasty."

"Listen. I know you sandbagged Spurgeon Robinson this morning."

Meomartino stared but said nothing.

"He's absolutely vulnerable to that kind of screwing," Silverstone said. "From now on, what you do to him you do to me."

"That's heroic of you," Meomartino said quietly.

"I'm equipped to handle that kind of situation, you see."

"I'll make a note."

"My motto is, 'Don't get mad, get even,'" Adam said. He nodded and moved on ahead, into the dining room.

Rafe made no move to follow. Instead of hunger he felt the kind of soul-darkness he hadn't known for years. He needed family cheer, he told himself; perhaps Liz's reaction to the news that he would try for the teaching job would wipe away some of the ugliness.

He called and asked Harry Lee to cover for him while he went home to eat.

It was an unprecedented request, and the resident did not quite succeed in concealing his surprise as he agreed. I should do it more often, Rafe thought. The little boy isn't going to know his own father.

The rush hour was long past and the traffic on the Expressway, although not light, moved steadily. He skirted the city in the car and then re-entered it to drive to the lane off Charles Street and park in front of the mews, the car almost but not quite blocking future traffic on the narrow street. His watch showed 7:42 as he climbed the single flight of stairs. Time enough, he thought, to grab a sandwich, kiss the boy, squeeze his wife twice and drive back to the hospital without even being missed.

"Liz?" he called as he let himself in with his key.

"She's not home." It was the baby-sitter whose name he never remembered, and a boy sitting next to her on the couch. Both were slightly rumpled and obviously interrupted. *Perdonen Vds., niños,* he thought.

"Where is she?"

"She said if you called to tell you she was meeting her uncle for dinner."

"Dr. Longwood?"

"Yes, sir."

"When?"

"She didn't say." The girl stood. "Ah, Doctor, I'd like you to meet my friend, Paul."

He nodded, wondering whether it was in his son's interest for her to have company while she baby-sat. Perhaps the boy planned to leave before Liz and her uncle got home. "Where's Miguel?"

"In bed. He just fell asleep."

He went into the kitchen and took off his jacket and draped it over the chair, feeling like an intruder in his own apartment as the conversation in the living room became a series of short whispered sentences and an occasional muted giggle.

There was bread, slightly stale, and the makings of a ham and cheese. There was also a Beefeater's bottle less than half full, containing martinis, which he realized she would have removed from the refrigerator before his scheduled return from the hospital next morning.

He made the sandwich and opened a small bottle of ginger ale and carried them through the living room and into his son's bedroom, closing the door against the curious stares of the two young people on the couch.

Miguel was asleep, a long orange stuffed serpent named Irving lying across his face, the pillow on the floor. He set the sandwich and the drink on the bureau and picked up the pillow and stood gazing at his son in the unsatisfactory dimness of the night light. Should he move the stuffed animal? He knew very well there was no danger of asphyxiation but he moved it anyway, giving him a chance to look at the small face. Miguel stirred but did not waken. The boy had dark, coarse hair worn Beatle-style even at the age of two and one-half, long in back and cut in a bang Liz loved and Rafe did not like at all. Liz's uncle hated the haircut even more than he disliked the boy's "foreign-sounding" name, for which he substituted the more acceptable Mike. Miguel had masculine, even ugly ears that protruded from his head and distressed his mother. Otherwise he was handsome, tough and wiry but with his mother's fair skin and his paternal grandmother's warm-blooded delicate features. The *Señora. Mamacita.*

The telephone rang.

He reached it before the baby-sitter and recognized Longwood's precise tones without need of further identification.

"I thought you were on the ward tonight."

"I came home to eat."

Longwood inquired after several cases and Rafe reported, each aware there was no possibility that the Surgeon-in-Chief would attempt to assume active direction of the patient's welfare. Against his ear in the background were restaurant noises, low murmur of voices, clink of metal against glass.

"May I say hello to Elizabeth?" Longwood said when Rafe was through.

"Isn't she with you?"

"Good grief, was I supposed to meet her?"

"For dinner."

There was a moment's silence, and then the old boy tried hard. *"Damn* that secretary. That girl has my appointment book completely screwed up. I don't know how I'll ever explain to Elizabeth. Will you give her my most abject apologies?" The embarrassment in his voice was genuine, but there was more, and Rafe realized with sudden distaste that the additional ingredient was sympathy.

"I will," he said.

After he hung up he retrieved the sandwich and the ginger ale and sat at the foot of his son's bed and chewed and drank and swallowed and thought about a lot of things, watching the gentle, steady rise and fall of Miguel's chest as he breathed. The child's resemblance to the *Señora* was especially strong in the half-light.

In a little while he abandoned the apartment to the young lovers and returned to the hospital.

Early the next morning Dr. Kender and Lewis Chin went into Mrs. Bergstrom and removed the bit of spoiled flesh that had once been Peggy Weld's kidney. They needed no pathology report to tell them the wasted organ had been completely rejected by Mrs. Bergstrom's body.

Afterwards in the surgeons' lounge they all sat and drank bitter coffee.

"What now?" Harry Lee asked.

Kender shrugged. "The only thing left is to try again with a kidney from a cadaver."

"Mrs. Bergstrom's sister will have to be told," Rafe said.

"I've already told her," Kender said.

When he left the lounge and walked to Peggy Weld's room Rafe found her packing.

"You're leaving the hospital?"

She nodded. Her eyes were red but calm. "Dr. Kender said there's no need for me to stay any longer."

"Where will you be going?"

"Only to Lexington. I'm not going to leave Boston until my sister is finished with this thing. One way or another."

"I'd like to see you some evening," he said.

"You're married."

"How do you know?"

"I asked."

He was silent.

She smiled. "She doesn't understand you, I suppose."

"I don't understand her."

"Well, that isn't my problem."

"No, it isn't." He looked at her. "Do me a favor?"

She waited.

"Use fewer cosmetics. You're very lovely. I'm sorry about the kidney. I'm sorry if I was the one who convinced you to give it."

"I am, too," she said. "But I wouldn't be if it hadn't been rejected. So you can stop feeling guilty, because I make my own decisions. Even about my makeup."

"Is there anything I can do for you?"

She shook her head. "I have things pretty well sorted out." She patted his hand and smiled. "Doctor, a girl with only one kidney can't afford to reach out to every man who wants to mess around."

"I don't want to mess around," he said unconvincingly. "I'd like to get to know you."

"We don't have a thing in common." The suitcase snapped shut with a hard, decisive click.

He went to the office and called Liz.

"What a shame I missed you last night," she said.

"Did you enjoy dinner?"

"Yes, but what a stupid thing. I got the dates confused. I didn't have a dinner date with Uncle Harland at all."

"I know," he said. "What did you do?"

"I finally called Edna Brewster. Luckily Bill was working late, so she and I ate at Charles's and then sat around their place and caught up. Are you coming home?"

"Yes," he said.

"I'll tell Miguel."

He cleaned the top of his desk and closed the door and changed out of his whites. Then he sat down and looked up Edna Brewster's number in the book.

She was Liz's friend, not his, and she sounded puzzled but pleased to hear from him.

"I've been trying to think of something special to get Liz for Christmas," he said. "You girls all have everything."

She groaned. "I am the worst one to come to for gift suggestions."

"Not suggestions. Just keep your ears open when you're with her. Try to find out if there's something she'd really love to have."

She promised to spy faithfully and he thanked her. "When are we going to see you people? Liz was saying just the other day she hasn't seen you for ages."

"Months. Isn't it terrible?" she said. "We never seem to have time to see the people we really want to see. Let's the four of us get together for bridge. Tell Liz I'll call her." She giggled. "On second thought, you'd better not tell her we talked. It'll be our secret. Deal?"

"Deal," he said.

Chapter 11: Adam Silverstone

Adam blamed his fury at Meomartino for driving him from his bed, but he returned to duty off-stride and brooding, inclined to remember at unlikely moments the way Gaby Pender had rested unsullied in the sun with her eyes closed, her perfect urgent smallness, her shy and broken laughter, as if she were uncertain she had a right to laugh.

He tried to push her from his mind by crowding in everything else.

Dr. Longwood informed him of the appointment that would be made in the surgical faculty and he understood suddenly what had happened to Meomartino. He told Spurgeon about it as they sat in his room and drank beer chilled in the snow on the window sill.

"I'm going to nail that job down," he said. "Meomartino isn't going to get it." His fingers throttled an empty beer can, making dents.

"Not just because you dislike him," Spurgeon said. "You can't dislike anybody that much."

"That's only part of it. I really want the appointment."

"It fits into the Silverstone Greater Scheme of Things?"

Adam smiled and nodded.

"The prestige job leading straight to one that pays the big money?"

"Now you've got it."

"You're just conning yourself, buddy-boy. You know what the Silverstone Greater Scheme of Things really is?"

"What?" Adam said.

"Bullshit and cow dung."

Adam just smiled.

Spurgeon shook his head. "You think you've got everything figured out, don't you, man."

"Everything I can think of," Adam said.

One of the things he had figured out was that Spurgeon's lack of
familiarity with the odontoid process was a sign the intern needed
to know more about anatomy. When he offered to work with him
Spurgeon accepted eagerly, and Dr. Sack gave them permission to
dissect in the pathology laboratory of the medical school. They
worked there several times a week, Spurgeon learning quickly and
Adam enjoying the drill.

One evening Sack wandered in and nodded a greeting. He said
little but instead of leaving he pulled up a chair and watched. Two
nights later he returned, and this time when they were finished he
asked Adam to come into his office.

"We could use some part-time help in the Pathology Department
at the hospital," he said. "Want to give it to us?"

The work wouldn't pay him nearly as much as moonlighting in
the Emergency Room at Woodborough, but neither would it drain
his energies or cut as deeply into his valuable sleep-time. "Yes, sir,"
he said without hesitation.

"Jerry Lobsenz did a good job on you. I don't suppose we could
lure you into Pathology next year?"

The offers were beginning to come in, signs that there was an end
to the endless struggle. "I'm afraid not."

"The money not big enough?"

"That's part of it, but not all of it. I just wouldn't want to do it full-
time." It wasn't in the Silverstone Greater Scheme of Things.

Sack nodded. "Well, you're honest about it. Let me know if you
ever change your mind."

So he had very little reason now to leave the hospital at all. The
old red-brick buildings became his world. His hours in Pathology
were irregular but not unpleasant. He enjoyed working by himself
in the singing silence of the white lab, aware it was an environment
in which some people could not function but where once again he
was able to work at high efficiency.

He divided his free time between Pathology and the animal lab,
where he was learning a great deal from Kender. He was struck by

the complete lack of resemblance between the two men who had taught him the most. Lobsenz had been a small, introspective Jew, with the slightest trace of German accent that became discernible when he was tired. And Kender . . .

Kender was Kender.

But perhaps he was trying to crowd in too much. For the first time in his life he was sleeping poorly on a regular basis, and he was dreaming again, not the furnace room dream, the diving one.

Always at the dream's beginning he was climbing the ladder into blinding sunlight. It was very real: he could feel the coolness of the steel frame vibrate in his hands whenever it was hit by the wind. The wind worried him. As he climbed he looked straight up to the perch at the top, where the ladder narrowed high above him like a pencil point, until the sun made his eyes tear and he had to close them. He never looked down. When he finally reached the perch he stepped onto it and looked out at the world stretching one hundred feet below him, his buttocks tight, his mouth dry, the platform swaying, shuddering in the wind, the swimming pool flashing tiny and hard in the sun, more like a dog-tag than a life net. He stepped off the platform, let his head fall back, spread his arms as his body twisted high, high in the air, and felt the wind catch him like a sail, pushing, destroying his balance, throwing him off just enough. He tried desperately to compensate, knowing he might as well miss the pool altogether as land anywhere but in the deepest part where the water was ten feet of shock-cushion. He would land badly, he thought dully, hanging grotesquely suspended, the water rushing up at him. He would be hurt and he would never be a surgeon.

O God.

The dream always ended halfway between the top of the tower and the water. He would wake and lie in the dark and tell himself that he was never going to do anything that foolish again, that he was already a surgeon, that nothing would stop him now.

Why was the dream recurring?

He could think of no reason until, one night in Pathology, he closed his eyes and breathing deep was transported by a scent, the raw essence of formaldehyde, through time and distance into Lobsenz's pathology lab, where he had first had the diving dream.

It was during his third year at the medical school in Pennsylvania, the period of his most extreme financial difficulty. The shame and disgust of the aging mistress and her dole were behind him. The coal-shoveling had paid his way through the cold winter, lasting until early spring when he began to fall asleep in class regularly, and then he had quit because if he had kept the job he would have been dropped from two courses. He became so accustomed to desperation that most of the time he was able to ignore it. He already owed six thousand in student loans. He was behind in his room rent, but the landlady was willing to wait. He eliminated lunches on the grounds that he was eating too much and for two weeks was annoyed by midday hunger and afternoon faintness, but then from the beginning of April until mid-May he pulled duty at the hospital and by cultivating the right nurses ate ward food at no expense.

In June he considered a job as a surgical technician but realized with regret that he couldn't take it; the meager pay wouldn't allow him to save enough to insure survival through the final medical school year. He had reluctantly decided to return to the resort in the Poconos when he saw a tiny advertisement in the Philadelphia *Bulletin,* seeking professional divers for a water show on the Jersey shore. Barney's Aquacade was a boardwalk attraction featuring two Filipinos and a Mexican, but they needed five divers for the show, and Adam was one of the two college divers who was hired. It paid thirty-five dollars a day, seven days a week. Although he never had gone off at one hundred feet, it was not at all difficult to learn how to scoop: one of the Filipinos showed him, in innumerable dry runs, how to throw his arms back as soon as he hit the surface of the pool and tuck his knees into his chest, so he would slide down the ten feet of water in an arc and end up gently sitting on the bottom.

The first time up the tower the height was the worst part of the experience.

The steel ladder felt too smooth, almost slippery, impossible to be retained in his grasp. He climbed very slowly, making certain that one hand had closed tightly around the rung before releasing the other hand and moving his feet higher. He tried looking straight ahead, toward the horizon, but the great dying sun was still there and it frightened him, a golden evil eye—he paused in his ascent, hooking a rung with the inside of his elbow while his fingers made the sign of the horns, *scutta mal occhio,* poo-poo-poo—and he resolutely looked up and fixed his gaze on the high perch, which grew in size and proximity with agonizing slowness as he climbed, but which he finally reached. When his feet were on the platform, letting go of the ladder and turning around was a very difficult thing to do, but he did it.

It was only the equivalent of five stories, he knew, but it seemed more; nothing lay between him and the surface, and all neighboring structures were built close to the ground. He stood on his aerie and looked to the right, where the boardwalk ended and the coast took a dip and a turn, and to the left, where far away and below, tiny cars crawled over a miniaturized roller coaster track.

Hello, God.

"ANY TIME," the impatient voice of Benson, the manager, floated up.

He stepped out.

The full gainer was very easy. There was so much more time than when doing it from the twelve-foot board. But he had never before held himself rigid through so long a drop. He began the scoop as soon as his toes touched the water. In another moment he had glided forward to land lop-sidedly on the bottom, on his right buttock. He bumped hard, but not too hard. He righted himself and sat there, bubbling and grinning, then pushed himself off the cement and shot to the surface.

Everybody seemed unimpressed, but after two days of practice he began to participate in the shows, two a day.

The other new man, whose name was Jensen, turned out to be a beautiful diver, former varsity at Exeter and Brown. He was in graduate school, creative writing at Iowa, and was an unpaid playwright at a nearby stock theater. He touted Adam onto an inexpensive boarding house where at night there were mice as loud as lions and some noise and scuffling, but the mattress was firm. The weather held and so did his nerves. A girl in the water ballet with beautiful breasts began to squeeze him with her eyes and he made plans to take her to his bosom and vice versa. He had long talks about Eliot and Pound with Jensen, who maybe would turn out to be his friend. He dove like a machine, thinking a lot about how he would behave when he went back to school an enormously wealthy man.

The stories of accidents seemed like fables. But on the fifth day Jensen scooped prematurely and landed in the pool on his back. He was white-faced with pain when he emerged, but able to walk away and call his own taxi to take him to the hospital. He didn't return to the show. When Adam telephoned, the hospital said his condition was fair and that he had been admitted for observation. The following day was gray but rainless, with a blustery wind that quivered the ladder and caused the platform to sway. They that stand high have many blasts to shake them. Shakespeare. Adam made his two dives without incident, and next morning was relieved to find that the sun was out and the wind had disappeared. That evening he made his first dive almost without thinking about it. During the second show he climbed the ladder and stood on the perch in the yellow illumination of the big spotlights. Far out to sea a trawler's lights revealed her mysterious distant presence to him, and the lights of the boardwalk stretched like scattered jewelry.

"You goddamned fool," he told himself.

He was not at all physically afraid. But he knew suddenly that he was not going to jump, simply because it would not be worth the money he could earn that summer if he were to injure himself in a way that would hamper him as a doctor or prevent him from becoming a surgeon. He turned around and started down the ladder.

"ARE YOU ALL RIGHT?" Benson asked over the microphone. "DO YOU WANT SOMEBODY TO COME UP AND HELP YOU DOWN?" The crowd's buzzing came up at him like an insect sound.

He paused and signaled that he was all right and needed no assistance, but this forced him to look straight down for the first time, and suddenly he was not all right at all. He proceeded downward very carefully. He was less than halfway down when the booing and jeering began; there were a lot of young bloods in the audience.

Benson was furious when he reached the bottom.

"Are you sick, Silverstone?"

"No."

"Then get the hell up there. Everybody gets scared once in a while. They'll give you a bigger hand than anybody if you go up again and dive."

"No."

"You'll never dive professionally again, you yellow little Jew bastard. I'll see to it!"

"Thank you very much," Adam said politely, meaning it.

The next morning he took a bus back to Philadelphia and the day after that he went to work in the hospital as a surgical technician, a job which allowed him to learn a great deal about operating room procedure.

Three weeks before the beginning of the fall semester he read a notice on the bulletin board at the medical school.

> *If you are interested in anatomy and*
> *need money I may have a job for you.*
> *Apply at the coroner's office.*
> Gerald M. Lobsenz, M.D.
> Medical Examiner
> Philadelphia County,
> Pennsylvania.

The County Morgue was an old three-story stone building badly in need of a sand-blasting, the Coroner's office a cluttered, dusty museum-piece on the first floor. A skinny Negro girl sat behind an oak desk and made a typewriter clatter.

"Yes?"

"I'd like to see Dr. Lobsenz, please."

Not pausing on the machine, she moved her head, indicating a man working in his shirt sleeves behind a desk at the rear of the room.

"Sit down," he said. He was chewing a cigar whose light had gone out and writing in a case book. Adam sat in a straight-backed wooden chair and looked around. The desks, the table tops and the window sills were clutters of books and papers, some of them yellowing. A coleus plant blazed in a cheap pink plastic container. Next to it was a small spray of dying foliage he couldn't identify, dry roots reaching desperately toward an inch of cloudy water at the bottom of a Pyrex lab retort. A whiskey bottle, half filled and tagged, stood on a pile of books. There was a worn bare linoleum on the floor. The windows were grimy and curtainless.

"What's your story?"

Dr. Lobsenz had faded blue eyes, very direct. His hair was gray. He had shaved badly and his white shirt had not been put on fresh that morning.

"I saw your notice at the school. I'm applying for the job."

Dr. Lobsenz sighed. "You're the fifth applicant. What's your name?"

Adam told him.

"I have a little work to do. Will you come with me? I'll interview you as we go along."

"Yes, sir," Adam said. He wondered why the Negro girl was grinning as she rattled away on her machine.

Dr. Lobsenz led him into the basement, a drop of two dozen steps and at least that many degrees of temperature.

There were bodies on tables and litters, some covered with cloths, some not. They stopped by the corpse of an old man, skinny and emaciated, with very dirty feet. Lobsenz pointed to the eyes with the unlit cigar. "See the white rim in the cornea? *Arcus Senilis*. Notice the increase in the depth of the chest? That's senile emphysema." He turned and looked at Adam. "Will you remember those things next time you see them?"

"Yes."

"Hmm. Maybe."

He went to one of the drawers that lined the wall, slid it open, gazed at the dead man within. "Fire death. About 45 years old. See the pinkish color? Two things do that. One is cold. The other is carbon monoxide in the blood. Whenever there's smoke or yellow flame, there's carbon monoxide."

"How did he die?"

"Tenement fire. Went in after his mother. All they ever found of the mother couldn't be differentiated from the other ashes."

He led Adam to an elevator, took him in silence to the third floor.

"Still interested in the job?"

"What *is* the job?"

"Taking care of them." He motioned with his head, downward toward the cold storage basement.

"All right," Adam said.

"And assisting at autopsies. Have you ever seen an autopsy?"

"No."

He followed Lobsenz into a room of white tile. There was a tiny figure on the white dissecting table, a doll, he thought, and then realized it was a colored baby, no more than a year old.

"Found dead in her crib. Don't know why she died. Thousands of kids do this to us every year, one of the mysteries. Damn fool of a young family doctor gave her mouth-to-mouth before giving up. Waited a day and then started to get cold sweats realizing that for all he knew she might have died of something highly contagious.

Hepatitis, t.b., who the hell knows what. Serve him right if we find something, the klutz."

He shoved his hands into gloves, flexed his fingers and then picked up a scalpel and made an incision that ran from each shoulder to the sternum and then down to the belly. "In Europe they do this from the chin down in a straight line. We favor the Y." The brown leather parted magically. Beneath it was a layer of yellow, baby fat Adam thought somewhat light-headedly, and beneath that, white tissue.

"The thing to remember," Lobsenz said, not unkindly, "is that this is not flesh. This is no longer a human being. What makes a body a person is life, personality, the divine soul. The soul has gone from this cage. What is left is clay, a kind of plastic material made by a highly efficient manufacturer."

As he talked the gloved hands explored, the scalpel slashed, he was taking samples, a dib here, a dab there, a little piece of this, a little slice of that. "The liver is beautiful. Did you ever see a prettier liver? Hepatitis would make it swollen, probably with spotty hemorrhage. It doesn't look like tuberculosis, either. Lucky klutz, that G.P."

He dropped the specimens in jars for laboratory testing and then replaced everything in the cavity and sewed up the chest incision.

It didn't bother me at all, Adam told himself. That's all there is to it?

Lobsenz led him down the hall, into another dissection room, a near-duplicate of the first. "When we're rushed, the diener sets up one room while I work in the other one," he explained. There was an old lady on the table, worn-out body, flaccid dugs, wrinkled face: my God, wearing a smile. The arms were folded across the chest. Lobsenz unfolded them, grunting with effort. "The textbooks tell you *rigor mortis* starts in the jaws and moves down the body in orderly progression. Take it from me, it never does."

When she was opened she did not emit four and twenty blackbirds. He kept his jaws shut tight—*rigor vitae*—and breathed as infrequently as possible, aware that his abdomen was convulsing over his empty stomach. Who reckoned being ill as one of the great pleasures in life? Samuel Butler. I will not enjoy myself, he told himself firmly.

Eventually, Lobsenz resewed the chest.

When they had returned to the office downstairs the medical examiner took two scratched glass tumblers from the middle drawer of his desk and poured them stiff shots from the tagged whiskey bottle. The tag said *Exhibit Number Two—Elliot Johnson.* They took the whiskey neat.

"To the john," Lobsenz said, removing a key from a nail in the wall.

When he was gone the skinny girl spoke without looking up from her typewriter. "He'll offer you a room and seventy-five a month. Don't take it for less than a hundred. He'll tell you he's got other candidates but he's had only one applicant who vomited halfway through the autopsy." The keys continued to clatter. "He's a terrific guy but he's full of shit," she said.

Dr. Lobsenz came back, rubbing his hands. "Well, what do you think? Do you want the job? You can learn more about the human body here than in four medical schools. I'll teach you as we work."

"Okay," Adam said.

"We've got a good room for you here. Seventy-five dollars a month."

"I want the room and a hundred dollars."

Lobsenz's smile faded. He looked suspiciously at the girl behind the desk, who continued to type. "I have other candidates."

Perhaps it was the liquor, which just about that time hit his empty stomach like a fist, making his head feel large and airborne, like a balloon. "Doctor, in a couple of months I'll be very hungry if I don't get a job right now. If not for that I wouldn't touch this fine position with your ten-foot pole."

Lobsenz looked at him and suddenly he smiled. "Come on, Silverstone, I'll buy you some lunch," he said.

The room on the second floor looked like an office from outside the frost-windowed door, but it contained a cot and a bureau. The sheets could be changed as often as he liked; he had access to the services of the county laundry for his personal needs, a wonderful bonus Dr. Lobsenz had neglected to mention. Cleanness of body was ever deemed to proceed from a due reverence to God. Francis Bacon.

The duties were not hard for somebody who had completed two years of medical training. In the beginning odors continued to bother him and he intensely disliked the rasping of the saw as it bit through the skull. But Lobsenz instructed as he worked and he was a good teacher. During the first year of medical school Adam had shared a pickled cadaver named Cora with six other students in an anatomy laboratory. By the time he had inherited Cora her parts and organs had been sliced and examined beyond all recognition. Now he kept his eyes open and listened carefully to Lobsenz who, noticing his interest, was obviously pleased but grumbled that he should be paid tuition. Adam was privately convinced that this was so; it was a first-class private lesson in anatomy.

In the beginning the nights were bad. The night telephone was in his room. From seven to eight-thirty undertakers telephoned, seeking the thirty-five dollars paid them by the county each time they unceremoniously buried an unclaimed body in a plain wooden box, the same price Benson paid for two dives.

The first night he took the calls from the undertakers, studied for two hours, set his alarm, lay down and went to sleep, and dreamed about the diving.

When he awoke he laughed at himself in the dark. Typical of the fool that he was, he thought: not caring a damn during all the high work, but now, in his bed, trembling over what might have happened.

The second night he talked on the telephone with the undertakers, studied until after midnight, set the alarm, turned off the light and lay there in the dark, wide awake.

He counted sheep, getting to fifty-six before each sheep turned into a body that floated slowly over the turnstile as he tallied. He counted backwards, beginning at one hundred and reaching one twice without the faintest sign of drowsiness, his eyes searching the darkness around him.

He thought of his grandmother, remembering her holding him to her flat chest as she rocked him to sleep in the kitchen. *Fa nana, fa nana,* go to sleep, Adamo. Pray to St. Michael, he will drive away the devil with his sword.

It was a large building. There were noises, the wind rattling windowglass, creaks and groanings, a kind of tinkling, the sound of footsteps.

Tinkling?

Footsteps?

He was supposed to be alone in the building. He got out of bed and put on the light so he could find his clothes. It was not spirits he worried about; as a scientist of course he did not believe in the supernatural. But the front door and the ambulance entrance were both locked. He had locked them himself. Therefore somebody had perhaps forced entry for who knew what purpose.

He left his room, turning on lights as he went through the building, first upstairs through the dissection chambers, then past the offices on the second and first floors. There was nobody.

Finally he went into the coolness of the morgue, groping hurriedly for the switch. There were four bodies on slabs outside the drawers, one of them the old woman at whose autopsy he had assisted Dr. Lobsenz. He looked at the frozen smile.

"Who were you, auntie?"

He walked to a very skinny Chinese man, probably tuberculous.

"Did you die a long way from home? Do you have sons in the Red Army, cousins on Formosa?"

No doubt the man had been born in Brooklyn, he told himself. The thought turned him back into a fool. He retraced his steps, shut the lights, went back to his room and turned on the radio, a lovely Haydn concerto.

He thought he heard them dancing and he could picture it, the old woman bowing in her nakedness to the oriental, the others peering from their opened ice-box drawers, the silent harlequin standing in his motley suit of lights, smiling and moving his head in time to the music.

Belled cap jingling.

In a little while he left the room again and turned on all the lights. He locked the door of the morgue. He set his alarm for six o'clock so he could turn off all the lights and unlock the morgue before the first person arrived the next morning, and then he went to sleep and dreamed about the dive.

The next night he left the lights off, and he did not dream. On the following night he forgot to lock the morgue, but the dream returned. Eventually he learned to identify knocking pipes and the jingling of loose panes of glass and other perfectly explainable noises, and he inhabited the dream no more and his slumber once again became deep and profound. The pattern of his existence came to seem to him unremarkable. Two months after he became a diener, wrestling with a Penn co-ed in her room, he was amused when she paused suddenly and buried her face in his chest. "You have the sexiest damn smell," she said.

"You, too, baby doll," he told her, meaning it, not bothering to mention that his was the faint, indestructible scent of formalde-hyde.

Now, working in Dr. Sack's Pathology Lab, he became accustomed again to the rawness of chemical preservative in his nostrils, and finally he dreamed no more when he went to sleep. Nowadays nobody got close enough to him to smell the essence of formalde-hyde. He considered dating the little blonde student nurse, Ander-son, but somehow he never got around to it.

He had tried to telephone Gaby.

He had been informed by Susan Haskell, her roommate, icily and repeatedly, that she was out of town and could not be reached.

Especially by Dr. Silverstone, the girl's tone had indicated.

He had written to her five days after they had returned from Truro.

> *Gaby,*
> *Time and again I have learned that I'm a disastrous fool.*
> *Will you please accept a telephone call or answer this note?*
> *I find that it's terribly different with someone you love.*
> *Adam*

But there had been no answering letter, and she remained una-vailable when he called.

The winter settled in. The snow fell, was sullied by the metropol-itan grime, fell again and was again sullied, the city cycle resulting in a layered white and gray effect when shovels cross-sectioned the drifts.

One morning in the surgeons' lounge Meomartino told the coffee drinkers of taking his son to see Santa Claus at Jordan Marsh.

"You a man?" Miguel had asked.

The bearded figure had nodded.

"A *real* man?"

Another nod.

"You got a penis and everything?"

The surgeons whooped and even Adam smiled.

"What did Santa say to that?" Lew Chin asked.

"He didn't say Ho-ho-ho," Meomartino said.

Boston merchants took note of the advent of the season. Department store windows bloomed with holly and came alive with animated tableaux, and green plastic wreaths appeared on the walls of the hospital elevators. Nurses hummed carols, and Dr. Longwood reacted to the joy of the season as if it affirmed his worst fears about the human frailty of young surgeons.

"I think Longwood's over the hill," Spurgeon told Adam.

"I think he's a great man."

"Maybe he *was* a great man. But now that he can't practice because he's sick, he's been acting as if he's a full-time, one-man Death Committee. That guy sees physician error every time somebody dies. You can tell the morning the Mortality Conference is scheduled, just by the way the entire staff is hypertensive."

"So we pay for his lousy luck with a little extra stress. It's a small price if it keeps him going a little longer," Adam said.

Ironically, two hours later he was with Meomartino when Longwood telephoned to question an appendectomy the two of them had performed two days earlier. The Chief of Surgery was not convinced the operation had been necessary. He ordered the case presented at Grand Rounds the next morning.

"Don't sweat it," Adam told Meomartino curtly. "The pathology slides show lots of inflammation and plenty of white cells. It's cut and dried."

"I know," Meomartino said. "I took the slides home yesterday and put in some microscope time. Oh, hell."

"What's the matter?"

"I forgot to bring them back. We'll need them to present."

"I go off duty in two hours. I guess I'll have to pick them up," Adam said.

"Would you? Take my car."

"No, thanks," Adam said. Still, it didn't bother him to accept favors from Spurgeon, and when he finished his shift Robinson drove him across the city in the Volks truck through the bleak winter evening. Meomartino had given them directions, but they had difficulty at the last moment; the street was more an alley, and banks of snow on both sides made it narrower still.

"Look, I can't leave the bus here, blocking the street. I'll wait for you," Spurgeon said.

"Okay."

Meomartino had good taste and the money to indulge it, he thought enviously as he rang the doorbell. The converted stables was a charming place to live.

A middle-aged Swedish maid opened the door. "Yes?"

"Is Mrs. Meomartino at home?"

"I don't think she can see anybody."

He explained his errand.

"Well, in that case you had better come in," she said reluctantly. He followed her into the house and, not knowing what else to do, into the kitchen, where a little boy sat at the table eating his supper.

"Hello," he said, smiling as he remembered the Santa Claus story. It was easy to see Meomartino in the child.

"Hello."

"I don't know anything about any slides," the maid said crossly.

"They would be with his microscope. Perhaps I can find them."

"In the study," she said, motioning with her head as she turned back to the stove. "Not the first door, that's the bedroom. The second door."

It was a nice room. There was a good Persian rug and deep leather chairs. The walls were covered with shelves. Most of the books were solidly medical, but there was biography and history, a mixture of English and Spanish titles. Very little fiction except one small section which also contained modern poetry.

The poetry must belong to his wife, he thought, glancing at the closed door between the bedroom and the study.

The slides were right next to the microscope. Some of them were still out and he returned them to the box. He was ready to leave when the bedroom door opened.

She was wearing her husband's pajamas and they were too large for her. Her hair was tousled and her feet were bare and perhaps she customarily wore glasses and missed them: she squinted at him comically. The overall effect was wonderfully attractive. He saw she was not the kind of woman who shrieked and ran for a robe.

"Hello," he said. "I'm not a burglar. I'm Adam Silverstone."

"Silverstone. Any relation to the Booksteins?"

Her voice was husky, but he saw that both the low register and myopic stare might be due to the fact that she had been drinking. She padded in and stood swaying.

"Hey," he said. He reached out to steady her and found a moment later to his amazement that she was leaning against him, her head on his chest.

"No relation," he said. "I work with Rafe. He forgot these slides."

She tipped her head back and looked at him without, he noticed, moving her body from his. "He's spoken of you. The competition."

"Yes."

"Poor Rafe," she said. "How do you do." She kissed him, her mouth warm and bitter with gin.

"How do you do," he said politely. This time he kissed her, and the idea was there before the kiss was done. Looking at her he knew it was possible, an absurdly classical demolishment of Meomartino: in his adversary's own castle, with Spurgeon waiting downstairs in the car and the servant capable of walking in on them at any moment.

From another part of the apartment he heard the little boy laugh happily.

Besides, the lady was drunk.

"Excuse me," he said.

He disengaged and gathered up the slides and left her standing there in the middle of the room. The little boy had finished eating and was watching television.

"Bye-bye," he called, not taking his eyes from Bozo the Clown.

"Bye-bye," Adam said.

Two days later she came to the hospital.

They were all coming into Adam's office from rounds and when he opened the door the first thing he saw was the mink coat thrown across his chair. She wore a smart black suit and looked like a Playboy version of the young Back Bay matron.

"Liz," Meomartino said.

"They told me I might find you here, Rafe."

"I don't believe you know these gentlemen," Meomartino said. "Spurgeon Robinson."

"Hello, there," Spurgeon said, shaking hands.

"Adam Silverstone."

She held out her hand and he took it as if it were forbidden fruit. "How do you do."

"How do you do," she said.

He couldn't look at Meomartino. Cuckoo, cuckoo: O word of fear, unpleasing to a married ear. Shakespeare. He muttered a goodbye while the other introductions were in progress, went back to the ward, worked hard, but was unable to drive away the thought of the woman offering herself up in her husband's pajamas.

In mid-afternoon when he was summoned to the telephone he knew before answering.

"Hello," she said.

"How are you?" he muttered inanely, palms damp.

"I'm afraid I lost something in your office."

"What was it?"

"A glove. Black kid."

"I haven't seen it. I'm sorry."

"Oh, dear. If you find it, will you let me know?"

"Yes. Of course."

"Thank you. Goodbye."

"Goodbye."

When he returned to his office fifteen minutes later he got down on his hands and knees and it was still under the desk where undoubtedly she had thrown it. He retrieved it and sat for a moment or two rubbing the soft expensive leather between his fingers. When he held it to his nose the perfume brought her to him.

She's sober now, he thought.

He looked up the number in the book and dialed it and she answered right away, as if she had been waiting.

"I've found it," he said.

"What?"

"The glove."

"Oh. That's fine," she said. And waited.

"I can give it to Rafe."

"He's so absent-minded. He'll never bring it home."

"Well, I'm off tomorrow. I can drop by with it."

"I had planned to go shopping," she said.

"I have some shopping to do myself. Why don't you meet me and I'll return the glove and buy you a drink."

"All right," she said. "Two o'clock?"

"Where?"

"Do you know The Parlor? It's not far from the Prudential Center?"

"I'll find it," he said.

He was early. He sat on a stone bench in the Prudential Center and watched the ice-skaters until his buttocks and feet became numb and then he gave up and walked down Boylston Street and into the lounge. At night undoubtedly there would be some serious drinkers and men and woman on the make, but now there were only students having a late lunch. He ordered a cup of coffee.

When she came in her cheeks were very red from the cold. He noticed for the second time that she had excellent taste. She wore a black cloth coat trimmed with beaver, and when he helped her off with it he saw with approval a beige knit dress, cut very simply, and a single piece of jewelry, a cameo pin that looked old.

"Do you want a drink?" he said.

She looked at his coffee cup and shook her head quickly. "It's really too early, isn't it?"

"Yes."

She asked for a cup of coffee and he ordered it, but when it came she said she didn't want it. "Shall we go for a drive?" she said.

"I don't own a car."

"Oh. Let's walk then."

They put on their coats and left the lounge, walking in the direction of Copley Square. He couldn't take her to the Ritz or the Plaza, any place like that, he thought. They were bound to run into someone she knew. It was very cold, they were both beginning to shiver. He looked around desperately for a taxi.

"I'm afraid I have to use the facilities," she said. "Do you mind waiting?"

Across the street was the Regent, a third-rate hotel, and he smiled at her admiringly.

"Not at all," he said.

While she was in the ladies' room he registered. The clerk nodded without interest when he said their luggage would arrive from Logan Airport. When she came back into the small lobby Adam took her elbow and led her gently into the elevator. They didn't speak. She held her head high and looked straight ahead. When he had opened the door of the room, 3 14, and they had walked in and he had closed the door behind them, he turned to her and they looked at one another.

"I forgot to bring the glove," he said.

Later, she slept while he lay next to her in the overheated room and smoked, and eventually she awakened and saw him watching her. She reached out and took the cigarette from his lips and ground it out carefully in the ash tray next to the bed and then she turned to him and they performed the rite again while outside the gray light deepened.

At five o'clock she got out of bed and began to dress.

"Must you do that?"

"It's almost time for dinner."

"We can call down. I'd just as soon skip dinner."

"I have a little boy at home," she said. "I have to see that he's fed and put to bed."

"Oh."

In her slip, she came and sat on the bed and kissed him. "Wait here for me," she said. "I'll come back."

"All right."

When she was gone he tried to sleep but he couldn't breathe, the room was too hot. It smelled seminal, of cigarette smoke and of her. He opened one of the windows, letting in arctic air, then he dressed and went downstairs and had a sandwich he didn't want and a cup of coffee, and he walked to Copley Square and sat in the Boston Public Library and read old issues of the Saturday Review.

When he went back at eight o'clock she was already there, under the sheet. The window was closed and again it was too hot. The lamps were off but the hotel sign outside the window blinked, the flashes making the room look like a psychedelic painting. She had brought him a sandwich. Egg salad. They shared it at eleven o'clock, the smell of the hardboiled egg becoming part of the rich odors that glued the day to his memory.

On Christmas morning Adam served alone in the OR as

standby surgeon. He was lying on the long bench in the surgery kitchen, listening to the lonely noises of the coffee-maker, when the telephone rang.

It was Meomartino. "You're going to have to do an amp sometime this afternoon. I'll be gone by then."

"O.K.," he said coldly. "What's the patient's name?"

"Stratton."

"I know him well," he said, more to himself than to Meomartino.

On the previous week they had tried to perform an arterial by-pass to bring the circulation back into Mr. Stratton's leg. The original plan had been to strip out the saphenous vein and use it as an arterial graft, reversed so the valves would open in the same direction as the arterial flow. But Mr. Stratton's veins had proven to be lousy, only two-tenths of a centimeter in diameter, about one-quarter the diameter they would have liked. They had cut out the big arteriosclerotic plaque that was blocking circulation and had rejoined the artery with a plastic graft, which would have been good for only a year or two at best, but it had gone wrong right from the start. Now the leg was a white, dead thing that threatened the patient's life, and it would have to come off.

"What time will he be up?"

"I don't know. We're trying to get hold of his lawyer, to get him to sign the papers. Mr. Stratton is married, but his wife is critically ill at the Beth Israel, so she can't sign. I guess he'll be up as soon as they can get the lawyer to come down. They've been trying since last night."

Adam sighed when he hung up, picked a green scrub suit from a pile on a table, and went into the junior surgeons' locker room to change out of his whites. The scrub suit felt familiar and comfortable. He picked up a pair of black plastic booties, ripping the perforated tops off and placing one of the resulting plastic strips between his stockinged foot and his shoe before fastening the boots to his ankles with elastic bands. Then, girded for action and booted and grounded against the possibility of an electric spark that could cause an oxygen-laden OR to go up in a fiery blast, he returned to his kitchen bench and his book, but not for long.

This time when he answered the telephone it was Emergency. "We're sending up a mesenteric infarct. You can start scrubbing. Dr. Kender's rounding up a whole mob to staff it."

"Louise," he called as he hung up. The scrub nurse sitting by the window set down her knitting.

"Merry Christmas," she said.

It was gratifying to know that they could assemble that much surgical talent on short notice. There were fourteen people—nurses, surgeons, anesthesiologists—crammed into the small OR along with a conglomeration of electronic equipment. The patient was gray-haired, unshaven and in coma. He looked to be in his late fifties or early sixties, powerful of body but with a great soft beer-belly. Known to be a cardiac and a taker of digitalis, he had been found by police in his apartment, in coma. It was assumed that his circulation had been impaired as a side effect of the digitalis dosage, although it was not known how much he had taken, or when he had taken it.

They had brought him up already receiving intravenous fluids, an anesthesiology resident squeezing an ambu bag to help him breathe.

Now Adam watched while Spurgeon Robinson scrubbed the man's chest. "Hey," Spurgeon said, beckoning. A tattoo. Adam peered over the patient with him, feeling ridiculously like a wor-shiper. DEAR GOD PLEASE TAKE THIS MAN TO HEAVEN . . . HE DONE HIS HITCH IN HELL. What kind of life would inspire the kind of despair necessary to cause a man to wear the thought as a suit of armor? He memorized it as Spurgeon wielded his swab, wiping it out under a smear of Betadine. If there was a source for the quotation, the computer failed him.

The patient was already hooked up to a pacemaker. Other equip-ment had been wheeled close to the table, a device to measure blood gases, a blood volume machine, an electrocardiographic monitor sounding a beep-beep-beep like a frantic glass-and-metal animal, the blips marching across its screen as the man's heart struggled on.

Kender waited impatiently until the sterile draping had been completed and then he moved to the side of the table, accepted the scalpel from Louise and made the incision swiftly. Adam was there with the suction, and the receptacle on the wall began to roar like Niagara as the peritoneal fluid was drawn into it from the patient's abdominal cavity.

One glance and he knew he was looking at peritonitis and gangrene. Kender's hands kneaded and moved over the swollen and discolored viscera like a man caressing a sick python. "Telephone Dr. Sack at home," he called to a fourth-year student. "Tell him we have a gangrenous belly, all the way down to the lower colon. Ask him if he can come to the hospital right away with his equipment."

"What kind of equipment?"

"He'll know."

Under Kender's direction they injected dye that would reveal under x-ray what was happening to the patient's intestinal blood circulation, and still another piece of apparatus was wheeled in, this time a portable x-ray unit.

Adam noticed that the blood in the operating field was very dark. The muscles in the patient's upper arms began to twitch as if he were a horse frightening flies. "It looks as though he's having trouble with oxygen," he said.

"How's he doing?" Kender asked the anesthesiologist.

"He has almost no blood pressure to speak of. His heart's arryhthmic as hell."

"What's his pH?"

Spurgeon checked. "It's 6.9."

"Better get the sodium bicarbonate ready," Kender said. "This guy's getting ready to go into cardiac arrest."

The yellow blips on the monitor, each a contraction of the dying heart muscle, bloomed into life with decreasing frequency, the little crests of light appearing as fainter lines with lower peaks until finally, as they watched, the blips flattened out.

"Jesus, there he goes," Spurgeon said.

Kender began the steady intermittent pressure on the chest wall with the heel of his hand. "Bicarbonate," he said.

Adam injected it into a leg vein. He watched Dr. Kender.

Bear down.

Lift off.

Down.

Off.

The regular, straight-armed pressure, the sight of the surgeon rocking back and forth reminded him of . . . what? Then he remembered his Italian grandmother kneading dough for home-made bread. In the kitchen (torn shades, faded yellow-on-white curtains, crucifix on the mantel, last week's *Il Giornale* on the old treadle Singer sewing machine, and the goddam canary always trilling); kneading bread on a big old wooden board with knife scars on it that were always filled with white hardened macaroni dough that had escaped the scraping after the last batch had been made. Flour on her brown arms. A curse for his father on the faintly-mustached Sicilian lips.

What the hell, he asked himself, dragging his mind back to the man on the table.

"Epinephrine," Kender said.

The circulating nurse flicked the glass ampule and broke it open with her fingers. Adam's syringe drank the hormone and he injected it into another leg vein.

Come on, you goddam muscle, he said silently. Beat.

He looked up at the OR clock, as still as the stopped heart. The clocks in all the OR's were useless. A hospital legend held that they had been tended for years by an old county engineer who knew how to keep them running, and that when he retired so did the clocks.

"How long has it been?" he asked.

One of the circulating nurses, unsterile and therefore able to wear her watch, glanced briefly at her wrist.

"Four minutes and ten seconds."

Oh God. Well, we tried, whoever you were, he thought. Now he looked at Kender, willing him to stop his efforts. After four minutes without oxygenized blood, what had been a brain had become a skull-contained turnip. Even if dragged back into life, this body would never think again, or feel; never really live.

Kender appeared not to have heard. He rocked on, the heel of his hand depressing the chest and letting it spring back.

Again.

And again.

And . . .

"Sir?" Adam said finally.

"What is it?"

"It's almost five minutes." Let the poor bastard go, he wanted to say.

"Try the bicarb again."

He injected the vein once more. Dr. Kender rocked on, giving

it the old Air Force try; no sweat, bombs away, never say die.
The seconds faded away.

"We've got a heart beat," the anesthesiologist said.

"Hit him with a little more of that adrenalin," Kender said, as if
telling him to drop the napalm.

Adam did so, his eyes carefully blank, his hidden mouth sullen
behind the mask.

On the monitor screen a nova appeared, and then another, and
the little blips of light began to march; they picked up the old
rhythm, the muscle contracting, refreshed, pulsing, beating in the
manner it had come close to forgetting for all time.

He is risen, Adam thought.

Dr. Sack arrived, bearing two cameras, one for slides, one for
color movies.

"Hold that incision wide," Kender commanded. Adam did. The
camera whirred and he flinched, a movie star.

It was a take. In a few moments the cameras were put away and
they became surgeons once again. He watched while they snipped
out the celiac ganglion and injected drugs to fight the muscular
spasm and try to bring the blood circulation back. The bowel was,
of course, inoperable. They gave him the honor of closing the
abdomen with wire sutures.

The job done, he and Spurgeon swabbed the field with alcohol.
As the blood and Betadine washed away, the letters slowly reap-
peared: DEAR GOD PLEASE TAKE THIS MAN TO HEAVEN
. . . HE DONE HIS HITCH IN HELL.

"I want two men with him at all times to keep him going," Kender was saying.

Adam helped them lift the patient onto the litter and then he
pulled the cloth mask from his sweating face and watched as, an
anesthesiologist squeezing the ambu bag to breathe for him, they
rolled the vegetable away.

There were days in which he practiced the surgery of life. The
operations he performed were for the living, procedures that would
make their lives easier, their existences more comfortable, free of
pain. There were other days when he practiced the surgery of death
and despair, opening the human shell to discover cells run wild into

ugliness that could only be closed up and hidden away, working desperately to coordinate his brain and hands with the knowledge that the best he could do was inadequate to prevent great suffering and eventual death.

This was such a day; he felt it.

Late in the afternoon Mr. Stratton was brought down to surgery. A man came with him, no doubt the lawyer whose permission had been necessary for the operation. The man wore a baggy brown suit; his shirt collar was soiled and the knot in his tie was much too large; he had a tired face that matched his hat, which was stained around the sweatband. He did not look at all like Melvin Belli or F. Lee Bailey. He stood in the corridor outside the OR, talking quietly to Mr. Stratton until Adam asked him to leave, which he did quickly, trying not to reveal his gratitude at the request.

"Hello, Mr. Stratton," Adam said. "We're going to take good care of you."

The man closed his eyes and nodded.

Helena Manning, the first-year resident, came in followed by Spurgeon Robinson. Adam decided to give her the experience of doing the amp. Since there was only one nurse on duty, he told the R.N. to circulate and asked Spurgeon if he would mind playing scrub nurse. In the scrub room there was another cheering note. The hot water supply couldn't keep up with the ancient plumbing system; now, as it did several times a week, often for as long as an hour at a time, the hot water taps gave out water that was icy cold. Gasping and cursing, the three surgeons scrubbed their hands and arms for the prescribed ten minutes under the frigid flow and then backed through the swinging doors into the OR, holding their numbed hands high.

The circulating nurse was relatively new and, she confided shakily, nervous because she was covering the OR alone for the first time.

"Nothing to it," he said, inwardly groaning.

He watched while Spurgeon opened the amp kit and arranged the instruments in neat gleaming rows, ties and sutures tucked under a sterile towel so they could be drawn one by one when needed. The woman resident positioned the patient and began to give a spinal under the eyes of the anesthesiologist.

Mr. Stratton moaned.

Helena Manning scrubbed the leg down and she and Adam draped.

"Where?" he asked her.

With her gloved forefinger she traced the route of the below-knee incision.

"All right. You're going to cut to make long anterior and short posterior skin flaps. So that when it heals he can walk on skin and the scar behind the skin. Go ahead."

Spurgeon handed her the knife and then began to slap snaps at Adam, who clamped the bleeders as fast as she cut through them. They worked steadily until there were ten or a dozen snaps running through the incision, then they paused to tie off the bleeders and remove the snaps.

"Fix the light," Helena said to the circulating nurse.

The nurse stood on a stool and adjusted the overhead lamp. As it swung on its axis Adam could see a shower of fine dust float from the ceiling-hung fixture and descend toward the surgical field. The OR lamps, like the OR clocks and the hot water supply, were relics of the past which bound Suffolk County General with another age. Ever since arriving from Georgia he had wondered how serious university surgeons could spend so much time and patience with scrubbing, disinfectant and other antiseptic detail and then casually shower the field with dust whenever the overhead lamp was adjusted.

Helena was doing a sloppy job, he saw, cutting too low. "No," he said, "you want to get the linea aspera up higher. If you push the periosteum up it will re-ossify and produce a spur."

She cut again, higher this time, adding minutes to the time of the amputation. The air conditioning whirred. The monitor sounded its lulling beep-beep-beep. Adam felt the first gentle stroke of drowsiness and forced himself into concentration. He thought ahead, anticipating the surgeon's needs.

"Will you get us some absolute alcohol?" he asked the circulating.

"Oh, my." She looked around wildly. "Ah, what do they need it for?"

"To inject the nerve."

"Oh."

The resident had located the femoral artery and tied it off. Now the circulating nurse returned in time with the alcohol. Helena found the sciatic nerve, crushed it high, ligated it and injected it with alcohol.

"Would you get the bone wax, please?" Adam asked.

"Aha." Faced with a new challenge, the nurse disappeared again.

Adam handed Helena the saw. At this point in time, to his great delight, the doctor became a woman. She did not know how to hold the saw. Grasping it daintily and with great dignity, she pulled it back and forth across the bone, the blade wobbling.

"You never made a footstool for your mother in junior high," he said. She glared, teeth clenched, sawing with determination.

The nurse came back. "We have no bone wax."

"What do you use to wax sutures?"

"We oil sutures."

"Well, damn it, she's going to need bone wax. Look in orthopedics." It was the end of their warm professional rapprochement, but she went. She came back with it in a few minutes.

"No bone wax?" he said, smiling.

"Well, there was none upstairs."

"Thank you very much."

"Anytime," she said coolly, leaving.

Helena sewed the flap nicely, having no doubt had a great deal of experience making dresses for her dolls.

"Mr. Stratton," the anesthesiologist was saying. "You can wake up now. Wake up, Mr. Stratton."

The patient opened his eyes. "Everything went just wonderfully," Adam told him. "You're going to be just fine." Mr. Stratton stared up at the OR ceiling, eyes narrowed, thinking the Christmas thoughts of a one-legged truck driver with a wife so ill in another hospital that she couldn't even sign a paper.

The nurse had wrapped the leg in two sheets. When Adam had changed back into whites he took it and Helena's path report and went to the elevator, which eventually arrived. Pathology was on Four. On the first floor a number of passengers entered the elevator and as the car rose toward Two he noticed a middle-aged lady, the kind of woman who croons babytalk to bulldogs, staring at the bundle in his arms.

"May I just peek at the little thing?" she asked, reaching out for the top of the sheet.

"No." Adam took a quick step back. "I wouldn't want to wake him," he said.

This child I to myself will take. Wordsworth. All the way to Four he tenderly patted Mr. Stratton's calf.

There was no word from Gaby. He called again and was warded off by Susan Haskell, whom by now he loathed.

He felt guilt about Liz Meomartino, realizing that he had used her, in his shoddy game of one-upsmanship with her husband, as surely as he had once used the Greek woman.

He never would call her again, he told himself with relief. It was an unworthy episode, but he would bury it in the past.

And yet he found himself thinking about her. She had been a great surprise. She was not the usual roundheeled woman. She had breeding, looks, taste, money, she was so marvelously sensual . . .

"Hello?" she said.

"It's Adam," he said, closing the door of the telephone booth.

They played the same charade, meeting at The Parlor, walking through the dirty snow to the Regent. He requested the same room.

"Will you be staying long, sir?" the clerk asked.

"Only the night."

"In three or four hours we're going to be full up. A national Legion meeting at the War Memorial Auditorium down the street. So I thought I'd warn you if you wished to reserve the room for the rest of the week."

The door of the ladies' room opened and he saw her coming back into the lobby.

Why not? He had nothing to keep him at the hospital when he wasn't working.

"Use the rate for the week," he said.

That afternoon they lay in Room 314, orchestrated by shrieks and laughter as invisible men in blue-and-gold overseas caps shouted insults and messages through doorways and bombed empty bottles and water-filled bags down the airshaft.

"What color was it originally?" he asked, stroking her strawy hair.

"Black," she said, frowning.

"You shouldn't have touched it."

She moved her head. "Don't. It's what he always tells me."

"That doesn't necessarily make it wrong. It should be your own color," he said gently. "It's your only flaw."

"There are others," she said.

"I didn't think you were going to call me," she said in a little while.

In the hallway they were marching and counting cadence. He studied the ceiling and smoked his cigarette. "I didn't intend to." He shrugged. "I couldn't forget you."

"It was the same with me. I've known a lot of men. Does that bother you? No," she stopped his lips with her fingertips, "don't answer that."

He kissed her fingers. "Have you ever been to Mexico?" she asked.

"No."

"When I was fifteen years old my uncle went to a medical meeting and I went with him," she said.

"Oh?"

"Cuernavaca. In the mountains. Bright-colored houses. A wonderful climate, flowers all year round. A pretty little plaza. If they don't sweep the sidewalks before noon they get citations from the police."

"No snow," he said. Outside it was snowing.

"No. It's only a short drive to Mexico City. Fifty miles. Very international, like Paris. Big hospitals. Great social life. A talented *norteamericano* doctor can do extremely well there. I have enough money to buy any practice that suits you."

"What are you talking about?" he said.

"You and me and Miguel."

"Who?"

"My little boy."

"It's crazy."

"It's not. You wouldn't mind about the little boy. I could never leave him."

"No. That is, I don't have to mind. It's impossible."

"Just promise me you'll think about it."

"Look, Liz . . ."

"Please. Just think about it."

She rolled over and kissed him, her body a summer in which he played, honeydews, blackberries, peach fuzz, musk.

"I'll show you Cortez' palace," she said.

Early Sunday evening Kender brought the peritonitis case back down to the OR, and when they reopened they found that the measures they had taken on Saturday morning had obviously stimulated the circulation. Enough tissue was free of gangrene to allow them to do a resection; they removed most of the small intestine and part of the large. Throughout it, the patient slept the sleep of the permanently comatose.

At breakfast Monday morning Adam heard that the man had suffered two more heart failures. He was receiving massive therapy, everything Kender could do to keep him technically alive. A minimum of two doctors was with him at all times, watching the vital signs, giving oxygen and drugs, breathing for him, dripping life-sustaining fluids into his veins.

That afternoon Adam stopped into the Surgery kitchen and saw that Kender sat in a corner chair, asleep or simply sitting very quietly with his eyes closed, he couldn't tell which. As unobtrusively as possible he drew himself a cup of coffee.

"Pour one for me, will you?" Adam handed it to the Associate Chief of Surgery and they drank in silence.

"A funny profession, this surgery of ours," Kender said. "I've spent years working my head and my tail off in the transplantation field. Next year there will be a new chair of surgery at the medical school. They want to fill it with a transplantation specialist, but I won't be in it. I'll be Surgeon-in-Chief."

"Do you regret that?" Adam asked.

Kender grinned wearily. "Not really. But I'm learning that Dr. Longwood didn't have an easy job. I've taken over all his cases."

"I know," Adam said.

"Do you also know the mortality rate for the combined cases of Dr. Longwood and Dr. Kender for the past three months?"

"It has to be high, or you wouldn't ask. Fifty per cent?"

"Try one hundred per cent," Kender said softly. He reached into his pocket and pulled out a cigar. "For three months. That's a very long time to go without a patient who survived. A lot of operations."

"How come?"

"Because, goddamit, the easy ones go to you guys. At a place like this the head man doesn't get them unless they're already ass-deep in the grave."

For the first time Adam saw that it was so. God. "Next time I get a hernia or an appendectomy I'll ask for your help."

Kender smiled. "I would appreciate that," he said. "Very much." He lit the cigar and blew smoke toward the ceiling. "We lost that fellow with the gangrenous gut a little while ago," he said.

Adam's sympathy dissipated. "We really lost him during that first six-minute cardiac arrest, wouldn't you say, sir?"

Kender looked at him. "No," he said. "No, I wouldn't say that." He got up and went to the window. "See that big red-brick mausoleum across the street?"

"The animal lab?"

"It was built a hell of a long time ago, before the Civil War. Oliver Wendell Holmes once dissected cats in that building."

Adam waited, unimpressed.

"Well, you and I and Oliver Wendell Holmes aren't the only ones who have worked there. For a long time now Dr. Longwood and Dr. Sack and some other people around here have been taking dogs dying of gangrene in their vitals, and by doing to them what we did to that fellow we had in our OR, they've been able to save some of those dogs."

"This was a man," Adam said. "Not a dog."

"During the last two years we've had sixteen such patients. Each of them has died, but each has lived longer than the last. This man lived for forty-eight hours. The experimental procedures *worked* for him. They turned an inoperable gangrenous condition into one we could handle through surgery. Who knows—the next patient, if we're lucky, may not go into cardiac arrest."

Adam looked at the older surgeon. He felt a number of things, all at once. "But when *do* you say to yourself, 'This man is gone, we can never bring him back, let him die peacefully and with dignity?' "

"Every physician makes up his own mind about that. I never say it."

"Never?"

"Goddamit, my young friend," Kender said. "Just take a glance at what's happened within a stone's throw of this hospital, within

the memory of people who are working here. In 1925 a young physician named Paul Dudley White began treating a 15-year-old girl
from Brockton. Three years later she was dying because her heart
was being choked by a leatherlike pericardial covering. He had had
her admitted to the Massachusetts General Hospital eight or nine
times, and everybody had looked at her and treated her, and nobody
could do anything. So he had her sent home knowing she must die
unless in some way the pericardium could be removed. As he pondered on this he had Katherine admitted to the M.G.H. just once
more, hoping that in some way surgery might prove possible. By a
stroke of luck—call it serendipity—right about that time a young
surgeon named Edward Delos Churchill had returned to the Massachusetts General from Europe, fresh from a year or two of advanced training in thoracic surgery, including a period under the
great Ferdinand Sauerbruch in Berlin. Churchill later was to become Chief of Surgery at the Massachusetts General Hospital, of
course.

"Well, Dr. White met him in the old brick corridor and persuaded him to come up to the ward to see Katherine. Nobody in the
United States had ever succeeded in doing anything about constrictive pericarditis with a knife or with medicines. But Dr. White
asked Dr. Churchill if he would try, and—" Kender shrugged—
"the girl was slowly dying.

"Well, he operated. And she lived. As a matter-of-fact, she's a
grandmother today. And a lot of people with constrictive pericarditis have had successful surgery over the past forty years."

Adam didn't say anything. He simply sat and drank his coffee.

"You want another case? Dr. George Minot. Brilliant young Boston medical researcher, nearly dead of diabetes back when there
was no effective treament. Then, just before the end, he got one of
the earliest batches of a brand-new hormone discovered by two Canadians named Dr. Frederick C. Banting and Dr. Charles H. Best
—insulin. He didn't die. And because he didn't die, he went on to
win the Nobel Prize for working out the cure for pernicious anemia,
and an untold number of *other* people were saved, who knows how
many of *them* in the nick of time." He slapped Adam heavily on the
thigh and blew cigar smoke in his face. "That's why I don't buy genteel concessions to easy death, sonny. That's why I prefer to fight
right down the line, even though it's ugly and it hurts."

Adam shook his head, unconvinced. "There remains a lot to say for not prolonging terrible pain and ugliness in the face of inevitable defeat."

Kender looked at him and smiled. "You're young," he said. "It will be interesting to see if your views change."

"I doubt if they will."

Kender blew a cloud of stinking cigar smoke at him. "We'll see," he said.

In the middle of the night, running in sweat-suit and gloves and muffler and arctic boots over soft new-fallen snow that glittered like ground glass under the street lamps, orbiting round and round the hospital, his sun, until the cold of outer space corroded his lungs and speared his vital center, he knew that Spurgeon Robinson was right: the Silverstone Greater Scheme of Things was bullshit and cow dung. Liz Meomartino was offering him the Silverstone Greater Scheme of Things on a platter, and he recognized at once that it was not at all what he wanted. What he yearned desperately to become in twenty years was a mixture of Lobsenz and Sack and Kender and Longwood, and that transformation wasn't going to occur in Cuernavaca or anyplace else with Liz Meomartino.

He called her in the morning and told her as gently as he was able.

"You're certain?"

"Yes."

"Meet me, Adam."

She thought she could change his mind, he knew. "I don't think so, Liz."

"Rafe is home tonight, but I'll get away. All I want to do is say goodbye."

"Goodbye, Liz. Good luck," he said.

"Be there. Please." She broke the connection.

He worked all day like an emancipated slave now in business for himself. Off-duty at six, he consumed dinner with fine appetite and put in several good hours in the animal lab.

When he got to the sixth floor he showered and lay on his bed in his shorts and read three journals and then he got into street clothes. He was searching for a fresh handkerchief when his hand closed on something in the bureau drawer and he picked it up and turned it over and over, examining it as if he had never seen the black kid glove before in his life.

This time the Regent was jammed with the Legionnaires and their wives, and he had to push his way through the lobby.

"Felix, do you have the tickets?" a fat woman in a wrinkled Auxiliary uniform shrieked.

"Sure," said her husband, goosing Adam with a cattle prod.

He leaped, causing general laughter, but was carried into the elevator.

They were in the corridor, on the stairs; he felt as though they were under his fingernails.

He fitted the key into the lock and as he opened the door of 314 the electric sign outside the windows flickered and snapped another psychedelic photograph, the focal point of which was the blue and gold overseas cap on the dresser.

Adam picked up the ridiculous hat. The man in the bed was looking at him warily. Not Vietnam. Too old even for Korea. Vintage World War II, Adam thought. Old soldiers, I know not why, seem to be more accostable than old sailors. Hawthorne.

The man was obviously very frightened. "What do you want? Money?"

"Just get out." Adam handed over the hat and held the door while the man skinned into his trousers and gratefully fled.

She looked at him. He could see she had been drinking. "You could have saved me," she said.

"I'm not even sure I can save myself."

He gathered up her stockings and placed them and the black glove in her handbag.

"Go away," she said.

"I've got to send you home, Liz."

"It's far too late." She smiled. "I told them I was just going for cigarettes."

She was wearing her slip, but the dress was an obstacle. He received no cooperation and it took a while to get everything in place. Halfway up, the zipper jammed. Perspiring, he struggled, but it was no good, it would neither let go nor close completely.

The coat would cover it, he told himself.

When he put on her shoes and pulled her to her feet, she wobbled. Arm around her waist, hers around his neck, he walked her to the door like a patient.

In the hallway, the generals were dispensing beer and highballs.

"No, thank you," Adam said politely, leaning on the elevator button.

When he got her into the downstairs lobby he saw the man with the cattle prod, preparing for hilarity.

"You touch that thing to either one of us, Felix," he said, "and I'll wrap it around your goddam neck."

Felix looked wounded. "You hear that bastard?" he asked the fat woman.

"I told you, the people here are cold, like the weather," she said as Adam moved away with his burden. "Next time they'll listen and hold it in Miami."

Outside, a snow like thin gruel drifted down. He dared not prop her against the building; clutching and holding, they swayed together out into the wet slush.

"Taxi!" he shouted.

The cars splashed by, among them several cabs.

"Taxi!"

"Ah, you failed me," she said.

"I don't love you," he said. "I'm sorry." His hair was already soggy; the snow was melting on his neck and wetting the collar of his shirt. "What's more, I don't see how you can feel that you love me. We hardly know one another."

"That doesn't matter."

"Of course it matters. You've got to *know* one another, for Christ sake. TAXI!" he screamed at a passing apparition.

"I mean loving. It's overrated. I like you so much."

"God," he said. He screamed again, aware this time that he was becoming hoarse. Miraculously, the cab stopped, but before he could move her a cunning capped ex-corporal had leaped in and slammed the door. The vehicle pulled away.

Another cab hove into sight, came abreast, sailed by but then, ten feet past them, stopped and two men began to get out.

"Come *on,*" he said, dragging her. "Before it gets away." He shouted for it as they slipped and slid but the two men were out now and they were coming toward him and he saw that one was Meomartino and the other was Dr. Longwood. The Old Man shouldn't be out on a night like this, he thought.

He stopped pulling her. They simply sagged and waited. Meomartino stared when he reached them but said nothing.

"Where have you been?" Dr. Longwood asked her. "We've been
looking *everywhere.*" He glanced at Adam. "Where did you find
her?"

"Here," Adam said.

He became aware that her arm was still around his neck, that he
continued to hold her around the waist. He disengaged and transferred her to Meomartino, who was silent as stone.

"Thank you very much," Longwood said stiffly. "Goodnight."

"Goodnight."

Sharing the burden, her husband and her uncle moved her to the
taxi. The door opened and finally closed, the motor roared, the back
wheels spun. Slush flew back like a punishment and struck him on
the right trouser leg, but it was already wet and he didn't care, remembering her stuck zipper.

"Taxi," he muttered hopelessly as an occupied Yellow Cab bore
down upon him out of the gloom.

In the days that followed, suffering with a heavy cold, he waited
for Longwood to send bolts of thunder at the seducer of his flesh
and blood. In a number of ways, the Old Man had the power to de-
stroy him. But two days after the disaster outside the hotel Meomartino stopped him in the surgeons' lounge. "My wife told me when
she was ill you were kind enough to go to considerable trouble to try
to get her a cab." His eyes challenged.

"Well . . ."

"It was fortunate that you met her. I want to say thank you."

"It was nothing."

"I'm sure she won't need your help again." Meomartino nodded
and went away, somehow the winner. Never had Adam felt so much
loathing or such respect. What had happened to his revenge, he
wondered.

Longwood's wrath did not descend. Adam worked hard, staying
in the hospital and spending his off-duty hours in his room or in the
animal or pathology labs. He inherited a flurry of surgical cases, an
appendectomy, a gall bladder, several gastrectomies, more skin
grafting for Mr. Grigio.

Mrs. Bergstrom received a holiday gift, a kidney. On the next-to-
last night of December a sudden Sunday blizzard dumped four

inches of clean whiteness on the grimy city. Across the river in Cambridge the sixteen-year-old son of a famed scholar, high on pot, stole a car and, careening away from the police vehicle gingerly pursuing him over snow-slick Memorial Drive, struck a concrete abutment and was killed instantly. His grieving parents, asking only anonymity to protect them from the mercilessness of publicity, donated the boy's corneas to the Massachusetts Eye and Ear Infirmary and one kidney each to the Brigham and to Suffolk County.

Adam sat with Kender and agonized over the problem of how much immunosuppressive drug to give Mrs. Bergstrom with the new kidney.

Kender decided on 130 mgs. of Imuran.

"Her renal function is very low," Adam said doubtfully. "Why wouldn't 100 mgs. be enough?"

"I gave her ninety mgs. last time," Kender said, "and she rejected the kidney decisively. I don't want to have to put her through this again." They operated after midnight and the new kidney was putting out urine when they took her from the operating room.

On New Year's Eve Adam was in the operating room again, preparing to do a splenectomy on the first of the drunken drivers, who had had the good sense to rupture his spleen on the highway only two blocks from the hospital. He stood with his gloved hands crossed on his chest and waited with Harry Lee, who would assist. Norm Pomerantz was giving the general anesthesia, which would be light but complicated because the man already had anesthetized himself with alcohol. It was very quiet in the OR.

"It's twelve o'clock, Adam," Lee said.

"Happy New Year, Harry."

The following evening, troubled by the drug dosage Kender had given Mrs. Bergstrom, he reviewed her records for hours but could find no solace in them, finally giving up and falling asleep over his notebook with his head on his arms. He dreamed of Room 314 and the woman, the figure offering herself to him merging with another, becoming slimmer and harder and less ripe until he was making love to Gaby instead of performing a rite with Liz Meomartino.

When he awoke, he laughed at himself.

Somehow, though, he had gained the knowledge that the man

who ended up with Gaby Pender would never have to worry about sending another doctor home to pick up some slides.

But of course she had other problems. He was well rid of the crazy little broad, he told himself.

An hour later he went to the telephone and dialed her number. He was expecting Susan Haskell but instead of the roommate's voice it was hers saying hello.

"Gaby?"

"Yes?"

"It's Adam."

"Oh."

"How have you been?"

"Fine. That is, I wasn't for a while, but I am now."

"Are you?" he asked wistfully.

"Yes."

"I'm not. Happy New Year, Gaby."

"Happy New Year, Adam."

"Gaby, I—"

"Adam—" They had spoken together, and now they both waited.

"I have to see you," he said.

"When?"

"I'm on tonight. Listen, come to the hospital parking lot at nine o'clock. If I don't show right up, wait for me."

"What makes you think I'll come running because you snap your fingers?" she asked coldly. "And wait around?"

He felt alarm, chagrin, great regret.

"Oh, Adam, I'm not fine either," she burst out. She was laughing and crying at the same time, the only girl he had ever known who was able to do that. "I'll be there, darling. Darling Adam." And hung up.

Book Three

Spring and Summer, The Full Circle

Chapter 12: Adam Silverstone

Adam had talked with Gaby quietly and at great length, sitting in the blue Plymouth in the hospital parking lot, with the heater on and the snow falling and an ambulance beacon blinking at them until a layer of white covered the windshield thick enough to shut out the rest of the world.

"It was all my fault," he said. "I'll never let us do this to one another again."

"You almost finished me. I couldn't even talk to another man."

He was silent.

But there were other unpleasant facts that had to be faced.

"My father is a hopeless alcoholic. Right now he seems to be making it, if you can call it that. But he's cracked wide open before and probably will again. When that happens I'll need every cent I can scrape together just to provide care for him. I can't get married until I'm in a position to earn some money."

"When will that be?"

"Next year."

She would never have Liz's driven sensuality, he knew, and yet she was so much more desirable to him. So dear. He had been careful not to touch her, and he made no move to touch her now.

"I don't want to wait until next year, Adam," she said steadily.

He considered talking to someone in the Psychiatry Department at the hospital and then he remembered that Gerry Thornton, who had been a classmate in medical school, was now at the Massachusetts Mental Health Center. He telephoned him and exchanged greetings and five minutes of gossip about the whereabouts of others.

"Ah—Did you call me with anything particular in mind?" Thornton asked him finally.

"Well, as a matter of fact," he said. "I have a friend. A very close friend who has a problem, and I thought it would be nice to chat about it with someone both congenial and psychoanalyzed."

"Actually, I still have several years of my own analysis left," Thornton said scrupulously. And waited.

"Gerald, if your schedule is tight it doesn't have to be this week . . ."

"Adam," Thornton said reproachfully. "If I came to you with an acute appendix, would you ask me to wait until next week? How about Thursday?"

"Lunch?"

"Oh, I think my office would be better," Thornton said.

". . . So you see," he said. "What I'm concerned about is the possibility that our affair will do her harm."

"Well, of course I don't know the girl. But I think it's safe to say that if she's seriously involved and you're just screwing around, if you will pardon the phrase . . ."

"That isn't the case. But I want to know, you smart-ass Freudian psychiatrist, what a long, drawn-out affair will do to a girl suffering from what appears to be a definite hypochondriasis."

"Hmm. Well, I can't diagnose for her any more than you can tell over the telephone whether a patient has carcinoma." Thornton reached for the tobacco and began to fill his pipe. "You say her parents are divorced?"

Adam nodded. "She's been cut off from both of them for some time."

"Well, it might have been that, of course. We're slowly learning something about imaginary illness. Some family doctors have estimated that as many as eight out of every ten patients in their waiting rooms are there for psychosomatic reasons. Their pain is just as real as any other patient's, of course, but it's caused by the mind, not the body." He struck a match and puffed. "Do you know the poetry of Elizabeth Barrett Browning?"

"Some of it."

"There are some lines she wrote to her dog, Fluff."

"I think the dog's name was Flush."

Thornton looked annoyed. "That's right, Flush." He went to a bookcase and pulled down a volume and searched the pages. "Here it is.

> But of *thee* it shall be said,
> This dog watched beside a bed
>   Day and night unweary,
> Watched within a curtained room
> Where no sunbeam broke the bloom
>   Round the sick and dreary.

"All the evidence indicates that for forty years she was a classical hypochrondriac. An invalid, in fact, so far gone she had to be carried up and down the stairs. Then Robert Browning fell in love first with the spirit of her poetry and finally with her, and he stormed old man Barrett's fortress on Wimpole Street and the hypochondriasis was gone with the wind—or perhaps the nuptial bed, I don't know. She even bore his child after she was forty years old. What's your girl's name?" he asked abruptly.

"Gaby. Gabrielle."

"Lovely name. How does Gabrielle feel at present?"

"Right now she's asymptomatic."

"Has she had any psychotherapy?"

"No."

"People with anxieties are being helped every day, you know."

"Will you see her?"

Thornton frowned. "I don't think so. I think it would be better if she saw a very bright guy over at the Beth Israel who has made something of a specialty of hypochrondriasis. Let me know if she's agreeable and I'll call him and set it up."

Adam shook his hand. "Thanks, Gerry."

Gerald, you'll end up a stuffed shirt, he prophesied as he waded through the pipe smoke and left the office. Then he grinned. Thornton would no doubt patiently tolerate that observation as a negative transference.

Gaby saw a lot of Dorothy. They had liked one another at once and often when Adam and Spurgeon were working the two girls got together. It was Dorothy who took her to the Beacon Hill neighborhood where she found the apartment.

"My sister lives not far from here," Dorothy said. "My sister Janet."

"Oh? Shall we stop in and say hello?"

"No. I don't do that. We don't get along."

She sensed that Dorothy was troubled but she asked no questions. Two days later, as she guided Adam up Beacon Street, excitement had driven the incident from her mind.

"Where are you taking me?" he asked her.

"You'll see."

The gold leaf of the State House dome imitated the burning bush in the morning sun but shed no warmth. In a moment she took his hand in her mitten and led him from the Common-born winds into the relative shelter of Joy Street.

"How much farther?" he said, his breath making frost puffs.

"You'll see," she said again.

She wore a red ski jacket and blue stretch pants that hugged what the previous evening he had described, stroking, as the loveliest gluteal area he had ever seen on or off an operating table; and a blue wool skating cap with a white tassel that he yanked when they were halfway down Beacon Hill to make her stop.

"I don't move. Not another step until you tell me where we're going."

"Please, Adam. We're almost there."

"Swear a sexy oath."

"On your thing."

On Phillips Street they walked halfway down the block and then stopped in front of a four-story apartment building with cracked stucco walls. "Watch these steps," she said, indicating the walkdown entrance.

"Suicidal," he muttered. The concrete stairs were covered with three inches of scarred ice, over which they moved gingerly. At the bottom she took a key from her pocket and opened the door.

The single window allowed very little light into the room. "Wait a minute," she said hurriedly, and turned on all three of the lamps.

It was a studio room. The wallpaper had been painted a brown that was too dark for the limited illumination. Under the dust the floor was brick-colored asphalt tile, cracked in spots. There was a fairly-new couch that undoubtedly opened into a bed, one over-

stuffed chair in faded damask and another chair that had been res-
cued from a set of wicker porch furniture.

She took off her mitten and bit the back of her thumb. He had
discovered it to be a characteristic gesture, used when she was
tense. "Well, what do you think?"

He removed her hand from her mouth. "What do I think about
what?"

"I told the landlady I'd let her know by 10 o'clock about renting
it."

"It's a cellar."

"A basement."

"Even the floor is dirty."

"I'll scrub it and wax it until it gleams."

"Gaby, are you serious? It's not as nice as your place in Cambridge. Not nearly."

"In addition to this bedroom-living room combination there's a
bathroom and a kitchenette. Take a look."

"You can't tell me Susan Haskell is going to like this better than
the other place."

"Susan Haskell isn't going to live here."

He thought about that for a moment. "She isn't?"

"We are. You and I."

They stood and looked at one another. "It's seventy-five dollars a
month. I think it's a bargain, Adam," she said.

"Oh, that is," he said. "It really is."

He put his arms around her.

"Gaby, are you sure this is what you want?"

"I'm positive. Unless you don't want it."

"I'll paint the walls," he said in a little while.

"They're ugly, but it's a fantastic location. The elevated station is
only a couple of blocks away," she said. "So is the Charles Street
Jail. And the landlady told me that in just three minutes you can
walk from here to the apartment on Bowdoin Street where Jack
Kennedy used to live."

He kissed her cheek and found it was wet. "That will be convenient," he said.

He had very little to pack. He took his things out of the bureau
and put them in the B-4 bag. There were a few garments on hangers
in the closet and some books that he placed in a brown paper bag,

and the job was done. The room looked just as it had the night he moved into it. He was leaving nothing of himself behind in the little cell.

Spurgeon was on duty in the ward and so there was nobody on the sixth floor to say goodbye to.

They drove to the place in Cambridge and Susan Haskell helped Gaby to pack her things while he emptied two bookcases into cardboard cartons.

Susan was very upset but she treated Adam with icy care.

"The plastic bucket is mine," Gaby said guiltily. "I bought a bunch of supplies and things but I forgot to get a bucket. Is it all right if I take it?"

"Of course. Take whatever you paid for, silly."

"We'll have lunch in a couple of days," Gaby said. "I'll call you."

They were both quiet as they drove over the Harvard Bridge and then followed the river on the Boston side of the Charles. The sky was ashen and their mood had withered but when they got to Phillips Street the physical activity of unloading the car broke the spell.

He performed a spirited little breakneck ballet on the icy stairs while carrying in the things, but managed not to fall. By the time the last carton was on the floor she had wiped down the bureau drawers with disinfectant and was lining them with butcher paper. "There's just the one dresser," she said. "Does it matter which drawers I put your things in?"

"Suit yourself," he said, suddenly happier. "I want to clear the ice from those steps."

"Great idea," she said, making him proud to be such a responsible householder.

When he came back into the house, cold but triumphant over the forces of nature, she stopped him from removing his coat.

"We're going to need sheets for the bed," she said.

So he went to Jordan's, where briefly he was haunted by the questions of white or colored, plain or contoured. Finally he plunged, settling on beige and contoured and buying four, two to use and two for the laundry.

When he opened the door he found her on her hands and knees, scrubbing.

"Stay close to the wall, darling," she said. "I left a space for you to walk on."

He circumnavigated the room. "Is there anything else I can do?"

"Well, the floors in the john and the kitchenette still have to be washed," she said. "You can scrub in there while I wax in here."

"Is that absolutely necessary?" he asked a bit faintly.

"We can't live in a place without cleaning it first," she said, shocked.

So he took the plastic bucket and threw out the used water and rinsed it and made new suds and got down on his hands and knees and scrubbed. The two floors were bigger when you got down to them but he sang at his work.

By the time he was through it was dark outside and they were both hungry. He left her waxing the bathroom floor and although he was sweating profusely he allowed gravity to carry his rubbery legs down the cold, windy north side of Beacon Hill to the roast beef stand next to the Charles Street Jail, where he ordered sandwiches and root beers to go and had the distinct feeling that the man behind the counter knew he was bringing the food next door to a prisoner.

When they had eaten he was ready for the locker room but she asked him to wash the kitchenette cupboards while she cleaned the closets and the bathroom fixtures.

This time he didn't sing. Toward the end each of them labored with mechanical grimness. She finished first and while she showered he waited in the wicker chair, too weary to do anything but breathe. When she came out in her robe he went in and soaked under the fine hot spray until it began getting cool fast and he entered a race with the dropping temperature, soaping and rinsing off one split second before the water was unbearably cold.

She had opened the couch and made the bed and she was lying there in a blue nightgown reading a magazine and marking recipes that she liked.

"That's a lousy light. You'll ruin your eyes," he said.

"Why don't you shut it?"

He made the rounds of all three weak-bulbed lamps and stumbled on her shoes in the dark on the way back. He eased into bed beside her, stifling a groan because his muscles had already stiffened dreadfully, and he had just turned toward her when somewhere a woman screamed, a long and terrified sound followed by a thump somewhere outside their door.

"My God."

He leaped out of bed. "What did you do with my bag?"

"In the closet."

She ran and handed it to him and he stuck his bare feet into his shoes and his arms into his robe and raced outside. It was very cold and he couldn't see a thing. From somewhere upstairs the woman screamed again. He climbed the front stairs that led into the upper regions of the building and as he entered the front hall, the door of Apartment One opened and a woman looked out.

"Yes?"

"We heard something. Do you know what it was?"

"I didn't hear anything. Who are you?"

"I'm Dr. Silverstone. We just moved in. Downstairs."

"Oh, I'm so pleased to know you." The door opened wider, revealing a short dumpy body, graying hair, a round flabby face with faint signs of hair on the upper lip. "I'm Mrs. Walters. The landlady. Your wife's a lovely little woman."

"Thank you," he said as upstairs the woman screamed again. "That," he said.

"Oh, that's only Bertha Krol," the woman said.

"Oh. Bertha Krol."

"Yes. Don't let her bother you. She'll stop in a little while." She looked at him standing there in his shoes and bare ankles and high-water pajamas and old robe and carrying the bag and her shoulders began to shake.

"Good evening," he said stiffly.

As he walked down the first set of front steps something hurtled downward and there was another thump as a bag of garbage split open in the middle of the street. Amazed, he observed now in the light of the street lamp the messy evidence of the first bag they had heard striking the ground a few minutes before. He looked up in time to see a head flick back into the window above.

"That's terrible!" he called. "You stop that, Bertha Krol!"

Something whistled by his head and clattered on the stairs.

A beer can.

Inside, Gaby was sitting in the chair, frightened. "What was it?" she asked.

"Only Bertha Krol. The landlady says she'll stop in a little while."

He put the medicine bag back into the closet and shut the lights and threw off the robe and stepped out of the shoes and they re-entered the bed.

"Adam?"

"What?"

"I'm exhausted," she said in a small voice.

"So am I," he said, relieved. "Stiff and sore, too."

"Tomorrow I'll get some liniment and rub you," she said.

"Mmmm. Good night, Gaby."

"Good night, darling Adam."

Upstairs, the woman howled. Outside, another can clattered on the icy pavement. Next to him she shivered slightly and he turned and put his arm around her shoulders.

In a little while he could feel her shaking under his arm much the same way as the landlady had shaken but was unable to tell whether in sorrow or mirth.

"What's the matter?" he asked gently.

"I'm so *tired*. And I keep thinking 'So this is what it's like to be a fallen woman.' "

He laughed with her, although it hurt in a number of places.

A small cold foot found its way into his instep. Upstairs the woman—he wondered, drunk or demented?—wailed no more. Occasionally a car went by outside, crunching his ice and Mrs. Krol's garbage and sending brief flaring shadow-pictures flitting across the wall. Her hand came up and dropped light and warm upon his thigh. She was sleeping, and he discovered that she snored but decided the soft, rhythmic sibilation was both musical and appealing, the moan of doves in immemorial elms, and murmuring of innumerable bees. It was a sound he already liked very much.

In the morning they awoke early and despite considerable musculoskeletal pain made delighted love under the layer of thick blankets in the still, chill room and then because there was as yet no food in the kitchen cupboards they dressed and walked down the hill, which had been covered in the night by soft white snow, and had a big breakfast in a cafeteria on Charles Street.

She walked with him to the elevated station, and kissed him goodbye for the next thirty-six hours and they could see on each other's faces how pleased they both were with the whole thing; but neither one tried to put it into words, perhaps out of superstition.

She went to the A&P and shopped, trying to be very frugal and sensible because he had a complex about their living on his check from the hospital, which she knew would not go far if she spent money with her customary disregard.

But when she saw the ripe avocados she couldn't resist and she bought two. Despite her shopping care and the fact that they were only two people, she was buying staples to fill a bare cupboard; she ended up with five full bags. She considered going home to fetch the car and then decided to ask the store manager if she could borrow a shopping cart. There was a store rule against it but he was overwhelmed that she had bothered to ask. He even helped her to load the bundles. It appeared a good solution until she started to push the thing up the hill. There was not enough traction for the steel wheels in the snow. They slipped and skidded and so did she.

A colored girl with a frosted streak in her hair came out of nowhere to her rescue. "You push on one side and I'll push on the other," she said.

"Thank you," Gaby gasped. Between the two of them they managed to reach Phillips Street.

"You saved my life! Won't you come in for a cup of tea?"

"All right," the girl said.

They carried in the groceries and took off their coats and dropped them on the couch. The girl wore faded blue jeans and an old sweatshirt. She had high cheekbones and lovely velvet-brown skin. She looked about seventeen. "What's your name?" she asked.

"Oh. I'm sorry. I'm Gabrielle—" She stopped, hung up about whether to say Pender or Silverstone.

The girl didn't appear to notice. "That's very nice."

"What's your name?"

"Janet."

Gaby was standing on tiptoes, reaching for the teapot. "Not Dorothy's Janet?"

"I have a sister named Dorothy."

"But we're friends!"

"Oh?" the girl said, almost without interest.

Gaby brewed tea in the kitchenette for the first time and opened a package of cookies and they sipped tea and had several cookies apiece and talked. Janet lived on Joy Street. "The name was one of the reasons we moved there. Into this big huge house."

Gaby laughed. "You make it sound enormous."

"It is."

"How many rooms?"

"I've never counted. Eighteen, maybe twenty. We need the space. I live with an unusually large family."

"How many people?"

She shrugged. "It varies. Sometimes people go away and sometimes other people come and stay on. I don't know how many we have right now. Quite a few."

"Oh," Gaby said, comprehending.

"It works out quite well," Janet said, helping herself to another cooky. "Everybody just does his own thing."

"What kind of thing?"

"You know. Make posters. Or flowers, or sandals. Anything you want."

"What do you do?"

"I dig. I'm a digger. I go out and bring back food."

"Where do you get it?"

"Oh, everywhere. Markets and bakeries. They give us stale stuff and spoiled vegetables and things. You'd be surprised how much good is left when you cut away the spoiled parts. And people around here get to know us and give us some things. There are five other diggers in my family. We do fine."

"I see," Gaby said faintly. In a little while she took the cups and things and placed them in the kitchenette sink.

"I'd better go return the cart," she said.

"I'll bring it back. I'm going there anyway."

"Oh, no, really . . ."

"You don't trust me to bring it back?"

"Of course I do."

"All right, then I will."

Gaby went into the kitchenette and put a jar of peanut butter and two jars of jam and a loaf of bread and—who knew why?—one of the avocados into a bag. "I'd like to give you these," she said to the girl, feeling ashamed for no reason she could understand.

Janet shrugged indifferently. "You've got a lot of books," she said, indicating the volumes stacked on the floor. "Orange crates make tremendous bookcases. Painted different colors." She waved her hand and left. When she was gone the apartment was quiet and empty. Gaby put away her order, aware that now she would have to go down the hill again for more peanut butter, jam and bread. She cut two strips of adhesive tape and typed GABRIELLE PENDER on one and ADAM R. SILVERSTONE, M.D. on the other and then fixed them both outside over the rusted black metal mailbox.

At the market she replaced the items she had given the digger girl and on impulse asked for and was given six orange crates. They filled the Plymouth to capacity. On the way home she made a stop at the hardware store and bought two brushes and paint thinner and cans of black, pumpkin, and white enamel.

The rest of the day was lavished on the project. She spread that morning's newspaper on the floor and worked meticulously and without stopping, painting two boxes in each color, wanting it to come out well so she could surprise Adam. When all six boxes were painted she cleaned the brushes and put them away under the sink with the paint cans and took a long shower and got into pajamas. She had been unhappy about her arrangement of their things in the dresser drawers and now she took half the things out of his drawers and half the things out of her drawers and swapped them around until all the compartments were co-ed, his socks nestling next to her stockings, her panties stacked primly beside his Jockey shorts. Under her blouses and bordering on his shirts she tucked the little round fake mother-of-pearl box containing the pills that were the touchstones of their relationship, the magic potions which allowed them their life together.

She studied until ten o'clock then locked the door, fastened the chain lock, took one of the horrible little pills, turned off the lights and got into bed.

Lying in the dark was loneliest, she decided after a while.

The apartment was semi-solid with the smell of paint. Mrs. Krol screamed three times but her heart didn't seem to be in it and she threw nothing out of the window that made a noise when it struck the ground. From the direction of the Massachusetts General an ambulance siren moaned and it made her feel close to Adam. When cars went by on Phillips Street their headlamps continued to make monsters that chased each other off the walls.

She had begun to doze when somebody knocked.

She leaped out of bed and stood behind the door in the dark, opening it just the bare crack that the little chain allowed.

"Who is it?"

"Janet sent me."

Through the crack by the light of the street lamp she could see a man, no, a boy. A very large boy with long blond hair that looked in the dimness to be almost the color of Janet's.

"What do you want?"

"She sent something." He held out a shapeless bundle.

"Can you leave it? I'm not dressed."

"All right," he said cheerfully. He set it down and his bearlike shadow bounded away. She put on her robe and turned on all the lights and waited a long time until her courage gathered, then she flung off the chain and snatched the bundle and slammed the door and locked it and sat on the bed with her heart pounding. Wrapped in a loose chrysalis of old newspaper was a large bouquet of colored paper flowers. Big blossoms in shades of black, yellow and orange. Just the right colors.

She went back to bed with the lights on and lay there admiring the room, less frightened. Eventually she stopped imagining she heard tappings on her door and soon after that she fell asleep, sensing for the first time that she was in her own home.

Chapter 13: Rafael Meomartino

When Meomartino was a small boy he had regularly accompanied Leo, the family factotum, to Saint Raphael's, a small whitewashed church surrounded on all sides by his father's cane fields, there to receive the cool wafer on the tongue from Father Ignacio, a *guajiro* worker-priest with bad breath, to whom he regularly confessed the sins of his early adolescence and received the gentle respectful penalties of privilege.

I have had evil thoughts, Father.

Five Hail Mary's and five Acts of Contrition, my son.

I have abused my body, Father.

Five Hail Mary's and five Acts of Contrition. Struggle against the weakness of the flesh, my son.

For weddings and funerals the family was accustomed to the pomp of the Cathedral in Havana, but on ordinary occasions Rafe felt at home in the small church, which had been built by his father's labor gangs the day he was born. Kneeling in the dark, damp interior before the plaster statue of his patron saint, he would make his penance and then ask the archangel to intercede for him against a tyrannical teacher, to help him to learn Latin, to protect him from Guillermo.

Now, lying haunch to haunch with the sleeping wife to whom he had given cold and despairing love an hour before, he thought of Saint Raphael and wished fervently that he were twelve years old again.

He had stopped believing at Harvard. It had been a long time

274

since he had confessed, years since he had really talked to a priest.

Saint Raphael, he said silently into the dark room.

Show me how I can help her.

Help me to see where I have failed her, why I do not quench her, why she goes to other men.

Silverstone, he thought.

He was a better man and a better surgeon than that one, and yet Silverstone threatened his existence from both directions.

He smiled mirthlessly, thinking that Longwood evidently had decided that there were worse things than a Cuban in the family. The Old Man had been quite shocked at the sight of Liz with Silverstone. Ever since that night he had been almost warm and friendly, as if trying to indicate that he knew that his niece was very difficult.

But now Longwood was putting more pressure on him every day to make certain that he and not Silverstone would win the faculty appointment.

Meomartino chewed on self-doubt.

Saint Raphael, he said.

Am I not sufficiently male? I am a physician, I know that at the moment we are finished with one another she is satisfied.

Indicate to me what I must do. I promise that I will make Confession, take Communion, that I will become a true Catholic once again.

It was quiet in the dark room, only the sound of her deep breathing.

He remembered that despite all his kneeling before the statue he had failed Latin and that his body customarily was black and blue with the bruises inflicted by Guillermo until the day he had grown strong enough to vanquish his older brother.

Saint Raphael had not helped him then, either.

In the morning, heavy-eyed, he went to the hospital and struggled through the early hours. His mood was already foul by the time he led the house officers through morning rounds, and it was not improved when he reached James Roche, a 69-year-old gentleman with an advanced carcinoma of the colon, who was scheduled for surgery early the following morning.

While nurses and dieticians hustled through the cavernous ward carrying trays, Meomartino quietly outlined the case, with which most of the house officers were familiar, and prepared to ask a few teaching questions.

But he stopped talking in mid-sentence.

"*Cristos.* I can't believe it."

Mr. Roche was eating his lunch. His plate contained chicken, potatoes, string beans.

"Dr. Robinson, why is this man eating what he is eating?"

"I have no idea," Spurgeon said. "The order to change his diet is in the book. I wrote it there myself."

"Please get me the order book."

When he opened the book the order was there, written in Robinson's neat, controlled hand, but it didn't assuage his anger.

"Mr. Roche, what did you have for breakfast?" he asked.

"Usual breakfast. Juice, an egg, little cereal. Farina, it was. And a glass of milk."

"Scratch his name from the surgery schedule for tomorrow morning," Meomartino said. "Reschedule him for day after tomorrow. Goddammit."

"Oh, and toast," the patient said.

Meomartino looked at the house officers. "Can you imagine what would have happened if we had gone into this man's colon with all that solid waste present? Can you imagine trying to clamp bleeders through a mess like that? Can you imagine the excess of contamination? Take my word for it, you can't imagine it until you've been through it."

"Doctor," the patient said anxiously, "should I leave the rest of my meal?"

"You finish your chicken and enjoy it," he said. "Tomorrow morning you'll go on the diet you should have been on today, a liquid diet. If anyone tries to give you anything more solid than Jello tomorrow, don't you eat it. You send for me right away, *comprende?*"

The man nodded.

Mysteriously, none of the nurses knew who had served Mr. Roche his breakfast and his lunch.

Twenty minutes later Meomartino sat in his office. He prepared a service complaint against the unidentified nurse who had served the two trays, and signed it with an angry scrawl.

That afternoon there was a telephone call from Longwood.

"I'm not at all happy with the number of post-mortem permissions you've turned in."

"I've done my best to get them," he said.

"Surgical fellows on other services have gotten twice as many permissions as you have."

"Perhaps there were more deaths on their services."

"On your own service this year another surgeon has gotten a lot more permissions than you."

He didn't have to ask Longwood to name the surgeon. "I'll try harder," he said.

In a little while Harry Lee came into the office.

"I just got my tail reamed, Harry. Dr. Longwood wants more post-mortem permissions from me. I'm going to pass that reaming along to any house officer working on one of my cases."

"We've all but gone on our knees to the family every time we've lost a patient," the Chinese resident said. "You know that. When they've agreed to a post we've gotten their signatures. If they have strong personal reasons for refusing . . ." He shrugged.

"Longwood indicated Adam Silverstone has been turning in lots more permissions than I have."

"I didn't realize you were in a race." Lee looked at him curiously.

"Now you realize."

"Now I realize. You know how some services get permissions?"

Rafe waited.

"They frighten the resistance out of the survivors, hint that the entire family may share some mysterious weakness that killed the patient, and that all the surgeon wants to do is save their lives by conducting an autopsy."

"That's disgusting."

"I agree. Do you want us to start doing that, too?"

Rafe looked at him and smiled. "No, just do your best. How many post permission slips did we hand in last month?"

"None," Lee said.

"Goddammit. That's exactly what I mean."

"We couldn't very well get permissions for autopsies," Lee said mildly.

"Why the hell not?"

"Because we didn't lose a patient on the service last month."

I will not apologize, he thought. "That means I owe you all a party."

Lee nodded. "You or Silverstone."

"I'll give it," Meomartino said. "I have an apartment."

"Adam also now has an apartment, I understand," Lee said. "At least, he doesn't live in the hospital anymore."

So that is where Liz goes, Meomartino thought numbly.

Lee smiled. *"Une nécessité d'amour,* perhaps. Even on Formosa we have such arrangements."

Meomartino realized to his annoyance that with the ball of his thumb he was rubbing the angels on the pocket watch again.

"You can spread the word," he said. "The party's on me."

Liz was delighted.

"Oh, I love parties! I'll be the kind of hostess who will get you Uncle Harland's job when he retires," she said, immediately curling the long legs under her on the couch and filling a scratch pad with lists of things to be attended to, liquor, canapes, flowers, help . . .

He was suddenly uncomfortably aware of the fact that most of the people on the service were not accustomed to large flower bills or servant fees when they entertained one another.

"Let's keep it simple," he said. They compromised on a bartender and Helga, the woman who worked for them regularly on a part-time basis.

"Liz," he said. "I'd appreciate it if you wouldn't . . ."

"I won't drink a thing."

"There's no need for that. Just don't overdo."

"Not a thing. You must allow me to do that. I want to prove myself to you," she said.

The truce with death didn't last. On Friday, the day before the party, Melanie Bergstrom developed pneumonia. In the face of a soaring temperature and evidence that both lungs were involved, Kender filled her with antibiotics.

Peggy Weld sat next to her sister's bed and held her hand under the bottom of the oxygen tent. He found excuses to enter the room but Peggy was not interested in him. Her eyes were fixed on her sister's face. He heard conversation only once.

"Hang tough, baby," Peggy commanded.

Melanie licked lips dried by her labored breathing. "You'll take care of them?"

The oxygen hiss was loud.

"What?"

"Ted and the girls."

"Listen," Peggy snarled, "I've done your dirty work all your life. You'll take care of them yourself."

Melanie smiled. "Ah, Peg."

"You're *not* going to give in to this thing!"

But she died in Intensive Care early the next morning.

It was discovered by Joan Anderson, the little blonde probationer. The student nurse was calm and lucid, but after she had reported to Meomartino she began to tremble.

"Send her home," he told Miss Fultz.

But the head nurse had seen hundreds of young girls suddenly become aware of mortality. For the rest of the day she assigned Miss Anderson to cover the most disagreeable of the ward's patients, men and woman brimming with bitter, complaining life.

Meomartino was waiting for Peggy Weld when she came hurrying into the hospital.

"Hi," he said.

"Good morning. Do you know how my sister is?"

"Sit down for a minute and talk to me."

"It's happened, hasn't it," she said quietly.

"Yes," he said.

"Poor Mellie." She turned and walked away.

"Peg," he said, but she shook her head and kept walking, out of the hospital.

Several hours later she came to collect her sister's things. She was pale but dry-eyed, he saw, which worried him. He had the feeling she was the kind of woman who would wait until she was completely alone, even if it took weeks to achieve the necessary privacy, and then become hysterical.

"Are you all right?" he asked.

"Yes. I've just been walking."

They simply sat for a little while.

"She deserved better than that," she said. "She really did. You should have known her when she was well."

"I wish I had. What are you going to do now?" he asked gently.

She shrugged. "The only thing I know. After . . . everything . . . I'll call my agent and tell him I'm ready to go back to work."

"That's good," he said, his relief in his voice.

She looked at him curiously. "What does that mean?"

"I'm sorry. I overheard a conversation . . ."

She looked at him and smiled wistfully. "My sister was very impractical. My brother-in-law wouldn't have me on a platter," she said. "He thinks I'm a loose lady. To tell the truth I've gotten so I can't stand the stuffy sonofabitch."

She stood and held out her hand. "Goodbye, Rafe Meomartino," she said, not attempting to mask her regret.

He took her hand and thought of the senseless time-patterns in which human lives crossed one another, wondering what would have happened if he had met this woman before the night Liz had taken a drunken stranger in out of the rain.

"Goodbye, Peggy Weld," he said, letting go.

That afternoon, with Dr. Longwood absent and Dr. Kender presiding, the service met in Mortality Conference, devoting the entire session to the case of Melanie Bergstrom.

Dr. Kender faced the issue squarely, attributing death to infection-susceptibility produced by the administration of too much immunosuppressive drug. "Dr. Silverstone suggested dosages of 100 mgs.," he said. "I decided the dosages should be 130 mgs."

"In your opinion, would pneumonia have resulted if you had given her the 100-mg. dosages suggested by Dr. Silverstone?" Dr. Sack asked.

"Probably not," Kender said. "But I'm reasonably sure that with only 100 mgs. she would have rejected the transplant. Dr. Silverstone has been conducting the animal studies, and he can tell you that it's not simply a matter of X units of body weight calling for Y units of drug. Other factors enter into the problem—the patient's stamina, the strength of her heart, her inherent resistance to disease, no doubt other things of which we're not yet even aware."

"Where do you go from here, Doctor?" Sack asked.

Kender shrugged. "There's a substance produced by injecting horses with ground-up lymph nodes from human cadavers. It's called Anti-Lymphocyte Serum, ALS. for short. There have been preliminary reports that it's very helpful in cases like this one. I think we'll start animal studies with it right away."

"Dr. Kender." It was Miriam Parkhurst. "When do you plan to give a kidney to Harland Longwood?"

"We're looking for a cadaver donor," Kender said. "His blood-type is B-negative. Donors are scarce enough, but with the added complication of a rare blood type . . ." He shook his head.

"It's a terrible obstacle," Joel Sack said. "Fewer than two out of every hundred donors coming to our blood bank are B-negatives."

"Have you notified the other hospitals that we're looking for a B-negative cadaver donor?" Miriam asked.

Kender nodded. "There's something else you people should know," he said. "We're able to sustain Dr. Longwood's physical condition on the dialysis machine. But he's emotionally unsuited to the treatment. For psychiatric reasons, he can't be maintained on dialysis much longer."

"That's my point," Miriam Parkhurst said. "We have to do *something*. Some of us have known this man—this great surgeon—as a friend and a teacher for years."

"Dr. Parkhurst," Kender said gently. "We're doing what is possible. None of us can do what is impossible." Obviously determined to restore professionalism to the meeting, he turned toward Joel Sack. "Has the Bergstrom post-mortem been completed yet?"

Dr. Sack shook his head. "I've received no permission for autopsy."

"I spoke to Mr. Bergstrom," Adam Silverstone said. "He refuses to consider post-mortem."

Kender frowned. "Do you think his decision is final?"

"Yes, sir," Silverstone said.

"I'd like to try to change his mind," Meomartino said suddenly. They stared at him.

"That is, if Dr. Silverstone has no objections."

"Certainly not. I don't believe he's likely to sign that paper, but if you want to try . . ."

"It can't hurt to try again," Kender said, glancing approvingly at Meomartino. He looked at the assembled surgeons. "Unless we have the results of a post, it's senseless to vote on this case. But it seems obvious that at our present level of knowledge concerning the rejection phenomenon, this death was unavoidable." He paused for possible objections and then, sensing general agreement, nodded to indicate that the meeting was over.

Meomartino made the telephone call from his office.

"Hello?" Ted Bergstrom said.

"Mr. Bergstrom? This is Dr. Meomartino, at the hospital."

"What is it?" Bergstrom asked, and in the voice Meomartino felt the subconscious hatred of the surviving relative toward the surgeons who were losers.

"It's about the autopsy," he said.

"I made that clear when I talked with the other doctor. It's over. We've all gone through enough. Her death will be the end of it."

"There's something else I think I should mention to you," he said.

"Go ahead."

"You have two daughters."

"So?"

"We don't believe they're in danger. We have no real evidence that a predisposition to kidney failure is hereditary."

"Oh, my God," Bergstrom said.

"I'm sure the post-mortem will indicate that there is absolutely nothing to worry about," Meomartino said.

Bergstrom was silent. Then from the telephone came a hoarse grunting, the sound of an animal in grief.

"I'll send somebody right over with the permission slip. All you have to do is sign it, Mr. Bergstrom," he said.

Meomartino sat and listened to the terrible sound for what seemed like a very long time and then, gently, he replaced the receiver.

That evening at 8:20 when the chimes sounded indicating the first arrival he answered the door himself.

"Hi, Doc," Maish Meyerson said.

Meomartino brought the ambulance driver in and introduced him to Liz. She had gone to the hairdresser's that morning and had surprised him by coming home with black hair.

"Do you like it?" she had asked, almost shyly. "They said it would grow out to my own color so that you'll hardly know."

"Very much." It frightened him a little, made her even more remote, a complete stranger. But he had been urging her to do it for a long time, and he was happy that she had done it for him, hopeful that it was a good sign.

Now Meyerson chose sour mash bourbon. They lifted their glasses to one another.

"Nothing for you, Mrs. Meomartino?"

"No, thank you."

They both knocked it back neat and gasped.

"What's it all about, Maish?" he asked.

"What?"

"The whole damn thing."

"I don't have the slightest idea." They grinned at one another and he filled Meyerson's glass and then his own.

The chimes sounded again and relief showed in Liz's face, but only momentarily. This time it was Helen Fultz. She let Helga take her coat and joined them in the living room but would take nothing stronger than tomato juice. The four of them sat and looked at one another and tried to talk and then mercifully the chimes began to sound regularly and the place filled. In a little while there were people standing all around and the noise was the kind made at parties. He found himself wondering if Peggy Weld had had a chance to weep yet, then as the host he began to drown in a pool of people.

Some of the house officers were married and brought their wives.

Mike Schneider, whose marriage was widely known to be on the rocks, introduced a slightly-obese redhead as his kissing cousin from Cleveland, Ohio.

In contrast, Jack Moylan was with Joan Anderson of the neat withers. The student nurse's eyes were a little too bright, Meomartino thought, but she appeared none the worse for her earlier trauma.

"I've never been drunk, Rafe," she said. "Can I change that to-night?"

"Be my guest," he said.

"Change is the key word. Down with the establishment," Moylan said, leading her to the bar.

Harry Lee, whom no one had ever seen with a girl before, was with Alice Tayakawa, the anesthetist.

Spurgeon Robinson, accompanied by a black Athena to whom he coolly introduced Meomartino, had arrived with Adam Silverstone and a small blonde with a Florida tan. Meomartino watched as their path crossed with that of the hostess.

His wife looked at her curiously. "How do you do?" she said.

"How do you do?"

The two women smiled at one another.

By 10:30 Meyerson had convinced Helen Fultz to try a screwdriver because orange juice contained vitamin C. Harry Lee and Alice Tayakawa sat in a corner and argued heatedly over the dangers of liver damage as a negative aspect of halothane anesthesia. "Have another," Jack Moylan called to Joan Anderson, who was sufficiently advanced in her program to be performing a remarkable version of the limbo under a curtain rod that had descended to within two feet of the floor, while Moylan and Mike Schneider sat and studied her clinically.

"Narrow pelvis," Moylan observed.

"Masters and Johnson should do a paper on the penis-receptivity of young nurses following an initial experience with death," Schneider said as the girl's back arched and, narrow pelvis pumping, she passed under the rod.

Moylan hastened to the bar to refill her glass.

"Can I get something for you?" Meyerson asked Liz Meomartino.

She smiled at him. "No, thank you," she said.

". . . And I sutured this slash in her deltoid," Spurgeon was saying. "And I said to her, 'So you got wounded in the fracas,' and she said to me, 'No, sir, in the shoulder.' "

It started a round of anecdotes about patients' fractured descriptions of their diseases: fibroids of the uterus transformed into fireballs of the Eucharist, sick-as-hell anemia instead of the sickle-cell variety, old maids with swollen glands who insisted they had the monks and children with rashes who had chicken-pops. Meyerson gave it reverse english by telling of a lady who had come to his uncle's neighborhood grocery in the West End for years to buy Aunt Vagina's Pancake Flour.

"Will you go back to Formosa?" Alice Tayakawa asked Harry Lee.

"When I finish my training."

"What is it like there?"

He shrugged. "In many ways they still hold to the old-fashioned customs. Respectable unmarried men and women would never meet in a gathering such as this . . ."

Alice Tayakawa frowned. She had been born in Darien, Connecticut. "You're a very serious person," she said.

He shrugged again.

"I would like to ask you a question," she said with shy formality.

"Yes?"

"Is it true what they say about Chinese boys?"

He looked at her in puzzlement. Then he blinked.

To his great amazement he found himself grinning back at her.

Her hair was a complete failure, Elizabeth Meomartino thought dully. When it had been blonde it had not compared to the sun-streaked light bronze of the little Pender bitch, and now that it was her own color again the Negro girl's African lustre made it look like what it was, dyed straw. She glared resentfully at Dorothy Williams and then noticed that Adam Silverstone and Gaby Pender were dancing with their arms around one another. Gaby smiled at something he whispered and touched his cheek with her lips.

"I believe I will have the *smallest* Martini," Liz said to Meyerson.

"It's getting so hot in here," Joan Anderson said.

"I'll get you another drink," Moylan said.

"I'm dizzy," she whispered.

"Let's get into another room, where there's more air."

Holding hands, they strolled into the kitchen and then beyond, into a bedroom.

There was a little boy asleep in the bed.

"Where can we go?" she whispered. He kissed her without disturbing the child and they wandered down a hallway and into the master bedroom.

"I think you ought to lie down," Moylan said, closing the door.

"There are coats on the bed."

"We won't hurt them."

They lay on their nest of garments and his mouth found her face, her mouth, her throat.

"Should you be doing that?" she said in a little while.

He didn't bother to answer.

"You should," she said dreamily.

"Jack," she said in a moment.

"Jack."

"Yes, Joannie," Moylan said, superbly confident now.

"Jack . . ."

"We don't want to spoil things by rushing," he said.

"Jack, you don't understand. I'm going to be sick," she said. And was.

On *his* coat, Moylan saw to his horror.

"Are there many Japanese on Formosa?" Alice Tayakawa said, squeezing Harry Lee's hand.

Rafe went into Miguel's room and fixed the covers around the small, thin shoulders. He sat on the bed and looked at the sleeping boy while from the living room there still came the sound of laughter and music and the whiskey-voiced singing of the redhead.

Somebody came into the kitchen. Through the open door he could hear ice being dropped into glasses, and pouring.

"You're all alone out here?" It was Liz's voice.

"Yes. Just making a couple of final drinks."

Spurgeon Robinson, Meomartino thought.

"You're too nice to be alone."

"Thank you."

"You're very big, aren't you?"

He heard her whisper something.

"Everybody knows about us talented colored folks." The voice had suddenly flattened. "That and tap-dancing."

"I don't know about tap-dancing," she said.

"Mrs. Meomartino, I've a neater, sweeter maiden in a greener, cleaner land."

There was a moment's silence.

"Where is that?" she asked. "Africa?"

Meomartino stepped through the doorway into the kitchen.

"Got everything you need, Spurgeon?" he said.

"Absolutely everything, thank you." Robinson left the kitchen with the drinks.

Meomartino looked at her. "Well, do you think you made me Surgeon-in-Chief?" he said.

Later, when finally they had gone, he could not lie down next to her. Instead, he took a pillow and blankets and lay on the couch in the deserted shambles that smelled of whiskey dregs and stale smoke. When he drifted into half-sleep he saw her body, the wonderful pale thighs blocked from view by a series of male backs in a variety of colors, some belonging to strangers and others recognized too easily.

Half-awake, in fantasy he killed her and knew he could not, any more than he was able to walk out of the apartment and drive away.

If it were narcotics, he argued with himself fiercely, would I desert her?

Now he was wide awake.

Saint Raphael, he said into the dark room.

He thought about it during the night and the next morning at the hospital he called one of the numbers in the Yellow Pages.

"This is Mr. Kittredge," a neutral voice said.

"My name is Meomartino. I would appreciate your getting some information for me."

"Would you like to meet me somewhere and discuss it? Or come to the office?"

"Can't we just discuss it now?"

"We never accept new clients over the telephone."

"Well . . . I won't be able to come to your office until around seven o'clock."

"That will be fine," the voice said.

So he asked Harry Lee to cover for him again during the dinner break and he went to the address given in the telephone book, which proved to be a creaky old Washington Street building that contained a lot of wholesale jewelry firms. The offices were very ordinary-looking business quarters that might have belonged to an insurance agency. Mr. Kittredge was about forty, conservatively dressed. He wore a Masonic ring and looked as though he never put his shoes on his desk.

"A domestic problem?" he asked.

"My wife."

"You have a photograph?"

He dug one out of his wallet: taken shortly after Miguel had been born, a picture he had been proud of, Liz laughing, her head tilted, good use of sunlight and shadow.

Mr. Kittredge glanced at it. "Do you want to divorce her, Doctor?"

"No. That is, I suppose it depends on what you find out," he said tiredly, the first concession to defeat.

"The reason I ask," Mr. Kittredge said. "I want to know whether written reports will be necessary."

"Oh."

"You understand that you no longer need bedroom pictures and all that nonsense?"

"I really know very little about it," Meomartino said stiffly.

"All the law requires now is evidence of the time, the place and the opportunity for adultery to have been committed. That's where my written reports would come in."

"I see," Rafe said.

"There's no extra charge for written reports."

"Just oral reports, I think," he said. "At least for the time being."

"Do you know the names of any of her friends?"

"Is that necessary?"

"No, but it might help me," Kittredge said patiently.

He was nauseated, the walls closed in slightly. "I think Adam Silverstone. He's a doctor at the hospital."

Kittredge made a note.

"My fee is ten dollars an hour, ten dollars a day for car rental and ten cents a mile. Two hundred dollars minimum, in advance."

That was why he took no clients over the telephone, Meomartino thought. "Is a check all right?" he asked.

"A check is fine, sir," Mr. Kittredge said politely.

When he got back to the hospital Helen Fultz was waiting for him. Without the benefit of alcohol, he thought, she was once again a careworn, aging woman.

A *tired* woman, he realized, looking beyond the uniform and seeing the person.

"I'd like very much to hand this back to you, Dr. Meomartino," she said.

He took the paper and saw that it was the service complaint he had filed against the unidentified nurse who had served Mr. Roche two meals on the day before surgery, against written orders.

"What do you expect me to do with it?"

"I hope you will tear it up."

"Why should I?"

"I know the girl who served those meals," she said. "I can take care of the matter in my own way."

"She deserves a reprimand," Meomartino said. "That old man has had it. With surgery we could only ease the pain of his last days. Because some bitch was too lazy to read the orders, he got two days of torture added to his sentence."

Miss Fultz nodded in agreement. "When I started out, we wouldn't have considered her a nurse. She's a cow."

"Then why do you defend her?"

"There's a nursing shortage and we need every cow we can keep. If the reprimand goes through, she'll quit, and she'll have another job in half an hour."

He stared at the paper in his hand.

"There have been evenings when I've found myself all alone in that ward," she said quietly. "So far we've been lucky. We haven't been caught short by an emergency. Don't spit on our luck. The cow has a pair of hands and a pair of legs. Don't deny my real nurses the use of those hands and legs."

He ripped the paper twice across and dropped the scraps in a waste basket.

"Thank you," Helen Fultz said. "I'll make certain she reads every chart from now on before she serves the meals." She smiled at him.

"Helen," he said, "how would this place function without you?"

"The way it always does," she said.

"You push yourself much too hard. You haven't been sixteen years old for a long time."

"Not very gallant today, are you, Doctor?"

"How old are you? Seriously?"

"What difference can that possibly make?" she said.

She was too close to the retirement age to want to discuss it, he realized. "It's only that you look tired," he said gently.

She made a face. "Age has nothing to do with it. I think I may be getting an ulcer."

He saw her suddenly not as Helen Fultz but as a worn-out old lady who was a patient.

"What makes you think that?"

"I've nursed enough ulcers to know the symptoms. I can't eat foods I used to. And I'm having a little rectal bleeding."

"Get into the examining room," he said.

"I will not."

"Look, if Dr. Longwood had taken routine precautions he'd be a healthy man today. Just because you're a nurse doesn't relieve you of responsibility to yourself. The examining room. That's an order."

He grinned as he followed her in, aware that she was furious at him.

She was difficult to examine but contained no surprises. She was hypertensive, 190 over 90. "Have you had any chest pains?" he asked, listening to her heart.

"I've known about that basilar systolic murmur for nine years," she said tartly. "As you said, I haven't been sixteen years old for a long time."

During the rectal examination, which she endured in mortified silence, he saw that she had hemorrhoids, undoubtedly the cause of the bleeding.

"Well?" she said, when her clothing and her dignity had been restored.

"I think you're probably a pretty good diagnostician," he said. "My guess would be a duodenal ulcer. But I'm going to make an appointment for you to have a G.I. series."

"Ah, what a lot of bother." She shook her head, unable to thank him, but she smiled at him again. "I had a good time last night, Dr. Meomartino. Your wife is very beautiful."

"Yes," he said. Unaccountably, for the first time since the news of Guillermo's death, he felt behind his eyelids a sharp salt sting which he ignored until, like everything else, it went away.

Chapter 14: Spurgeon Robinson

When Adam moved into the apartment on Beacon Hill, Spurgeon had been left all alone and lonely on the sixth floor and he began to play the guitar more and more to the old walls, the music a funhouse mirror that distorted his soul's reflection. He was desperately in love, he should have been ecstatic. But the songs he played chortled with the kind of joy that meant he was so sad he couldn't bear to think about it. To make happier music he would have had to buy a banjo and work in the fields.

It was everywhere around him and each day he saw it more clearly.

"Can you tell me," Moylan asked him one morning, "how something like this can happen *here?*" He was looking at a baby with a fascination compounded of horror and fear, the kind of expression Spurgeon remembered on the faces of medical students examining for the first time the textbook photographs of abnormal fetuses.

This baby was colored. It was hard to determine his age, because malnutrition had eaten away the infant fat that is a birthgift, leaving the spare, wrinkled visage of an old man. His muscles had atrophied and he lay there weak and dying, his matchstick limbs accentuating the swollen little belly.

"It can happen anywhere," Spurgeon said. "Anywhere at all where a kid doesn't get enough nourishment to stoke the fire."

"No. I can understand how you might find something like this in a sharecropper's cabin in Mississippi," Moylan said.

"Can you, man?"

"Hell, you know what I mean. But here, in *this* city . . ." He shook his head and they walked away from the sight together.

Spurgeon couldn't flee far enough.

When he was through with his thirty-six hours, almost against his will he took the elevated into Roxbury and got off at the Dudley Street station and started to walk, passing the Ace High without going in, continuing destinationless until he no longer saw a face that was white, only skins that were tan to black in many in-between shades.

He found himself reliving bits and pieces of his childhood in individual sights and stinks and sounds, the tired houses with broken steps, the refuse and offal in the streets, the savage screams of children, a cracked window with a heartbreaking tomato-can planter on the sill.

What had become of fat-thighed Fay Hartnett, Petey and Ted Simpson, Tommy White, Fats McKenna?

If he had the power to see the people who had made up the fabric of his childhood—as they were right now, at this moment—would he want to?

He knew he would not.

They were likely to be dead or worse: whore, pimp, pusher, junky, human flotsam known in the records of the Police Department, almost certainly caught up in, if not killed by, the easy escape offered by drugs.

A little nappy-haired boy came barreling around the corner and swivel-hipped like a running back to avoid him, brushing past with a short, mocking curse. He stood and watched with a sad smile as the boy scuttled away.

No matter how fast you run, sonny, he thought, unless you meet a Calvin J. Priest of your own you're a fly caught in hot tar, already in the shadow of the steamroller. Calculating the odds against escape, he looked around him with fresh, frightened awareness of his own miraculous deliverance.

When he returned to the hospital he checked for mail and found only a free catalogue from a pharmaceutical manufacturer, which he opened in the elevator and sampled as the old car fought against the pull of gravity.

There was someone waiting in the hallway outside his room, a short redfaced man in a black overcoat with a velvet collar, carrying, he noted with disbelief, a derby hat.

"Dr. Robinson?"

"Yes."

The man held out an envelope. "This is for you."

"I just picked up my mail."

The man chuckled. "Special delivery," he said. Spurgeon took the envelope, noting that it bore no stamp. He groped for a coin, but the man replaced the derby and turned away, smiling. "I'm not a messenger," he said. "Deputy sheriff."

Deputy sheriff?

Inside, Spurgeon sat on the bed and opened the envelope.

COMMONWEALTH OF MASSACHUSETTS

SUFFOLK, SS: SUPERIOR COURT

To Spurgeon Robinson of Boston, within our County of Suffolk. Whereas Arthur Donnelly of Boston within our County of Suffolk has begun an action of Tort against you by writ dated February 21, 1968, and returnable in the Superior Court holden at Boston within our County of Suffolk on Monday the twentieth day of May, 1968 in which action damages are claimed in the sum of $200,000.00 dollars as follows:

TORT AND/OR CONTRACT FOR MALPRACTICE

as will more fully appear from the declaration to be filed in said Court when and if said action is entered therein:

WE COMMAND YOU, if you intend to make any defense of said action, that on said twentieth day of May, 1968 or within such further time as the law allows, you cause your written appearance to be entered and your written answer or other lawful pleadings to be filed in the office of the Clerk of the Court to which said writ is returnable, and that you defend against said action according to law.

Hereof fail not at your peril, as otherwise said judgment may be entered against you in said action without further notice.

Your goods or estate have been attached as security to satisfy any judgment which may be recovered against you in said action.

Witness, R. HAROLD MONTANO, Esquire, at Boston, the

twenty-first day of September in the year of our Lord one
thousand nine hundred and sixty-seven.

Homer P. Riley
Clerk

The first thing he did was telephone Uncle Calvin, trying to tell
the story calmly, neither sparing himself nor overlooking any of the
important points.

"You just leave everything to me," Calvin said.

"I don't want to do that," Spurgeon told him.

"Insurance is my business. I know a lot of people. I can take care
of this without fuss or feathers."

"No, I want to take care of it myself."

"Then why did you call me?"

"Oh, Jesus, Calvin, can't you understand me for once? I wanted
advice. I didn't want you to handle it for me. I just wanted you to
hear my problem and tell me what to do."

"The insurance company will have a good attorney based in Boston. You get in touch with him immediately. How much coverage
do you have?"

"I'm all right there. I've got $200,000, which is twice as much as
most of the guys here have." It had been Calvin, he realized, who
had insisted that he take out at least that amount of malpractice
coverage.

"Okay. Do you need anything else?"

Calvin felt rebuffed; Spurgeon could tell from his voice. "No.
How's my mother?"

"Roe-Ellen?" The voice softened. "She's okay. She's spending
her mornings in the gift shop at the United Nations. Having a ball
selling jungle tom-toms to little white pullets from Dubuque."

"Don't mention this to her."

"I won't. You take care, boy."

"So long, Calvin," he said, wondering why, having called, he felt
more depressed than ever.

Four days later they were in Boston.

"Calvin had to come on business," Roe-Ellen told him when she
telephoned him at the hospital. "He thought this would be a good
chance for me to see my son," she said meaningfully.

"I'm sorry I haven't been home more often, Momma."

"Well, if the mountain won't come to Mohammed . . ." They were at the Ritz-Carlton. "Can you meet us here for dinner?"

"Yeah, sure."

"Seven o'clock?"

He made lightning calculations, figuring how long it would take him to get to Natick and back. "Eight o'clock would be better. I'd like to bring somebody."

"Oh?"

"A girl."

"Why, Spurgeon, honey! How nice."

What the hell, he thought resignedly. "On second thought, I'd like to bring three people."

"Three girls?" she said hopefully.

"She has a mother and father."

"Wonderful."

He read the caution that crept into her voice during the single word.

But when Roe-Ellen saw Dorothy, Spurgeon noticed her immediate relief and he knew his mother had been afraid he had become entangled with some little white nooky. The Priests looked at her in her simple brown silk dress and her short African hair and they warmed to her at once. They liked her parents. The Williamses had never been anyplace like the Ritz, but they had dignity and Calvin and Roe-Ellen were simple people. By the time dessert was served the four of them were friends and the New Yorkers had promised to come to the house in Natick for dinner next time they were in Boston.

"Can you stop back for a nightcap?" Calvin asked him as he prepared to leave to drive Dorothy and her parents home.

"Will you still be up?"

Calvin nodded. "Not your mother. But I've got some paperwork."

"Sure, I'll come back," Spurgeon said.

When he knocked at the door, Calvin came at once and held a finger to his lips.

"She's asleep," he whispered.

There was a sitting-room, but they decided to go across the street to the Public Garden.

Outside, the late night air was sufficiently chill to cause them to turn up the collars of their topcoats, but they found a bench next to a bed of hyacinths that blazed under the lamplight. They sat facing Boylston Street and watched the late traffic drifting by.

"That's a nice girl," Calvin said.

Spurgeon smiled. "I think so."

"Your mother's been worried about you."

"I'm sorry," Spurgeon said. "The internship year is the roughest one. I haven't had much time off."

"You could call her on the telephone, once in a while."

"I'll call more often," he said.

Calvin nodded. "This is a nice park. Any fish in that pond?"

"I don't know. When it gets to be summer there are paddleboats. With big white swans on them."

"Did you see the lawyer?"

"Yes. He said not to worry. He said for a young doctor nowadays a malpractice suit was routine, like you weren't a man until the first time you got the clap."

Calvin looked at him. "What did you say to that?"

"I told him I had seen some mighty ugly cases of the clap, and some of them were owned by mighty poor excuses of men."

Calvin smiled. "I'm not worried about you," he said.

"Thanks."

"I worry more about myself," he said. "Why are you always turning me away, Spurgeon?"

Across Boylston Street voices were raised in song and laughter, and car doors slammed.

"That's the Playboy Club," Spurgeon said. "Lots of dicty broads with cottontails on their ass."

Calvin nodded. "I've been to the one in New York," he said. "But thanks for the definition."

"It's hard for me to put into words," Spurgeon said.

"I think it's time you did," Calvin said. "I couldn't love you any more if I was your flesh-and-blood daddy. You know that."

Spurgeon nodded.

"You never in your life asked me for anything. Not even when you were a kid."

"You always gave things to me before I could ask. You know what Rap Brown and Stokely have been saying about whitey cutting our balls off?"

Calvin looked at him and nodded.

"Well, it's something like that."

"I cut off your balls?" Calvin said faintly.

"No, no, that's not what I mean at all. Look, you saved my life. Everywhere I look, I see that. You saved my life."

"I'm not a lifeguard. I want to be your father."

"Then listen to what I'm saying. And try to understand. You're a special guy. Letting you do things for me for the rest of my life would be easy. Like drowning."

Calvin looked at him hard and nodded. "Yes. I can see that."

"Let me be a man, Calvin. Offer me no more help."

Calvin still looked at him. "You'll telephone your mother? You'll come home when you get a chance?"

Spurgeon smiled and nodded.

"And if you ever need me—really *need* my help—you'll ask? As if I were your blood father?"

"I promise."

"What would you have done if they had hated me?" Dorothy asked him a few days after Roe-Ellen and Calvin went back to New York.

"They didn't hate you."

"But if they had?"

"You know," he said.

Without the necessity of many words an understanding of interdependence had grown between them, but he found it increasingly difficult to treat her as though they were adolescents, a difficulty compounded by the fact that they were seeing a great deal of Adam Silverstone and Gaby Pender, who were so obviously reveling in fleshly pleasure he sometimes felt like a voyeur in their presence.

On quiet afternoons the four of them explored Beacon Hill, sharing it, wandering over it with a sense of ownership. They admired it all, the stylish old Boston orderliness of Louisburg Square, the smooth cobblestones that pre-dated politically-awarded road contracts, the pompous fat pols arguing over coffee checks in the drug store behind the State House, the lovely preserved lanterns on Revere Street, the feeling on dark nights that on the other side of the crest lay the year 1775, waiting. Always, when they returned to the raffish north side of the hill, *their* side, tenanted mostly by working people and a fast-growing colony of beards and weirds, they agreed it was the best side of the two, the liveliest, the juiciest.

One morning the four of them walked through a cold spring rain as fine as mist, following directions Gaby had gotten from her landlady, and found the ordinary-looking town house at 121 Bowdoin Street where an extraordinary President of the United States had maintained his voting address, and they wondered to one another what might have happened to the world if the young man had been allowed to grow older and wiser.

Dorothy turned suddenly and ran.

He went after her and caught up to her on Beacon Street, on the steps of the State House, and he put his arms around her and kissed her wet face, tasting salt.

"The governor of the whole state can be watching us right now from one of those windows," she said.

"Let's give him something to watch," he said, pulling her to him so they stood tightly together, rocking slightly, on the steps in the rain.

"I'm sorry," she said.

"It's all right. He was quite a man."

"No, you don't understand," she said. "It's not mourning Kennedy. I was crying because you've made me so happy and I love you so much and Gaby and Adam are so cool and beautiful and I know this perfect time isn't going to last for any of us."

"It will last," he said.

"But it will change. Nothing ever stays the same."

There were beads of moisture on her brown skin above the upper lip and with his thumb he smoothed them away the way he had wiped away dried salt that first day on the beach. "I want things to change between us," he said.

"Poor Spurgeon," she said. "Is it awful for you?"

"I'll survive. But I want desperately for things to change."

"Marry me," she said. "Please, Spurgeon."

"I can't. At least not until I finish the internship in July."

She looked at the rain-dulled golden dome of the State House.

"Then we can use the apartment on Phillips Street, sometimes. Gaby and I have talked about it."

He took her wet, woolly head between his palms. "I could buy them a dog. We could arrange to visit them while they walked the dog around the block."

She smiled at him. "They could walk the dog twice around the block."

"We could name the dog Bim-bam," he said.

"Oh, Spurgeon." She began to cry again.

"No, thank you, ma'am," he said. He buried his face in the black wool. "We'll be married in July," he said into her wet hair. In a little while he took her hand and they waved goodbye to the Governor and walked back and found Gaby and Adam. They hadn't discussed it, but by unspoken mutual consent neither of them said anything to the other two people about the remarkable change which had taken place in the world.

Next morning he picked her up and drove with her to the Roxbury ghetto. He parked the Volks and they walked slowly along the streets, feeling no need to talk. The rain had stopped during the night, but the sun was cruel.

"Why did you bring me here?" she asked finally.

"I don't know," he said. "I come here once in a while."

"I hate it here. Please take me away."

"Okay," he said. They turned and started back toward the car.

Some boys were playing baseball in the street, burying winter. "Hoo, Charlie," the one at bat jeered to the pitcher. "You ain't fucken Jim Lonborg. Your ass too sunburn."

"Up you," the pitcher shouted, throwing wildly.

"You ain't fucken Looey Tiant, neither. You ain't even fucken Jim Wyatt."

When they reached the car, he drove out of Roxbury without detours.

"I couldn't stand bringing up a child in that place," she said.

He hummed bright snatches of music. "It's not only poor people who live there. Lots of professional people live there, too. They manage to bring up their kids."

"I would rather not have the children."

"Well, don't worry about it," he said irritably. "You won't have to raise your children in a place like that."

"You once promised me an island and frangipani in my hair."

"I'll deliver," he said.

"Why couldn't we *really* go?"

"Where? To a desert island?"

"Hawaii."

He looked at her, sure she wasn't serious.

"There's no race thing there. That's the kind of place I want to raise my children."

"Your grandchildren would have slanty eyes."

"Oh, I would love them. They'd have your nose."

"They'd better."

"I mean it, Spurgeon," she said in a little while.

He could see that she did. He was beginning to get used to the idea, to examine it for flaws. "I still have a three-year residency to do," he said.

"Couldn't we go after you finished your residency? I'd keep working after we're married and we'd save our money like tight-wads, maybe take a trip there in a year or two to look around and make plans." She was very excited now, certain they were blue-printing their future.

"It might work," he said cautiously, caught up in her happiness.

He discovered when they got to Natick that while the car had been parked in Roxbury somebody had stolen the hubcap from the left rear wheel. All the way back to the hospital he sang at the top of his lungs.

Chapter 15: Adam Silverstone

Adam loved the orange-crate bookcases. Inspired, he bought white paint and a roller-and-pan and before the old aches had left his body he had acquired new ones, but the white walls opened the room up, made it a completely different room. On Newbury Street Gaby bought two inexpensive prints, a Käthe Kollwitz reproduction of a peasant mother holding a child, and a colored abstraction of globes and cubes that went well with the paper flowers.

She saved an avocado pit and studded it with toothpick spears and placed it in a glass of water—something she had read about in a magazine—and waited, checking it anxiously. Nothing happened for three weeks but then, just as she had decided she would have to throw it away, it germinated, a little light-green snake of life, a sprout and then a leaf that turned darker-green and glossy after she had transplanted it into rich black dirt she bought in a bag at the supermarket. The avocado added two more leaves, pinnate and shiny, spoonfed on love and plant food in the transitory patch of sun from the single window.

The basement apartment became the frame of their lives; they would not have exchanged it for the White House. They made love happily and very often and with only a little discernible guilt, becoming increasingly knowledgeable of one another. She felt strong and free, a pioneer woman. She knew they were the first and only lovers in the world, even though Adam told her that despite her fantasies and all the books he had read in medical school they would never create an original sin.

For the first time in her memory she was unconcerned about her own body. The only discomfort she suffered was due to the hormonal stresses of the pill, to which she was not yet attuned and which at times brought on wracking bouts of morning sickness. Adam promised her the symptoms would go away.

She was proud of what they had done to the apartment and would have liked to entertain all the people they both knew, but trusted herself only with Dorothy and Spurgeon. Susan Haskell came to lunch and was awkward and miserable, so obviously waiting for juicy revelations about how Adam mistreated her that Gaby knew she would never repeat the invitation. But she found she maintained a kind of intermittent salon for some of their neighbors from Joy Street. Janet Williams dropped in frequently but not so often that she created a nuisance. Several times she brought another digger, the big blond boy who had delivered the paper flowers. His name turned out to be Carl, and he was gentle and polite and knew a lot about music and art. Another time she brought a scraggly-bearded somebody named Ralph, who looked as though he hadn't bathed for a long time and was groggy and distant, obviously high on something. Janet appeared not to notice. She treated him just as she treated Carl. Or Gaby, for that matter. After every visit the diggers left with a small portion of her grocery budget.

Inevitably, they came one evening when Dorothy and Spurgeon were there.

"Hi," Janet said to her sister.

"Hello," Dorothy said. She waited while everybody was introduced and then she said, "Don't you want to know how Midge and Dad and Mama are?"

"How's Midge?"

"She's all right."

"How are Dad and Mama?"

"All right."

"Great," Janet said.

Everybody was very polite. Adam offered and mixed drinks, passed the salted nuts, joined in the talk. The problem arose when Spurgeon said something about the national election.

Ralph frowned and blinked. He had climbed onto his chair and now sat on the back of it with his feet on the seat, as though on a throne looking down at them. "If everybody would only *listen* to us," he said. "And turn on and tune off. The bastards wouldn't have anybody to govern. We try to tell you, but you won't *listen.*"

"You don't really think that would work," Spurgeon said to him mildly.

"Don't tell me what I *think,* man. I think everybody should just bugger off into the woods and get high and do his thing."

"What would happen to the world if everybody got high?"

"What's happening to the world right now that's so crazy swell, with all you squares dead straight?"

"You need all us straight squares just to exist," Adam said. "Without us you couldn't do your thing at all. We feed you, pal, and make your clothes and the houses you live in. We put the things in the cans you buy when you sell enough flowers and posters to buy cans, and we deliver the fuel oil that keeps your pads warm during the winter. We make you well when you screw up the fine bodies God gave you." He looked at Ralphie and smiled. "Anyhow, if we all became like you, you'd want to be something else. You couldn't stand being like the rest of us."

"That's guano, man."

"Then why the hell are you sitting like that, way up there like a high guru looking down at the world?"

"This is the way I like to sit. It doesn't hurt anybody."

"It hurts Gaby and me," Adam said. "Your shoes have made a mess of the seat of our chair."

"Don't psych me," Ralphie said. "I can turn that thing right around. You're a real aggressive cat, you know? You'd probably be working as a butcher instead of a surgeon, taking out all your aggressions sticking knives into cows instead of people, if you hadn't had wealthy parents to send you to college and medical school. Ever think of that?"

Gaby and Adam had been unable to control their laughter, nor did they attempt to explain it.

Janet never brought the other diggers back or came again herself in the evening, but she continued to drop in occasionally for morning coffee. She was sitting on the couch one day when nausea drove Gaby from the room. When finally she returned, white-faced and apologetic, Janet looked at her with a face like Mona Lisa. "Are you preggers?"

"No."

"I am."

Gaby gazed at the girl and then spoke very carefully.

"Are you sure, Janet?"

"Uh-huh."

"What are you going to do?"

"Let the family raise it."

"Like Midge?"

The girl looked at her coldly. "My real family. Here on Joy Street. Everybody will be its parents. We think that will be lovely."

The conversation haunted her. Would Carl be the child's father? Or Ralphie? Or a more frightening thought: Did Janet know who the father really was?

Of one thing she was sure. The girl would need medical care, starting immediately. When she spoke to Adam, he closed his eyes and shook his head. "Damn. Somebody didn't know how to do his thing."

"We're hardly in a position to make remarks like that."

"You don't see any difference?" he asked her.

She wilted. "Oh, Adam, of course I do. But I won't sleep nights unless we do something for that little fool. Shall we tell Dorothy?"

"I don't think so. Not yet, at least. If she'll come to the hospital I'll make sure she's examined and gets her vitamins and things."

She kissed him and waited eagerly for Janet's next visit, but the girl did not come back. Six days later, trudging up the hill with a bag of groceries, she saw Ralphie coming the other way.

"Hi, there. How's Janet?" she asked.

His eyes were glazed. "What, the kid?" he said. "Her family's taking care of her." He walked off, marching to a different drum.

Two days later she saw Carl delivering posters and asked again about the girl.

"She's not living with us anymore."

"Where is she?"

"I think Milwaukee."

"Milwaukee?" Gaby said faintly.

"This cat she met came and took her away."

"Do you have her address?"

"I've got it written down somewhere back at the house."

"Could you give it to me sometime? I'd like to write to her."

"Sure. I'll do that."

But he never did.

She missed the coffee visits. Mrs. Walters would have been glad to come in and sit and gossip if asked, she felt certain, but she didn't like the landlady and avoided her. She became fascinated by another inhabitant of the building, a small bent woman who scuttled forth under her shawl every few days and always came back carrying a single paper bag. Her face was pinched up tight as if against a hostile world. The poor thing looked like a hung-over witch, Gaby thought, and knew instantly who it was.

One morning she opened the door and moved to intercept her. "Mrs. Krol," she said.

Bertha Krol trembled as Gaby's hand touched her elbow.

"I'm your neighbor. Gabrielle Pender. Won't you come in and have a cup of tea with me?"

The frightened eyes searched Phillips Street like birds seeking escape from a cage. "No," she whispered.

Gaby let her go.

It rained a lot, a wet spring. The nausea caused by the pills disappeared. The earth shifted and the days became longer and less cold; the rain fell every few days and the run-off rushed down the hill's cobblestoned gutters and made little waterfalls into the old sewers and drains. At the hospital Adam assisted at a series of thoracic cases and was affected by open heart surgery as if it were LSD. At night when they lay in bed and talked softly in the dark he told her of placing his hand into the chest incision and feeling through the thin rubber of the gloves the throbbing of the twisting pink pump, the living heart.

"What was it like?" she asked him.

"Like touching you."

Adam had stopped naming the dogs. It was one thing to go to the animal lab and learn from Kazandjian that Experimental Surgical Procedure No. 37 had been a failure; it was something else to be informed of the death of a living creature called Lovely or Max or Wallace or Flower Child. He forced himself to ignore the canine tongues that sought to kiss his hand and instead to concentrate on the microcosmic wars raging between antigens and antibodies within the dogs.

After months of trusting him to work alone, Kender had begun to haunt the laboratory and was watching him closely.

"Things must be getting very ripe on the faculty appointment," he said to Gaby one night, telling her about Kender while she basted herself with baby oil under the sunlamp.

"Perhaps it isn't that," she said, turning on her stomach and handing him the oil. "He may simply be so interested in the experiments he can't stay away."

"He's always been interested in the experiments without observing me," Adam said. His oil-carrying palm made liquid sucking noises as it rubbed his favorite spot, the small hollow where her spine ended and the gluteal rise began. He breathed the odor of the oil on warm flesh and neither of them could stand it when he tried to do the backs of her knees. When finally she turned he got greasy stains on his clothing and on the following day when he went to work his shirt chafed the slight burn on his back and his neck.

Two nights later, when Kender asked him to explain a procedure he had already described in detail in the notebook, Adam was certain.

He ran through the experiment orally and then looked at the older surgeon and smiled.

"So far as I'm concerned, you pass," Kender said.

"How do you think I'll do with the other people who count?" he said, gambling on an intuitive feeling that this was a moment in which candor was permissible.

Kender unwrapped a cigar. "It's hard to predict. I can tell you this: it's a small field. They're considering only you and one other man. I suppose by now you know who he is?"

"I'm pretty certain."

"You each have a lot going for you."

"When will we be notified?"

Kender shook his head. "That isn't the way it works. Only one doctor is notified, the man who receives the appointment. The other candidate will hear about it through the grapevine as scuttlebutt. He will never be told why he didn't get the appointment himself, or learn who voted against him."

Kender shrugged. "That's the system," he said. "At least it allows the unsuccessful candidate to console himself with the thought that perhaps he lost out because some prejudiced bastard didn't like his choice of neckties or the color of his eyes."

"Is that possibility part of the system, too?"

Kender puffed. The cigar tip glowed like neon and the atmosphere of the lab became foul with smoke. "I suppose it's happened," he said.

Later that night Dr. Longwood came into the Animal Laboratory and Adam steeled himself somewhat irritably for further appraisal and examination.

But the Old Man merely asked his permission to examine the lab book on the Anti-Lymphocyte Serum series.

He sat like a tragic caricature and read while his hand in his lap trembled and Adam was forced to look away. Perhaps he sensed this; the hand began to play with his key ring while he read, the keys making a gentle jangling noise like . . . what?

The Harlequin's bells, Adam thought.

"You keep the horses here, in another part of this building?" Dr. Longwood asked.

"No, sir," Adam said. "The hospital owns the animals, but they're kept at the state biological laboratories. We collect lymph nodes from human cadavers and grind them and send them to the state labs, where they're injected into the horses to produce the serum."

Dr. Longwood tapped the notebook with a thin finger. "You've gotten some results."

Adam nodded. "The serum retards the rejection mechanism. When we use it we can give powerful immunosuppressive drugs like Imuran in doses small enough to leave the animal some protection against infection."

Longwood nodded, apparently having learned what he had come for. "You like this work, with the animals?"

"It's making me a better surgeon, I think."

"It will do that."

Adam suddenly felt the force of his eyes.

"Where are you going next year, when you leave us?"

He took the question badly, realizing that Longwood had decided it was all over. Then he was comforted, remembering that Kender obviously had not felt that way.

"I don't know yet."

"Why don't you decide on a geographical area and let me know. I'll be glad to help you find something."

"Thank you," Adam managed.

"I would like you to read something." Dr. Longwood reached into his briefcase and took out a box. "It's about two-thirds of a book manuscript. For a text on general surgery."

Adam nodded. "Whatever a Chief Resident's opinion is worth, you'll have it."

"Some very senior surgeons in other parts of the country have read portions of it. I want to see how it strikes a man not too many years out of medical school."

"I'm honored."

"One thing." The eyes held him again. "I want none of our staff men told about this. I can't have my working hours rationed because of my condition. I can't afford the time."

God, he thought, what do I say to that? But it was unnecessary to say anything, because Longwood nodded and drew himself out of the chair.

"Good night, sir," Adam said.

The Old Man didn't seem to hear.

He medicated some of the animals, took readings of vital signs, brought the lab book up to date. It was very late when he finished, and he was tempted to put off reading the manuscript, but he knew if he did not at least start it while he had the chance he might never read it. He called in and told the paging operator he would be in the lab. Then he sat behind the old oak desk and took the manuscript out of the box. The coffee bubbled on the Bunsen burner, the old building creaked. In the cages some of the dogs bit for fleas; others moaned and yipped in their sleep, perhaps chasing slow dream rabbits or mounting the heated bitches who in the cold wakeful past had driven them off with bared fang. The noise awakened some of the animals, and in a moment their barking had aroused the others. The laboratory rang with the canine protest.

"It's all right," he said. "Quiet down now. Go to sleep, go to

sleep." Absurdly, talking to them as though they were human patients and could understand the soothing tones.

But they quieted.

He poured himself a cup of hot black coffee, sat again, sipped
gingerly, began to read.

Most of the chapters filled him with awe. The writing style was
trenchant and deceptively simple, the kind of easy scientific reading
that is hard writing. Longwood had distilled a lifetime of first-class
surgical experience and had not hesitated to call upon the work of
many other surgical leaders. When Adam was one hundred pages
into the manuscript the telephone rang and he was filled with regret
at the thought that he might be called away. Fortunately it was
Spurgeon with a request for advice that he could give without leaving; he returned to the manuscript eagerly.

He read through the night.

When he had finished the last three chapters the windows of the
laboratory had lightened to a murky gray.

Perhaps, he thought, it was because he was tired. He rubbed his
eyes, heated the coffee and drank another cup, and slowly reread
the three chapters.

It was as if they had been written by another person.

With his limited experience, he still was able to find glaring errors. The writing was murky, the construction tortuous and difficult
to follow. Great gaps appeared in the material.

He read the pages still another time, and now a kind of grim progression became obvious to him, a picture of the dwindling of a
formidable intellectual capacity.

The disintegration of a mind, he realized, shaken.

He tried to catnap but for once he couldn't fall asleep. He left the
laboratory and, Maxie's first customer, ate an early breakfast, then
he walked back to the animal laboratory through the ruined dawn
and carefully replaced the manuscript in its box.

He was waiting, three hours later, when Kender came into his
office.

"There's something I think you should read," he said.

The following night, lying in the dark with Gaby, he told her
Longwood had resigned that afternoon as Surgeon-in-Chief.

"Poor man," she said.

"Can't anything be done?" she asked in a moment.

"Chances of getting a cadaver donor with a rare blood type are slim. He can be sustained by dialysis, but Kender says the machine is the cause of his psychiatric failure."

In a black sea and looking up at a black sky, they hung suspended, side by side.

"I don't think I'd want the machine for long if I were," she said.

"You were what?" he said drowsily.

"Doomed."

He was asleep.

In a little while she brushed him with her toenails, twice, until he awoke and turned to her. Her wild cries sent sound-ripples across the black sea.

Afterward she floated with her head on his chest while he slept again and his beating heart spoke into her ear.

Alive, it said.

Alive.

Alive . . .

Chapter 16: Spurgeon Robinson

The man was bent and black and weeping, none of which made him a strange sight in the hospital, but Spurgeon paused by the bench.

"You all right, old timer?"

"They done kill him."

"I'm sorry," he said gently, wondering whether it had been son or brother, highway accident or homicide.

He did not at first make out the name.

"Shet him up for good. Our leader, the King."

"Martin Luther?" he said faintly.

"White mothers. Get us each and every one, in the end."

The old black man continued to sway. Spurgeon hated him for creating so monstrous a falsehood.

But it was true. Soon the radios and televisions all over the hospital were confirming it.

Spurgeon wanted to sit down on the bench himself and weep.

"Oh, God, I'm sorry," Adam said to him. Others spoke similar words. It took him a little while to realize that people were offering condolences to him the way he had offered them to the elderly patient, in the belief that he had suffered a loss which somehow would leave them essentially untouched. He did not feel rage at this until later.

He had no time for the luxury of shock. Dr. Kender called in all off-duty personnel. Suffolk County General Hospital had experienced racial conflict only once, the year before, and on that occasion it had been unprepared. Now wards were left with skeleton crews while every operating theater was readied for immediate use. Each ambulance was stocked with extra litters and supplies.

"I want an additional doctor in each vehicle," Dr. Kender said. "If all hell breaks loose I don't want you to come back with one patient when it's possible to bring in two or even three." He turned to Meomartino and Adam Silverstone. "One of you stay here and run the Emergency Room. The other one can go with the ambulances."

"Which do you want?" Meomartino said to Adam.

Silverstone shrugged and shook his head as Moylan came in with a report of roof sniping, monitored on the police radio.

"I may as well stay in Emergency," Meomartino said.

Adam assigned the ambulance crews and placed himself in Meyerson's ambulance with Spurgeon. Their first pickup was an anticlimax: on the Expressway, a three-car collision, two people injured, neither seriously.

"Your timing is lousy, you know that?" Meyerson said to one of the drivers as they carried him to the ambulance.

But when they returned to the hospital they found that things were quiet. The reports of gunfire had been incorrect. The police Tactical Force continued to mobilize, but nothing had happened.

Next time they went out it was to Charlestown, to bring in a girl who had stepped on a broken bottle.

But the third dispatch was to Roxbury, where there had been a shooting in a bar.

"I ain't goin' out there," Meyerson said.

"Why not?" Spurgeon asked.

"I don't make that kind of money. Let the bastards kill each other."

"Off your ass," Spurgeon said.

"It's up to you," Adam said mildly. "If you don't drive tonight you're through around here. I'll see to it."

Meyerson looked at them. "Boy scouts," he said.

He got up and walked slowly out of Emergency. Spurgeon thought that perhaps he would walk right past the ambulance, but he opened the door and got behind the wheel.

Spurgeon let Adam sit in the middle.

Some of the store fronts on Blue Hill Avenue were boarded up. Most were dark. The lighted ones had hastily-painted lettering splashed across the windows: SOUL BROTHER, BLACK OWNED, OWNED BY A BROS. They passed a liquor store already looted almost clean, a carcass stripped by ants, children emerging from the glassless windows carrying bottles.

Spurgeon's heart broke for them. Mourn, he said silently. Don't you know how to mourn?

Not far from Grove Hall they ran into their first mass of people, so large it spilled across the road for half a block, like cattle, groups milling from one side of the street to the other, pushing and shoving. The sound flooding through the open windows was a carnival roar, shouted insults and Mardi Gras laughter.

"We won't get through this," Meyerson said. He honked.

"We'd better turn off Blue Hill Avenue and go around them," Adam said.

Behind them the road was already closed off by bodies.

"Any other ideas?" Meyerson said.

"No."

"Boy scouts."

Under the street light some of the men and boys began to rock a parked car, a black four-door sedan. It was a heavy model, a Buick, but in a little while it teetered back and forth like a toy, two wheels lifting off the ground after every push and then crashing down again, until finally it went over to screams and cheers and a scramble to get out of the way.

Meyerson pressed the siren button with his foot.

"The man!" somebody shouted.

Other voices took it up and immediately they were an island in a sea of people. Hands began to hammer on the metal sides of the ambulance.

Meyerson rolled up his window. "They're going to kill us."

In a moment the ambulance began to rock.

Spurgeon released the handle and shoved his shoulder against the door, sending somebody outside flying. He got out of the ambu-

lance and scrambled onto the hood and stood there, his back to the
two men within.

"I'm a brother," he shouted into the strange faces.

"What are *they*—cousins?" somebody called, and there was
laughter.

"We're doctors, on our way to pick up a man who's been hurt. He
needs our help and you're keeping us from him."

"Is he a brother?" a voice shouted.

"Hell, yes, he's a brother."

"Let them through!"

"Hell, yes!"

"Doctors gonna help a brother!" He could hear the word being
passed.

He sat on the hood: nine years of higher education to become a
radiator ornament. Inside, Meyerson turned the spotlight on him.
Very slowly, the ambulance moved forward, the people parting before, as if he were Moses and they the waters.

Soon they were clear.

Meyerson made certain they were half a dozen blocks away before he stopped the ambulance and allowed Spurgeon to get back
inside.

They found the bar. The wounded man was lying face-down on
the floor, his trousers sodden with dark blood. There was no sign of
anyone who might have shot him, nor was there a weapon. The on-
lookers denied knowledge.

Spurgeon cut away the bloodsoaked pants and undershorts. "The
bullet passed clean through the gluteal maximus," he said in a moment.

"You sure it still isn't in there?" Adam said.

He touched the wound with a fingertip and nodded as the man
bucked and groaned. They placed the patient on the litter on his
stomach.

"Is it bad?" the man gasped.

"No," Spurgeon said.

"You got shot in the ass," Meyerson said, grunting as he picked
up his end of the litter.

In the ambulance Adam gave the patient oxygen and Spurgeon
sat next to Meyerson. Maish didn't use the siren. A few minutes af-

ter the return ride had begun, Spurgeon realized they were approaching "frontier" territory in North Dorchester, an uneasy neighborhood where the black population was spreading into hitherto white streets.

"You're taking the long way," he told Meyerson.

"It's the shortest way out of Roxbury," Meyerson said; he swung the wheel and the ambulance turned a corner and then squealed to a stop as he jammed his foot on the brake. *"Now* what the hell?" he said.

A parked car, door open, blocked one end of the narrow street to traffic. The other side was equally cut off by two boys about sixteen, one colored and one white, standing toe-to-toe and flailing each other.

Meyerson sounded his horn and then growled the siren. Oblivious to anything but the single enemy, they stood and fought. There was no art to their fighting. They simply punched one another as hard as they were able. There was no telling how long the fight had been in progress. The white boy's left eye was closed. The black boy was bleeding from the nose and he was sobbing nervously.

Meyerson sighed. "We'll have to break the stupid bastards up or move the car," he said. The three of them got out of the ambulance.

"Don't get clobbered," Meyerson warned.

"Let's take them now," Adam said as the boys went into a clinch and grappled.

It was surprisingly easy. They put up only ego-soothing resistance, each undoubtedly relieved the ordeal was over. Spurgeon had grabbed the white boy's arms from behind. "Is that your car?" he asked.

The boy shook his head. "His," he said, indicating the other combatant. For the first time Spurgeon noticed that Adam was holding the colored boy's arms while Meyerson's large pale hands, clenched in kinky black hair like Dorothy's, forced his head back.

"That isn't necessary," he said sharply. The white boy whimpered. Glancing down, he saw his own familiar black fingers digging into freckled flesh. Amazed, he opened them and the boy walked away like a freed animal, stiff with false nonchalance.

The black boy gunned his twin carburetors in defiance as they got back into the ambulance.

He felt again like the old man weeping on the bench.

"We chose sides," he said to Adam.

"What do you mean?"

"I couldn't leap fast enough to handle the white punk and both of you brave ofays roughed the colored kid."

"Don't be a paranoid asshole," Adam snapped.

On the way back to the hospital the wounded man occasionally groaned, but none of the occupants of the ambulance spoke to one another.

In Emergency there were three cops who had been struck by thrown rocks, but otherwise still no sign of the predicted onslaught. Their ambulance was sent back to Roxbury to pick up a carpenter who had sliced his hand on an automatic saw while cutting boards to nail over store windows. Then they were dispatched to bring in a man who had suffered a coronary outside North Station. At 9:20 they went out again, to get somebody who reportedly had injured his back in a fall from a ladder while painting his apartment ceiling.

The next call was at a city housing project in the South End. Waiting for them near the large, splashing pool was a boy, about the same age as the street-fighters but very skinny and wearing a dirty white Nehru jacket.

"Right this way, gen'men," he said, moving into the darkness. "I'll take you up to him. Look like he's really hurt."

"Shall we take the litter?" Spurgeon asked.

"Hey," Adam called to the boy. "What floor?"

"Fourth."

"Is there an elevator?"

"Broken."

"Hell," Meyerson said.

"Stay here," Silverstone told him, reaching for his bag. "That's too far to lug the litter if we're not going to need it. Dr. Robinson and I will take a look at him. If we need the litter one of us will come down to help you carry it."

The project was a series of boxlike concrete structures. Building 1 1 was the one next to the pool; not old but already a slum. Graffiti and anatomically-improbable crayon drawings covered the walls of the lower entry but could not be seen on upper landings because darkness covered the void, the bulbs having been snatched or broken. On the second floor the darkness contained the reek of old garbage and something worse.

Spurgeon could hear Adam catch and hold his breath.

"What apartment?" he asked.

"Just follow me."

Somebody upstairs was playing a savage thing by Little Richard, wild horses stampeding to a big, driving Motown sound. It grew louder as they climbed. On the fourth level the youth walked down the hallway to a door behind which the music played. Apartment D. He hammered on the door and inside somebody took the needle off the record.

"Open up. It's me."

"They with you?"

"Yeah. Two doctors."

The door opened and the kid in the Nehru went in and then Adam. As Spurgeon followed he heard Adam's warning.

"RUN, SPUR! GET—"

But he was already inside and the door had been slammed shut behind him. There was a single lamp. In its pool of light he saw four men; no, five, he realized as another walked out of the dark into his cone of vision, three white and two colored, not counting the boy. He recognized only one of them, a lean brown man with zulu hair and a pencil-line mustache, holding a kitchen knife that had been filed down until it was a very thin shiv.

"Hello, Speed," he said.

Nightingale smiled at him. "Come in, Doc," he said.

They moved into the room and faced the men.

"Didn't know it was going to be you, longhair. No need for trouble. All we want is your friend's bag."

"What a stupid waste," Spurgeon said. "Somebody who plays piano the way you do."

Speed shrugged but grinned, complimented. "We got a couple of cats in a bad way. They need something fast. Matter of fact, I been without it too long myself."

"Give them the bag, Adam," Spurgeon said.

But Adam moved to the window.

"Don't do anything stupid," Spurgeon said. "Give them the lousy bag." He saw with fright that Adam was looking down at the pool. "Nobody's that good a diver," he said.

Somebody laughed.

"Splat," said a voice from the darkness.

"That's a wading pool, mister," the kid said.

Speed walked to Adam and took the bag from his hands. "You all through fucken around?" he said benevolently. He handed the bag to Spurgeon. "You find it for us, Doc."

He opened it, found a bottle of Ipecac and held it out. Nightingale took off the top, stuck the tip of his tongue into the bottle and spat.

"What is it?" one of the men asked.

"Something to make us sick, I reckon." He looked at Spurgeon without smiling this time, and began to move in.

Adam already was swinging wildly.

Spurgeon tried to throw a punch but he was less skilled even than the young street fighters. Now hands held *his* arms and he was overcome by a profound sense of déjà vu. As the big black fists moved toward him the world turned full circle and he was once again fourteen years old and rolling a drunk in a dark doorway on West 171st Street with his friends Tommy White and Fats McKenna, on that occasion taking the place behind the victim. The man who now served in the role then occupied by Fats McKenna was going to do an excellent job, he realized as the great force smashed into his stomach and he could no longer breathe. Something jolted against the side of his head and he scarcely felt the rest of it. He saw as in a dream the man he might have been but for the grace of God and Calvin, kneeling on the floor and scrabbling through the medical bag, finally turning it over and dumping its contents on the floor.

"You got it, baby?" a voice asked.

Spurgeon didn't get to hear whether Speed Nightingale had it. Somebody put the needle back down on the Little Richard thing and the wild horses of sound ran right over everything, including him.

He regained consciousness twice.

The first time he saw Meyerson when he opened his eyes.

"I don't know," Maish was saying. "It's become harder to get the blanks. I may have to go up a buck. Six dollars a prescription isn't too high."

"We're not arguing price," Speed said. "Just deliver, man. Deliver."

"You can queer the whole deal by rousting these two guys," Meyerson said.

"Ain't no need to worry about them," a voice said contemptuously.

He wanted to know how it was all going to come out, and as the voices faded away he felt an angry kind of regret.

The face he looked into the second time was big, Irish and ugly. "The shine's going to be all right," it said.

"So's the other lad. But I think his dignity's hurt."

When he sat up he vomited weakly and he saw that there were two police officers in the apartment.

"You okay, Adam?" he said, his head aching.

"Yeah. You, Spur?"

"I'll live."

Speed and his friends had already been taken away.

"But who called you?" Adam asked the officer.

"The fella said he was your driver. He said to tell you the ambulance keys are under the seat."

The two policemen drove them back to the hospital. In the lobby, Spurgeon turned to thank them. He was as amazed as they were when he spoke.

"Don't you ever call me a shine again, you thick bastard," he said.

He slept late, awaking to bruises and stiffness and a feeling he had forgotten something.

The riot.

But the radio informed him there had been no full-fledged riot, no Newark, no Detroit, no sniping. A few stores torched, a minimum of looting. Jimmy Brown was in town and the Mayor had asked him to put on a telethon from Boston Garden. The people who would have been burning were staying home and watching Jimmy on the television. The other people were already holding meetings, working to cool it.

He stayed in the shower almost an hour and was toweling between the bruises when the hall telephone rang.

The police had picked up Meyerson. He could be freed on two

hundred dollars bail. He needed twenty dollars, the ten percent for the bail bondsman.

"I'll come down," Spurgeon said.

At Police Headquarters on Berkeley Street he paid the money and got a receipt.

"You look tired," he said when Maish came out.

"Lousy mattresses."

The morning held a first hint of spring warmth and the air was lemon-tinted with sunlight, but they walked through it in uncomfortable silence until they were crossing Park Square.

"Thanks for calling the cops," Spurgeon said.

Meyerson shrugged. "I didn't do it for you guys. If they had killed you I would have been an accessory."

That had not occurred to him.

"You'll get your twenty bucks back," Maish said.

"No hurry."

"I got money tucked away in my room, my seein' an' raisin' money. They were waiting for me last night when I went to pick it up. I'll mail you the double-saw."

"You're going to jump bail, aren't you?" Spurgeon said.

"There's another thing that happened long ago. This time it would mean a term."

Spurgeon nodded. "Some philosopher," he said sadly.

Meyerson looked at him. "I'm a bum. I told you. But if you were really a nigger you wouldn't have said that."

They had been walking down Boylston Street toward Tremont. Now as they stopped and stared at one another a bearded, barefoot prophet approached them off the Common and announced that unless they gave him a dollar he would eat no breakfast.

"Starve, shmuck," Meyerson said, and the boy wandered away without offense.

"You don't know what it is to want things so bad you'll do anything to have them," Maish said. "You're a white *shvartzeh,* that's why you don't understand the niggers. That makes you as bad as the rest of us, the white ones who just don't give a damn because we're thinking of number one. Or maybe you're worse." He turned and started for the subway kiosk.

I'm not, Spurgeon assured himself.

Neither is everybody else.

"THEY AREN'T ALL LIKE YOU, MEYERSON!" he shouted. "THEY AREN'T!" But Maish had already disappeared down the stairway.

An old lady with blue-gray hair struck him with an Anglo-Saxon look like a rock. "Hippies," she said, shaking her head.

Against his will, he was drawn to the ghetto.

The wind blew from the south and before he had crossed the frontier the faint bitter perfume of burning entered the Volks. Not all the people had stayed home to watch Jimmy Brown.

He drove very slowly.

The boards over the store windows looked pathetically ineffectual by daylight. Some of them had been torn off. At a package store a metal protective gate had been pried away at its hinges. The plate glass was broken and inside he could glimpse bare shelves and ruin on the floor. A sign on the front door—SOUL BROTHER—had been X'd out and replaced by another: DAMN LIAR.

The first fire was not far from the Aces High, a tenement, no doubt torched by someone who had had enough of rats and roaches.

The second fire he came upon was half a mile beyond, and no longer a fire. Half a dozen firefighters played two hoses over the scene of a lost battle. All that was left was the blackened brick foundation and a few charred spars.

He parked the car and walked to the ruin. "What was this?" he asked a fireman.

The man glanced at him coldly but said nothing. One for Maish, he thought.

"A furniture store," one of the other firemen said.

"Thank you."

He squatted on his haunches and looked at the smoking remains for a while, and then he got up and began to walk.

It was more of the same, block after block of shops barricaded against the whirlwind. Most of the stores that were not boarded were vacant. One had a painted sign that made him smile: AID STATION. The door was unlocked and he went in and the smile faded. It was no joke. In a cardboard Kleenex carton there were rolls of crude bandages, hardly aseptic, cut no doubt from old shirts and aprons by black women in their tenements, part of the greater plan of some Panther Napoleon, probably a Vietnam veteran, who had not led the Big One this time but who undoubtedly was looking toward The Next Time.

He wondered if they had antibiotics, blood donors, trained people, and decided sadly it was improbable that they had more than a few empty stores and hidden weapons and homemade bandages and the notion that they had waited long enough.

It was a large store.

Centrally located in the black community.

He remembered how Gertrude Soames, the hooker with the dyed red hair, had signed herself out of the hospital with carcinoma of the liver because she didn't trust the white hands that poked and hurt, the white man's eyes she thought really did not care.

He thought of Thomas Catlett, Jr., whose little black ass he had smacked in the ambulance parked on the bridge, who had eight brothers and sisters and whose unemployed father by now must have planted the seeds of number ten in Martha Hendricks Catlett's flaccid womb because orgasm was free and no one had taught them how to make love without making babies.

He wondered if wasted people like Speed Nightingale could be reached by somebody in the neighborhood who was ready to help a junky try to break loose.

The sign-writer had dropped some broken pieces of chalk on the gritty floor and he picked one up and played a little game, drawing partitions and creating a waiting room by the door, a reception desk, an examining room and emergency surgery, an x-ray corner and, in the toilet inhabited by thick spider webs and three dead moths, a darkroom.

Then he squatted on his haunches again and studied the white lines on the dirty floor of the empty store.

That afternoon he hung around the Surgical Department until he spotted a pharmaceutical detail man he knew.

His name was Horowitz, a nice fellow and good enough at his job to know that young interns had a way of turning into important customers in a relatively few years. He sat over a cup of coffee in Maxie's and listened while Spurgeon spoke.

"It's not so wild," he said. "Frank Lahey started the Lahey Clinic in 1923 with only one surgical nurse." He frowned and began jotting figures on a paper napkin.

"I could get you certain items free, because the pharmaceutical industry supports things like this. A supply of drugs, bandages. Some of the equipment you could pick up second-hand. You wouldn't want x-ray, you could send them to the hospital—"

"No, you *would* need x-ray," Spurgeon said. "The whole idea would be to have a black neighborhood clinic they'd come to willingly, with complete trust that it was *theirs*. And these people have tuberculosis, emphysema, all kinds of respiratory problems. Hell, they live in the contaminated air of the core city. You'd have to have x-ray."

Horowitz shrugged. "Okay, x-ray. You could pick up old furniture for the waiting room. You know, folding chairs, an old wooden desk, things like that?"

"Sure."

"You'd need an examining table, a treatment table. Surgical instruments, an autoclave to keep them sterile. Examining lamps. EKG. Diathermy. A couple of stethescopes, an otoscope, a microscope, an ophthalmoscope. Darkroom and developing equipment. Probably a few odds and ends I haven't thought of."

"How much?"

Horowitz shrugged again. "That's hard to say. You can't always find these things second-hand."

"Don't figure second-hand prices. These people haven't had anything in their lives that was first-class. Old chairs, okay, but figure on new equipment."

The detail man did some more adding and put away his ballpoint pen. "Nine thousand," he said.

"Um."

"And you'd have to be able to keep going once you opened up. Some of your patients would have medical insurance, but most of them wouldn't. A few would be able to pay a very small fee."

"And there will be rent and electric bills," Spurgeon said. "Figure twelve grand to get through the first year?"

"Sounds reasonable to me," Horowitz said. "Let me know if there's anything else I can do."

"Yeah. Thanks."

He sat there and had a second cup of coffee, and then another. Finally he paid his check and asked Maxie for a dollar's worth of change. He hummed as he dialed for the operator but his stomach was crampy with nervousness.

He had no trouble placing the call until he reached the final bas-tion, the icy-voiced English secretary who protected Calvin Priest from mortals.

"Mr. Priest has somebody in with him, Dr. Robinson," she said in the voice that always sounded disapproving. "Is it terribly important?"

"Well, no," he said, and immediately felt self-disgust. "Well, yes, as a matter of fact it *is* important. Will you tell him his son is on the phone and needs his help?"

"Oh, yes, sir. Will you hang on or shall I ask Mr. Priest to return your call?"

"I'll wait for my father," he said.

He took Dorothy to see the store the next day. By then he had had a night in which to develop doubts and invent many dragons, some of which he had not been able to slay with reason. The block and the store looked somehow bleaker than it had when he had left it. Somebody had stolen some of the chalk and had drawn on the sidewalk a number of depictions of a couple in the various positions of sexual embrace, or perhaps it was more than one couple, a sidewalk orgy. The artist had left the chalk and now two little girls, ignoring the bacchanal, played tic-tac-toe with a desperate intentness. Inside, the store was less spacious than he remembered, and dirtier.

She listened to him and she looked at the chalk lines on the floor. "It sounds rather long-term," she said.

"Well, yeah."

"You couldn't do it as a short-term thing," she said. "I can see that." There was a silence in which they regarded one another with mutual thoughtfulness, and he knew she was saying goodbye to Hawaii and the carefree little grandchildren with slanty eyes.

"I promised you frangipani," he said guiltily.

"Ah, Spurgeon," she said. "How would I have known it when I saw it?" She began to laugh and in a moment he was laughing with her, loving her fiercely.

"Are you afraid?" she said.

"Yeah. Are you?"

"Scared stiff." She came into his arms for comfort and he closed his eyes and buried his face in the nappy black wool. The two little girls on the sidewalk watched them through the window.

When he had finished kissing her he went to the Ace High and borrowed a broom from the bartender and she swept the floor for him. While he evicted the spider and the moths from the darkroom she wet her handkerchief and shredded it washing the coupling figures from the sidewalk, and then she gave the little girls an art lesson. When he came out the sun had dried the concrete clean and the sidewalk was covered with chalk flowers, a field of lilies.

Chapter 17: Adam Silverstone

When April came it was as if a clock within Gaby had begun to need just a little winding. She panted a bit more as she climbed the hill, she was slightly less ready for love-making, she began taking leaden naps in the afternoon. A year before, she would have gone sleepless with worry and then raced for the doctor. Now she told herself firmly that all that was behind her, she was a hypochondriac no longer.

She believed she had had too much winter, that she was gripped by spring fever. She said nothing to Adam or to the nice young psychiatrist at the Beth Israel who listened to her once a week and was now hearing the interesting story of her parents' marriage, occasionally asking a question in a sleepy, almost disinterested voice; sometimes a single answer took weeks and hurt unbelievably as it cut through scar tissue she hadn't even known about. She began to hate her parents less and pity them more. She cut a few classes and waited for the softer weather to change the Public Gardens and the little private courtyards on the hill, to bring green strength to the shrubs and the flowers and to her. Within the apartment the avocado plant began to turn yellow, and she fed it fertilizer and water and worried about it. Making the bed, she bumped her shin and won a bruise like a hickey; it wouldn't go away even though she kneaded it with cold cream.

"Are you all right?" Adam asked her one morning.

"Do you hear me complaining?"

"No."

"Of course I'm all right. Are you?"

"I've never had it better."

"Good, darling," she said proudly. But when the time for her period came and the period did not, she knew with a frozen certainty what was bothering her.

Somehow the damned pill had failed, and they were trapped.

Despite her feeling of general fatigue she went sleepless and then in the morning—the syndrome of events she had wanted to avoid —she called the student health service and they gave her an appointment to come in for an examination.

The doctor's name was Williams. He was gray-haired and paunchy and wore two cigars in his breast pocket.

Much more of a father figure than her own father, she thought. Therefore when he asked her the nature of her complaint she was able to tell him quite calmly she suspected that she was pregnant.

He had been a college doctor for nineteen years and before that had served for six years as physician at a private preparatory school for girls. In a quarter of a century he had never learned to receive this news without sympathy but he had become somewhat accustomed to it.

"Well, we'll see," he said.

When a drop of her urine—mixed with a drop of antiserum and then two drops of antigen—agglutinated on a glass slide in two minutes before their eyes, he was able to tell her that she was not about to become a mother.

"But my period," she said.

"Sometimes they're like slow trains. Wait for it and it will arrive eventually."

She smiled at him in her silly relief and made ready to leave, but he held up his hand. "Where are you running to?"

"Doctor," she said, "I feel so stupid. I'm one of those idiots you physicians sometimes refer to with gallantry as an over-anxious patient. I thought I'd gotten over screaming at shadows, but I guess I haven't."

Dr. Williams hesitated. He had seen her before on a number of occasions and he knew that what she said was true; her file on his desk in front of him was thick with the reports of imagined illnesses stretching back six years to her first term as an undergraduate.

"Tell me how else you've been feeling lately," he said. "I think as long as you're here we might as well run a few tests."

"Well," she said to him almost an hour later. "Can I go confess to my psychiatrist that I did it again?"

"No, you can't," he said. "You feel tired because you're anemic."

She felt a silly surge of triumph because it appeared she was after all not merely a silly neurotic.

"What must I do, eat lots of rare liver?"

"I want to do one more procedure," he said, and handed her a johnny.

"I have to undress?"

"Please."

He summoned the nurse and presently she felt the cold kiss of an alcohol swab on her hip above the left buttock, and the prick of a needle.

"That's all?" she said.

"I haven't done it yet," he said, and the nurse chuckled. "I gave you some Novocain."

"Why? Will it hurt?"

"I'm going to take some bone marrow. It'll be a bit uncomfortable."

But when he did it she gasped and her eyes watered. "Hey."

"Baby." He slapped on a Band-Aid. "Come back in an hour," he said, unperturbed.

She wandered through the stores, looked at furniture but saw nothing she liked, bought a birthday card to send to her mother.

When she got back to the office Dr. Williams was very occupied with paper work.

"Hi. I want to arrange for you to have some blood transfusions."

"Transfusions?"

"You have the type of anemia known as aplastic. Do you know what that is?"

Gaby folded her hands tightly in her lap. "No."

"The marrow in your bones for some reason has stopped producing enough blood cells, and has become fatty. That's why you're going to need the transfusions."

She thought about it. "But if a body doesn't produce blood cells . . ."

"We have to supply them in transfusions."

Her tongue felt a little strange. "Is the disease fatal?"

"Sometimes," he said.

"How long can a person live with a condition like mine?"

"Oh . . . years and years."

"How many years?"

"I can't predict something like that. We'll work very hard to get you by the first three to six months, and after that it's almost always clear sailing."

"The people who die. Most of them die in three to six months?"

He looked annoyed at her. "One has to look at the positive side of something like this. Many, many people make complete recoveries from aplastic anemia. There's no reason why you can't be one of them."

"What percentage recover?" she said, aware that she was making it difficult for him and caring not at all.

"Ten percent."

"Well." My dear God, she thought.

She went back to the apartment and sat without turning on any of the lights even though the single window did not allow sufficient illumination to read by.

Nobody came to the door. The telephone did not ring. After a long while she became conscious that the tiny patch of sun that fell on the avocado plant for three hours each afternoon had disappeared. She examined the yellowing plant closely and thought about giving it more fertilizer and water and then decided not to do either. That was the trouble, she thought; she had overfed it and drenched it and no doubt at the bottom of the pot the roots were rotting away in a tiny bog.

A short time later she saw Mrs. Krol approaching the front stairs and a few seconds after that she snatched up the avocado plant and hurried to overtake her in the front hall.

"Here," she said.

Bertha Krol looked at her.

"Take care of it. Maybe it will grow for you. Put it in the sunlight. Understand?"

Bertha Krol gave no sign that she did or did not. She merely stared until Gaby turned away and went back to her own apartment.

She sat on the sofa and wondered why she had given the plant away.

Eventually she understood that although she had believed a moment ago that she was pushing time away toward morning, when Adam would come home, she had known she would not be there when he arrived.

She packed only her clothes. She left everything else. When the suitcase was closed she sat down and wrote a note, hastily, for fear she would not be able to force herself to write it at all if she took her time. She placed it on the couch, weighted down with the vase of paper flowers so he would be certain not to miss it.

She was unaware of driving out of the city. When she looked around she was on Rte. 128 but heading the wrong way, north, toward New Hampshire. A reaching-out toward her father? No, thank you, she thought. She got to the other side of the split highway in Stoneham and drove south again, her foot jammed down on the fuel pedal. Neither the tough cop who once had given her a ticket on this road nor any of his colleagues materialized to humble her as she made the Plymouth a projectile, wondering idly about the great concrete abutments of the overpasses through which the car flashed.

One saw them pictured in the newspapers and on television, immovable objects with what was left of the vehicles and people they claimed periodically. But she knew she had a charmed life, destined to trickle away, not end in a flash of light or a clap of thunder; her hand would not obey her if she decided to turn the wheel slightly as she approached an overpass.

It was later, weaving at breakneck speed in and out of the swift traffic that pushed down Rte. 24, that she realized how stupid it had been to have given the plant to Mrs. Krol. Almost certainly Bertha Krol would get drunk and scream her screams and throw the plant out of the window. The black store-bought dirt would be scattered over Phillips Street with Bertha's garbage and the plant would never grow to be an avocado tree.

He knocked when he found the door locked and then grunted in surprise as he saw that the morning paper had not been taken in.

The apartment was murky but he spotted the note at once under its floral marker.

> *Adam,*
>
> *To say that it's been fun would be to insult both of us. I'll cherish it as long as I live. But we had an agreement that if either of us wanted out, it was all over. And I'm afraid I need out, very badly. I've wanted to break this off for some time but hadn't had the courage to tell you to your face. Don't think too harshly of me. But think of me sometimes. Have a wonderful life, Doctor Darling.*
>
> > *Gaby*

He sat on the sofa and reread the note and then he telephoned the psychiatrist at the Beth Israel, who could tell him nothing.

He saw how little she had taken. Her books were here. The television set, the record player. Her sun lamp. Everything. Only her clothes and suitcase were gone.

In a little while he called Susan Haskell and asked her if Gaby was there.

"No."

"If you hear from her, will you let me know?"

There was a pause. "I don't think so."

"What is that supposed to mean?"

"She's left you, hasn't she?" There was triumph in her voice. "Otherwise you wouldn't be calling me like this. Well, if she comes here you won't hear about it from me."

She hung up on him, but she didn't matter, Gaby hadn't been there. He thought for a little while longer and then picked up the phone again and dialed the university.

When the switchboard operator answered, he asked her to give him the student health service.

He borrowed Spurgeon's Volks and by the time he drove it lumbering over the Sagamore Bridge he was afraid of what he would find when he got out of the car. Once he passed Hyannis he kept his foot on the floor, driving the way she drove. It was too early in the season for traffic and the highway was almost empty of cars. In North Truro he swung the bus off Rte. 6, drove down the narrow macadam road and then, praying, just after sighting the Light turned onto the sand road that led to the beach.

When the Volks topped the rise he saw that the blue Plymouth was parked by the door.

The cabin was unlocked but deserted. He left it and walked the path to the cliff. From the high lip he could see the white beach below for miles in either direction, wind-scoured and covered with the jetsam of winter storms. The sandbar was missing. There was nobody in sight.

There were whitecaps, as far out as he could see.

Could she be somewhere out there, below the surface of the water? He pushed the thought from his mind.

Then as he turned to go back to the house he saw her walking slowly along the cliff top about a quarter of a mile away. Weak with relief, he ran to overtake her; before he caught up, she sensed a presence and turned.

"Hello," he said.

"Hello, Adam."

"What happened to the sandbar?"

"It's shifted about a quarter of a mile. Toward Provincetown. Sometimes the winter tides do that."

She started to walk in the direction of the shack and he walked along with her. Later in the season there would be berries here. The plants crushed by their feet filled the air with blueberry spice.

"Oh, Adam, why did you have to come? You should have let it break off swift and clean, without . . . this."

"Let's go inside and sit down and talk."

"I don't want to go inside."

"Then get in the car. We'll take a ride."

They went to the Plymouth, but he held the door for her on the passenger's side and got behind the wheel himself.

He drove without speaking for a while, back to the highway and then north.

"I talked to Dr. Williams," he said.

"Oh."

"I have a number of things to say to you. I want you to listen carefully." But he didn't know what came next, he had never loved one of them before, and he found suddenly that love made a difference in contemplating impending death as well as in bed. God, he prayed, panic-stricken, I've changed my mind, from now on I'll think of every patient as someone I love, only help me to say the right words now.

She looked out the window.

"If you knew I might be killed in an automobile accident, would you refuse yourself the precious time that was left with me?" It sounded weak even to him, somehow patronizing and not at all what he had been trying to say. He saw that her eyes were bright but she would not allow herself to cry.

"Dr. Williams told me you tried to pin him down on a prediction. In your type of case you could easily live out your normal span. We can have fifty years together."

"Or one, Adam? Or none?"

"Or one. That's right. Maybe you have just one more year to live," he said flatly. "But damn it all, Gaby, don't you see what that means today? This is the edge of the golden age. They're already taking the human heart out of one body and transplanting it into another. And kidneys, and corneas. Now the lungs and the liver. They're working on a little machine that will be taking the place of the heart in a very short time. For a patient today, every week is a very long time. Somewhere in this world a team of people is making progress on every important problem you can think of."

"Including aplastic anemia?"

"Including aplastic anemia and the common cold. Don't you see?" he said desperately. "Hope is what medicine is really about. I finally learned that this year."

She shook her head. "It's no good, Adam," she said quietly. "What kind of marriage would it be with *that* hanging over our heads? Not only for you. For me, too."

"We have things like that hanging over our heads anyhow. The son of a bitch of a bomb may go off tomorrow. I could die in the next year or be killed in half a dozen different ways. There are no guarantees. You just have to live life while you can, take it in both hands and squeeze it to get the last drop of juice out of it."

She didn't answer.

"You need guts to do that. Perhaps you prefer Ralphie's way. Just tune out. That's easier."

He had no other arguments. He felt exhausted and futile and he drove in silence, not knowing how to make her understand.

In a little while they became aware of something up ahead, a convention of gulls, wheeling and squawking and dropping toward the ground as if they thought they were hawks. There were cars parked all along the right shoulder of the road.

"What is it?" he said.

"Where are we, Brewster? The herring run, I guess," she said.

He parked and they got out and went to the edge of the stream. He had never seen anything like it. The fish were stacked almost solidly, bank to bank, facing upstream, a fantastic flotilla of dorsal fins splitting the surface of the water, beneath the dorsals the greenish-grayish-silvery bodies iridescent, the ventral fins gracefully fanning, the forked tails, hundreds of thousands of forked tails, waving in gentle rhythm as they waited—for what?

"What are they?" he asked.

"Alewives. My grandfather used to take me to see this every spring."

The herring gulls screamed and feasted. On the banks human predators dipped flapping fish from the brook with nets and pails that could not miss. Some of the children were flinging the live fish at one another.

As quickly as a hole was formed in the almost-solid mass of fish it was filled in by the patient, slow-swimming bodies moving up from the sea.

"From how far away do they come?" he asked.

She shrugged. "Maybe New Brunswick. Or Nova Scotia. They come back to lay their eggs in the fresh water where they were born themselves."

"Think of all the natural enemies they had to pass through to make it," he said, awed. "Killer whales, sharks, stripers, all the other big fish."

She nodded. "Eels. Gulls. Man." She walked upstream. He followed and soon was able to see the reason most of the fish below were not moving. The stream rose in a series of fish ladders, perhaps a dozen, that fell from holding pools in tiny cataracts wide enough to hold one fish at a time. The herring swam up the flowing spout of water into the quiet of the pool above, each ladder harder to swim through because the preceding leaps had taken their toll in effort and strength.

"My grandfather and I used to choose one fish and go up with her," she said.

"Why don't we do that?" he said. "You choose."

"All right. That one."

Their alewife was about ten inches long. They watched while she patiently waited for a clear shot at the ladder and then squirted forward and flickered up through the water that poured down from the pool above, where she waited again. She climbed the first six ladders with apparent ease.

"You picked a winner," he said.

Perhaps the remark jinxed the alewife. As she strove to swim up the next ladder the falling stream of water had too much force; it halted her momentum, carried her, flapping clumsily, back into the pool.

She made it next time, but the ladder above required her to leap three times before it was behind her.

"Why do they fight so, just to lay their eggs?" he wondered.

"Preservation of the species, I suppose."

Their fish moved more slowly now, between attempts, as if even swimming took too much effort. They felt that she made each successful leap through the force of their wills, but the strength obviously was being drained from her own torpedo-shaped body. By the time she reached the pool below the final ladder she rested on the bottom almost motionless, only her pumping gills and the balancing ventral fins indicating she was still alive.

"Oh, God," Gaby said.

"Come on," he encouraged.

"Come on, poor thing."

They watched as she made four vain attempts to clear the final obstacle. Each time the rest period was longer than the last.

"I don't think she's going to make it," Adam said. "I think I could just reach in and pick her up and carry her over."

"Leave her alone."

A gull dropped down and moved past them toward the fish.

"Ah, you won't!" Gaby cried, slapping at the bird. She was suddenly weeping. "You won't, you bastard!"

The gull rose, squawking indignantly, and went downstream for easier gorging. As if sensing the recent danger the alewife spurted forward, started upward but was battered and flung gracelessly back. This time she went at once without resting, surged forward once more and hurled herself upward through the descending fall. She hung poised at the top and then, wriggling, splashed over into calm water on the other side.

Gaby was still weeping.

In a moment the tail convulsed and gave a triumphant wiggle of ecstasy and the herring flickered from their sight into the deep water of the pond.

He held her tightly to him.

"Adam," she said into his shoulder, "I want to give birth to a child."

"There's no reason why you can't."

"Will you let me?"

"Let's get married right away. Today."

"What about your father?"

"We've got to live our own lives. Until I can afford to take care of both of you he'll just have to take care of himself. I should have known that before."

He kissed her. Another herring plopped over, an athlete, and flashed up the final ladder as if riding an elevator.

She was laughing and crying at the same time again. "You don't know anything at all," she said. "You have to wait three days to get married."

"We've got plenty of time," he said, thanking God and the battered fish.

On Tuesday morning she walked down Beacon Hill and over the Fiedler footbridge to the Esplanade, where she felt it had all begun. At the river's edge she opened her purse and took out the pill box. She threw it as hard as she was able, and the fake mother-of-pearl flashed in the sun before it hit the water. It was a lousy throw but it would serve. She sat down on a bench by the water's edge and was pleased by the thought of the little box in the soft-flowing water of the Charles, perhaps nuzzled curiously from time to time by a mud turtle or a fish. Maybe it would be moved by the tidal currents out into Boston Harbor, to be found by somebody at some far distant date on the Quincy shore, along with sand dollars and mussels and the shell of a crab and the jaw of a dogfish and a sandworn returnable Coke bottle and placed somewhere under glass as a relic of *homo sapiens* a long time ago, as far back as the twentieth century.

That afternoon, as if somehow she knew it was a wedding present, Bertha Krol knocked on their door for the first time and returned the plant as mutely as she had accepted it. She had not thrown the avocado out of the window. Furthermore, the foliage no longer drooped, although nothing they could think of would induce her to speak when Gaby asked her what she had fed it. Beer, Adam thought.

They were married on Thursday morning, with Spurgeon and Dorothy standing up for them. When they got home from City Hall the first thing Gaby did was rip from under the mailbox the tape bearing her maiden name. The missing strip left a pale unweathered mark which she cherished as long as they lived in the small apartment on Phillips Street.

One night shortly thereafter Adam was in the animal laboratory when Kender came in for a cup of coffee.

"Do you remember a conversation we once had, about sustaining life in a patient with a terminal disease?" he asked.

"Yes, I remember it well," Kender said.

"I want you to know I've changed my mind."

Kender's eyes gleamed with interest and he nodded, but he didn't ask what had brought about the changed opinion. They sat and drank their coffee in companionable silence, Adam restraining himself from asking about the faculty job, which he now not only wanted desperately but needed as a means of staying where better men than he could fight for her with everything that came along.

Chapter 18: Rafael Meomartino

Meomartino had the feeling that subtly and in ways he did not understand the atoms of his life were rearranging themselves into patterns over which he had little control. He met the private detective at a second-floor pizzeria on Washington Street and they conducted their business over salty linguini marinara and resinous wine.

Kittredge had observed Elizabeth Meomartino going repeatedly to an apartment building on Memorial Drive in Cambridge.

"But do you know that she met anybody?"

"I just followed her to the building," Kittredge said. "Six times I waited outside, she went inside. A couple of times I rode the elevator with her, as if I lived there. It's a very nice building, professional people, upper middle-income."

"How long does she stay?"

"It varies."

"Do you know the number of the apartment she visits?"

"I haven't been able to learn yet. But she always gets off at the fourth floor."

"Well, that should help," Meomartino said.

"Not necessarily," Kittredge said patiently. "She could walk up to five, say, or down to any other floor."

"Does she know you're following her?"

"No. I'm positive."

"Well, let's assume she goes to the fourth floor," he said in disgust, beginning to despise the detective's professionalism. "She doesn't have the skills of an international spy."

"All right," Kittredge said. He took out his notebook. "Why

don't I read the names of the individuals who live on that floor and see if one of them means anything to you."

Meomartino waited tensely.

"Harold Gilmartin."

"No."

"Peter D. Cohen. That's Mr. and Mrs."

"Keep going."

"In the next apartment are two unmarried girls, Hilda Conway and Marcia Nieuhaus."

He shook his head a bit indignantly.

"V. Stephen Samourian."

"No."

"That leaves only one. Ralph Baker."

"No," he said, depressed that he should be playing such a game.

Kittredge shrugged. He took a typewritten list from his pocket and handed it to Meomartino. "These are the names of every other tenant in the building."

It was like reading a page in the telephone book of a strange city. "No," Meomartino said.

"One of the men on the fourth floor, Samourian, is a doctor."

"That's no help. This is the first time I've heard his name." He paused. "Is there any chance she could be doing something completely ordinary, like going to the dentist?"

"On two occasions, both when you were on duty at the hospital, she went back to your home around dinner time and then returned to the Memorial Drive building to spend the evening."

"Oh."

"Do you want me to give you written reports?" Kittredge asked.

"No. Don't rush me," he snapped. At the detective's request he wrote a check for one hundred and seventy-eight dollars, each stroke of the pen more difficult than the last.

That night at eleven o'clock Helen Fultz came to him.

"Dr. Meomartino," the old nurse said.

He saw that she was pale and sweaty, slightly shocky-looking. "What is it, Helen?"

"I'm afraid I'm bleeding quite a lot."

He made her lie down with her legs elevated.

"Did you ever have those x-rays taken?"

"Yes. I've been going to the clinic here," she said.

He sent for packed red blood cells and for her records and films. The x-rays had shown no ulcer but had revealed a small aortic aneurysm, a tiny ballooning in the main trunk arising from the left ventricle of the heart. The clinic people had believed the aneurysm too small to be responsible for the bleeding, which they had felt was caused by an ulcer that didn't show in the x-ray. They had placed her on a bland diet.

He examined her abdomen, allowing his touch to become his sight, and he knew they were wrong.

He wanted a senior surgeon's advice. He saw on the bulletin board that the Visiting Surgeon on call was Miriam Parkhurst, but when he telephoned he was told she was on her way to the Mount Auburn Hospital in Cambridge.

He called Lewis Chin and learned that the Visiting was in New York City. Dr. Kender, he knew, was attending a transplantation conference in Cleveland at which he expected to hire his own successor. There was no other senior man available.

Silverstone was in the hospital.

He had the Chief Resident paged and they examined her together. He guided Adam's hand until it had found the aneurysm. "How large, would you say?"

Silverstone whistled soundlessly. "At least nine cms., as a guess."

The bloods came and Silverstone set up an I.V. for them while he tried the telephone again, this time reaching Miriam Parkhurst. They had had to summon her out of the scrub room at Mount Auburn and she was very testy about having wasted four minutes of abrading her hands, but she quieted when he informed her about Helen Fultz.

"God, that woman was a ward nurse when I was a house officer," she said.

"Well, you'd better get here as soon as you can," he told her. "The aneurysm can let go at any time."

"You and Dr. Silverstone will have to start repairing it yourselves, Dr. Meomartino."

"You're not coming?"

"I *can't.* I have an emergency of my own. One of my private patients, a large bleeding ulcer involving the duodenum and the pylorus. I'll come over to you as soon as I can get done here."

He thanked her and called the OR to tell them he would be

down with an aneurysm case, and then in swift succession telephoned for a medical consult and an anesthesiologist.

Helen Fultz smiled at him when he told her. "You and Dr. Silverstone?" she said.

"Yes."

"I could be in worse hands," she said.

They had to wait after they were scrubbed while Norman Pomerantz got her anesthetized with agonizing slowness, but finally Meomartino was able to begin. He made a long midline incision, cutting through the skin and between the rectus sheaths. Wherever a tiny bleeder appeared, he clamped and Silverstone tied.

He went through the peritoneum carefully, and once they were into the abdomen he could see the aneurysm, a large, pulsating swelling on the left side of the aorta.

"There's our baby," Silverstone murmured.

It was leaking blood into the intestine, the cause of her bleeding.

"Let's get it out of there," he said. Together they bent over Helen Fultz's big beating aorta.

Miriam Parkhurst came bustling into the OR office after Silverstone had taken Helen to the recovery room. She listened to Meomartino, trying not to look pleased. "I'm glad we're able to help *somebody* on this staff. Did you use retention sutures?"

"Yes," he said. "How did your Mount Auburn emergency go?"

She smiled at him. "We both had a good evening."

"I'm glad."

"Rafe, what is going to become of Harland Longwood?"

"I don't know," he said.

"I do love that old man," she said tiredly. She waved good night at him as she left.

Meomartino simply sat there, listening through the open doors to the nurses talking quietly as they cleaned the operating room.

There was no other sound.

He closed his eyes. He was sweaty and rank but he felt almost post-coital, released, fulfilled, qualified by an act of love to claim a place on the earth. The idea came to him that what Liz had once said to him was correct: the hospital claimed him as a human mistress could not.

What a shabby old trull, he thought, amused.

When he opened his eyes the concept embarrassed him and he pursued it no farther. He took the green cloth cap from his head and dropped it to the floor. There was a tape recorder on the table and he picked up the microphone and leaned back in the chair and placed his feet, still encased in the black static-proof operating boots, on the table next to the machine.

Pressing the button on the microphone, he began to dictate the operative report.

It rained. All the next day and into the evening, the kind of rain that is greeted by New England farmers with joy and then with fear and finally with anger as the seedlings wash away. That night he lay and listened to the rain and in a yellow silk nightgown she drifted like a bright shadow into the dark room.

"What's the matter? Are you angry with me?" she said.

"No," he said.

"Rafe, I have to change or perish," she said.

"When did you decide that?" he asked, not unkindly.

"I don't blame you for hating me."

"I don't hate you, Liz."

"If only we could turn the clock back and avoid making our mistakes."

"It would be nice, wouldn't it?"

Outside the rain began to drum with increasing intensity. "My hair is almost all grown back. My own hair."

"It's fine and soft," he said, stroking.

"You've been so kind to me. I'm sorry for everything, Rafe."

"Shshsh." He turned and took her into his arms.

"Remember that first rainy night?"

"Yes," he said.

"I want to pretend," she said. "Will you let me pretend?"

"What."

"That you're a boy again and I'm a young girl and we both have never."

"Oh, Liz."

"Please, please, make believe neither one of us knows a thing."

So they played like children and he knew again the palest imitation of the discovery and the fear. *"Amoroso,"* she called him finally. *"Delicioso, mágico, marido,"* the words of love he had taught her in the first weeks of marriage.

Afterwards he laughed and she turned away and wept bitterly. He got up and opened the french doors and went out onto the little balcony in the rain and broke a blossom from its stem in a flower pot, a calendula, and came back and put the flower on her navel.

"It's cold and wet," she complained, but she allowed it and stopped crying.

"You do forgive me? You'll let me try to make a new start?" she asked.

"I love you," he said.

"But do you forgive me."

"Go to sleep."

"Say yes."

"Yes," he said happily. He would call Kittredge, he thought drowsily, and tell him his services no longer were needed.

He fell asleep holding her hand, and when he awoke it was morning. During the night she had rolled over and the flower was crushed, there was a mess of orange petals on the sheets. She was sleeping heavily, her limbs sprawled, her hair black and tumbled, her face without trouble, washed in the blood of the lamb.

He got ready without waking her and left the apartment and went to the hospital, a new man for a new day.

At noon he telephoned but there was no answer. In the afternoon he was very busy. Dr. Kender had come back, bringing with him from Cleveland a pair of visiting professors named Powers and Rogerson, and they all went on afternoon rounds together, a long-drawn and formal affair.

At six o'clock he telephoned again. This time when nobody answered he asked Lee to cover and drove to the apartment off Charles Street.

"Liz," he called as he let himself in.

There was nobody in the kitchen; or in the living room. The study was unoccupied. In their bedroom he saw that certain bureau drawers had been left open and were empty. Her dresses were gone from the closets.

Her jewelry.

Hats, coats, luggage.

"Miguel?" he called softly, but his son did not answer, he had gone wherever his mother had taken all his things.

He went downstairs and drove to Longwood's apartment,

to which he was admitted by a gray-haired woman, a stranger.

"This is Mrs. Snyder, an old friend of mine," Longwood said. "Marjorie, this is Dr. Meomartino."

"Elizabeth is gone," Rafe said.

"I know," Longwood said calmly.

"Do you know where?"

"Off with another man. That's all she told me. She said goodbye to me this morning. She said she would write." He looked at Meomartino with loathing.

Rafe shook his head. There seemed to be nothing else to say. He started to leave, but Mrs. Snyder followed him into the hallway.

"Your wife called me on the telephone before she left," she said.

"Yes?"

"That's why I came. She told me Harland had to go to the hospital today for treatment on some kind of a machine."

He nodded, looking at the concerned aging face without real comprehension of what she was saying.

"Well, he won't go," she said.

What do I care, he thought angrily.

"He absolutely refuses," she said. "I think he's very ill. Sometimes he thinks I'm Frances." She looked at him. "What shall I do?"

Let him die, he thought; didn't she know that his wife had left him, that his son was gone?

"Call Dr. Kender at the hospital," he said. He left her standing in the hallway, staring after him.

On the following morning he was paged at the hospital and when he responded was told that a Mr. Samourian was at the reception desk and wished to see him.

"Who?"

"Mr. Samourian."

Ah, he thought, remembering Kittredge's list of fourth floor tenants. "I'll be down in a moment."

The man was a disappointment, in his mid-forties, with anxious brown spaniel's eyes, a balding head and a mustache flecked with gray; it was unbelievable that his home had been broken by this short, pudgy person. "Mr. Samourian?"

"Yes. Dr. Meomartino?"

They shook hands self-consciously. It was a few minutes after ten o'clock, both the coffee shop and Maxie's would be too crowded for privacy, he thought. "We can talk in here," he said, leading the way to a consultation room.

"I've come to see you about Elizabeth," Samourian said as they sat down.

"I know," Rafe said. "I've had the two of you observed by a detective for some time."

The man nodded, watching him. "I see."

"What are your plans?"

"She and the boy are on the West Coast. I'm going to join them there."

"I was told that you're a doctor," Rafe said.

Samourian smiled. "Of philosophy. I teach economics at M.I.T. but in September I'll be teaching at Stanford," he said. "She plans to file for divorce immediately. We're hoping that you won't contest."

"I want my son," Rafe said. His throat thickened. Until that moment he had not realized how much he wanted him.

"She wants him, too. Generally divorce courts feel it best for children to stay with their mothers."

"Perhaps that won't be so this time. If she tries to keep him from me I'll contest and file on my own. I have sufficient evidence. Written reports," he said, thinking glumly that Kittredge was the only winner.

"We should keep in mind what is best for the child."

"I've kept that in mind for a long time," Rafe said. "I've tried to keep my marriage going to make some kind of a life for him."

Samourian sighed. "I'm just trying to make things as easy as possible for *her*. She's very fine-drawn. She won't survive too much of a battle. Her uncle's illness has affected her terribly, as of course you know. She loves him very much."

"If that's so, she left at a peculiar time," Rafe said.

The other man shrugged. "People show their love in peculiar ways. She couldn't stay here and see him suffering." He looked at Meomartino. "I understand there isn't a great deal of hope."

"No."

"When he dies I'm afraid I'm going to have a very hard time keeping her stable."

Meomartino studied him. "I'm afraid you are," he said. "I didn't realize you knew her that well."

Samourian smiled. "Oh, I know Beth," he said quietly.

"Beth?"

"It's what I call her. A new name, a new life."

Rafe nodded. "There's only one thing wrong with that picture," he said. "She has the same old little boy, and he's mine."

"Yes," Samourian said. "These things are likely to take time. Lawyers and judges don't hurry. I give you my word that until everything is decided Miguel will have a good home. As soon as we have an address in Palo Alto I'll send it to you."

"Thank you," Rafe said, finding it impossible to hate him. "What does the V stand for?" he asked as they stood.

"The V?"

"In V. Stephen?"

"Oh," Samourian smiled. "Vasken. An old family name."

They walked outside together. On the sidewalk the sun struck them twin blows and they blinked as they shook hands.

"Good luck, Vasken," he said. "Watch out for young Mexican gardeners."

Samourian looked at him as though he were mad.

That afternoon, with the visiting professors from Cleveland attending, there was a conference about the week's surgical complications. Rafe scarcely listened to the ebb and flow of their voices. He sat and thought of many things, but in a little while he realized it was Longwood they were now discussing.

". . . I'm afraid he's reached the end of the line," Dr. Kender said. "The machine can go on sustaining him but he refuses more treatment, and this time he means it. He chooses to face uremia and then death."

"We simply can't allow that to happen," Miriam Parkhurst said.

Sack grunted. "It would be nice, Miriam, if we had some sort of choice about all these matters," he said. "Unfortunately, we don't. We can offer a patient dialysis, but we can't force him to accept it."

"Harland Longwood is not just a patient," she said.

"He is a patient," Sack said, pained as usual by emotionalism. "He must now be considered by us *only* as a patient. No more, no less. That's the best thing we can do for him."

Dr. Parkhurst refused to look at Sack. "Forgetting what Harland already has given to each of us and to surgery," she said, "there's a compelling reason why we cannot allow him to do this to himself.

Some of us have read the manuscript of a book he's been working on. It's a genuine contribution, the kind of text that will affect whole generations of young surgeons in the most important way."

"Dr. Parkhurst," Kender said.

"Well, the lives of people not in this room will be affected if this man is allowed to die."

She was right, Meomartino remembered.

She looked at the two visiting professors from Cleveland. "You people are kidney men," she said. "Can you suggest anything we might try?"

The doctor named Rogerson leaned forward. "You must wait until a cadaver donor with B-negative blood type becomes available," he said.

"But we can't," she said scornfully. "Haven't you been listening?"

"Miriam," Dr. Kender said. "You must accept the situation. We can't obtain a B-negative cadaver. And we're not going to be able to save Harland Longwood without a B-negative donor."

"I'm B-negative," Meomartino said.

They dwelt too long, he thought, on the chances of decreasing his life expectancy. "I have kidneys like a horse," he said. "One will last me as long as two would have."

Kender and Miriam Parkhurst talked with him in private and gave him every opportunity to withdraw the offer with honor.

"Are you certain?" Kender asked for the third time. "Generally a donor is a relative."

"He's my uncle by marriage," Meomartino said.

Kender snorted but Rafe smiled. There had been enough conversation for him to know that they had argued themselves out. Their consciences were satisfied and they would accept his kidney eagerly.

Kender confirmed it. "An unrelated live donor is so much better than a cadaver," he said. "We'll have to run tests on both of you." He looked at Rafe. "You won't have to worry about the surgery. No one has ever lost a live donor."

"I'm not worried," Rafe said. "I have one stipulation. He's not to know from whom the kidney is coming."

Poor Miriam looked bewildered.

"He wouldn't take it. We don't like one another."

"I'll tell him the donor doesn't want publicity," Kender said.

"Suppose he still won't take it," Miriam said.

"Just repeat your speech about the work of genius his finished book will be," Meomartino said. "He'll take it."

"We'll use Anti-Lymphocyte Serum this time," Kender said. "Adam Silverstone has the quantities worked out."

The only possible obstacle was crossed when samples of tissue from his body and the old man's were cross-matched and found to be well within the range of compatibility. In what seemed a frighteningly short time he was lying on his back in OR-3, feeling that this was an odd thing for him to be doing in that place despite the anesthetic Norman Pomerantz had kindly and painlessly slipped into his haunch.

"Rafe," Pomerantz said to him, the words bubbling down into his ears.

"Rafe? Can you hear me, buddy?"

Of course I can hear you, he tried to say.

He could see Kender approaching the table, and Silverstone. Cut well, my enemy, he thought.

Content for once to let others do the surgery, he closed his eyes and went to sleep.

Convalescence was a slow-moving unreality.

Liz's absence became increasingly obvious and people now seemed to understand that their marriage was over.

He had a flood of visitors which diminished to a trickle as time wore on and novelty wore off. Miriam Parkhurst gave him a small dry kiss and a basket of fruit that was far too large. With the passing days the bananas turned black and the peaches and oranges developed creeping white rot and gave off an effluvium that forced him to throw away everything but the apples.

His kidney was functioning beautifully in the Old Man. He made it a point never to ask, but they kept him abreast of Harland Longwood's progress.

Television offered temporary refuge. One day he was searching through *TV Guide* when Joan Anderson came into his room with icewater. "Is today's ball game on television or just on radio?" he asked.

"Television. Did you hear about Adam Silverstone?"

"What about him?"

"He's been appointed to the faculty."

"No, I hadn't heard."

"Instructor of Surgery."

"Nice. What channel is the game on?"

"Five."

"Would you get it for me? There's a good girl," he said.

He spent a lot of time just lying and thinking. One afternoon he saw an announcement in the *Massachusetts Physician,* and he read it several times with increasing interest as the idea took hold.

The day he was released from the hospital he took a taxi to the Federal Building and had a very pleasant interview with a representative of the United States Agency for International Development, at the conclusion of which he signed the papers for eighteen months of duty as a civilian surgeon.

On the way to the empty apartment he stopped at a jewelry store and bought a red-velvet box not unlike the one in which his father had kept the watch when he was a small boy. When he arrived home he sat in the quiet study with pen and paper and made several false starts, changing *My Dear Miguel* to *My Dear Son* and finally compromising:

> *My Dear Son Miguel:*
>
> *I must begin by thanking you for giving me more of the joy of loving someone than I have ever known. In the short time of your life you have demonstrated to me all the finest qualities of my family and of myself, and none of the tawdry weaknesses with which, alas, you will discover the world has always been riddled, and we along with the world.*
>
> *If, at some date when you are old enough to understand it, this letter is given to you to read, it will be because I do not come back from the journey which I now contemplate. For if I return I will overturn the legal world to gain custody of you, and should that world prove impossible to overturn I will arrange to see you regularly and often.*
>
> *It is possible, however, that you will read these words. Therefore I wish that I were able to make them a creed by which to live, the essence of what a father gives to a son during a lifetime, or at least substantial wisdom with which to ease the precious pain of existence. Unfortunately, I cannot. I can only advise you to try to live your life so as to inflict as*

*little damage as possible. Attempt to make or mend some-
thing before you die which would not have existed except
for your presence on the earth.*

*As for myself, the thing I have learned best is that when
you are afraid, it is best to face the thing you fear and move
toward it resolutely. I recognize that to an unarmed man
facing a hungry tiger this may sound like questionable advice. I am going to Vietnam to meet the tiger and discover
whatever moral armament I possess as a human being and
as a man.*

*The watch that accompanies this letter has been passed
for many generations to the eldest son. I pray that, through
you, it will continue to be handed down many times. Occasionally, polish the angels and oil the works. Be good to
your mother, who loves you and will need your love and
support. Remember the family from which you have come,
and that you had a father who knew that very good things
would come from you.*

> *With my deepest love,*
> *Rafael Meomartino.*

He wrapped the watch carefully, first stuffing the box with wads
of *The Christian Science Monitor* to guard against shocks. Then he
wrote a short, explanatory covering note to Samourian.

When he was through he sat and looked around the cool pleasant
room, thinking of subleasing, thinking about furniture storage. In a
few minutes he went to the telephone and called Ted Bergstrom in
Lexington and asked for and received, if with some coolness, a telephone number in Los Angeles. He placed the call immediately, but
he had not reckoned on the three-hour time lapse.

It was not until ten o'clock that evening that his telephone rang
and the call was completed.

"Hello, Peg?" he said. "This is Rafe Meomartino. How are you?
. . . Good . . . I'm fine, just fine. I'm divorced, or that is I will be
at any moment, I guess. . . . Yes. Well . . . Look, I'm passing
through California in a couple of weeks, and I'd love to see
you . . .

"You would? Marvelous! Listen, do you remember telling me
once that we had nothing in common? Well, this is the damnedest
thing . . ."

Chapter 19: Adam Silverstone

Impending fatherhood had turned Adam into a stomach feeler. "Let's go to the Common and watch the people," he said to his wife one Sunday morning as he stroked her belly. Gaby was only three months along, and her small pod scarcely showed; she said it was gas but he knew. Pregnancy had turned *her* into a miniature Rubens woman, lending for the first time in her life a hint of heaviness to the small breasts, giving a prominence to her hips and buttocks, and causing in her gut where the payload was carried a definite outward ellipse, far too beautiful to be gas. There was nothing for his worshiping palm to feel but the smooth skin of his wife's immature flesh-bud, broken by the inward plunge of her umbilicus, but in his mind he could see down through the layers to the tiny living thing floating in the amniotic fluid, now a little fish but soon to develop her features, his features, arms, legs, sexual accessories.

"I don't want to go to the Common," she said.

"Why not?"

"You go. Take a walk and look at the girls and while you're gone I'll make breakfast," she said.

So he left their bed and washed and dressed and on a lovely summer's morning ambled over the hill. San Francisco was history. This year it was the Boston Common, and some of the people were Haight-Ashbury veterans and some were newcomers and some were fake hippies who put on the costume occasionally, but they were all fun to watch. The men were far less interesting than the women, and the reasons were not all physical, he told himself virtuously; the males tended to be slavish conformists in their non-conformity, bunching together under a limited variety of hirsute tribal markings. The women showed more imagination, he thought, trying not to stare at a bongo-smacking redhead wrapped Indian-fashion in a gray blanket despite the heat; she sported a feather in her beaded hairband and as she walked by him on marvelous bare feet, on the back of the blanket the letters U.S. NAVY moved up and down to the rhythm of the tom-tom. He made the tour of the Common but not even the most breathtaking of the juicy female hippies made him regret his wife.

Nowadays he spent a lot of time being silently grateful for what they had. With each passing day, her chances were better.

When he and Gaby had learned that the instructorship was his, they had felt momentarily rich. One of the girls she knew at school was giving up a first-floor apartment on Commonwealth Avenue, much nicer by any standard than the basement apartment on Phillips Street, larger and in a converted town house with a venerable magnolia behind the tiny iron fence. But they had decided against taking it. Eventually they would move; they agreed it would be nice for a child to know grass and more open space than the city provided. But they had the beach place in Truro whenever they could get away to it, and for now they wanted to preserve what they shared on Beacon Hill. Gaby determined thriftily that each month she would lay aside the additional money they would have spent on the Commonwealth Avenue apartment ("Is that why they call it a layette?") and by the time the baby things were needed they would be paid for.

For his part, he found the excuse he had needed to give up smoking. Instead of hoarding guilt because he was a physician who used tobacco, at reasonable intervals he dropped the price of a pack of cigarettes into a cardboard container designed for pathology specimens, saving toward the purchase of an English baby coach like one he and Gaby had admired on walks in the Public Garden. The financial aspects of the confinement were taken care of. Gaby was under the personal care of Dr. Irving Gerstein, chief of the hospital's Ob-Gyn Service, who was not only the best obstetrician Adam knew but was extremely good with expectant fathers. One day Adam sat with him in the hospital cafeteria discussing Gaby's narrow pelvis and drinking coffee while Gerstein ate watermelon. Taking a slick black seed between his thumb and forefinger, Gerstein had pinched and the ovule had squirted out. "That is how easily your baby will be born," he had said.

Now, as Adam re-entered the apartment, he was content and enormously hungry. He ate the grapefruit, eggs and crisp bacon she gave him and heaped lavish praise on her supermarket brown-and-serve rolls, but she was curiously reticent.

"Is there anything wrong?" he asked as he started his second cup of tea.

"I didn't want to spoil your breakfast, darling."

Miscarriage, he thought numbly.

"It's your father, Adam," she said.

She wanted to come with him, but he insisted that she remain behind. He gave most of the English coach money to Allegheny Airlines and flew to Pittsburgh. The smoke that once had covered everything had been banished by technology and the air seemed no more impure than the air of Massachusetts. There was nothing new under the sun: the traffic was the same as Boston's; the taxi let him out at a hospital very much like Suffolk County General; on the third floor he found his father in a bed provided by the taxpayers, looking like any of the other derelicts Dr. Silverstone saw every day in the ward.

He was sedated heavily because of delirium tremens and would not come out of it for some time. Adam sat in a chair pulled close to the bed, staring at the gaunt face, its pallor accented by the telltale tinge of jaundice. The features, he saw with a chill, were his own.

Such a waste of human resource, he thought. One man could do so much or throw it all away. And yet human wreckage was often given long life without deserving it, while . . .

He thought of Gaby, wishing he had the power to pluck disease from one body by substituting another.

Ashamed, he closed his eyes and listened to the sounds of the ward, here a groan, there a scornful delirium-chuckle, heavy breathing, a sigh. A nurse came by and he asked to see the resident.

"Dr. Simpson will be along later, on rounds," she said. She moved her chin toward the figure in the bed. "Are you related?"

"Yes."

"When they brought him in he carried on terribly about some things they left where he lives. Do you know anything about them?"

Things? What could he own of that kind of value? "No," Adam said. "Do you have his address?"

She didn't, but fifteen minutes later she was back with a slip of paper.

It was something to do while waiting. He went downstairs and took a taxi, feeling no surprise when the cab brought him to a three-story facade of chipped red brick, an old apartment building that was now a boardinghouse.

Through a grudging crack in the door he talked with the landlady, who after mid-day was still in an old brown robe, her thin gray hair in metal curlers. He asked for Mr. Silberstein's room.

"Nobody lives here by that name," she said.

"He's my father. You don't know him?"

"I didn't say that. He was the superintendent here until a few days ago."

"I came for his things."

"They were just rags and clutter. I burned them. I got a new super coming in the morning."

"Oh." He started to turn away.

"He owed me eight dollars," she said, and watched him as he took out his wallet and counted out the bills. A hand snatched the money when he held it out. "He was a drunken old bum," she hurled like a receipt through the closing crack in the door.

When he got back to the hospital he saw that his father was conscious. "Hello," he said.

"Adam?"

"Yes. How are you?"

The bloodshot blue eyes attempted to focus, the mouth smiled. Myron Silberstein cleared his throat. "How should I be?"

"Be well."

"Are you here for long?"

"No. I'll come again soon, but I have to go right back. Tonight's my last shift as Chief Resident."

"You a big man yet?"

Adam smiled ruefully. "Not yet."

"Going to make lots of money?"

"I doubt it, Pop."

"That's all right," Myron said awkwardly. "I got everything I need."

His father thought he was minimizing his financial prospects to protect himself from parental claim, he realized in disgust. "I went to try to get your things from your room," he said, not sure what was missing or how much to tell him.

"You didn't get them?" his father said.

"What did you have?"

"Some old things."

"She burned it. The landlady."

Myron nodded.

"What kind of things?" Adam asked curiously.

"A fiddle. A *siddur.*"

"A what?"

"*Siddur.* Hebrew prayers."

"You pray?" Somehow he found the idea incredible.

"I found it in a second-hand bookstore." Myron shrugged. "You go to church?"

"No."

"I cheated you."

It was not an apology, Adam knew; simply the flat statement of a man who had nothing more to gain by untruth. Yes, you did, in so many ways, he thought. He wanted to say that he would replace the lost things but he saw that the delirium tremens were beginning again. His father was shaken as by a wind, the thin frame arched under the precordial pain and began to thrash, the mouth opened in silent scream.

"Nurse," he said, thankful that Gaby was not there to observe. He helped to administer the hypodermic, a lighter sedative this time, but in a few moments the storm was over and his father slept again.

For a while he simply sat looking at the figure in the bed, an old man who had roared for a violin and a used prayerbook. Eventually he noticed that his father's hands had not been properly cleaned. Grease or something similar had become engrained long ago and the admitting team had not attempted to remove it. He helped himself to a bowl of warm water and Phisohex and gauze, letting the hands soak one at a time and washing them gently until they were clean.

As he dried the right hand he examined it almost curiously, noting the scratches and the broken nails, the bruises and the calluses, the fact that the once long and slender fingers had gnarled and thickened. Despite everything, he reflected, this hand never had struck him. Against his will he remembered other things, in memory felt again the fingers stroking his hair and gripping the back of his neck, tight with love and agony.

Poppa, he thought.

He made certain his father was still asleep before he touched the damp hand with his lips.

When he let himself into the apartment in Boston he found his wife on her hands and knees, painting a crib he had never seen before.

She scrambled to her feet and kissed him. "How is he?" she said.

"Not very well. Where did that come from?"

"Mrs. Kender called this morning and asked if I could help in the Auxiliary thrift shop. When I got there she pounced on me and showed me this. The mattress was ghastly and I threw it away, but the rest is in perfect condition." They sat.

"How bad is it?" she asked.

He told her what the chart had revealed when the resident had showed it to him. A disfunctioning cirrhotic liver, anemia, possible damage to the spleen, d.t.'s compounded by malnutrition and sleeplessness.

"What can they do for a man in that condition?"

"They can't release him, one more bout of drinking would kill him." He shook his head. "His only chance is concentrated psychotherapy. The state hospitals have good men but they're overcrowded. It's doubtful that he'll get it there."

"We shouldn't have made the child," she said.

"It had nothing to do with it."

"If we hadn't been married . . ."

"It wouldn't have mattered. He won't be eligible for Medicare for a year and one-half, and a private facility will run to more than forty dollars a day. I'm not going to come close to earning that much as an instructor." He sat back and looked at her. "The crib looks nice," he said wearily.

"It's just the first coat. Will you paint the finish?"

"All right."

"And we'll get some funny baby decals."

He got up and took a shirt and a clean set of whites from the bureau and went into the bathroom to shower and change. He could hear her dialing the telephone and then the rise and fall of her voice as he turned on the water.

When he came back into the living room, knotting his tie, she was sitting and waiting.

"Is there a good private hospital for him around here?" she asked.

"There's no use discussing it."

"Yes, there is," she said. "I just sold the place in Truro."

He abandoned the tie. "Call them back."

"It was the Realtor in Provincetown," she said calmly. "He gave me what I think is a very fair price. Twenty-four thousand. He says he'll make only three thousand dollars on the turnover and I believe him."

"Tell him you've had a talk with your husband and you've decided not to sell."

"No," she said.

"I'm aware what that place means to you. You want your children to know it."

"Let them find their own love nests," she said.

"Gaby, I can't let you."

She understood him so completely now. "I'm not keeping you, Adam. I'm your wife. You've learned to give to me, but taking from me is harder, isn't it?"

She took his hand and pulled him down to where she was sitting. He put his face between her breasts; the old Radcliffe jersey smelled of turpentine and sweat and the body he knew so well. Looking down, he could see on her bare foot an imperfect circle of dried white paint that he reached for and peeled away. My God, I love her, he thought wonderingly. Her skin was fading. She had given up the sunlamp when she became pregnant, and now as the summer progressed his wife was turning lighter in inverse proportion to the rate other people tanned.

He touched the warm, round stomach. "Aren't these jeans too tight?"

"Not yet. But I won't be able to wear them much longer," she said a trifle smugly.

Please, he thought. Let me give to her and receive from her for a very long time.

"I know it won't be the same, but some day I'll get you another place down there."

"Don't make promises," she said, stroking his head, the only time she was tempted to mother him. "My Adam. Growing up hurts like hell, doesn't it?"

He was slightly late getting to the hospital but it was a quiet evening and he spent the first hour in his office. He had been working toward this shift for weeks and almost all the clinical reports had been completed. Now he annotated the last of the case histories and realized that twelve months of his life were on paper in these files.

Behind the door waited four Campbell's Soup cartons he had begged from the supermarket on Charles Street three days before, and he used them as receptacles for the books and journals on the shelves and then, with dread, faced up to the task of cleaning out the desk, each crammed drawer the result of his pack-rat tendencies. The decisions about what to save and what to discard were difficult, but he took a hard line and the level of the waste basket rose. The final item to emerge from the last drawer was a small, smoothly-polished white rock, a gift from one of his patients when he had given up smoking. It was called a stress stone, rubbing it was supposed to relieve tension when nicotine addiction nagged. He was confident it was worthless but he enjoyed the weight and texture, its message that things survived the ages. Now it backfired; he was reminded by it and ridden by the insistent urge for a cigarette.

Some fresh air would be good while he had the opportunity, he decided.

Downstairs in the ambulance yard Brady, the tall, skinny man who had replaced Meyerson, was caressing his ambulance with a chamois. "Evening, Doc," he said.

"Evening."

Darkness was falling. As he stood there the outside lights flickered and flashed on, and almost immediately great moths made the exodus out of the gloom to dance around the bulbs. From nearby neighborhoods they could hear the war-movie sound of firecrackers, a rattling like rapid-fire from remote sectors of the front, and he thought with guilt and wonder of Meomartino already heading for a place with a name like Ben Soi or Nha Hoa or Da Nang.

"Fourth of July still four days away," the ambulance driver said. "You wouldn't know it to listen to those stupid bastards. Fireworks illegal, too."

Adam nodded. The patient census in Emergency would be up for the rest of the week because of the holiday, he thought idly.

"Hey," Spurgeon Robinson said, drawn out of the building to the ambulance.

"What do you know, Spur?"

"I know I'm about to take my last rides in this damn thing," Spurgeon said.

"A full-fledged resident in the morning," Adam said.

"Well, yeah. I've got to tell you something about that. A funny thing happened to me on the way to the residency. I left the Surgical Service."

It jolted him; he had invested a lot of his professional faith in Spurgeon. "Where are you going?"

"Obstetrics. I asked Gerstein yesterday and luckily he has a place for me. Kender released me with his blessing."

"Why? Are you sure it's what you really want?"

"It's something I can't do without. I have to know things surgery can't teach me."

"Like what?" Adam said, ready to argue.

"Like everything I can learn about contraception. And the embryo."

"What for?"

"Man, the fetus is where the whole damn mess is perpetuated. When expectant mothers are undernourished, the fetal brains don't develop enough to permit adequate learning later on, after the babies are born. And then there's a general increase in the number of hewers of wood and haulers of water. I decided if I was going into this thing I'd better get to the source."

Adam nodded, admitting to himself that it made sense.

"Listen, Dorothy found us an apartment," Spurgeon said.

"Nice?"

"Not bad. Inexpensive, and near the clinic in Roxbury. We'll have a big housewarming bust the night of August third. Write it down."

"We'll be there unless something happens in this wonderful place to keep me away. You know . . ."

"Sure," Spurgeon said.

In the ambulance the radio crackled.

"That's us, Dr. Robinson," Brady said.

Spurgeon got into the ambulance. "Hey, you know what I just realized?" he said, grinning through the window. "I may be able to help deliver your baby."

"If you do, whistle Bach," Adam said. "Gaby likes Bach."

Spurgeon looked pained. "You don't *whistle* Bach."

"Maybe if you ask Gerstein he'll let you move in a piano," Adam said as the ambulance began to move. It carried the intern's laughter out of the yard.

He smiled after them, too tired and too contented to move. He was going to miss working with Spurgeon Robinson, he realized. When things began to get hairy in a large teaching hospital, people on different services might as well be on different continents. They would see one another occasionally but it wouldn't be the same; they had arrived at the end of a good interlude.

For each of them it was also the beginning of something new that would be very good, he was certain of it.

Tomorrow the new interns and residents would descend on the hospital. The Old Man's administration was over, but Kender's was just beginning and Kender would be as satisfying to work under as Longwood, as tough and challenging and probing whenever the Mortality Conference met. Tomorrow all the other staff people would be there and this time he would be one of them. He would teach surgery to the house officers in the ward and in the operating room until September, when his first students would arrive at the medical school.

He stood in the empty yard and rubbed the stress stone and thought of that important first class and of all the classes to follow, a lifeline into the future that would link him to men like Lobsenz and Kender and Longwood. He remembered with some embarrassment that he had promised Gaby enormous achievements from medicine, solutions to problems like aplastic anemia and hunger and the common cold. And yet he knew that, through the nameless and faceless young physicians whose lives he would touch, it was not unlikely that he would be close to awesome accomplishment. He had not lied to her, he thought as he turned and went back inside the building.

Upstairs, in the disassembled office, he sat in the chair with his head on the desk and for sweet minutes, dozed.

In a very short time he started, pulled awake. The firecrackers were sounding again, a longer illegal burst this time, and in the final crack he heard through the open window the first banshee wail of a far-off siren, an ambulance coming in, but these things had not awakened him.

In his lapel pocket the paging device beeped again, and when he called in he learned that one of Miriam Parkhurst's patients was in pain and demanding unauthorized opiates. "Call Dr. Moylan and have him take a look at her," he said, curiously reluctant to leave the office and aware that the intern was on duty and had first call. When he returned the phone to its cradle he sat back in his chair. His books were in the cardboard cartons. The file cabinets of case histories were locked and the scratched metal shelves were bare. The office was exactly as he had found it, down to the old coffee stain on the wall.

The pageboy buzzed again, and this time he learned he was needed in Emergency for a surgical consultation.

"I'll be right down," he said.

He took a last slow look around.

There was a ball of paper on the floor and he picked it up and balanced it on the full waste basket, then he opened the empty middle drawer of the desk and dropped in the stress stone, a gift for Harry Lee, who would be Chief Resident in the morning.

The paging device signaled again as he stood and stretched painfully, wide awake now. It was a sound he would always associate with this room, he thought, louder than sirens, louder than firecrackers, loud enough even, God willing, to drown out the faint, mocking tinkle of the Harlequin's bells.

His fingers involuntarily made the sign of the horns, and he grinned as he closed the door behind him. *Scutta mal occhio,* poo-poo-poo, he thought, accepting his grandmother's help in warding off the enemy as he waited by the elevator shaft for the slow, creaking monster to come and carry him to Emergency.

Noah Gordon, author of the bestselling novel *The Rabbi,* holds a Bachelor of Science degree from Boston University (1950) and a Master of Arts degree in English from the same institution (1951). Mr. Gordon was a reporter on the *Worcester* (Massachusetts) *Telegram* for two years before he joined the *Boston Herald,* where he was the Science Editor for four years. He is Editor and Publisher of *Psychiatric Opinion.*

Mr. Gordon now lives in Framingham, Massachusetts, with his wife and three children, Lise Ann, Jamie Beth, Michael Seay, and is currently at work on an historical novel set in ancient Israel.